This Room
Is Made of Noise

This Room
Is Made of Noise

Stephen Schottenfeld

THE UNIVERSITY OF WISCONSIN PRESS

The University of Wisconsin Press
728 State Street, Suite 443
Madison, Wisconsin 53706
uwpress.wisc.edu

Gray's Inn House, 127 Clerkenwell Road
London ECIR 5DB, United Kingdom
eurospanbookstore.com

Printed in the United States of America
This book may be available in a digital edition.

Library of Congress Cataloging-in-Publication Data

Names: Schottenfeld, Stephen, author.
Title: This room is made of noise / Stephen Schottenfeld.
Description: Madison, Wisconsin : The University of Wisconsin Press, 2023.
Identifiers: LCCN 2022028879 | ISBN 9780299341343 (paperback)
Subjects: LCGFT: Fiction. | Novels.
Classification: LCC PS3619.C4548 T48 2023 | DDC 813/.6 23/eng/20220—dc16
LC record available at https://lccn.loc.gov/2022028879

Book epigraph: Gina Berriault, excerpt from "Women in Their Beds"
from *Women in Their Beds: Thirty-Five Stories*. Copyright © 1996, 2017 by
Gina Berriault. Reprinted with the permission of The Permissions Company,
LLC on behalf of Counterpoint Press, counterpointpress.com.

On your way back into life, do you fit yourself into who you were always expected to be, for a safe return?

—GINA BERRIAULT, "Women in Their Beds"

This Room
Is Made of Noise

I

I WAS DRIVING PAST THE BIG HOUSES on Thomas Avenue when I caught, across the street, these pretty shades glowing in a window. A twelve-light table lamp. A Tiffany Lily, it looked like, but a copycat, I was sure. I'm no guru of lamps—I'd started buying and selling them recently (a little side business, to help with the hole I'd dug)—but I figured that's what I was only seeing. Valuable, nonetheless, and I reversed direction and swung my van up the driveway to try to acquire what wasn't real.

There was an old lady in the front room, seated in an armchair, and when I rang the bell I waited a full five minutes till she got up and made her way over. The loud talk inside was the TV. I heard the lock unlatch, and then the door opened slowly. She was ninety, ninety-plus maybe, younger than the lamp if it were genuine. "Hello," I said, holding the screen, and she repeated the greeting, but it sounded more like "Oh . . . ," like an echo of what I'd said. I asked about the lamp in the front window, whether it was for sale. She shook her head. "Too bad," I said, "I was going to offer you eight hundred for it." Then her small eyes brightened and she pointed her finger at me and said, "Sold!" She cackled like hell.

I want to be clear that eight hundred is not a low-ball offer for a Tiffany reproduction.

I asked if I could inspect the lamp first before making a purchase. "My guest," she said. She flicked her hand in an invitation.

I entered the house and followed behind her bent body. She didn't use a walker or a cane, but every step was thoughtful and assessed, her hands touching the backs of furniture and the surface of an end table for support, her foot carefully lifting off the ground and onto the area rug, so as not to drag and trip—which made me conscious of my eager feet charging forward. She stopped in the middle of the room. "Over there," she said, and I maneuvered around her, orderly and restrained, hiding my energy as I went past for the lamp. She stepped to her chair and positioned herself not to stumble. I heard the TV shut off; the clicker tapped against a plate. I watched her wobble before dropping back onto the cushion. Her chair was padded with back pillows. I do a lot of work for the elderly, and there are times when I feel not just sorry for their condition but also lonely for how my life might end up, captive, my body frail and shutting down, everything difficult. Certain customers, I've felt like I was abandoning them after I got paid and left.

But the lamp: the Tiffany stamp was on the base, but I figured the other company name had been soldered off, and what I was seeing was just fake marks. I learned this the hard way, when I took a mushroom lamp that said Tiffany to the antiques dealer, and he explained that I was looking at a look-alike. "Sorry to break your bubble," he said, "but ninety-nine out of a hundred are reproductions."

I studied the condition of the lilies. The shades had a nice silky feel.

"It was my father's," I heard her say, and my mind couldn't think of an appropriate response, how to comment or be nice without making a mistake. Nodding seemed enough. "He didn't want to give it to me," she said. "He was . . ." She pressed her thumb hard against the arm of the chair, which I guess meant that he was tough and cruel, that he put the screws to her. Which was good—I mean, not about his treatment but her sentiment, that she wanted the heirloom lamp and even the memory out of her house.

"My dad's like that," I said, and it was mostly true.

"Bossy," she said. We nodded agreement. "I was supposed to be a boy," she added.

The metalwork and patina looked good. I told her I'd be right back, and she said, "Ha ha ha," and I realized I was turned sideways, and she'd probably faked hearing, so I faced her directly to communicate. "I just need to go to the bank," I said, louder, and she replied, "Good idea!"

I went home for a box and some packing paper, then to the ATM, and came back with the cash. "Remember me?" I said, and she smiled at my return. "The lamp man," she said, in a commanding voice, and I was maybe surprised, her being ninety or beyond and not needing reminding. I was happy that I'd been recognized and didn't have to explain myself and start over as a stranger with a price. "The lamp man," I smiled back, like it was my new name and our private joke.

We stood in the vestibule together. I handed her the money but she told me to put it on the nearby dresser, which I did, on top of a mess of papers and mail. "I'm putting it right here," I said.

She looked over at the clutter and rolled her eyes. "I have enough bills to wallpaper the world."

I walked across the unvacuumed rug, busied myself with the lamp. First, I switched it off. For some reason, I thought back to the rug, how it was too thick for her stiff steps, and that she might want to replace it with a thinner one, so she could step more easily, or better yet, shift the braided one away from the walking lane.

"My nickname is slow motion," she said. She was moving toward her chair, halfway there—she had already stepped across the uneven ground—and if she'd looked at me I would have smiled, but she was focused on her feet.

So, back to the object. I removed the shades, wrapped them in paper, and nested them in the box like a dozen baby birds. I unscrewed the lights, quick twists on the still-hot bulbs, and set them on the paper. "Hurt yourself," she said, and I knew what she meant. "Don't . . . burn." She reached the chair, teetered before falling in. The TV noise went quiet. Her plate still held some leftover scraps; a squeezed ball of aluminum foil. She sat in her chair the way my grandmother did, when I'd visit her, crumpled up and reduced, and I felt like I was supposed to talk while taking what I'd paid for. But I didn't want to linger, and I needed to concentrate on this fragile thing.

"If he has a job, and he doesn't beat you, you can marry him."

I turned to see a finger shaking. Then she nodded at me, sure that I understood the meaning. I tried to decipher where she'd looped back to. My mind grasped nothing. "What?" I said.

"My father." She looked surprised, almost bothered by my confusion over her out-of-the-blue thought. Her voice tremored, but I hadn't heard enough of her to know if this was emotion or just regular speech. "Said that."

"Oh." I nodded as if I'd missed the beginning, then gestured at the lamp as if it were the reason for my forgetting, and for not saying more. I removed the last bulb.

"But my husband wasn't like that at all. Jim was the pick of the litter."

There were pictures on the mantel, years and years of their marriage—the young faces of the wedding, next at middle age, then recently old—but I didn't ask how long it had been only her. I didn't notice any photos of children, so maybe it was just them alone together the entire time, if you don't count pets. And she had pictures of dogs but mostly cats, although I hadn't detected any presence now, no sounds or sheddings or, worse, a reek.

I pulled the plug, freed the cord from the wall socket. I took the base and wrapped it in a protective sleeve of paper and set it gently atop the other bundles. All finished.

"I'm weighing steaks in the basement," she said.

The line felt less cryptic, or maybe I was just getting used to her skipping thoughts. "Your husband?" I guessed, at the subject.

"No," she corrected, laughing. "My father." And I laughed, too, over not telling the difference. "He owned a tavern. He was always in the basement. When there was trouble. When there was a fight. When there was something bad. No one could find him. Weighing steaks. That's what we said about him, when he was never around."

I liked the story. And it seemed safe to hear now. Plus, it reminded me somehow of my ex-wife's father. His saying: "You can't make chicken soup from chickenshit." I used to laugh about it with Renee. Only, when we started fighting, when we got near to separating, she said it about me. I didn't want to remember it anymore—but I also wanted to be friendly here. Still, it felt wrong to repeat a swear. I tried to think of other talk.

"But you're right," she said. "It was a joke between me and Jim."

Since the divorce, Renee still says it. Only shorter, just the curse. Chickenshit. Actually, that's not true, we've stopped talking. So the words are just in my head.

I gathered up the box, and nodded leaving, and carried the contents across the room, moving closer to her, then away. The box—it wasn't one of the boxes I had used when I'd moved out, but I guess the association (box, house) was there, only this time I hoped I was going somewhere good.

"Goodbye," I heard her say from behind. I turned back. Her hand was in the air. I said the same, and I told her I'd get the door. "You can handle that," she said, and I glanced at the big chair anchoring her body, and I wasn't sure if she'd meant a statement or a question. Outside, I propped the box against the house to pull the door shut. I reached my van, moving normal, but because of her it felt like a hurry.

The dealer buzzed me in and I set the lamp, which I'd reassembled, on the counter, but instead of a quick dismissal—he'd purchase it but only after knocking it down as common—he showed greater interest by staying silent. This was a first. He detached one of the lilies from the stem, held it in his hand. Then he walked it over to the window, which he'd never done with a replica, and I watched him study the pigment in the better light. He didn't shake his head. I couldn't believe what was happening—I was sure I'd missed something—and I stopped thinking about a minimum offer. "Good color," he said, after he'd scrutinized all twelve lilies, and my mind climbed steeply. I added a digit to the worth. He turned over the base and nodded at the number, as if he were identifying it—I mean, authenticating it—in his mind. He looked at the porcelain sockets, and then he screwed back the bulbs. There were some chips in the upper rim, but the damage disappeared when you reset the shades onto the stems. He plugged in the lamp. He tested the switch to see if the settings functioned. I watched the twelve lights turn half on, half off, then all on, all off: a full working circuit. It was a fun electrical pattern, clusters of lights blinking bright and dark, like strands on a Christmas tree.

"Where did you get this?" he asked, and I told him it was a family lamp. I didn't tell him what family. I figured he was just seeing if I got it at auction. It's funny, because I heard myself, or even her, the two of us, replaying "the lamp man" like a shared language. When he said the thing about 99 percent of Tiffanies being fakes, he added that I'd got the one. "What are you looking to get out of this lamp?" he said, and I joked, "The max."

I watched him manage a smile. "Anybody else look at this?" A female antiquer with artificial hair glanced up from her browsing. She frowned, jealous, as if the collection of vases in front of her just switched from treasure to trinkets.

I wasn't sure what the right answer was, so I said yes. When he asked me who, I confessed nobody, but it didn't matter. He shrugged. He didn't mind that I'd been caught in a cheap lie, because the lamp was telling only a rich truth.

"Are you prepared to sell it now?"

When I said yes, he said, "I'm prepared to give you fifteen thousand dollars." He was a tiny man, but when he said that figure, well, his personality got very big. And I increased with him. I didn't even make a counteroffer, because he'd already said so much more than the double I'd originally hoped to clear. He suggested splitting his payment into two checks, the second one postdated, to avoid a tax hit on a ten-thousand-dollar transaction, which sounded sneaky and sensible.

Maybe the payment terms made me assess what was hers and what was mine, because instead of keeping all the money—which, believe me, I felt like doing, fifteen thousand changes your life for a while . . . although it *would* have, if not for the mistake I'd made earlier this year. It was just after the separation, when maybe my head was messed up a bit, I'd gotten discombobulated, because I forgot to make an insurance payment. Which had never happened before. And then of course bad luck happened—a roof leak, some error at the ridge, and of course the homeowner had renovated their attic, so the water could damage every expensive thing. A twenty-thousand-dollar claim. I didn't even know I'd let my insurance lapse, and it wasn't like I'd ever needed anyone, or Renee, to remind me to pay my insurance (not saying I was like clockwork, but I always got the check in the mail on time), but I think the problem was that I'd always written the checks when I was living in one place, and I wasn't there anymore. So I didn't have that reminder. I almost felt like Renee had conspired with this wife (the client, with the bad roof and a good lawyer), devised some alimony payment, which I hadn't had to make, because the kids, Renee's, weren't mine. It was pointless to curse anyone but myself. That roof, I'd probably done ten jobs on that one day, and a hundred while I was driving around uninsured, but the one job that went bad was the worst payout I could have imagined. It was like the same odds as the Tiffany lamp being real. Almost called my dad to ask for cash—which would've been childish, here I am, such a middle-aged kid, so I didn't. Just took on extra work, and added the side business of buying and selling.

Anyway, the lamp. I calculated a sizable profit, took five for myself (which finally finished the debt and put me in the plus column, barely, although I still couldn't spring for a newer van, and I wasn't about to strain my resources to rent a better apartment), and brought the bigger share back. I've knocked on doors a bunch—*I can clear those leaves from your gutters. Miss, you've got little trees growing out of them*—but never to deliver ten grand. At her doorstep, I felt hesitant and generous. There was a part of me, I confess, that wondered if I should've banked the upper number, or even divided it half-and-half. But another part was excited—kind of giddy—to show her what happened. "Look what I did with your lamp!" I was thinking. "Look what I turned it into!"

The door opened faster, although she might've remembered my van, which is all lettered up, or maybe she'd been up already, waiting to greet the mailman, like my older customers sometimes do. I fanned out the money like sweepstakes.

"Here again, and again," I said. I showed her the thousand-dollar stacks, and started explaining the transaction, how I was returning a large sum because I had undervalued the worth, the reason being—and I stumbled over my words, as if making a bad pitch for a repair job—that I thought her lamp was imitation.

"Imitation?" she asked.

I tried talking simpler. "A fake."

"A fake?" she shouted. She sounded almost strangled. "Why would it be that? It's a lamp." Her eyes bugged out in alarm.

I tried to clarify that names get erased and replaced with the Tiffany signature, that I wasn't insulting her or her possessions, but speaking of the one-in-a-hundred ratio of real antiques. I shook the bundle again to signal there was no reason to be upset.

"Well, come in," she said, and left the doorway, and because I'd felt scolded about the lamp, which wasn't hers anymore, and because I was still holding the money, which was, I followed.

The money—the eight hundred, I mean, from before—was still right there on the table, only now peeking out of an unlicked envelope, which hardly seemed like theft prevention. I wanted to tell her to stow it away safer, that somebody could take that, but it wasn't really my business to interfere. Instead, I placed the bundle beside it. The unevenness of the stacks against the envelope made me think, again, that I should have taken more from the total, that it was a mistake to bring this extra money to someone already wealthy. Then I reminded myself that I'd pocketed over four grand, which still felt like a big winning bet, and I was happy again. And she was, too. She said, "Look at that." And I did. We both beamed. But then I realized the room was dimmer.

The lamp was gone. Of course it was—I bought it and took it out and exchanged it for a cash windfall—but it was still strange to see it not there, and stranger to think about what was missing from a house, from a person, I hardly knew. A good part of the room was now dark.

There was just an unreachable overhead, with burned-out bulbs, and then a floor lamp throwing a weak light. I'd treated her house like a shop window. I almost regretted turning the lamp into cash. Ten grand was useless to her. I wished two things: that I had kept all the money, and that I had brought back the lamp. "Do you have another lamp?" My voice sounded apologetic.

"We'd be rich!" she said.

But I only meant to bring down from the attic, not for cashing in valuables. I gestured at the poor lighting.

I watched her squint at the only light. We were both silent and that's when I heard a plumbing noise. "Do you have water running?"

"Water?"

"I can hear a sink," I said. "A toilet, maybe?"

She concentrated. "I can't hear anything," she said, and I glanced at her hearing aids. "I can't hear stones!"

"Is there a bathroom downstairs?"

"Why, yes."

"Would you like me to inspect the problem?" I explained that I was a handyman.

"To the bathroom we go." A finger saluted the air. "I will lead the way."

We walked deeper into the house, past inner rooms, and I watched the effort of her slow steps navigating the hallway, as if we were taking a long uphill route. Her hand balanced on the wall. When she appeared to stumble, my hand reached for her elbow, but she righted herself before I made contact. Still, I thought about the need for a rail. The noise hissed louder. She nudged the bathroom door open and entered the room. She leaned against the sink counter. I lifted the tank lid, set it down on the seat. The water level was low. Easy diagnosis: a leaky flapper.

"What is the matter?" she asked.

I crouched down to shut off the water. "Your flapper is defective."

"Oh, my."

"This won't take but a moment." I flushed the toilet. Then I un-hooked the chain from the handle, removed the bad flapper. I dropped it in the small trash bin. My fingers were wet and black from the grime beneath the valve, and from circling and scraping away the grit on the valve seat. She offered me a hand towel from the rack, but I just wiped the gunk and deposits on myself.

"I do not have a clean complex," she said.

After insulting her lamp, I didn't want to reject her towel, which was white and rooster-patterned, so I wiped my hands, even though my fingers weren't dirty or dripping anymore.

"I had no idea this was acting up. I didn't . . . notice anything was wrong!"

"Have you checked your water bill?"

"Have I what?"

"Your water bill. It might be high. Depends on how long you've had this leak."

"Well, I don't know."

I rose from my knees and walked without her back down the hallway, past the unsecured money and out the door, and out to the van to retrieve a better device. From outside, I eyed the empty spot in the window. It was just a dark area with the lamp not there. I wondered: If a neighbor passed by, would the room seem like a different place? The furniture was still visible, but it looked as if she had begun moving out. Or, I don't know, that the neighbors' houses were farther way, which of course was nonsense. (And, anyway, they already *were* far away, because it was that kind of neighborhood.) Still, I could imagine someone driving down this street, at night, and missing turning in to the driveway because the familiar window didn't look the same— because the lamp wasn't there. Thinking that thought, it jogged my memory of driving in here, earlier, and not seeing it, the unique marker.

What could I do? Maybe I could find online an identical fake as a replacement. Some cheap match. Because the darkness was my responsibility. I grabbed a new flapper, but also my stepladder and a pack of 60-watt bulbs, and carried the equipment inside. The coffee table needed to be angled out of the way in order to position the ladder below the overhead. I spread the legs and set the bulbs on the tray.

Then I walked back to her in the bathroom. I told her what I was doing. I explained every step. Some of my customers are really interested in the whole operation. After I connected the chain to the lever, it took me a couple of pushes on the flusher before I measured out the correct chain length. The attachment needed to be loosened.

"Thank you for wrecking . . ."

"Excuse me?" I said, and she was shaking her head. I turned back on the water. I flushed, and the tank water rose and leveled. The sound stopped. I tested it again, the water sucking down to the bottom then deepening up. The lid scraped when I secured it in place.

"Fixing," she said, but she was still shaking her head. "For rectifying. Rectifying. Not wrecking. Oh, God."

I stood and stepped to the rack and dried my hands on the towel. And then I looked at her in the mirror. Her eyes were shut. When they opened, she stared at the toilet, frightened, as if the tank might crack and the water would rush out, flood her feet and swallow her. Her eyes were saying, *This toilet is dangerous*, and I was about to assure her that all was running properly, but she seemed to recover. Her expression lifted. She smiled, satisfied. "The problem is gone!" And suddenly she wasn't just pleased but astonished. She pressed a button in the air. "Poof," she said. "A magician." This time, her fingers made an invisible cloud of smoke. I laughed at my bag of tricks. "Thank you for giving it attention. The toilet is now cooperating. Let's settle up."

"No worries," I said. "On the house."

But she ignored me, or hadn't heard, my words too quiet or her ears too deaf. So I was just talking about cost to myself. I looked in the mirror. I thought back to her reflection, when her eyes were closed and she didn't see me.

She had already started moving forward, trekking back in a crouch and feeling the wall for stability, and I didn't want to call from behind to upset her footing.

We walked along the distance of the hallway. Her arm was out. She needed something to grab; she needed a grab bar in the half bath, too. There were many things I could do. She must shower upstairs, but how did she manage the steep hazards of a two-story house? Unless she didn't. Just sponge-bathing, a little bit here, a little bit there.

When we reached the living room, she turned to me without teetering. "What do you feel is appropriate?"

"Five bucks," which I meant as a joke about expenses, because she didn't owe me a dime.

"For the trouble. What is your wager?"

"My wage? My rate?"

"That is the word."

I told her I charge forty-five an hour, but this job was only a fraction of that time. She glanced at the room. The place looked changed, by the lamp and the ladder, two items brought out and in. If she was confused, it was understandable.

"Well. I must pay," she said, and she reached for the money, which embarrassed me, because I didn't stop her, and I glanced away, to the line of photos on the mantel, my eyes pulling to the oldest one, of the bride and groom. They probably didn't live here yet; they'd move in later. When I looked back, I saw the age added to her face. She was having trouble with the bank strap. "This . . . tape," she said. So instead she went to the other money, the same denomination, and tried slipping a hundred from the envelope. It was hard for her fingers to separate a bill, but it was easier than breaking the strap's adhesive. "I used to stitch at the senior center. I made slippers, caps, scarves. I made eleven patterns. One time, I won the apple basket raffle." All the money stacked there made her seem immensely wealthy. I asked her if she still sewed. "Bonnets," she said. Her fingers formed a crown on her head. "For babies. For the newborns. Over at Rochester General." She turned over her gnarled hand, the fingers going out like tree branches. "Can't even play solitaire. I don't even know where the . . ." She gripped a hand and bobbed it up and down. "Needles," she said, and I realized her hand was holding an imaginary basket. "Basket," I said, and I copied her grip. "My sewing basket," she said, and she smiled like we'd solved the puzzle, and I saw more of the old photo reappear on her face. And when that happened, I glanced once more at the smiling bride and almost expected to see the picture reanimate. "Knitting is hard," I heard her say.

I wanted to refuse the money when she placed the bill in my outstretched hand. It felt like a payment and a refund and a raffle ticket.

"Can you make change?" she said.

I reached into my pocket, unfolded my uncrisp bills, and counted out fifty-five.

She looked at the stacks. "That didn't cost. I paid with your money." I guess that was one way of looking at the cash. The currency bands just sitting there on the table: it seemed like I'd walked into an open vault.

"No, it's *your* money," I said, and she waved her hand like there was no difference.

"*Ours*," she said back, and she laughed, and I joined in.

I thought of the antiques dealer, the way he'd separated the payout to avoid red flags.

"Fifty-three," she said, and I realized by her glance that she wasn't miscounting the money but was reading the clock correctly on the mantel.

"It certainly is," I said, minus the hour. The way she said the number, you might have thought her mind was elsewhere, or she was calling out the lotto. And it made me wonder her exact age. Ninety-three? Ninety-four, I guessed again, as if the numbers were on a spinning wheel that hadn't yet stopped.

"What is *that* doing here?" she said, and I agreed: the ladder really looked like a mysterious apparatus. Heck, if someone brought it into my house without telling me, I might think I was hallucinating. *What is that monster?* Although, I didn't live in a house anymore. But this room—the rotated table, the ladder split open in the center—looked redesigned.

I walked over to the ladder, sidestepped the table. Fifty-three, ninety-three, ninety-four, the set of numbers spun in my mind like a combination lock. "Shiny new lights," I said. Then I climbed up to the ceiling fixture to swap out the spent bulbs.

2

SHE CALLED ME TWO DAYS LATER. I had left my business card, which has my picture on it. It makes customers, especially the elderly, feel comfortable, seeing a face. I wasn't surprised to get the call. I had mentioned installing a hallway banister, and she said she would give it some thought. More importantly, I'd sensed that a bond was formed.

"This is Millie Prall," she said, to my voice mail. I was on another plumbing job when her call came in. "My windows are cold." There was a long pause, and then she said, "Call me back." She didn't give her number, but my smartphone remembered it. I called her from my office: my van. I have two offices actually: my front seat and the customer's kitchen table.

"Hi, Millie. This is Don Lank. I fixed your toilet. You called me about your windows."

"You are the lamp man."

"That's right," I said. I didn't think she was smiling when she said it, but I did, because I liked the fondness of the name. "Sounds like you're losing some heat."

"They are all shut. I need the other ones. Not shutters. The windows are thin. I need the extras. The second windows. They need to be covered with heat."

"Okay. I can get to you in a few hours. I'm on another job."

"You are close by?"

"I am. Not far."

"Good. You will find the time. I will be home today. I am here until then."

The lamp man. That really was me. Meaning, not just the one I took, but the one I was hoping to bring back. Because, after I left her house, I'd searched around online. I wasn't really doing anything with my nights anymore.

For a while, after the divorce, I felt liberated. Wake up in the morning unmarried and no one's making demands. It was good being alone. And I thought I'd have some fun at bars, make up for the year of gloom and doom, but one of the first gals I met, she was like, "Hi, I'm forty, I got eight kids, want to get married?" Sure, and why don't I just put my foot in a bear trap, too.

Still, I kept trying, and hooked up a bit, and then I went on some dates and I thought maybe there was something good between me and this one girl, lady. A spark. I had found myself recently sort of saying our names together, "Don and Beth, Beth and Don," throughout the day. Until she told me over the phone, "I'm not feeling it." Which sure felt like a slap. I had some questions, but I didn't ask them. I wanted to say, "Wait," but I didn't know what to say after. I was only seven years older, and she was average in looks, which I don't mean as an insult—I thought we were rated equal, is all—but I guess she was saying I was inferior. Or I'd overestimated me. When the call ended, I was a little dizzy. Like, the person you thought someone else was seeing when they looked at you—it wasn't you. And which one is the *more* you? I was sort of reviewing the time with her, and I didn't see any event or issue. No mind games.

So, because I couldn't really find a cause, I took the breakup with Beth as karmic payback for cheating on Renee. (Renee cheated, too, just after and not as bad. Full story, she cheated between the times I cheated on her.) Still, it stung a bit. But I'm not that hefty, and the hair's still there. Okay, my nose, but the rest of me is decent. I kept wanting a little more information, proof for why I got dumped. I called once, but she never answered.

Whatever, we're through. I try to put a door between me and my problems. A steel door with a lock on it. I don't hate her. It's not like she rejected me right away. We had a good fling. I took a break from dating and companionship, stopped drinking at the overpriced bars. Well, that's not true. I returned a couple times, until this one guy, he was spouting like he was on stage, like everything that came out of his mouth was a punch line or a hit song. When I looked at him, I felt older and out of place. Like I was left out of some party that started three generations ago. Which was strange, because I'd gotten there first. I'm not a hateful guy—I'm not even really an arguer (I walk away, which sometimes means at work I don't get what's due)—but this guy, in the center of the room, I imagined that he was really flammable or something. That the fringe of his collared shirt could somehow get singed, by the lighter in my pocket, and you would watch him catch fire. And then I thought—I probably shouldn't be out in public with my pyro fantasies. A good time to scatter. Skedaddle. Well, first I finished my beer. Three's my limit. He stood over there, unharmed, his shirttails not burning.

I went nowhere, except to work. Around the clock, no free time. I had just gotten this referral to an apartment complex, so that was keeping me busy, thirty units. I know it's my fault I'm alone. But loneliness can take you right out. I'd been thinking about getting a prescription for the personality stuff.

But, in the meantime, I had searched for a lily lamp for the woman who I now knew was Millie. I located a close-enough substitute. But I just couldn't click "buy." It seemed too pricey—which probably makes me sound like a stingy giver. I had a door repair out in Henrietta, so I drove an extra mile to the mall and checked out the product line at Penney's. They sold Tiffany re-creations. A different Tiffany. Not Louis Comfort, but Dale. They had a single-lily lamp, which was made in China and chintzy—it was marked down, plus I could use a store app to make it cheaper still—but I was hoping that the thought counted, and the nickname she had for me was justified. I liked its definitiveness. It was something you could put on a business card, to state what you were or did, and it sure sounded better than Beth's "I'm not feeling it," which told you nothing except a negative, and was so vague it spread everywhere, out to the far edges, like the whole world was in opposition. And I guess if I'm talking about everyone, it felt like The Lamp Man was a kind of correction to the contempt of Renee's chickenshit. (Or, if both statements were true, maybe I could make one truer.) But with Millie, with the lamp, with her hands, maybe it would be simpler to work a single, only having to change out one candelabra bulb rather than futzing with a dozen. And the pull chain would be easier than turning a switch.

The newspaper was on the stoop. I opened the mailbox and collected the mail. I rang the doorbell and stood there on the front step like the mailman, the paperboy, and the deliveryman all wrapped into one. She recognized me, but when she looked at the lamp, she didn't. If the lamp was unfamiliar, then maybe I was another kind, too. "That is not mine," she said.

"No," I said, although I was hoping that it was.

"You have made a mistake," she said. And I guess I had. I felt strange and nameless holding this lamp. I wasn't a handyman come to hang windows, but a visitor at the wrong address. I still had the receipt, and returning it seemed easier than explaining why it belonged here. Or I could just keep it for myself. It wasn't bad—well, it was pretty tacky, but I was still furnishing my new place.

"It is yours?" she said.

"I bought it for you."

"For me?"

"It's in the style of the other one," I said, "that you had. It's a Tiffany lily. It's a gift."

"Oh," she said, and her voice rose. "It's beautiful. It works?"

"It sure does."

"It's a dummy?"

"What? It's a—"

"Well, bring it in. I know you by now. It's dark in here."

I brought the lamp inside. I set the newspaper and the mail down where the money used to be. The money, all of it, was gone. Deposited or put away. Which was good. Truth is, I get nervous when customers leave stuff out. Purses. Jewelry. Twenty goes missing, and people suspect the handyman.

"Would you like to trade knees?" she said.

I told her my knees weren't too great, either. Actually, they're shot. After twenty years of this, the joints of a sixty-year-old. In another few years, I'll probably get a helper, somebody to do the heavy lifting. Except, with a helper, I'll make less. Workers' comp, payroll fees, taxes. So maybe hiring a person isn't the answer. I'd like to get to where I'm just doing the sales, the deals. Farm out the work to subcontractors. Let him take the liability. I do the quotes, give the order, and make a percentage, and the customer's still happy. And I've got other plans, too.

Anyway, I put the lamp where the other lamp was. The light was obviously smaller, but gave a decent glow. Still, I couldn't help but think of the bigger light gone out, how I was only restoring a small portion. But I found myself adding up this lamp and the overhead bulbs, and wondering if I'd offset the darkness.

"The eagle has landed."

The TV clicked off. The same plate with toast crumbs, but no compressed ball of foil. There was a phone nearby, but I'd never heard it ring. I thought of it ringing when I called her. Then I thought of her calling me, and waiting. She was wearing a sweatshirt that said, "Let's go to Paris." Beside the phone was a rosary. Maybe it had always been there, and I just hadn't seen it from this angle, but it made me re-think the pillows and blankets beneath her body on the Barcalounger. This was where she slept now, and she'd removed the rosary from her bedpost. Tucked alongside the recliner was a plastic shopping bag. If I was aware of it before, I'd thought mistakenly it contained garbage, but now I could see it had clothes. Socks and underwear, probably a couple of tops.

"My life," she said, "interferes with my naps."

I laughed. Then I pointed at the single-paned windows. Somebody had put the screens up for the warmer weather. Maybe her husband, a neighbor, or someone like me. Maybe the same person who helped with the missing money, to take it to the bank. She couldn't be still driving. Someone must be delivering her groceries, getting her to appointments. "Looks like we need to put the storms up," I said.

"The what?"

"The storms. For the winter."

She nodded. "There are windows in the basement. I can't go get them. I had energy coming out of my ears! My strength can't lift windows."

"How do I access the basement?"

"You can take them from there. They are under the stairs. My husband would put them in. Every year, up and down. He would move. So fast. We used to be such traveling nuts. Pick up at a moment's notice."

"Someone put these screens on?"

"Huh?"

"The screens."

"The heat," she said. "Patchooo," and she rubbed her hands fast, to signal warm air escaping. "A neighbor did that," she said. She shook her head, as if he'd hung them wrong. "He helped out. A favor. I made him a pie. But he moved. To ... *Georgia*," she said, laughing. "He mowed the lawn, too. He had family down there. Who can blame him? You drink coffee?" I nodded and she said she would make me some.

The storms were where she said. Propped on two-by-fours, away from the damp or flooding risk. A dozen windows, each one labeled on the frame, by her husband, probably. There were two numbering systems. One—the first labeling—was in a faded pencil, and then a subsequent system, in black marker, written over the gray lettering.

When I found Window #1, I saw a helpful diagram, "L→R," and the arrow symbol would save me time with directions and orientation. The numbers were disordered, but I'd sort them upstairs. Two of the storms were plexiglass, and I imagined they'd been replacements after an accident, the husband climbing, or descending, every other season, and maybe one of them slipping from his grasp because he couldn't carry two at a time, or maybe banging the frame against the landing or wall or table corner, or the glass face coming into contact with any number of objects, some hard, unintended touch.

It took me over an hour to install them, and, at some point, I emerged from the stairs and found her in the kitchen. She stood with her back to me, her shoulders frozen in a shrug. A percolator was now on the counter. She probably made instant for only herself, but she wanted to prepare more. Each time I came up the stairs with a window or went back through the kitchen with a screen, more items appeared: the cups, the saucers, the matching creamer, the sugar, the whole set. Cookies. A plate for the cookies. Then she carried the items, one by one, to the table. Once, as I hauled two windows, I noticed she held just a spoon. As I worked, I thought about her time and effort, her slow and endless back and forth, all the minutes passing as she paced the kitchen space. When I glanced at the armchair, I remembered her wobbliness before sitting there. I saw the plate and the crumbs, and I thought about the deliberation of what she was doing in the kitchen, the whole production of it, the percolator, the measuring out of the coffee, the cookies arranged on a plate.

When I finished, I came back to find her seated, napkin in her lap. "I've made a mess," she said.

But the room was clean. I didn't see any spill on the table, or anything dropped on the floor and in pieces. No broken cup. The only smell was coffee. But her head was bowed like a penitent. I thought of the rosary, but then my mind went backwards to something else. A month ago, I rang the doorbell for another customer, an elderly man, and I heard him shout for help. The door was fortunately unlocked, and I came inside and followed his screaming body to find him in the bathtub, butt naked. He hadn't fallen. He was just stuck on the floor. No water in the tub. He'd been there all morning. He should be forbidden from taking baths. Two hundred fifty pounds is a lot of bulk to lift, but I climbed in and rescued him, got him over the side. And soon after, I did a bathtub cutout. But right then, all he kept saying was, "Don't tell my brother about this!"

I wondered if maybe she'd got stuck. "You couldn't get to the bathroom?" I asked her, even though I probably should've just asked if she was okay, and I couldn't see all of her legs or any wet on what was visible.

"What? No! Not mess. Penmanship!" She lifted a pen and the napkin, which wasn't a napkin but a slip of paper. She shook it. The writing looked like some code or message. Maybe a list or recipe. I approached above her and saw she'd scrawled her name at the top, and then below there were letters, the alphabet. She'd stopped at s.

"What's wrong?" I asked. The order was right, and the writing was a bit wiggly but generally neat.

"The letters are mixed up."

I still couldn't see the problem. And I'd already been wrong about the accident and the napkin, and been blind about the shopping bag. "You stopped?"

"I started with upper-class, and then I switched to lower."

I looked back at the inked slip and saw what she meant, the letters shrinking. What's the word? Cases. Uppercase.

"My penmanship is very bad now."

"Hey, you should see my chicken scratch." Which made me think of chickenshit. I wondered how long that insult would linger in my head. And then I wondered if anything I'd said would linger, too. I sat down across from her.

She folded the paper and flung it off to the side, almost to the edge of the table. We were face-to-face. "Do you take anything?" she said. "In your coffee?" I shook my head. She had already poured the cups. Carefully, it seemed, since there were no signs of spatter. She placed a napkin in her lap. I kept mine on the table.

"Like my husband," she said. "Without. He never took cream and it became his habit."

"It's good," I said, after sipping. And it was. Much better than the customers who scoop instant into a pot of boiling water.

"I was a good ninety," she said. "I'm a bad ninety-four."

Which is how I found out her age. I'd been right. Wrong and right, if you count both guesses. Strangely, I thought again of the combination-lock sequence. "I don't believe it," I said, and she smiled.

"You put the"—her hand pushed out, a wall—"barriers up."

"I did. Sealed tight."

"Good. No more windy house." She thanked me. Then she said, "Batten down the hatches!" But her smile faded. Her fingers gripped her throat. She looked outside like it was raining, or dark and she was lost in it. I stared away, too. But my spirits weren't low. Not just because of the surprising sunshine. It was a nice landscape, a good half acre out there.

"Your bathroom," I said.

"It is down the hall."

"No, I don't need to use it." I sipped again. The sugar cookies sparkled. I tried one. They were sweet and stale, but I liked the taste. I wanted another. Vanilla. Which was Beth's favorite flavor. Which—I really needed to quarter-turn that in my mind, shut the remembering. Sometimes you just don't know what happened. You can't find fault.

One of my elderly customers, he didn't want grab bars in his bathroom. No way. Except his daughters did. One daughter met me at the house, while the other took him to lunch, so I could put them in before he got home. And that was fine, because the time before, when I was fixing a shower valve, the guy was just f-bombing the two of them, how he didn't want anyone knowing how much money he had and making any changes to his house, so I'm happy to be some handyman ghost. With Millie, with me asking these questions, it's not wrong to push with good intentions.

"Are you having any trouble with it?"

"You fixed it."

"No, I mean—"

"You put that trap. Contraption." She tapped her forehead. "My radio waves are jammed up."

"Mine, too." And I felt like they were, moving from Renee to Beth. I was about to knock my skull when she frowned.

"What's your excuse?"

"Don't got one."

"You're young. I didn't even know I was in my late eighties until I was brushing my teeth one night."

I opened my mouth to ask: "Is getting off the toilet hard for you?" But I winced when I heard myself say it. So I didn't. It's just, after I installed the grab bars for the irate man, he called me the next day to ask for more. Now he's got one for the three steps from his garage to the kitchen. Those steps used to be no problem, but they'd become trouble: two minutes and a lot of pain, and if he fell he might not be seen for a week. So I've eliminated or minimized a risk. Another customer, he's got stitches over his eye; the grab bar beside his bed, which he *now* has, might have prevented that injury. Of course, I hadn't been through anything like this with Millie, but sometimes I'm in so many houses, with so many elderly people, and you blur particular widowhoods, or that you're ever at something like a beginning, or that there's even a point to being cautious with questions when someone might get hurt for not asking. At times I thought it was so strange that I asked these kinds of intimate question with near strangers when I never asked them with family. I didn't know if asking these questions made me a better person, or worse, since there was always a job, with money involved, depending on the answer.

My napkin was still on the table. I stared at it and thought, okay, and placed it on my lap. On the one hand, I felt a childishness doing it, because I was following her example, obediently. On the other, I felt like we were suddenly having a meal, no, we were out at a restaurant, a fancy one. Some occasion. Looking at the oven, I could imagine a big meal in a broiling pan.

And then I asked the question I had stopped myself from asking before, and even though it was my second time thinking it, I still felt myself blush. I felt like I had a split personality, two behaviors: the politeness of the napkin in my lap, and the rudeness of what came out my mouth. Having the napkin in my lap somehow made the question more proper and allowable. But it also made it feel even more of an oddity.

"It is not fun," she said. "Getting off the john."

"The old toilets are lower," I said. I thought if I talked in a technical way, it wouldn't sound so private and bodily. But then, just thinking of that word, bodily, made me think of seeing the plastic bag in the living room, the underpants, and how it was even more embarrassing and indecent for me, to see such clothing alone.

"How's that?"

"They just were. Would you like a raised seat? I can put arms on the side, for getting up easy."

"That's all I do is sit in a chair. You sit in a chair, you get to look like a chair." She shook her head. "If you don't keep busy, it's bad business."

I nodded, glanced away, down at the floor. The corners were dirty. The center of the floor was clean, but the unreachable perimeter was filthy. I imagined the mop stopping, the superficial sweeps. "How about the stairs? Do you have trouble walking up them?"

"I'm breathing."

"Right."

"If I'm breathing, I can do it."

"Good for you."

"I sit on the stairs and inch my way down." Her hand descended in levels. "On my fanny. I'm a tough old lady."

"You sure are."

"I am not an ox." Her face hardened.

"Me neither," I said. I thought about another old customer. She used to lasso her recyclables bin with a rope and pull it down to the curb.

"The staircase. That mountain. I fell. But I got over that. Re . . . recovered. I did my rehab. The . . . strengthening. The X-rays are always fine. I'm a tough old bird. I have . . . strong arms. That's why I lasted. I didn't go back to the exercises. No more. Because I'm back together. But I don't like my symptoms."

One more. I chewed, swallowed. The second cookie was enough. She had taken two bites, but then nothing. "Have you ever thought about a stair rail?" Because I had an alarming thought—her standing at the precipice at the top of the stairs, ready to take an unsupported step.

"A wheelchair?"

"You sit in a chair and it brings you up and down."

"That sounds like big bucks."

"I guess it depends on how you look at it."

"Somebody sees one of those in your house, they think they should put you in a home. I am not going *anywhere*."

"No, of course not." That's what the elderly man—the bathtub—was so scared about, with his younger brother.

"This is it. I will die right here!"

"Miss. Millie." But she shook her head, furious.

"I will be carried out of here. No nursing home. No one will dump me in a home. No one can kick me out of this."

"I understand. I'm just asking about mobility." If no one asked these questions, what became of her? I didn't want her toppling and taking a header. Things were not all right with this house. Accommodations were necessary. The laundry was in the basement. Another staircase to negotiate. I'm sure she was devising a way, but it was still dangerous. And her doorknobs could be switched to lever handles. Modifications—simple and sensible. If there's no daughter or son, no helping hand, who else was around for decisions?

A third cookie—I couldn't help myself. There were three left, which were all hers, if she wanted them.

"I can get from here," Millie said, "to the other side of the house. I manage that trip. And I don't get lost. Breakfast, lunch and dinner—

everyone says I need a walker. I need better *shoes*. I stopped going to the senior center. You see a lot of walkers there. Everywhere. They all said I needed one. Those . . . wheels. They don't go straight until you turn them straight. I walk *without* something."

I nodded. Cookie in hand, I thought about the weight of a carried spoon. I set the cookie on the saucer's edge. I'd already touched it, so I couldn't put it back on the plate. I took a sip, thought of the room where the mock Tiffany burned a faint light. The mantel, with the photos of what she used to be and have. Another sip, down to the lukewarm sediment. I looked away, to the folded piece of paper where she'd written her name. Down to the floor, which at first view I mistook for all clean. Her cup wasn't yet empty, and she would offer me another, and I glanced at the percolator, and I imagined it brewing while Millie moved through her slow routine, and then I could feel my legs tapping because I imagined it was *me*, waiting and waiting for the percolator to brew like the clock had gone backwards, and the percolator *itself* felt like I'd gone back decades, which made me feel that whatever I was supposed to do had long stopped, and my leg tapped faster, enough to vibrate the chair, because I had looked at the oven and thought of the meal again and imagined some timer set for *hours*—I stood up to get paid and get going. Time is money, and this didn't count as time. Not to be impatient, but I'm not a charity and I don't have a salary, either. I set the napkin back on the table.

"It is time to leave," she said.

I nodded. I was glad she understood my signal. The napkin, I refolded it, set it back to how it was when we started.

"Would you please help me?"

"Of course."

"My television. I can't get my stations."

She rose slow and hunched to her feet. I waited while she changed positions but stabilized. "Let's see what's the matter," I said.

"It's that darn control. That gizmo."

We would navigate back and I would reprogram the TV. When we got there, I would point out the storms, how the drafty air was gone.

3

A LONG TIME AGO, Renee had something weird happen to her on Facebook. This was before I'd met her, but not so long. (Within the year, if my memory was right.) What happened was, she got a message from a stranger, a woman, who told her that she'd been dating a guy, who'd stated he had a kid. A son. The guy started doing things that made the woman distrustful—she didn't explain what the actions were—and it got so bad, she became so suspicious, that she began to doubt that he really had a kid. She'd never met the child (he lived with the ex-wife, was what the guy had said), and the only evidence of his existence was a Facebook photo of him, on the guy's page. Just a single photo, with no one else in the shot. So, she decided to do some detective work. She did a reverse-image search, which is how she came to contact Renee, because the image traced back to Renee's Facebook page. It appeared that the man (I don't remember his name anymore, Gary or Barry something-or-other) had taken a photo that Renee had posted of Jack, and he'd copied it to his own Facebook page, and, if I'm remembering it correctly, he'd even written something below the photo, something like "My boy, my life." Renee had no idea who the guy was. She'd never seen him before, never heard of him, had no mutual friends. She hadn't a clue as to how he'd stumbled across her, much less his motivation. She thought about sending him a message, saying WTF, but instead she contacted Facebook and told them to make him take the photo down. Obviously she adjusted her privacy settings. And she considered deleting the photo, but then she thought, Why should *I* have to delete it?

When she told me the story, the takeaway was, sure, what a creep, but mostly it was about being careful with social media because of course there were nutsos out there. She thanked the woman for alerting her, and she never heard whether the woman called the guy out or just broke it off with silence. By the time Renee mentioned it, it was just a story, no real freak-out or vulnerability, and we kind of played off of it, how she and the woman should have set the guy up, arranged to meet up at Renee's house, and Renee, after the guy entered and got himself comfortable, would say, "Hey, you wanna meet my kid?" And then they'd bring Jack out, from the other room, like one of those gotcha TV shows. But then we agreed that you wouldn't want that kind of guy in your own home, so you should do it in a neutral site, like a restaurant, or maybe in that staged house where the TV host did it.

All of this came back to me when I was on Facebook looking at photos of Beth. I'd never done that before, but I guess I was having a "What's She Been Up To?" moment, maybe because I'd seen the photos again of Millie's marriage as I was at the door, preparing to leave, after I finished with the storms, so I typed her in, Beth's full name, in the search bar, and there were six of her, and she was the first one, and I clicked on it, her, and, sure enough—I don't know why I said that—there were pictures of her with a new guy. In one, they were both wearing wigs, matching ones, black hair with gray at the tips, like they'd worn them for some costume party, and the two of them were grinning. Actually, he was grinning at her. It took me a second to realize that, because I first stared at Beth, who was grinning at the camera. It was a smile I remembered seeing her make at me, though obviously not much at the end. Her upper lip would always disappear. Just like it was doing here. In the photo. She looked the same—of course she did, it hadn't been that long—although, in some ways she even looked younger, because of the smile, like she was reverse aging. She was younger. Than *me*, I mean. When she first asked me my age, I confess, I rounded it down. A few years, no harm done. But soon after, I told her what I really was, and I didn't think it made a difference. Beth had never had kids, but on Facebook it now looked like she did. Meaning, the kids were his, I'm assuming, and she'd posted photos of them, too, and one of them, the girl, oddly, was the spitting image of the dad (Beth's boyfriend—which is a weird phrase to say, when I'm not talking about myself), but the son looked totally different, probably like the mom, whoever she was. So even though their relationship was at the beginning, Beth was already, according to these pictures, some kind of step-girlfriend, if that's even a term. I didn't want to stare too long at this stuff, especially the photos of the guy, and there were a few more of them, one where he was expressionless, standing with his arms folded like he was the head bouncer, blocking the door, and then another where he looked like he's being a DJ—I mean, he's *actually* being a DJ, he's got headphones on, and he's gazing down at the record player, and his fingers were on the knobs, or the controls, or—like I even care what the word is—and he's smiling at what he's doing, he's really in the moment, and I just almost laughed at him, like, Sure, as if you could trust *that*. Oh, sure, why don't you go fall in love with a guy who loves a turntable.

I didn't think of Renee's story while I was looking at Beth's pictures. It was moments after, when I logged out, and I felt this instant tug to log back in and look more at Beth. Or maybe read some of her comments. Which was always a hazard, because I knew I'd just see everyone gushing about how they were the perfect couple, and sending heart emojis. I wondered, when she dumps him, or when he dumps her (because, come on, the guy's a DJ), when would she delete his photos? And what about the kids? Would she just delete them, too, right along with him? Of course she would. And that's when I thought of Renee's guy, of kids' photos getting erased or duplicated. Maybe the guy, I'll call him Gary, no, I'll call him Gerald, even though I'm positive that's not his name, had been married before, and he'd had kids, and he'd lost them, they'd disappeared, through death or divorce, and—

I'm not excusing it—and, no, I guess if he was divorced, they'd still be his kids, unless his situation was closer to mine. Which gave me a jolt—finding a resemblance. A kinship, like the way I'd seen the facial features, the eyes and cheeks, the genetic inheritance, of the girl to her father. And I didn't know how he (Gerald) found his way to Renee, but maybe he'd done some Facebook search, like I'd done with Beth, and the name he was looking for, it was *close* to Renee's, so he wondered who that was, too, or maybe it was identical to Renee's but a different person, the next one, like I'd seen with Beth when there were six of her. So he clicks on the one below, the one that's *not* the person that he knows, and explores the photos because they're not hidden, and he sees this kid, and I wouldn't have known which image he'd seen, so now I'm going off my own memory, of one of the earliest pictures Renee had of Jack in her house. Seated on a tricycle, bundled up. And Gerald, Jerry, wants to feel like a dad, even just online, maybe he's thinking it's only his online identity, and maybe even for a little while—it's like when you hear one of those stories about a guy who it turns out led a double life and had a secret family, except in this case, it's the mirror image of that, it's a guy saying what he had when he didn't.

Millie called me the next morning. I was finishing up at Home Depot. The place is like my warehouse, and I know the store better than the workers do. I had grabbed some shark bites for a water-heater job, plus a garbage disposal and a whole configuration of pipes and joints because some amateur expert had done a cob job under a sink with all these kinks and bends so the water wouldn't drain. Then it was over to lumber to find a close replacement for a molding. At the Pro Desk, there was a knot of contractors jockeying. I recognized most of them, because we're always here. One of the guys, his cart was huge, with cement, posts, fence pieces. And he also had a platform cart—his helper did—with high-end stuff, a spa tub with nozzles and jets, three thousand dollars, plus an expensive sink and vanity. Another guy saw all this and said, "You got your work cut out for you."

"What are you working on?" the two-cart man said back, and he said electrical, and he pointed at the brushed-satin finishes and said the customer was giving him some liberty to pick out fixtures. "I'm backed up," the spa man said, and he waved at the carts, the helper, all of it. "You do electrical—this job I'm working on could use somebody. You available for a couple of days?" Then he looked past him to me, and my eyes fell to my materials list. Set of curtains. Grout. I didn't really need to participate in this BS. I thought about walking back to hardware, for some specialty screws or even specialty pliers for getting into a weird angle. Personally, I wouldn't have hired the other guy, because I thought he sounded like some fly-by-nighter. From the corner of my eye, I watched them exchange business cards. The aproned cashier rang them up, and I waited for my turn. Finally, it was me. "Find everything?" she asked.

What Millie wanted was a grab bar in her shower, but she was concerned about colors. The options were white and biscuit. "Biscuit," she said. Biscuit sounded nicer. I was booked out for the week, but things had slowed for the holiday season. A couple of yucky jobs the next afternoon, and this one lump who liked to stay in his tighty-whities while I worked. His closet-door rollers were off-track, so I rescheduled his nonemergency to get to her. The lamp was on when I arrived—I couldn't help but think about the deep discount—and I was mostly glad it was being used.

We said hello. I saw the rosary beads that I had failed to see. "It is what it is," she said when I asked about her day.

I went to work. A grab bar is a quick installation, and when I told her I'd finished, she said, "Well, that was duck soup!" She laughed, and I told her I was a fast worker.

I stayed longer again for coffee. Why? I didn't intend to. I think when I agreed to the coffee I just assumed I would add extra minutes to complete the day. But when I glanced at my phone and saw the jobs that were left, a couple of doors—a balancing and a replacement— they looked identical, and it didn't seem to matter if I did both of them or just the one. Of course, it would matter to the customers, and to

33

me—not necessarily monetarily, since both were small jobs so the money wasn't significant, but it would ding my reputation if a customer went on Angie's List and said, He didn't show up when he said he would. Unreliable.

Millie made the same presentation, and I sat in the same unscrubbed corner. I noticed some paint flaking at the baseboards. The coffee, like I said before, wasn't the best but it wasn't sludge. The chair was comfortable. Again, the plate of cookies, three each, and she offered the plate to me so I'd pick mine first. I set the napkin in my lap.

"You are not married," she said. She pointed at my ringless finger, and I explained one reason I was without one—catch a ring on a saw, you lose whatever goes with it. "But no," I said, "I'm not married," and I told her about the recent divorce.

"I was married sixty-eight years," she said.

"That's long. I only made it to the eight part."

She shook her head. "People don't know how to take bumps. Three fights and they're gone."

"Well," I said, "we had more than that."

"You marry someone sixty years, you get used to that. I'm not used to this." She glanced outside. "I am ready to cross the bridge," she said, and she didn't understand why the Lord hadn't taken her. "My husband bought five graves. My father is in this one. My mother is in this one." She counted them out on her fingers. "I'm here but not there. I have my monument already built. The words are already in the stone. 'Gone on a new adventure.' He died in 214," she said, which I knew meant two years ago. "His third attack took him. His second one—he died and they brought him back to life. Re . . ." Her eyes shut as she struggled to find the word. "Resuscitated," she said, and her eyes popped open, and her finger pointed.

I wasn't sure, but the table seemed odd, not rearranged but straightened, centered. Maybe it was just the way I was positioned, but it felt as if it had been inched toward her side, to make more room for my chair. I imagined her strong arms pulling.

"Down for the count," she said. Then she asked if I had children. I wasn't surprised that we were talking like this—or that *she* was. Customers, the older ones, the widows, can go either way, telling you nothing or everything, although in both cases they usually didn't ask much about me. I didn't mind avoiding that subject.

But now I said, "My wife did. My ex. They're teenagers. I guess I'm a former stepdad now." And I remembered my recent online activity, and I even thought of the guy again, and I felt my head shake, not because of the whole episode, of thinking about Beth or Renee, but because I'd been wrong about him, that a guy who does something like that has never had kids of any kind, and a guy who does that is probably doing a heck of a lot of things worse. I did a lot for them. Erin and Jack. Paid to send them to space camp, over at the science museum. I tried. Jack was old, too old when I first met him. I was never gonna be his father.

When I glanced down at my napkin, I didn't think about how I'd placed it in my lap earlier than before. Or, I mean, I had already registered that. Instead, I thought about when Millie had written out her broken alphabet, the letters looking one way, then another, and I remembered all that I'd misunderstood in the moment, including the napkin that wasn't a napkin. And I remembered the husband's numbering and notation on the window frame, indicating which is what.

I stared at my phone again, at the contact numbers. At some point, I would need to call, and the customers would either say it wasn't a bother if I was late or even had to postpone, or that it was a terrible inconvenience. Only two jobs, and more like one because, like I said, they were both doors, although I think what I really felt was that I'd done the job so many times it was more like a hundred, and I felt fatigued by the thought of that effort, as if they were all, every door, made of granite, and so I didn't think it was wrong to delay the second one, if that was all I was doing, although they both felt secondary. Skipping one, I suddenly had more energy, but maybe that was just the cookies, and even though they were the same, I felt like I enjoyed them more.

"We were supposed to have kids," she said. "He wanted me to stay home and take care of them. But there were no kids. But I still stayed home. I was home every day, because he didn't want to die alone. I kept house. Made sure there was dinner. We were patrons of everywhere. When they started the zoo. We attended functions."

I looked outside. The trees were tall and bare. No rotting swing set. The leaves were on the ground, and I thought about offering to rake them, which was strange since I was just thinking about what jobs to decrease, but for some reason the thought didn't bring with it a tiredness. I checked the phone for bad weather. All clear. But when she offered me a second cup, I was reminded of time and lateness, and I looked at the percolator and then the stove, and a part of me reexperienced that earlier fear about a clock—and my life—stopping, and my leg started motoring up again, and in my mind I was already in my van doing fifty down St. Paul to get back on schedule. But another part of me—the part of me that didn't decline the coffee, because I liked drinking it with her—didn't feel quite so much urgency to leave, to get to somewhere next. I could just count our conversation as some late lunch hour. No, I argued with myself, I'd already had that meal, and unless my appetite had increased and I was an eater of second lunches, unless money was suddenly unimportant, unless I didn't need it to live or pay rent, unless my landlord was throwing some rent holiday I didn't know about—I had to make up this hour. Because I wasn't some volunteer who sat at homes for free, to be shown snapshots of someone's old life for an afternoon. Or I could, as long as I extracted some bigger payment elsewhere. Still, I didn't lift my napkin or think about an escape route. I resolved to get tougher with delays tomorrow.

I looked at my phone and my schedule, to locate some other justification beyond the forecast, since I'd already checked that, and I couldn't blame rain, but I had to say something about an overrun, and exaggerate why I wouldn't be able to travel to them today.

Millie had a brother, she said, but the navy got him. Which I learned later meant asbestos. "His family is out in California," she said, and she drifted her hand. "He just got on a plane and went somewhere else. He went way out on the other side of the world. I have never been on good terms with his wife. I don't think of them as family. They never even sent a card. When Jim died."

She called me again, about another grab bar. And one more.

"How's your day?" I asked, and she said, "Good enough."

Usually, once I was there, she had additional tasks. Changing the smoke-detector batteries. Cobwebs where she couldn't reach. Heights. And then, her hospitality, and our prim napkins in our laps, the coffee, the refills, and the numerous cookies. The table felt different. Which I didn't mean repositioned, again—but this time I had an even more absurd thought than of Millie pulling it from the wall. The tabletop seemed smaller. As if the circumference had been cut, the edges sanded down, some inner circle carved out. In thinking about Millie and carpentry, I guess I was saying that I imagined her as *me*. But I guess what I really meant, what I *only* meant, was that the table seemed smaller because it was familiar. Or not a table anymore but two chairs.

And here was another confusion: When I looked over at her, and I thought about the decisions she was making alone, I said, *No spouse or kids*—and then I stopped. Because I realized I could just as easily be talking about me. Who are you talking about, I thought, her or you? Because it sounded like both. The sentence I'd started to say was: No spouse or kids, so it's just me, I'm everyone. But when I finished that thought, it sounded both clarifying and confusing.

"I will pay you for listening to all of this," Millie said, shortly after saying, "I'm in love with my dead husband." She insisted when I said no. "I expect you to charge me for your time," she said, the next visit, which I appreciated.

It would always take her a long while to reach and locate the checkbook in the cabinet, and to find the next check. "Here we are," she said. "Success at last."

One time, the date on the check said 1916. I pointed it out, made a joke about backdating.

"I meant . . ." she said. "That is not what I meant."

I tried to explain that it was nothing to correct the error, but she ripped out the check, tore it into tiny pieces.

Another time, she wrote the date inside the dollar box. I suggested voiding it, but again she shredded it into confetti strips.

The next visit, I told her the amount, but she didn't understand. She just looked down at the checkbook. She tried to focus, and figure what was due, what went where. "Would you please fill this out?" she said. "I'm not seeing well today. You have young eyes."

So I did. I filled in the blanks, wrote the date, the numbers, and my company name: Don's Fix-It. I spelled out the amount and said the figure aloud. "You just need to sign it here," I said, and I handed her the pen, pointed her to the signature line.

4

I'M NOT TRYING TO TARGET SENIORS. Okay, I've got my ad in the 55 *Plus* magazine that you see on the Wegmans rack. And I've left my business card and fridge magnet at some of the senior centers. And, for a while, I even advertised on the oldies station. But if you've ever heard stories of someone following an old lady back from stores—not to rob them, just to see what the house looks like, if it's deteriorating—that ain't me. And the scam artists that fix the outside and rob the inside—they're unforgivable scumbags.

But customers can be deceptive, too. The penny pinchers with the brand-new house and the new cars, the fancy patio, the double ovens in a kitchen you'd die for: When these people tell me they're on a fixed income and they got no money and they want a senior discount, I'm sorry, but the rate just went up. Because my prices are fair to begin with. Not padded. So stop asking me to take another ten percent off when that's my profit.

Some of the work you do is not always clear-cut. An old house, there's a spot on the wall, moisture, termites, and you end up replacing the wall. The surface is not what it appears to be. But now the customer is gonna write me up a bad review. Said I butchered the job. Switched it. No, the *job* switched. The deception is there.

"You have anything else?" I asked.

Millie always did, written out in a daybook. Today, it was a loose cabinet hinge. When I finished, she had one more thing, her answering machine.

"Is it broken?"

"No," she said. "I want to change the message."

We walked over to it, and I found the record button and asked if she was ready.

"Would you leave it?" she said.

"Leave what?"

"You be the one to talk."

"Me?"

"Yes. You be the speaker."

I said people would think they'd reached the wrong number. She said she liked to hear a man's voice on the answering machine.

"What do you want me to say?"

She laughed, as if I'd asked a silly question. "Tell them I am not here."

I pressed the button and heard the beep. "This is . . . this is Millie," I said, which sounded weird, like I was some dubbed voice. "Wait, that's not right." I wondered if I should have listened to her old outgoing message, and just duped her words. "This is the residence of Millie . . ." But I still felt like some impersonator. I deleted it, tried again. "This is the Prall residence," I said, and I looked at her and she smiled. The machine blinked time on its display; there was a gap of silence before I added, "Please leave a message."

I stopped the tape and played it back to make sure. We listened to my voice and the dead air and my voice again. I always sound nasally and distorted on machines, but who hears their recorded voice and thinks it's them? Still, if someone called up, they'd want to know, Who is this man pretending to be?

"Maybe I should have said your number," I said. "Instead of your name."

"No." She shook her head. "This is better. This way they will know it's me."

Millie said she was yesteryear. And I felt that way, too, because my twenties were a big success. Not that I banked the money. I bought a new truck, a snowmobile, took too many trips—I can't believe how much I spent. But now I was forty-five and my earnings capabilities have maxed out. I can't work more hours, and I've gotta sleep. I've plateaued. I thought I'd be farther, into the bigger projects. Six-figure construction jobs. Sometimes, I feel like a failure, the monetary part, doing all this small, putzing-around stuff. Maybe I'm just like Millie, finding my limitations. But the guy I was twenty years ago—he'd shake his head at me. Tell me I was flunking life. Come to think of it, the way he'd speak to me would be far worse than Beth's vague snub.

Customers like Millie make me feel smart. Her especially. I change a lightbulb, she's so thankful, it feeds my ego. After the divorce and the dating . . . with Millie, I get rid of a dimmer switch that's hard on her hand, and I've gone from zero to hero. Even more, she called me an angel. She said God had brought me here.

But I'm no saint. Never have been. When I got started in this business, I worked for an outfit that was expert at driving up costs. Never looked like you were preying over the job. But you were. A little repair, you bump it up to bigger. Sell the repair, sell the bigger repair. Spiking the job, was what my bosses called it. You were encouraged to turn that little piece of rot into a three-thousand-dollar framing job. I loved rot, because I knew when I opened it up, there were gonna be carpenter ants. And carpenter ants were your friends. I would say it was more questionable than corrupt. Not fraud, but leading you into the steps of where the job can go. The vision needs to be wide-angled. Look at the whole house. See the rotted posts on the deck.

The checkbook was missing from the usual drawer. "I've lost five things today," she said. "I can't find anything." And when we looked, I found something else: the money, first hidden, then forgotten, never deposited. It was strange to hold the stacks again.

"Millie, you shouldn't keep this around."

41

She stepped forward, bent in front of my discovery. Her eyes went down to it, then over to me. "I have been meaning to take that to the bank," she said.

"You have a way to get there?"

"Well, of course I do."

"You're still driving?"

She didn't answer. "I haven't renewed my driver's license. Re . . . re-registered . . . I'm shopping for new insurance."

I nodded.

"I can drive, but I don't want to mess with all of it." Then she said, "Give up your license, give up your life."

"I could drive you," I said. I wasn't sure why I said that. Part of it, part of *me*, might have been responding to Millie's face, the moroseness, when she talked about giving up this and that, the one thing that became everything. Or maybe I felt that she had to go to the bank because of me. Because of the lamp, the deal. But I knew it was something else—meaning, I knew we had *become* something else by my driving her, because when I was in her house, I was on my schedule, and now it felt like I was on hers, although I guess in both cases I'd be compensated, because she'd already clarified that. I don't know, I just knew that by going outside with her, for the first time, by driving with her, I was somehow already doing those things again, and often.

"The age is against me," she said.

I told her again I would drive.

So I did. I backed the van out of the driveway, swung it around and reversed it in, to shorten her walk to the passenger side. I checked my schedule. Two more appointments—a toilet repair, and then stripping wallpaper out of a bedroom. I could get to the toilet later today, but I'd have to push back the wallpapering.

"This is the second time you've canceled," the old lady said, and I didn't think her memory was right. Mine said it was the first. I apologized. "I'm calling someone else," she said, and I said I understood.

I kept the van running for the heat and stepped back inside. Fortunately, last week's snow had melted, but I threw some salt on the steps.

The steps were crumbly and in need of repair. I'd get to them in the spring. Which jolted me. To think so far in advance. This inner thought was almost more confusing to me than the outer one I'd had when I offered to drive, or to what I'd heard the lady say about me being a double canceler.

Millie didn't know where her winter coat was. I went to the closet and called out some colors. She said black, and I brought it to her. "That's the one," she said. I held the coat sleeves low, so she could more easily slip her arms inside, and then I gently hoisted the coat up and around her shoulders. She didn't look bigger or fuller with the coat— mostly, it looked like it dwarfed her—but she looked older. Or *younger*. What I mean is, seeing her in the coat, I could imagine her past, not just winters but all the time she went out more, did things, was married, not widowed. I went back to the closet for a basket of hats, and I remembered her knitting hobby. "You made all these?" I asked.

She stared over at the memory. "I did." Then she glanced outside. "It looks like I need five mittens."

"No," I said, "it's not that cold."

For the first time, we walked to the front door together. "My purse," she said, and I realized she was right, that she would need ID, and then I realized I'd forgotten about the money.

I grabbed her purse and went to the cabinet for the cash. I collected all of it, the ten bundles and the enveloped eight hundred, until I remembered the earlier sale. I didn't know if this would be a similar red flag, a too-large deposit, and I didn't want this transaction to lead back to the lamp, so I returned the envelope to the drawer. "What are you doing?" she asked. I turned around. I couldn't tell what she saw. And I wasn't sure how to explain my action. "I'm getting the money," I said.

"Oh, good. We need that."

In leaving some of the money, and not telling her why, I felt like I wasn't only stashing it but taking it. Which was strange, since I was in her house. But I figured she could use this cash to pay me in the future, without having to worry about the checks, and the time it took to record the information. I found a paper bag in the closet and put all ten bundles inside.

We left the house together. She struggled with the steps, but I helped her down. At first, I was unsure how to do that. I held my arm around her shoulder, not touching, almost like how the coat had come down on her, but that didn't seem right, it seemed unsupportable, or worse, that it might push her forward, so next I brought my left arm out from behind and held it at her side, to act as a railing, and she threaded her right arm inside and set her hand on my bicep, and then she gripped her left hand onto my forearm. When we stepped down, I felt the pressure on the upper and lower parts of my arm. The shuffling on the salt sounded like pain. "I need a voodoo person," she said.

I was glad that I was thinking ahead to the step repair. Now, with her mobilizing, and with our combined weight, it seemed the steps were in even more need of fixing, and if I used compressed sand at the joints, it would require more maintenance, the occasional sprinkle and a quick broom sweep, but it would last longer over time if you stayed on top of it. And then, I thought, what did that mean, *years*, now?

When I got her in the passenger seat, I realized that I should have propped a blanket beneath her, so she wasn't sitting down so far, so getting out would be easier. I was surprised at myself, for thinking something like this, but if I drove her again, I would get one of the blankets from the back. I got the seat belt and handed it to her, right in front, so she wouldn't have to twist and grab. I pulled the slack, so she was able to click the buckle shut. Which she did. I told her she had strong hands, and she grinned. "You would not want to meet me in an alley."

And then I walked around to my side and climbed in. "You're in for the ride," she said.

I set the paper bag between us. I asked her what her bank was, but she couldn't remember.

"The letters."

"Yes?" I said.

"First . . ."

"First Niagara? That's *my* bank."

"No. The first letter."

"Oh, the first letter?"

"What is the first letter?"

"Millie, do you mean *A*?"

"The bank. The bank is letters."

"Oh . . . HSBC."

"No. It is not that."

I wasn't sure if I was supposed to say the alphabet, or if it might be easier to just call out banks. "Canandaigua. Key Bank," I said. Both guesses were wrong. "Genesee Regional Bank. That's GRB."

She didn't say anything. And I couldn't think of any others. "Millie . . . I'm trying . . ." I started searching my phone for every bank.

"It is two letters."

"Millie."

"*M*," she said.

"Yeah?"

"That's the bank."

"*M*?" I said.

"*M* is the start."

"M&T."

"That's the one!"

"*M* is for Millie," I said. We both laughed. "That's how we'll remember it."

My phone gave me an address. I kept the radio off. She said, "It's a nice street," but then she got quiet, just looked out at the scenery. I wondered how long it had been. Houses and buildings and traffic, cars filing into parking lots, pedestrians departing from stores. Fast-food restaurants, a winter jogger. Everything that's out here. At some point, she asked where we were going, and I told her we were nearly there, just around the corner. Without the radio, M&T turned into alphabet jingles in my head: M&M's, *A* is for Apple. I remembered back to when we recorded her phone message: *This is the Prall residence.*

45

When we reached the branch, I realized I didn't have a handicapped sticker—a car honked behind me, for failing to signal—and while I could have maneuvered around to the drive-through, it seemed like the wrong way to do this transaction, with me at the wheel like a go-between. I wondered if I would want to get a sticker soon. For her. I asked if she had one, and she said, "I'm not driving."

I escorted her inside, and then I stopped a few steps behind her. I was unsure where to stand. No one was looking at me yet, but I felt that soon they would, and everyone would be thinking: *Who are these two?* No, just: *Who is he?* Millie carried her purse, and I handed her the bag—I should have looked for a different one with handles—and she took it to the window. She removed the bundles. Ten grand, in bank straps, a heap on the counter, but the lady teller wasn't shocked. Millie was just an ordinary old lady finding huge money in her house. If the money were mine, or going into my account, that would be another story.

"I want to deposit this money."

"Certainly. Can I see some ID?"

Millie fumbled in her purse and withdrew her wallet. She tried to remove the driver's license from the plastic, but the teller said she didn't need to take it out.

"Thank you, Mrs. Prall. Who's with you today?" the teller asked.

Millie looked to her left to see that I wasn't there. I wasn't sure if I was supposed to wave or step forward. "Oh," she said, and half turned. "This is my friend."

The teller glanced at me and then at Millie, for any sign of distress. Then she studied her computer. "And which account would you like to deposit this in?"

"The savings."

The teller filled out the deposit slip and handed the pen for Millie to sign. Then she broke the straps and counted the money.

"Would you like your balance on the account?"

"That would be very nice."

"And do you need help with anything else?" she asked, and Millie said she didn't.

I listened to the machine print out the data. The money went in the drawer. When I saw that, I thought about things from Millie's house, *money* things—the checkbook that *wasn't* in Millie's drawer until we found it beneath mail, the cash that should have been in a drawer, or, really, should have been here, which is why it was a good thing that we *were* here, together. A second teller, with her back turned, faced the drive-through window and talked into the microphone, to the customer in a car, who, from my vantage point, I couldn't see, and maybe because I couldn't see them, I imagined, again, that it was me and Millie out there, which still seemed wrong, but also not, simpler.

The teller, Millie's teller, handed her the slip of paper. Millie folded it in her purse. She began to walk toward me when she stopped. "Wait," Millie said. "I have made a mistake."

"You did?" the teller asked.

"We did something wrong." Her voice trembled. It sounded loud, or maybe just loud to me, microphoned like the second teller's, who now turned around because of Millie's noise.

Both tellers angled their faces at me. The man in the office, on the phone, looked out warily to the lobby.

Somehow, Millie had remembered the other money, and I couldn't explain why it was missing. Was I supposed to drive back? Suddenly I was in two odd places, here in the bank with Millie, and, in my mind, alone, in Millie's house.

"I need to pay you," she said.

"Oh, that's okay," I said. Which snapped me out of it, but not in a good way, because I didn't like that Millie was talking about payment, *my* payment, here.

"You have taken time from your day. How long have we been?"

"I guess a few hours. All told." The truth was I hadn't timed it. I'd forgotten when we started. Some half hour. Now it was a quarter past.

"Fifty. Fifty." She turned to the teller. "I need a hundred dollars."

"Certainly," the teller said. "Would you like me to take that from your checking or your savings?"

"Checking," Millie said, and the teller reached for another slip. More information taken down. The pen changed hands again. Her nameplate said Gwen. Next to the plate was a flyer for rates of interest. Credit.

The second teller said, "Have a good day" into the microphone, and I could envision the customer reaching out their car window to collect the cash or the proof of a deposit slip. And then I had a strange thought. I mean, another one, about Millie. I imagined that she had known about the money, that right after she'd said something was wrong, she had covered up my deception, to spare me the attention. Which I knew was not how her mind would work. Nonsense. Mounted behind the teller's head, a flat-screen TV aired cable news, muted, without captions, a story no one heard or understood.

"Would you like that in fifties?"

"What?"

"You said fifty-fifty. I can give you five twenties, if it's easier."

"I need a hundred dollars."

No more reasoning about how to break the money, in half or smaller. The system printed again, and Millie took the second receipt.

The TV was a split-screen. Two people, one asked questions and the other provided answers, and both were silent. Their quiet felt like my quiet.

I think Millie was trying to figure out what to do with three things: the bag, the hundred, the purse. How to carry them all. She put the money in the paper bag. I imagined that the single bill was somehow ten thousand, a magic trick that changed the denomination. All those thick stacks that were once inside there, and now this thin note— whose face was on it?—added up to the same. I imagined taking it back to the teller. I knew what she would say: Where did you get this funny money?

I watched Millie walk back to me. She held the bag out. I thought again of the changing face value. Another customer approached the window. The other teller stood backwards at the drive-through. The man in the office stared only at his monitor. He wore a tie to make him look like bank president. Of course, there was always the camera over us. I stared at its eye. And then I studied Millie, in her heavy coat. Her hair was out of place, and I realized her hat was missing from her head. It wasn't at the window—I had to step sideways to peer past the customer, which drew suspicion from the teller, Gwen, who wondered if I was sneaking a look at numbers. I wanted to glare back at her, to say I'd done nothing wrong. I didn't like the accusation. "Hey Gwen," I wanted to say, "you better not have fast-counted Millie's money."

The hat wasn't on the lobby floor. "Where are you going?" Millie asked. Her face wore an expression of concern: *Where have you strayed?* No, more intense than that, somewhere between anger and fear: *Don't you dare leave.* Because of the closeness of us in the car, which was even closer than us at her small table, but also with how we walked, down her steps with my arm as a crutch—now it felt like a big deal, that I was across the room from her, in a foreign building. And what about *my* face? Did it look like I was disoriented, gone batty? I tapped my head to signal.

What would the tellers say when I left? Would they say, *What was that? Did something just happen?*

Both tellers were now at their identical windows, the drive-through was empty, and when I glanced at the microphone stand, I imagined the tellers voicing their anxieties over the intercom.

Fine, let them talk. I understood.

I would search for the hat on the walk back to the van. It was most likely wedged between the passenger seat and the console, or on the other side by her door. I would check both places. I would help Millie find what was gone.

5

LAST WEEK, I DROVE BACK TO MY HOUSE. Not Renee's, because I didn't want to be spotted, but my childhood home. Maybe "drove back" is the wrong wording, and "detoured" is better. The house wasn't really on the way from anywhere, but I guess I convinced myself I was in the area, nearish, and I drove till I was. I just wanted to see what it looked like. I figured a lot of people did this kind of thing, some after-hours reminiscing, and I think the reason I went is that, after leaving Millie's house, I didn't feel like arriving yet at an apartment (mine).

The house was unchanged. The neighborhood too. It wasn't the kind of place where homeowners built massive additions, although I suppose most of the houses had turned over, with new families regenerating, so it was young kids again, the proof being a plastic slide here, a soccer goal there, some mini geodesic dome for climbing. I didn't get much from staring at my house. Not sure what I expected—the ghost of me staring out from a bedroom window? And, actually, it was hard to think about that window (and only that window) not being mine, belonging to others. I went from room to room, picturing the layout in my mind, although I kept interrupting my thoughts, wondering whether they'd renovated a bathroom or kitchen, until I was aware of sitting back in the car, on some memory stakeout, a surreptitious act, which reminded me of the trip to the bank, even though I'd done nothing wrong there.

The neighbors on each side had been a typical mixed bag. The family on the left (on my right, from my angle) was a nice family. Their kids were older than me, although I remembered making the best igloo with the youngest son—maybe the shape of the dome was what triggered the memory—the kind of place you dreamed you were gonna live in forever, so much so that I can still recall the sadness when the roof collapsed, because we had spent so much time padding and supporting the structure. I could almost hear the echoed thump of my gloved hands packing the snow, just like I still could hear the teenager laughing when it broke on top of us, which wasn't how I felt at all. (It's funny to think of him as only a teenager, because in my mind at the time, he was a grown-up, but I guess that's what he was.) We had worked on it for two days, and I remembered trying to sleep that first night. I couldn't wait to get out to the house the next morning. Their house—I mean, their actual house—looked kind of dismal now, like whoever was living there wasn't the same kind of people, which seemed unfair to the Craigs, to their memory, even though, if this family paid the asking price, what did the Craigs care? (And I guess there could have been multiple occupants in between.) And maybe the house was always this small and plain, but it was filled with the activity of four kids, so it looked more alive in my head.

On the other side, to my left but on my old house's right, the house looked better than I remembered, even though I had liked this family less. I think I expected (or even hoped?) that the house might have fallen apart. The front door was the same. The same vertical translucent windows, on either side of the door, funny what you remember. The house now had a basketball hoop in the driveway. They weren't mean, exactly, the people, and actually they did a lot with Christmas lights—although, I'm not sure what one has to do with the other. When I thought about the decorations, the lights, I remembered, oddly, Millie's lamp (even though it was mine at that moment, the circuits switching on and off for the dealer). It wasn't entirely unexpected that Millie would pop into my head, since I'd just come from there and I'd been spending so much time with her, but thinking about her here, it felt almost like she'd existed all the way back in my past, out of my childhood.

As if to prove that point to myself, my attention jumped three houses down, to where an elderly couple had lived. I couldn't name them. They weren't childless, but when I was growing up they were empty nesters, which felt like they *were*, as if the kids hadn't merely moved out but had never really been there in the first place. The family seemed so distant from my childhood timeline, miles from the starting point of my life, just *beyond*, even though these lots were much smaller than Millie's avenue. Now, in fact, the house, because of *Millie's* house, or because of her *life*, my job, had a special weight, and the more I stared at it, the more I thought of Millie, and the more I thought of Millie, vice versa. The family didn't seem apart. They seemed as close, as present, to me as the sequence of pictures on Millie's mantel, of a couple, kids or no kids, following a natural course from older to old. For some reason, because I couldn't remember their names, I counted up the house numbers (skipping ahead by evens, adding six to my own), almost as a consolation, just to have known something more about them. The numbering system, and maybe the thought of windows, my bedroom window in front of me plus the ones I'd installed, made me think of Millie's husband, and, on the one hand, it made sense to think of him, to think of them both, since I was thinking about this other married couple, but on the other it made as much sense as Millie's napkin writing. Not a napkin.

I turned back to the immediate family, the one with the Christmas lights. This family, they mostly kept their distance, which when I was growing up felt like a kind of meanness, and I do remember my dad getting in some kind of dustup with Mr. Martinengo, something trivial, a property-line dispute or about maintenance, although that's probably not right, sounds too recent. Their kids were older, too, and when I was growing up, I felt like I was living in the wrong spot, because no one my age was near me, although there was a group up the street, so what did it matter? Still, I remembered when I was really young asking my parents if we could move up there so I could be closer to everyone. They had a son who was trouble. I'm talking about the Martinengos still. And that's what my dad said about him, although all I could remember was the way he drove, tearing out of the driveway. No idea what he turned into, if he was in jail or a cop or selling real estate. Their daughter, I had a crush on her. She was a few years older than me, and really good at cartwheels. She seemed so light. I'd barely known her. I must have seemed like a child to her, if she ever thought of me at all, and I remembered how, at the time, I wished I was older, or at least a taller child, or that I wasn't so weak that she'd look at me and see something laughable. Maybe laughable is too strong a word. More like unseen. Like she was in the center of the yard, hit by sun, and I was hidden in shadow.

How weird to not hear noise from the house now, because they had a dog who barked constantly from their backyard, where he was chained up. In some ways, it was harder to imagine the dog not being here than the people, and maybe it was just the dog who *sounded* mean than the people being it, and now I was remembering it's what my dad must have fought about, telling them to bring the dog inside, although I guess they could have argued about both things, and even more.

So I was sitting here wondering when I was going to leave, and maybe the word "leave" is what did it—but, if that's the case, you'd think it would trigger a memory of my dad leaving, but instead, it made me think of another house, and it made me think of me. It was when Renee and I sat the kids down, in the living room, because we figured it was something we should do together, to explain the breakup, even though we really weren't. Explaining it. We weren't going to talk about our behavior, certainly I wasn't going to talk about mine, only our decision. Which was Renee's. And I hadn't had a leg to stand on to convince her otherwise. Renee went first, and then me, and then more of Renee, and it was strange to hear us talking together, taking coordinated turns. I guess in any other circumstance the back-and-forth would have been encouraging. At some point, Jack said, "Not again," and left the room. So it was just Erin. After she heard our story, Erin got real quiet. Her head was down. Renee asked if she was okay, and Erin lifted her face, and her expression was so open it frightened me. We were silent. And then Erin said, "I have an unfamily." And Renee said, "No, no," and then she looked at me, like, help, although her inner thoughts were probably worse than that, and I didn't know what else to say, because I'd already said everything, and because I didn't anticipate seeing her much, because, according to the separation agreement, I was considered a third party, and I couldn't prove extraordinary circumstances to have any type of relationship, and I hadn't adopted them, so I wasn't obligated, and Renee had already told me she was so looking forward to my disappearance. "No," I said, "that's not the word at all." And when Renee squeezed her hand, Erin's, it seemed enough of a gesture for both of us, her grip. Erin lowered her head again, and Renee stole a glance at me, and her teeth gritted, which I guess I interpreted as I hope you're suffering right now, and after.

And now I couldn't believe that I had driven here to my childhood to remember this, that if I was so interested in making myself sad, I should have driven directly to Renee's—I was almost mad at her because I'd wanted this to be private, instead of her being all over my mind. I was hoping I'd remember something if not quite happy then maybe festive, like the Martinengos' colored lights, which blinked everywhere, and I realize they wouldn't be glowing in the daytime, and it was only sunset now, but I thought, as far as memories go, this house would be easier. I thought it would be less.

There were a million things wrong with Millie's house, and through the winter I fixed a host of them. A sink repair. Squeaky floors where the floorboards were loose. A hot-water tank replacement. Cracked windows. Peeling paint. I was troubleshooting everywhere. Doors in need of weather-stripping. Outlets that couldn't hold plugs.

Other things weren't wrong, but Millie insisted they were. She wanted her basement waterproofed, even though she only had the seasonal seepage, but she said a neighbor's basement had flooded. I didn't ask when. She said she was afraid of mold. It was almost like

Millie was some plumber or basement inspector using scare tactics, pointing to a wall or foundation, saying, "I don't like what I'm seeing." Except, Millie was the one saying it, and saying what she couldn't see. Still, I dug a trench.

She wasn't like my other older customers, who tended to have a different value of my time, where I'm worth four dollars an hour, and not forty-five. I dropped the apartment complex. It was a mutual decision between me and the employer. I wasn't fired. It was mostly just changing out lock cylinders. Leaky faucets. I had more important things to do. I scheduled many days around Millie.

One day, her doorbell rang. I was closer, so I answered it. Her delivery guy. I'd been wondering how she was getting food. "Hello," he said. He held bags in both hands. "I'm here for Millie." He was younger than me, but not by much. I moved aside while he stepped in.

"Hi, Millie," he said.

"Hell . . . ohh."

He was the first person I'd met with her that knew her, at least by name. The teller at the bank had needed ID. Looking back on that transaction, I had an uncomfortable thought, which is that I was *comforted* by the unfamiliarity, that if the teller didn't know Millie, she didn't know *me*. Then again, thinking about it now, what did it matter if they didn't, they had the important personal information, her financials, which meant, in some way, that they knew her better than I did. I wasn't sure where I was going with this train of thought, thinking about bank statements—until suddenly thinking about hers made me think of mine, which was, like I said long before, on the positive side, solvent, because of the lamp, but was still low, lower than where I thought it would be if I'd asked myself, when I was twenty, Where did you think you'd get to?

He went straight to the kitchen. The deliveryman. I heard cans clunk down on the counter, the fridge open. He was back empty-handed in a few minutes, because it wasn't a lot of food.

Millie was watching one of her programs. She looked like she preferred to not get up. "How much does she owe you?" I asked. I could pay with my own, and just have Millie reimburse me with the supply of cash in the cabinet, which was another reason to have it handy.

"All set," he said, which meant she had an account there. I hadn't thought of that. A system where she wouldn't have to handle money. His voice, his demeanor, it reminded me of the first job I'd done for Millie, the toilet, when I acted like it was nothing, on the house.

After he left, I checked the fridge to see what he'd brought. Macaroni salad. Milk. The produce bins were empty. The freezer was filled with frozen dinners and Eggos. If this was my fridge, I'd be starving. There were two milks. Two half gallons. The new one was tucked behind the old (I could see the lower level), and I grabbed the closer milk (the sell-by date said today) to see if it was bad. I twisted open the cap and smelled for sourness, but it was still okay. When I closed the cap and returned the container and shut the fridge door, I thought about what I'd just done—not testing a fridge, but the contents inside, making sure they were safe for a customer, for Millie, which was a new task, smaller but somehow bigger at the same time.

And then I thought about the bags. Or, rather, I thought about his hands, empty-handed. So, where did they go? The bags. The kitchen garbage, but the bags weren't there, and then I remembered coming up the basement stairs and seeing them hanging on a hook. The bags he carried were the same kind Millie had used for storing her clothes by her chair, which was a strange association to have. It felt intrusive. Like the bags themselves, and not the undergarments, were intimate, and shouldn't be seen.

"They are very nice," she said when I asked about him. "He knows what to twist open for me."

"How's the program?" I asked.

Millie shrugged. "Crime this, crime that."

She was watching the local news. I expected to see some story about an arrest or trial, the reporter standing outside the police station or courthouse, but it appeared they'd moved on to the next story, and Millie was talking about the previous ones, so who knows what it was, or where. Convenience-store robbery? Some dumb crime committed in broad daylight, the guy maybe masked but hardly untraceable.

The deliveryman. He seemed nice, and human contact is good, but why should she trust him? A guy like that could be casing the joint. The word *valuables* popped into my head, and maybe the word triggered an image of the Tiffany lamp. When he was standing at the door, saying goodbye, he didn't seem to notice it was gone, and maybe I was overreaching here, but I drew two conclusions: One, he was probably more honest than the suspicions I had about him, and two, and more importantly, he didn't really know Millie if he didn't know what lights were here and what weren't. He didn't know anything.

"I like the meat counter," Millie said. "I used to know the butcher there. But he is gone."

But maybe there were things that Millie wanted to see for herself and pick. Not this product, but the other one, better brand.

"I could take you shopping," I said. I knew I'd offered something beyond even the bank errand, because she already had a person getting her groceries, so in some ways I was interfering. Maybe I was still in dialogue with the other guy, weighing the risk factors, or that I was imagining me as a replacement, like the lamp, to her. But as soon as I heard the statement from my mouth, I knew it wasn't a mere bank run. (Maybe bank run is the wrong phrase to use with Millie.) I'm just trying to make a point about quickness. Speed. Because we wouldn't be standing in a room, but slowly crawling from aisle to aisle, it felt like some journey or expedition, making our way around and along the aisles of the stores felt like as much mileage as the drive to get there. An entire morning or afternoon, but for some reason I didn't mind it, and not only because I'd be compensated, although we'd already solved, once and for all, the problem of delay. It felt like I was taking her to a place that wasn't just about money, although I was undercutting that fact if I kept talking about getting paid.

She wouldn't need this helping hand. If I was here, there wasn't any point in him being here, too. Two was redundant. Not if I took the extra step. It didn't mean much for me to say that I could do more than the deliveryman, because who was he anyway? But it meant something to say that I could do more than *me*.

I got a handicapped permit—or Millie got it. We did. We got a signed statement from her doctor and brought it down to the DMV. We kept it in her car, because it was easier for her to sit in the lower seat. "This is a gas guzzler," Millie had said, about my van, and she laughed, and I did, too, it didn't feel like an insult at all. Her Cadillac felt like a boat, but I didn't say that, because I thought it might confuse her. The battery was dead but I jumped it. The car was actually younger than my van, which was on its last legs. I saw, and also sensed, a lot of new doors opening—the car doors, the garage door swinging up. I adjusted the seat to make room for me. Somewhere I heard my younger self say something about driving Miss Daisy, and I told him to talk to me after he went out on his own.

Sitting in the driver's seat, it felt like many things. It felt, when I first squeezed into a scrunched position, that I was Millie. So I was in her seat, and I thought of her living room armchair, and I thought of me sitting there, too. But when I moved it back, the car seat, the adjustment, to straighten out my legs, it also felt like I was in a similar position to where the husband must have sat, when he was driving, when he was alive. Maybe the proper way to describe the sensation is that when I released the lever and slid back, I felt like I had grown into him, and I almost lifted the lever again, to sit back—I mean *up*—to find a closer or middle spot all my own. Although, what did I know about his height, other than from the mantel pictures, and his being approximately a head taller, and so what, if we're in the same place. I tried not to make too much of all this, because I guess any old car feels like a time machine. A better way of thinking all this was that the car was no longer abandoned.

I didn't know you worked for Rent-a-Husband.

I guess he—younger me—was still piping up. Go climb a roof, I told him, get going on your young man's work.

Really, this is quite an achievement.

Him again. Apparently he had a lot to say to me.

The way you sniffed that milk, a new area of expertise for you. Wow, you're becoming a sniffer, I see a bright future for you as a bloodhound. You're really using that nose to an advantage. Who knows what you'll do with the rest of your carcass.

Once he got going, he wouldn't stop, and I could imagine him throwing up his hands, but I could throw up my hands, too, or a single finger, a signal for him to leave. I was done with that, him. He really needed to grow up, this taunting twenty-year-old. I'd screw my head on straight. I was done talking to that kid.

6

THE CLOCK NEEDED TO BE RESET, because of the dead battery.

We listened to the golden oldies station. Me and Millie. It was the same station I used to advertise on, and I imagined at any moment the commercial might come on between the songs. The guy's voice hadn't been mine, but better, he sounded not just confident but conversational, likable—it helped that there was this light guitar in the background, that it was a happy thing that you didn't have time or know-how to do your repair work, because here I was—that's what the guy was telling the listeners. I think it was guitar, maybe it was banjo. Some comfy, throwback music. I hadn't thought of that ad in a while, but thinking about it now, that guy being me was sort of like me being Millie on her machine. Renee liked the ad. She thought the guy sounded upbeat. But she also said, "He doesn't sound half like you."

"They painted their house yellow," Millie said when we drove down her street. Millie's.

She would do this sometimes, prove to herself that she remembered things. Landmarks. Changed facades. She didn't like the expressway. Everything moved too fast and she didn't like going over forty. So I took back roads, side streets. Sometimes, or maybe just initially, holding the steering wheel gave me the same sensation as when I'd shifted the seat back and felt like I was him. What I mean is, when I gripped the wheel and placed my hands in the standard positions, ten and two, I could almost feel the traces of his clamped hands, and then hers, before me, as if the wheel were worn at the spots beneath my fingers. But what was I to do, I couldn't hold my hands at some ridiculous positions on the curve, or at the top and bottom, twelve and six, because it wasn't my car, and I wanted to show caution in handling this boat. Of course, it was smaller than my van, and it didn't have the strong smells of my jobs coming in from the back. In fact, while the car's exterior had all sorts of dents, the inside smelled surprisingly odorless, but that might have had more to do with the months of idleness.

I could feel my posture twitch in the seat. Millie didn't have to adjust at all—or have *me* reposition her, since the lever might be too difficult—but I guess she had gone back to the passenger seat she was in when her husband was alive and driving, that is, before she sat here, where I was. I shook my head at the musical chairs. I liked looking outside with her, and seeing what was remembered. But I didn't like to look at the gray interior. It's not that I thought it was private or unseemly, like underclothes, but sometimes being inside the car was like being trapped, the old seat belt tight across my chest, the position of the driver's seat between his setting and hers. It felt like less of me, or me blurring into them, their past, and even though the car was fairly recent, and I'm sure they'd been through a series of them, it felt like *all ages*, like this model held the entirety of their marriage, and when I eyed the rearview mirror, I felt like I was in the first one and I could almost hear the Just Married cans rattling on the asphalt. When I half looked at the AAA books tucked in the side panel, for destinations like Toronto and Montreal, I felt like we were crossing over the border. "You recognize any of these buildings?" I'd ask, to shift my attention to street scenery, because I liked how she'd referenced the blue house that had been previously yellow. It was like she was revealing a secret, the unseen layer. I wanted to see if she knew more. It's a house, she only shrugged. Or she'd say nothing, as if she were watching a colorless slideshow, and I'd wait, until she'd turn from the window, her eyebrows knitting, and I'd nod at her, as if to communicate agreement that there was nothing worth mentioning. Sometimes we'd arrive sooner than I expected.

In the parking lot, we walked side by side, but in the store I kept behind, shielding her so no one on their cell phone bumped into her. It made me feel good, bringing her out to get some exercise, to shop for nutrition. I helped her reach anything high, and lowered her items into the cart. "My . . . cuff. I've got cuff issues," she said. "Row. Rotate. I fell and disorientated my shoulder." She took a long time studying the brand and the price and the packaging. Sometimes, I'd watch her examining things in her hand, and I felt like she wasn't reading ingredients but deciphering the thing itself. This is a can. This is a box of cereal. This is a strawberry.

An elderly woman smiled at me. Other women did, too, wives my age. They looked at me, stopped halfway down the aisle, like I was spending time with my dear aunt. And then they pushed their cart in the other direction. They were wrong, of course, about our relationship, but I didn't want them to be wrong about me. I was the guy they were seeing. Actually, I wanted to be with them—with her, the wife who was maybe divorced—talking about him, what a nice guy he was. I wanted what I was doing with Millie to bring someone over. Then again—and sure I felt the itch, it had been a while—I didn't know how to relate to them. I felt so slack when others wheeled past me down the aisle, the world going fast without me, but I reminded myself that I was getting paid for going nowhere.

It was odd, but somehow being with Millie made me see more of the kids' food: the Jell-O, the alphabet soup. It felt like I was aging backwards to my childhood. Oscar Mayer bologna, chocolate milk, Kraft Singles. Honey-Combs. Millie made a joke about being too old to buy green bananas. She made lots of jokes about expiration dates. I asked about oranges. The big bag was cheapest, but she said she couldn't eat that many. So I told her I'd buy the bag, and she could take three. In that way, I reintroduced fruit to her life. I brought substance. Sustenance, I mean. When we returned to her house, I restocked her fridge, and I enjoyed the sound of the fruit tumbling into the produce bins, like the start of an arcade game.

But sometimes, when we were still there, back in the store, in an aisle, with customers weaving around our inertia, she'd forget what the bag was for. (And I think I was feeling my own bewilderment as well, not about the bag, but the cart itself, which wasn't loaded up, and so it was similar to the Home Depot one, which hadn't been loaded up, either.) "I can't eat all this," she'd say. And I'd remind her how we were splitting them, that I was taking most. "Remember the beginning?" I'd say, and I'd gesture back to the produce. She'd press her forehead, and her troubled face would clear. Then she nodded and smiled, like the bag was a souvenir or prize. She said something about Florida. And sunshine. I asked if she'd ever been.

"No," she said. She stood thinking. "And I don't have my passport."

I wasn't sure if she was joking.

"Did you need anything for yourself?" she asked.

Sometimes, I did, just a few items, never a full shop, just enough that I thought of it as payment for the time spent, even though she was already paying me. These items usually went in with Millie's stuff, but I didn't bother telling the cashier to separate mine, since I could always sort them out once I got back to Millie's. I could use one of her bags, once I'd emptied the contents. Millie didn't really like the noise and crowdedness of the checkout lane, and the refrigerated section was shivery cold, but she liked to get sweets. I asked what she wanted today. "I haven't had cake in a while."

I asked what kind. She said, "Upside-down pineapple cake." I'd never heard of that, but she said she knew the formula. We got the ingredients. I added them to the shopping list, which was always me doing the writing now, so it wasn't Millie's squiggles, which were hard for her hand and hard for my eyes.

We prepared the recipe together. From scratch. She said the cake was her husband's favorite. I liked it. It seemed like something my grandmother would have made. Sunday nights, sometimes, I would get a pizza for us, and help her with laundry. How that happened was, we'd returned from the store, and I was stuffing the plastic bags where the other guy, Mister Nameless, had put them. And I noticed one of the bags was down on the basement floor. When I peered closer, I saw clothes inside, almost like what I had gotten used to seeing by the chair in the front room.

I called Millie over. I stared at the bag while I waited. "What's that?" I said, and she said, "Laundry." "How do you mean?" I asked, and she said that was how she got it there. And she showed me with an imaginary throw. "Good throw," I said. "You have strong arms," and she smiled when I said it, but I didn't know if she realized I'd used her same words—probably not—or if she just liked the compliment. The laundry: I'd thought about it, but I *hadn't*. We'd been talking all these days, but not really, not enough. I could have saved her the trip, the potential accident, and once I thought of the word *accident*, I saw *her* down on the basement floor, no bag. I could feel it in my body right now, light-headed, heavy-legged, the tumble from the top step.

I should have thought of laundry so many times—like when I'd asked her what her hobby was, and she said moving stuff around. "Put you back over here," she'd said. She said her other hobby was forgetting things. She used to do the puzzle books, but now it was mostly television.

We talked more about her husband. "He worked for . . . up up up. Retired as manager."

"Kodak."

"What?" Millie said.

"That's where he worked." Because I already knew that.

"He worked at Kodak."

I nodded, as if we were first having the conversation. She asked me again why I was divorced. She said, "Didn't you say 'I do'?" She thought that was supposed to mean something. These days, she said, everyone's just out the door.

She had a point. I remember asking my dad about it, why he hadn't lasted with Mom. He said some people stay in a building when it's burning—but that wasn't him. I didn't really blame him for that out-look. Mom had always been a bit of a crab. *"How you doing, Mom?"* *"It's Monday morning again."* Dad had advice not just about ditching marriages, but about how to run a legit business. He said, steal some-thing small every day. Steal a pen at the bank. A gumball. At the bulk section of the supermarket, eat a couple of peanuts. Eat a grape out of the bag. That way you never have the urge to do anything bad. That was Dad's advice on being honest.

But here was Millie being faithful to her dead husband, when me and Renee cheated on each other, had affairs left and right—not say-ing it was even, it was more like left and right and left, with me being *left.* Anyway, what made Renee so different from Millie was that she probably *wished* I was dead. I hadn't really thought much of a failed marriage. The word, I mean. Failed. We'd just broken up. Split.

Me and Millie were eating upside-down cake again.

"This was Jim's favorite," she said. "And bread and butter. That was his best friend. That's why he had a double stomach. When he retired, he got bored."

"Did you make this on his birthday?"

"Of course. Our first anniversary . . . the first anniversary, when he died. After. I wanted the full nine yards. But not now. He called me his first wife. That was his joke, for sixty years."

My birthday was two months back, but I'd skipped it. I asked her when hers was, and she told me it was coming up.

I found out they'd honeymooned at the falls.

"Niagara?"

Of course, she said. It felt stronger than when she'd said it just before. Her words almost sounded like an exclamation, because she wore the same face as when I'd tried to explain how I'd thought her lamp was a fake.

They met at a church dance. They vacationed once at a dude ranch, and countless times in the Poconos.

"Ninety-five."

"What?"

"You'll be ninety-five," I said. "That's something."

She nodded. "Purse. Purse severe. I have persevered." She frowned. "I would like my brain to come back," she said. Then she shook her head. "I ask God to take me in my sleep. Every night. And wake up in heaven."

It was understandable for Millie to say all this, but less so for me, to be spending time with someone who was nightly praying for the end. For clarity's sake, I pushed my thoughts back to her perspective. It may have sounded contradictory, wishing for your mind to come back at the same time you wished so hard to depart, but I thought it made total sense. And if I were her, or had her life, it would be exactly the two things I'd hope for. Even if they sounded mutually exclusive.

"That's winning the lottery," she said.

She became the bulk of my income. "If you see anything, go ahead and fix it," she said. Some things, like the baking element of her stove, were too old to fix, the parts were discontinued, and she asked if I would get her a new appliance. Normally, I didn't do that, but for her, I did. The winter was slow (people were waiting for their tax-return money), but I was slowing things down, too. Or narrowing them. Weeding out people and jobs. I stopped going into the middle of the city, where you can't leave your truck unlocked, and where you might not get paid. And I eliminated the longer drives, where I'm wasting gas to make fifty dollars, just to do a dishwasher diagnosis out in Brockport. I cut down my work radius. A guy could make a living off of three good customers. After a while, though, it's like she became my one.

We'd go on these outings. Once in a blue moon we got a hamburger. She liked clams. And her appetite was surprisingly good. Like me, sometimes, she even cleaned her plate. Once, when the waiter took it, she startled like he'd come from nowhere. "His arm just came out of a cave," she said when he left.

I agreed. It was like he'd swooped down from another planet.

"Where did he come from?" she asked.

"I didn't see him, either," I said. "Cave city." We laughed about it together. A city where all the waiters lived.

Millie smiled. "That must be where he is from. Where she came from."

I nodded—he, she.

"She came from the elevator."

I knew there wasn't an elevator in the restaurant, and maybe she was making a joke about waiters taking elevators from the cave to get to here, men and women, which was kind of funny. But she wasn't smiling anymore.

"That's where he met her."

"The waiter?"

She shook her head. "She wore lipstick at work. Every day. I was home. Always. Some . . ." She frowned and circled her hand around her front, like she was full. "Some top. To clean out the garage. And she's some chicky. Dressed up for work. They drove around in twin Cadillacs."

I was curious. Or beyond that. The curiosity I felt was bigger than when I saw the laundry bag on the basement floor, or even when I stumbled on the cash that hadn't yet been banked. I didn't think I was exaggerating the second point. It's just, what Millie said, or was trying to, it was like something my mom or grandmother might have said, a story from their lives, my own family history, and I was surprised at the merging. Although, I still wasn't even sure if I was right, if Millie was contradicting the version of Jim. About Jim being the pick of the litter. "Millie, um . . ." I felt like I was on the precipice of something. Maybe her mind had slipped, and she'd somehow switched her life to mine, like I'd told her a story I'd forgotten about. That is, forgotten that I'd told her. Except, we didn't come from Cadillacs. "Your husband drove around with a woman with two Cadillacs? He bought her a car?"

"*They* had Cadillacs. *Her* husband. He was a tyrant. Because they talked about him. That's what they were doing, over coffee. Can you believe that?"

I told her I couldn't.

"He would've had a rope around her wrist, if he could've. That's how she talked. He wanted a ranch hand."

I couldn't tell if Millie was confused, or the story was just confusing. "That's how she softened my husband up. By telling her sob story. The Jerk—that's what she called her husband. He went to lunch with her." She looked around the restaurant, like it had been a place just like this, Jim sitting with another woman, having a conversation.

"How . . . how did you find out?" Which was a question I've asked before, or haven't, but always got answered.

"I didn't realize Millie cut her hair and colored it blonde."

I shook my head, and Millie did, too, but we were shaking for different reasons, and I'd lost her again, lost myself. "I'm sorry, you're talking about yourself. So I got confused. That's what you told *him?*"

"What?"

"About your hair?"

"That's what my friend told him."

Right, I thought. The friend told Millie, because she saw them. Together. Or she walked up to Jim and said that. Or both things happened, one after the other.

"I don't want to talk about this!"

Which jolted me. And a few other tables, too. I nodded. I bounced my hand in the air to lower our voices. "Of course," I said, whispering, even if I hadn't been the one to bring it up first.

"In my days, you didn't upset the cart. You didn't speak if you had a mouthful."

So we didn't, even after going back to the burger place, or anywhere else.

Who covered the meal? It depended. Sometimes me, more often her, at times we split it fifty. If I tried to pay more, she explained, "My money doesn't mean anything." Mostly, we charged it. But sometimes we paid cash, and the waiter brought back change. I helped her calculate the tip. The staff recognized us. We had become regulars, and I thought I recognized some of the other tables, too.

We ran errands. The pharmacy drive-through. She gave me her husband's tools. Which were so old, and normally I'd give them to the scrapyard, or donate them, but these, I kept. One time, I brought her cinnamon bread. Sunday nights, we ate together. I cooked a meal for her. I made chicken, and the first few minutes, she sat there pulling off the skin. "I call that the overcoat," she said. But after she took a bite, she told me it was tasty. Actually, I thought it was pretty bland. "Real food," she said. "This didn't come from the factory." She insisted we use cloth napkins. I did the dishes after. I checked my voicemail. One of the messages was the tighty-whities guy, saying he needed rooms painted. Sorry, go show someone else your loincloth.

I became Millie's go-to guy. Her go-get-the. There had been another lady, I used to bring her cigarettes. I was her cigarette boy. Oh, I'll miss you, she said. You can set a tent up in the back. It was a funny joke. But her life wasn't. One time, I went over there, she was living with one lightbulb. She didn't want her kids to know. So, I changed all of them.

Still, sometimes there were days in a row when I was tied up with other jobs and I couldn't see Millie. Even though, in truth, I preferred her. She told me I was the grandson she never had. And I felt the same way; she reminded me of my grandmother. Not the one I knew, really, but my dad's mom, Grandma Dot, who had lived hours away in Utica, and we rarely saw. I think we drove there twice. She died when I was six. I only knew her a few years. But she mailed me stuff. She took a vacation once to a Caribbean Island, and she brought me back a model sailboat. My mom's mom we knew more, but she was mostly crotchety. I don't know why Millie reminded me of her. My other grandma, that is. Dot. For Dorothy. No, wait, she was Doris. I can't remember a single word she said. She always had gum and candy. And she coughed a lot. The only time she was scary was when she coughed. These attacks she'd have. She cooked food. I'm trying to remember what. The smell. Millie smelled of lavender. I can't remember what my grandmother smelled like. Cigarettes, of course. I hadn't thought of that sailboat in years. It was like treasure. I wished I still had it.

But money-wise, like I was saying, I couldn't always be with Millie. I was doing a basement remodel. Good pay, but the customer—the husband—was being ridiculous. I'd built the exercise area, the office, installed the drop ceiling and the recessed lighting, but now he wanted a projector. And he wanted this extra at no extra charge. The projector, the screen, the speakers—they were all an afterthought, but he wanted me to throw them in because I was already here. I showed him the contract, which just made him irate. He still owed me half. It was dead of winter, and this was a profitable job, but I was still annoyed he was asking for a freebie. I should have known. I'd painted his house last year, and he inspected everything. He's a dentist, and I am *done* with dentists.

Millie called. She called me a lot, at all hours. She said her toilet was clogged. But I got there and it wasn't. I had to rush back to the dentist for the donated time. Which was strange, twisted: I was going back there, to run speaker wire for free, but here I was getting paid to do nothing. This—a phantom call—had happened already with a water mark Millie'd seen on a wall that wasn't moisture but shadow. In both instances, she insisted on paying me for the false alarms. But she called me again about the toilet. When I returned the message, I got her machine. And heard my voice. Which shouldn't have surprised me—right before it clicked on, I remembered recording it— but I wasn't ready to hear it when I *wasn't* right next to it, and her.

"This is the Prall residence," my voice said. Sure, it felt like I was calling myself. And that I was in two places at once. Which made me feel like I was nowhere. And because I didn't live there, it seemed like nobody did, that the voice was coming from a dead space, not just the machine but the entire house. *Please leave a message.* I didn't. I wasn't sure how to talk. And it seemed crazy, talking through my recorded self to talk to her. I called back, and I didn't want to hear the message again. I realized that when I wasn't there, I was, a piece of me, my voice, was implanted, waiting to be switched on. Millie picked up on the third ring, which was good, because I was worried. She might be in trouble on the floor. More than that. I felt like she was gone.

"Hello?"

"Millie?"

"Yes?"

"You called me about your toilet. This is Don."

"There are problems with it."

"I just called you before," I said, and I didn't know why I was bringing that up. "You said your toilet was stuck yesterday."

"Yes."

"And it wasn't."

"It is stuck now."

"Okay."

"It cannot flush."

"I'll be there soon."

"Good. I'm ready when you are."

I wanted to tell her to change the message, that it was too strange, but maybe it was only strange for me. "I'll be there soon," I said again.

"It cannot flush."

I heard her voice, but I was too distracted with the echo of my own.

"Hello?" she said, but I didn't answer, which felt like I was denying I was here. I almost felt that I was acting—or being—her, in the passenger seat, when I'd asked her what was outside and she responded with nothingness.

I got there, and she was right. I plunged the toilet, but I couldn't get it unplugged, and then I ran the snake down. I pulled up some hand towels. They were rooster-patterned. I looked over at the rack and saw what was missing.

A few years ago, I was fixing a garbage disposal; the motor had burned out. I found this handful of change in the disposal—the owner's kid had thrown it down there. But this sewer backup: I'd never had a customer deliberately hurt their house, just to bring me back. I was, in a weird way, flattered. If Renee ever broke something in the house, not that she did, it wouldn't be to keep me around, or have me return. And when I told Beth I was a handyman, she said, "Oh, good, that might be useful," but it never got to that point. But maybe she, Millie, didn't comprehend her actions. One time—too long ago to say when—an old lady called me about her broken dryer. But it wasn't broken. She had taken her wet clothes out of the washer, put them in a bin, rolled them to the dryer, and then forgot where she was in the process. So she made a U-turn and washed them again. How many times? *Why are my clothes still wet?* She had kids and they stepped in.

But Millie, I felt like she knew what she was doing. Or didn't. Either way, things were getting out of hand. And sometimes you walk away from a job. You call in the experts, who have experience with bigger procedures. Except, who in this instance was in over their head? Not me, really? Was I in over my head because Millie was having problems with hers?

When we had our coffee, which, as usual, I poured and brought to the table, I remembered how she talked about the senior center. Bingo and card games. Kings in a corner, she called it.

"Maybe there are other people at the center you could talk to," I said now, because she had told me her lady friends were all gone.

"Well, of course there are." She shook her head. "I already know all of their business."

I asked her about church. She used to be on the altar guild; church members would bring things by.

"I remember Father Anderson, but I've heard they have a new priest, and I've heard nothing from them."

"What about neighbors?" She had mentioned a doctor who organized a street picnic.

"One of them—their dog is always pooping in my yard."

"Really?"

"Just this morning. They never pick it up."

"I . . . I could look for it." I almost felt like she was my dad, complaining about the Martinengos' dog, and I never would have made that association if I hadn't driven to my old house. "Do your neighbors know you're here? Alone?"

"Well, why wouldn't they? I don't say six words to them. Everyone else is too busy with their own lives. And it's not their fault."

Her former mailman was very kind, she had told me, but he changed routes, and the new man was not as nice. "Have you thought about getting some help in here? A health person?"

I didn't want to make her angry, but I was strangely happy that she was. Her head shook furiously, and mine did, too, because I was trying to figure out my strange happiness. Seeing Millie was like the flip side of hearing Beth, her breakup flippancy: *I'm not feeling it.* I wished, after Beth had said that, when it was my turn, I could have said, "Yeah, I'm not feeling it either," just so it sounded even. Even if it wasn't. I almost wanted to call her up now, she was still in my phone, and tell her what I meant to say. Or say, "We're not feeling it," like I was speaking for both of us, like we'd teamed up to say the words. No, even better, I'd steal the line. I wished I'd said it first.

Millie said, "I don't want someone I don't know in my house." And I agreed with her, but part of me was agreeing with the statement because of my childhood drive, and how I'd felt when I stared up at my window. No one wanted anyone there, in place of you. "And . . . they're thieves," she said. Which, mostly, we were in agreement on, or at least how they could be. For example, the deliveryman, even if he wasn't, he just as easily was, although the main problem with him was not that Millie didn't know him but that *I* didn't. "You hear horror stories. They stole her entire silver set."

Our eyes met. Locked. "Who? From who?"

"Across the street." She pointed in different directions. "Way over. One piece at a time, going out in her *purse.* Most of the caregivers don't speak English . . . They're babysitters. And they gouge you. I *had* an aide, but she quit."

"Oh, you did?"

"They put money in her face, and she left." Her eyes stayed big.

Her judgment—they were crooks and looters—felt wrong or right.

"Do you have *anyone* looking in on you?"

She looked at me, but didn't speak. I glanced away. But then I returned her stare. I nodded, even before she said, "You."

What I felt, what I knew: she'd latched onto me. I'd become indispensable by inches. She had said to me once, "You live here, but people forget you're living." But it wasn't like that. She had put herself on an island. And she wanted only me there, and a lot of me, more and more, wanted to be there, too. Despite the isolation.

The wet towels. "I remembered those towels," I said, hardly out loud, almost to myself. What I meant, with the remembering, was that I was in so many places. I was back in the bathroom, with the wet towels, pulled from the toilet, on the floor, but I was also down in the basement, adding them to the laundry, where, in a couple of hours, the towels, having been washed and dried and returned upstairs, would be draped, neatly and evenly, on the rack, just as they had once and always been. And of course I was here, with Millie, across from her. (I could hear, below the floor, the washing machine, now on spin cycle, almost like how, from the front hallway, I'd heard that leaky flapper months ago.) When I glanced at Millie, her frail, strong arms, I was back in the hallway, the back one, thinking she didn't need to use small, throwable bags anymore. I guess I was here but also elsewhere, everywhere.

She needed me to be more than a handyman. But a handyman, it's never been what I thought I should only be. Decades ago, I thought I'd move up, I'd widen my scope. Now, I could be a different kind of more. I could coordinate something bigger. Maybe she was my purpose. My mission. Maybe this house was where I fit.

7

—————

I CALLED MY DAD. It wasn't odd for me to do that, since we talk semiregularly, but what was uncharacteristic was that I would call him from here. I told Millie I had to take a business call, but then I didn't step out to the van. Instead I asked, pointing with my thumb behind me, "You mind if I use your kitchen?"

"I don't care what you do," she said.

But then I realized I was lying to her, so I added, "Actually, if you don't mind, I just need to call my dad first." Which sounded more like the truth, or truthful.

But why here, for the call? Maybe the answer was the cupboards. I don't mean, digging around, Oh, look, here's the corkscrew. It was just, all the coffee cups, the rows of them, going back, and the stacks of plates: I felt connected to that history. Whereas, with my apartment, it wasn't just the spareness, or the bareness, it was that everything had been furnished from Craigslist. And sure, the couches and tables were now mine, or maybe a trace of secondhand, but they all felt anonymous, or the place itself felt that way, like there's too little of me, or anyone. Or there was the crowd of everyone who had come before, and then me, and then everyone after, but it still added up to nothing, certainly less than this kitchen. If I didn't want to call from the apartment, I could still have opted for some parking lot, but maybe

I liked how I *sounded* here, more grounded, or like the long marriage, hers, made me feel stronger, than him (Dad) or myself.

Dad's retired from UPS, and he spends most of the year down in Florida. He owns an RV. Roughing it smooth, he calls it. He got a girlfriend, recently, although I didn't know if they were still an item. She's, like, thirty years younger. They go to concerts. Honestly, I didn't know what she saw in him.

After he picked up the phone, I realized I only wanted to talk about Grandma Dot—I wasn't going to mention my drive home—which was odd since, with my dad, we didn't do the ancestor thing. So instead I just asked how he was doing. Maybe that's why I called from here: I needed to be in an old house to ask about an unfamiliar elder.

"Well, I don't see a tag on my toe."

I laughed, even though it was an old joke. I played along, said something about the undertaker.

He asked about business. I told him it was good. I said I was doing work for someone who reminded me of his mom. But because Grandma was so unknown, I had to lie about Millie to make them sound alike. "She's a smoker," I said, and it was strange—more than that, plain wrong—to be talking about her, to be lying about her, especially when I was here, but I was just trying to get to someone else. Still, I was glad Millie couldn't hear me from the other room. I said there was a candy drawer. To my dad. "She likes cake," which felt like a double truth, not only that she liked it but also that I helped with preparation, and I felt like I'd evened out the balance sheet with the lies about smoking and candy. But then I didn't know if my grandma did. Liked cake. "She cooked meatballs, right?"

"Sure, she cooked meatballs. What grandmother doesn't make meatballs?"

"Yeah, I don't remember much. I got less memory of her."

"Less memory than who?"

"My other grandma."

"Oh, that's right. Well, your memory ended—what were you? You were pretty young."

I told him I was six. He said he didn't realize it was so early, and no wonder it was such a blur. I told him I remember the coughing.

"The coffin?"

"Cough*ing*." Then I told him about the sailboat. "I just remember her as really nice."

"She was. Dad was mean. An SOB. And she loved him to pieces. I mean, she could be real stubborn. Especially at the end, when she got sick. She'd throw her pills away. If a pill didn't work after the first day, she'd throw it down the toilet."

When he said toilet, I guess I pictured towels. "Slow day?" he asked.

"No, I'm working. Just a free hour." It was, and it wasn't. I'd—or we'd—eaten lunch here earlier, and I told Millie I'd get to the bowls and plates later, when we had our coffee. I'd combine the dishes. But I could see all of it now, the percolator, cups, napkins, even Millie in the chair, even though she was in another one, in another room.

"I'm heading over to Stacy's in a few minutes."

"You're still dating?" I wasn't sure if there was something underneath my voice, not just surprise but annoyance.

"Sure."

"I thought maybe it was some fling."

"No, it's more than that. We're together. We're serious."

"How old is she again?"

"She's not old at all. *I'm* the one that's old. That's why I'm taking my love potion."

"All parts working. Everything goes *up*."

"I might go all the way with her. Marriage, I mean."

"Really."

"Why not?"

"She been married before?"

"Sure. She's not *that* young, that she's never been married. I'd be number two. We'd both be."

I pictured the "JUST MARRIED" cans trailing his RV, the young/old pair honeymooning somewhere out west, and my mind veered out to the garage and Millie's rearview, the vision of her early days. I'd wanted to have this conversation in the kitchen, but now I sort of *wasn't*. I was in Millie's last car that felt like her first. To return me here, I stared at my hands, cupped them as if a coffee cup were inside them, which it would be later.

"You with anyone?" he asked.

I told him no.

"I thought you were. Weren't you dating some gal? Thought you were steady. Getting to be. I should probably remember her name. Sorry."

"No, it was casual. Whatever it was. Not anymore. Ancient history."

"Oh, that's too bad. Well, I think it's still a good thing, that you jumped ship from Renee. A lot of hostile fire. You needed to get out. But alone is—"

"Yep. That's me. A fresh start. New life. I might go raise llamas."

He took some time to answer. "Anything wrong?"

"Why would anything be wrong?"

"It's Wednesday. It's two o'clock in the afternoon. You're talking family tree. You're talking grandmother."

The two bananas on the counter were already overripe. Millie couldn't eat them fast enough, so we'd have to buy more, but next time, maybe purchase less. "She gave me this model sailboat."

"You've already said that."

"I know what I've said. I'm just being sentimental. Childhood toy. My mind went back to it. That's why I'm saying it twice."

"Okay. I don't remember. I'm . . . sorry she didn't live longer. They were an odd combo. Mom and Dad. Your grandparents. They didn't match. Donny . . . honestly . . . I can't tell if you sound like an old fart, because you're talking about your grandparents, or if you sound like a four-year-old, same thing."

"Must be the phone."

"It's not the connection. You . . . need—"

"I've never asked you for money." Not even when I'd botched the roofing job and the insurance payment and made a mess and a hole, I never mentioned any of that mistake.

"I'm . . . not talking money."

"You've got me wrong. I'm working steady. For some heiress." I didn't know why I said it that way, why I called Millie that. She was in her chair, watching TV, deaf to anything beyond the one room, but in my mind I turned the volume up louder so she wouldn't overhear.

"Oh. Okay."

"I'm not making less," I said. "Don't worry about my paycheck."

"I was just thinking, if the winter's slow, why don't you come down and visit me? I know those winters."

"Florida. Sure. I'll go get my passport."

"Ha. I'm just saying. You ain't that far away. And those Rochester winters are too long. They make people crack. All that snow makes folks stir-crazy."

"We're not getting any snow. One storm. And it warmed right after, so it's not even like it buried us."

"Go figure. No snow in the snowbelt."

"Look at the numbers. Snowfall's been less than forty inches."

"Well, down here, it's zero. No counting up. No math. And all sun."

"We're getting sun, too. More than usual."

"Believe me, I remember. I know that old weather. Too many gray days. Blech."

"It's been sunny," I said, which was a lie, and I didn't know why I was lying to him, although I sort of liked it, he probably deserved a little of that. I didn't want him to have better weather. "I'm telling you, it's been warm."

"Listen, from where I'm at, it's cold up there. I don't have to check temperatures."

I looked outside at the yard, which had become such a familiar view. The giant tree at the back corner was a hazard, two trunks split at the base in a V and leaning; it should probably be taken down as a precaution. An expensive job. The ground was green but muddy; the trees wouldn't bud for another month. Millie was comfortable. She was watching her TV, and I was watching her lawn. A bird flew across it. I could see green shoots coming out of the beds. I had no idea if

Grandma Dot gardened. Grandpa Carl grew vegetables. I wish I'd known her better.

"You still in that rental?"

"Yeah. I moved out of Renee's."

"Right. You should think about property. You had to move out, but you don't want to get stuck in that spot. You know, short-term is how you should be thinking. An opportunity comes along, somewhere else, you can buy, you're out. You're moving."

I didn't answer.

"Hey?"

"It's not a long-term lease."

The TV was louder, like a headache—a commercial must have come on—and now I wanted the volume lowered. Before, I'd wanted it raised so she couldn't hear me say heiress, but now I wanted the opposite so sound wouldn't travel over the phone and my dad wouldn't ask where I was, inside.

"Never mind," I heard him say. "It's your life."

"I'm fine. I'm just like you. I got my own May–December thing."

"What? Oh—wait, what is she, twelve?"

"Something like that. Actually, you've got the wrong number. Way off. Wrong way." I felt embarrassed for thinking that, even if it was a joke no one understood. I was more embarrassed than when I walked into the bank with Millie, with no good place to stand, and now I felt *doubly* embarrassed, because I was thinking about money, and thinking about it here. And I wanted to blame my dad for that, for bringing up needs, even if he said he'd meant something else.

"Oh, she's *older?*"

"Actually, I'm taking a break."

"You're taking a break. But you're in a relationship? Donny, those are two different things."

"I'm saying I'm not available."

"Will you stop talking gibberish."

"I'm fine."

"You sound—"

"I went by the old house," I said, and then I realized I'd told him because it was something he couldn't do, because he wasn't here now. But then I instantly regretted it, so I said I didn't stop but kept going.

"Okay."

"It looked . . ." And I was trying to figure out a lie, but then I thought, why bother, let him fill in the blank.

"When you said the old house, for a sec, I wasn't sure if you meant Renee's or, you know, where you grew up, where we . . ."

I decided not to answer him—have him figure it out for himself. It had been a while since I'd listened to someone else search for words. Someone other than Millie. Or me. Martinengos on the left, Craigs on the right. Us in the middle. Let him picture himself there.

"Where we *what?*" I said.

"What?"

"You were about to say something about the house."

"Yeah. I . . ."

"You sound out of it." I liked using the line he'd tried to use on me.

"*I* sound out of it. No, *you* do. I'm just trying to follow."

"I'm right here." I was surprised the bananas were already spotted and brown. It seemed like, day before yesterday, the skin was green, or yellow green, but maybe Millie had accelerated the ripening with the heat, the temperature—the high thermostat she set this house on— which reminded me, my memory growing, of the heat escaping from the windows, months ago, and the installation job I did. It *was* warm in here, stuffy, and I looked at the fridge, and maybe it would be better to nix bananas altogether, and just stick with refrigerated fruit, so you weren't so rushed to eat. "Like I said, I'm working. I'll call you . . . what day is it?" I was playing a game about forgetfulness, acting dumb about what day. "Next Wednesday. Our usual phone call." And I guess I was making a joke about how it wasn't, we'd never been that way, doubt we ever would, but I sort of wished I'd kept the criticism to myself. I didn't know why I was being so negative. "Our regular thing. We'll continue about my heritage. Grandma's meatballs." I turned on the kitchen sink. There were dirty dishes to get to. "It'll be my regular surprise."

"All right," he said. "All right," he said again. "I'll go find a family album. Hey—next time, no oddball stuff. Honestly, I'm not sure how I'm feeling right now."

The call ended. Dad had told me it was good I was divorced, but it was also good if he remarried. Which wasn't what I wanted to know more of. I guess I could say I felt gained on and passed. Or that Dad's life was reversing. To cover me. So there was no me. But I wasn't upset. Or maybe I was. Because, instead of them being thirty years apart—because why stop at thirty?—maybe he should go for full-on ridiculous. Fifty. Fifty would make quite a statement, and after he got married, I could tell him that, I'd probably even have to repeat it because he couldn't hear so good with his ears, or maybe, minutes later, I'd have to repeat it because his memory was wiped out.

My meanness—where was it coming from? I was glad it only existed in my head, although some of it had spilled out earlier when I'd flipped his line around on him. I knew I was getting ahead of myself, or himself, with his decline, and I was grateful for him not being there, and hoping it would be some time. I'd only wanted a simple conversation. But I guess asking someone to remember a half century—"Hey, tell me a story about Old Cousin What's-His-Name"—isn't so simple.

He taught me to drive. Dad did. What else? Shared his wisdom about minor theft and legitimate businesses. Pocketing gumballs. Steal the bank pens. I laughed to myself, but then I didn't, because the joke put me back in the bank. I saw Millie ahead of me, and imagined myself, lurking behind, like some purse snatcher, or worse.

The TV was still loud, another commercial, and maybe she'd switched channels, unless the program was all ads. And then I was back in the car, with Millie, imagining my radio commercial that stopped airing years ago.

I tried to use my dad's tone of voice on myself. Stop with the nonsense. Ridiculous. As ridiculous as Dad with his age spread. Maybe I was being too mean. To me. So I was thankful for my dad for bringing me back, even though I wouldn't tell him that, when we talked whenever, or even next. As for marriages, my dad would be the first to go second. Fine. He's my dad; I guess he should be married more.

I set the dishes and utensils on the rack. It felt like neither of our lives was real. Just numbers. My two hands on this one bowl. The bowl she used again and again. Just a fraction of the total, with so much more stacked away in the cupboard. So, good for my dad, his life, seventy years old, engaged, with an erection. He found someone else. A second chance. He's using all of himself. I pictured him in an advertisement, for May–December romances, for performance enhancements—my boosted father—in the 55 *Plus* magazine, right next to the handyman ad I used to run. Father and son, both of us, meeting up in one place on the same page.

8

THE WINTER MONTHS ENDED. I rebuilt a soffit. I did a stucco repair where the stucco had broken off. The trees leafed. I got the garden turned over. A bush in the backyard was getting crazy; Millie wanted me to take it out.

She called me and said she smelled gas. I got there and didn't smell anything. The next time, or soon after, she complained about a noise in the wall. I told her it was probably just a water hammer. She insisted I investigate, so I climbed up to the attic and pulled insulation, searched for a nest or droppings. "No varmints," I told her, back downstairs.

"Where did you go?" she asked, and I pointed up to the place she'd sent me.

I took her driving up along the lakeshore. Sometimes, we went downtown and parked, the car idling, to look at High Falls, to watch the water plummet.

Once, when we were in an old part of the city, and she hadn't said anything for a time, I pointed to a store and said, "That shop's been there forever." Millie didn't answer, which wasn't surprising, but I kept talking, which kind of was. "I'm surprised that mom-and-pop's still there," and I realized I was saying this for my own dislocation. *I don't know how they stay in business*, I thought to myself. *I don't know how they survive.*

We went shopping. The laundry soap felt heavy.

We got our usual burgers. "I'm all done," she said, after only a few bites.

"Aw, you can do better," I said. "You barely touched your plate."

"I couldn't eat another tidbit."

"What about your fries?"

She looked down, surprised they were there. "I don't like to get involved in all that."

It was a line that meant a lot to me, something I'd probably said, or at least communicated, to Renee, when we were separating, or something that she communicated to me, about what I *wouldn't* be doing going forward, and it's probably a line that I should have said to myself *before*, when we were still married, when she didn't have any idea what I was doing, or up to.

She seemed gaunt. Millie. Her clothes were hanging off her. Her hair, already thin—but was it thinner at the crown? It was strange to think of someone so old still changing so much.

It felt wrong to be in public and have her pay. I might insist, even if I had paid last time, or I might reimburse myself from the eight hundred in the drawer. And when that was gone, I could just add it to any number of jobs I did around the house, if I remembered. Sometimes, I didn't. No, that's not true, I always did.

One day in April, she called me, frantic. The power had gone out. "Did you pay RG&E?" I asked.

"I don't know. I've always paid them."

"Is power out at your neighbor's house?"

"I'm sitting here in the dark!"

"Okay."

"I called 911. But no one answered."

"I'll be right over."

The mail was in disarray, a scatter of papers on the dresser, and more fallen behind it. "I've made hay of . . ." she tried to say. I found the overdue bills, the warning, the final shutoff notice.

"I don't want this to happen again."

"It won't," I said.

"I've made hay of it. The mail. Would you help me? Separate the junk from the real? I don't know the bills. I don't know what I owe."

When I opened the bank statement, I saw the pot of money. Six figures. A crazy number. More than halfway to seven.

"My checkbook. Adding and minus. Would you help me balance?"

I told her I would.

"Thank you." She stopped crying. She looked at me like she'd seen her great reward.

Seeing a number like that, there's no way to unsee it. Maybe in some ways I suspected it was there, maybe I'd known what decades of Kodak could add up to, and them not having kids, but I don't think I'd thought of the money *on top of* the house. I reminded myself I hadn't done anything wrong by seeing it, that she'd even directed me to the statement. I thought, I only know what the bank knew, but they didn't know how she was living, or wasn't, which meant I knew much more.

It almost didn't feel real, not as real as the actual money I'd seen months before, the cash I'd brought from the bank, to her. It felt more like the kind of figure you'd see when you get that bogus Publishers Clearing House letter, with all the zeroes in the window, telling you you're the big winner, and then you open up the letter to learn you're only eligible, which meant never—and, if I thought about it more, which I did, this situation was exactly the opposite, because I'd torn the envelope to see the number that *wasn't* showing on the outside, or maybe it was just different, because it was only Millie, not some company with a catch. I saw the money a lot. I mean, it was on my mind, I didn't need the paper as reminder. It was so much easier to see it than when I'd been outside my old house and I was trying to move through old rooms, and I kept getting mixed up with my work, my job, the fixes I'd done for other people. But then I'd tell myself, it was just a sequence of numbers. Nothing more. It had nothing to do with me.

I got rid of the temptations: the donation requests, the sweepstakes, the magazine subscriptions. I separated the real mail—the medical bills, the health insurance, the statements, the policies. (The water bill reminded me of us at the near-beginning, and the noise I heard.) I saved her money by avoiding penalties and late payments. I opened all the important documents, the stock reports; arranged them in colored file folders. I treated her mail—her bills—better than I treated my own when I'd lapsed on the insurance payment. Extra careful. Millie never answered her phone when I was there (it rarely rang anyway), and I'd never seen her check her machine, so, when I saw the light blinking, I asked if she wanted me to play her messages, in case the doctor's office or someone important called.

"Be my guest," she said.

So I did. I got a pen and paper and wrote down whatever was important, and erased whatever wasn't. "Here I go," I said, the first few times I played them, because I wanted to make sure she heard every one, because these people weren't calling for me. "Are you listening?"

"Of course," she said.

But I couldn't get her to eat. The meat, the sides. "Maybe the fruit cup?" I said.

"I have eaten to your heart's content." She stared down at the plate. "Look at these bag of hands." She turned her fingers, wiggled them in the air.

The waiter appeared at his position. *Cave City, Millie, did you remember that?* Did she need a box? the waiter asked.

She looked at me.

"For the leftovers," I said.

She shook her head. "I'm full."

Now it was the waiter's turn to be unsure. I waved away the wasted food. He picked up the pieces of silverware and set them on her plate. "All finished?" he asked me. I nodded. He cleared my side. I glanced at the other tables. Another waiter came and went. The families, large and small, the work friends, the daters, the new sweethearts, the couples hanging on, long past attraction, all the different combinations and companions. And us. What were we?

She wept a lot. If she forgot a word, or lost her train of thought, or sometimes just because. "Why am I on this side of the grave?" she'd ask. I couldn't comfort her. Or I could, by staying, always. But her house: If it was the place I most wanted to be, it was also the place I most needed to leave. All she wanted me to do was sit. The slowness—I couldn't take how long a task lasted. For her to stand up, it was like asking her to lift a hundred pounds. Then she'd take a breath. I felt the effort, sitting there. Felt it on my chest, like the lead vest at the dentist's office. Nothing ever happened. Nothing new. The boredom. Making it from today to tomorrow—that was it. Or a spill, which happened all the time. When she napped, I felt like such a failure. And we didn't share the same tastes in shows. "I have no idea who can sing what," she said, while we watched a program about an opera singer. "I used to make that," she said, to the demonstration of deviled eggs. I got so tired of the voices being only hers and the television. "Don?" she said. "Don?" she said again, when I was fetching her a Kleenex. When I was carrying away her bowl. "What?" I answered, too loud, like a TV switching to commercial.

I had an uncle like that. A sitter, I mean. With a loud voice. Always calling for his wife. "Ro?" "Ro?" "Ro?" Like a stutter. Like a nursery rhyme. He'd repeat it again and again. "I'm right here," she'd say back, sometimes impatient, but he just kept at it. Her kids—my cousins— made fun of him. To their mom. They had grown tired of decades of his outbursts, even if he wasn't yelling anymore. When I was young, he terrified me. He screamed as he stalked through their house, bossing everyone. He was in a wheelchair now. His hands hardly worked. Useless fists. But his kids had lost all sympathy. Neither lived close, and when they'd visit, they'd cover their ears and mockingly say, "Can't hear you." And then my aunt would get angry at *them*. "You are talking about my husband," she would say. Dignified but resentful. And the kids were like, "Mom, we're on *your* side." Fine, they murmured to each other. We won't go there. It was hard when Millie said, "I can't do a damn thing," when she said it every day, multiple times. It was hard to listen to her tell me about every dog. It was hard telling her things up and down. Or resetting the remote control, because she kept hitting the wrong button.

I liked helping her so much; I was always so glad to leave. I was so impatient to get out of there, couldn't wait to get away from her litany of troubles and complaints—I felt like a horse held back—and I'd speed home, feeling released, the radio, *my* stations, cranked up, only to arrive and collapse in a recliner and think, What was the rush? To sit in my temporary home, alone and uncompensated, for what was left of the day? That's when I felt sorriest, that I'd deserted her, that I'd *been* deserted, that I'd had a better financial life in my twenties, a better personal life in my thirties, and both versions had left me, or I'd left them. There was so much less of me. No wife, kids. I'd run a bath, sit in a vat of dead water, till the warmth went out of it, and I'd get out and with my wet feet I'd imagine slipping and going down. I felt like I was having the same night; I was the same small figure in a chair. Except for the beer. And, except for sitting in my underwear like the customer I didn't see anymore. My shoulder and neck were sore, from bending down to Millie, so she could take my arm, so we could wrap elbows, when we walked. I'd probably need a chiropractor. Because my posture was all compromised. I thought about calling Renee or Beth, both of them, and telling them I was getting married. Which made no sense. But I wanted the confusion. To confuse them. The way I'd briefly confused my dad, but more so. I wanted them to know they didn't know me anymore. But what would I say? Tell them about my flatlined life? "So what's new?" they'd ask. *Nothing.* Instead, Millie called me. I didn't have to answer. "Hello, Millie." She told me she made a spill, and I told her I'd get the Rug Doctor tomorrow. She asked about her breakfast, and I reminded her where it was, all set out, sequentially, on the top shelf of the fridge. The Tupperware of fruit, the cottage cheese container, the mason jar of coffee, the glass of OJ for her medicine. "I can't see what's outside," she said, and I reminded her it was nighttime. "Nobody can," I said. "I hate it," she said. "Your clothes are on the couch," I said, and I pictured her turning to the closest cushion: underwear, bra, support stockings, pants, T-shirt, sweatshirt. Laid out in order, by what she would put on first. Then we said goodnight. I killed the television, knowing that she'd keep hers on, a living voice, even if she left the room, and I would brush up and think about her not knowing she was old till she looked in the mirror.

She looked the same—meaning, she wore the same clothes too often. Even if I set the fresh clothes out, she might ignore the change. But she was also different, worse. There were bad smells I could detect. Trails on the carpet. The hair didn't look right, or as clean. There were dark spots on her shins, the dead skin like tree bark.

"We should order," she would say, when we already had. And when the food arrived, she studied it as if it were someone else's. The sandwich, the triangles on her plate, was a foreign object, split in two. She scanned the angles and coordinates. "Where are my shoestring potatoes?"

"You didn't ask for that," I said.

"I didn't?"

"No." I nodded at her symmetrical sandwich.

"Did they change the menu?"

"You ordered your usual."

"This was Jim's favorite," she said, and she pointed at the bread basket, and suddenly I remembered Grandma Dot talking about hoboes knocking on their back door, to ask for bread and butter. I couldn't believe it, how it came back to me. I told Millie.

"Who?" she asked, and I repeated who she was. Dot must have been a child with this memory. Depression-era, a teenager at most. "You are like the grandson I never had," Millie said, again. I smiled and stared off at a vacated table. When I looked back, I saw her coffee mug, about to fall.

"Your coffee—don't keep it at the table edge."

"Don't yell at me!" she said.

She called me to complain about the heat, that it was too hot, and when I came over the stove was on. "Let's go to the amusement park," she said when she meant a different attraction, the waterfall. She asked me four times what time the appointment was. "I don't remember the day I'm supposed to go to that chitchat." More words slipped, turned cryptic. More was wrong with her. But things were wrong with me, too. Who doesn't have something wrong?

I mentioned that my van was rusting out. It was true, but I shouldn't have mentioned it. "Oh, Don, let me pay for the truck. That way you can still come to me."

A few years back, I did some work for an old widow. She lived alone, had no kids, but she had this niece who hung around and wanted money. The widow was getting rid of the car, and the niece was saying how good she'd look in the car. I'll confess, I thought of this story when I listened to what Millie was doing now. If you see a sailboat sitting in the yard, do you want it? Who doesn't ask, What's in it for me? Who doesn't think about what their grandmother might have to give to them?

I did a chimney rebuild. I cut the lawn. Did some gutter work, a crushed downspout. I wondered if she'd backed the car into it, if that's what stopped her driving. I stained the deck. I got her a new recliner with a boost.

"This must have cost four thousand dollars," she said.

"No," I said. I told her it cost three. To be with her so much, I had to make a grand margin like that.

"Oh, this chair is a wonder," she said, after I showed her the positions, all the things the seat could do.

When I worked for that company, way back, we might tell a customer we needed special asbestos dumpsters from Canada. An extra cost. Beefing up the contract. The dumpsters weren't necessary, but they weren't gonna hurt the job either. I helped Millie more than I hurt her. I don't even know if she'd call it hurting. And I'm the only one here to help. I've never ripped anybody blind, but I've never been Humanitarian of the Year either.

She woke up from another nap. "Is this a short street?"

"Thomas Avenue?" I said, pointing outside. "No. It's long."

"We lived on a short street."

"When you were first married?"

"No, you dummy," she said, smiling, which didn't bother me, although when Renee screamed idiot, it sure did. "We couldn't live here when we were first married. It was too big!"

"Okay."

"When I was a kid. We went ice skating a lot. I want to go ice skating. Now I'm just in this one spot."

Did my grandmother ice-skate? Sure, why not. I told Millie she did.

"Who?" she asked.

Of course she'd forgotten. The name, the person. I couldn't be hurt by her memory loss.

I brought her her food. "You ate so little. How about more?" I thought I sounded like Renee, encouraging the kids to eat vegetables.

"I don't buy into this program."

"You sure? This is what you wanted," I said.

She shrugged. "This is a whole full of meal. I have pigged it out." She spooned applesauce, but it spilled on her shirt. "Look at this gob. Now I have pig stuff all over me." She wiped at it, left a dark patch. "Look what fell down the front of me." She swiped at it again, then flung her hand indifferently, as if she were saying farewell to the whole mess. Then she gazed into the distance, and her expression seemed both sad and numb, as if she'd gone in the wrong direction, which was both unfortunate and no real concern. "I want you to take over."

"Take over what?"

"All of it!" Her agony was so sudden I thought she'd lunged at my face. "I don't want to do anything. I can't make decisions. My affairs. You need to help me with them."

I nodded. I glanced at her stained shirt. Twice recently, she said her coffee was tea. "I want black and white in my coffee," she said once, and

I knew she meant cream. Sometimes, when she used the wrong words, it was funny, like when she said she needed to renew her subscription at Walgreens. I mostly got her train of thought. When she called a blanket a washcloth, I understood. But then I remembered, last week, when she said she wouldn't eat the meal in the fridge because it was poisoned. I chucked the food. I thought she meant spoiled. I thought it was just another word slip.

9

THE LAW OFFICE WAS A CONVERTED HOUSE. We both had dressed up for the meeting: a flower dress for Millie, and me in respectable pants, no overalls. The receptionist brought us into the conference room. The attorney entered. "Hi, Millie," he said, "it's good to see you again." She introduced me as her friend. Nothing about my line of work, and there was no paint spatter, no identifying tar on the hands. He gave me a once-over. Sure, he had the standard tie and arrogance, but it was his job to judge the situation. An old woman about to sign over her life to a nonrelative fifty years younger. I could see his antenna working. The guy out of the woodwork. The new best friend. He would like to replace me with a husband or son. If no direct kin, perhaps a nephew, a second cousin twice removed. Some long-lost heir. Because I'm nowhere on the family tree.

"I need to meet with my client," he said, and motioned me to the door. I waited in the hallway, like a guard. I wondered who else had stood out here, how many surrogates and odd proxies? Not just the trusted neighbors, the valued friend, but the longtime hairdresser? The personal trainer who helps with water aerobics? The nice fella you sat beside in jury duty? Quite an illegitimate lineage.

Here was a funny thought: The last time I could remember waiting out in the hallway for something was during a school meeting with one of Erin's teachers. (By the time I left, Jack was older, and we didn't have those kinds of one-on-ones.) In those meetings, I didn't change my clothes if I was coming from work, because the stakes were lower, although Renee was always nervous, and I guess I was, too, because there was always a part of the meeting that felt like it was about *you*, and what you had or hadn't done at home. (I can't imagine either of my parents giving that a second thought.) And Renee might ask if I had any questions for her, the teacher, and I really didn't because I figured she was the expert, and I probably just shrugged and said, "I guess we'll just listen." And I think Renee would agree with me. I think I was already picturing myself inside the room, in one of the tiny chairs, nodding and saying nothing, looking smarter through silence.

I thought about Millie's state of mind, but I'll admit, I also thought about my life ticket. She was not delusional. But she was something. Less intact. I should tell him about my concern. Of course, I get nothing from telling him—and what did she get? Protection from me. But she is safe there. I will think of her best interests. If this is a stupid decision, well, I've made stupid decisions. We're all free to make them.

I heard voices—hers—not through the wall, but in my mind, defending me. It wasn't surprising that her voice would be so familiar. She was telling him how I helped with the house, assisted with bills. "He does lots of stuff." It's what she had already said to me. *I have no one else.* Good answer, I thought, but for him maybe not correct enough. I wasn't the judge of her mental exam.

Can you be more specific? he might counter. The name of the utility company? The phone company? I felt her focus on the difficult questions. Her mind searched for the sequence of initials. "RG&E," I said, or my inner voice did, but I imagined for Millie it was blurrier, as hard as the bank initials, and I thought, Stop with that. Now.

"Why would I need to tell you that?" she would say. "Why would *anyone?*"

Maybe he would apologize, but he would still insist on knowing, and that's when she would feel insulted. *What an obnoxious routine. We* were separated, so I couldn't feed her any lines. "The phone company— begins with the letter *A.*"

Renee was the one who began the divorce proceedings. Of course I'd be thinking about her, and that, sitting here. You learn a whole new batch of words when you deal with lawyers. Words like equitable distribution, which in terms of Renee and me meant we were roughly the same wealth, and we didn't need to exchange funds, so the divorce wasn't complicated or messy, financially speaking.

Not time yet. Maybe he was scribbling notes, some lawyer shorthand.

I had an impulse to want to read his thoughts, to see his behavior, but I couldn't because, of course, the door separated me—I remembered Millie's illegibility from across the kitchen. Now, I realized, and maybe only because I had been thinking about Erin, and teacher meetings, that what Millie was doing was like what Erin used to do, what any kid did, when you're practicing letters, the alphabets big and small, when you first learned handwriting. I almost wanted to ask Millie that now, is that what you were trying to write or remember? She said she'd gotten mixed up, with cases, but maybe it sort of wasn't a mistake. She was just trying to do two things at once.

Which made me think about other, more recent questions I should have asked her, the difference between two words, spoiled and poisoned. Because when I chucked the spoiled food (that wasn't), the food that Millie called poisoned (when maybe she meant something else), when I opened up the container, I was about to sniff it when I heard, in the distance, a voice, vaguely familiar, actually not really a voice but a dull buzzing, trying to say something about my skill as a sniffer. I answered it by walking away. I carried the container over to the garbage and flipped it over and shook it down, thumped the container on the inside of the pail to get all the bad food out. The sound, the thumping, was low but also echoing, and think I was turning the sound up on any other noise I might have heard. I just didn't see the point in talking to anyone.

But now, with time for that conversation, with Millie, about her wording, how would my questioning have even gone? *Millie, when you said what you said—that word—did you mean a different one? Because*

if you think it was poisoned, it wasn't, and we should talk about why—
I cut myself off. What did it matter, if either way, if *any* way, *every*, I could ensure her safety. I could be comprehensive.

Spoiled and poisoned, they're close. Sound-wise. Not saying they're right next to each other, but the association is there. When Millie ripped up the paper, I almost wanted to collect the confetti pieces and tape them together (oh, wait, that was the check she shredded) . . . Fine, but what I would tell Millie now, about her mistake that was really semi, was that I understood she was just trying to do two alphabets at the same time. It reminded me of sitting in one of the early classrooms, one of Erin's, I mean, and seeing the posters of the letters, both types, upper and lower, side by side. If I had a fresh piece of paper, which reminded me of Erin crumpling up her homework in frustration, usually over a math error, I'd say to her, to Millie: It's okay, try again, I knew what you meant to do. Start over with the letter *A*.

The door opened. The lawyer summoned me back inside. I sat down in the seat I'd been kicked out of. I could see Millie was upset. Which meant he'd already rendered his verdict.

"I have encouraged her to explore other alternatives. There are agencies who are insured, bonded." His eyes narrowed. "This would really protect both of you. If money is missing, if accounting doesn't match up, if there is a suspicion, adult protective services would come in."

When he looked at me, I nodded, because what he was saying sounded reasonable.

"These people are strangers to me," Millie said.

He cupped his hands. "I'm not comfortable doing this. I'm sorry." He seemed very fatherly. "You'll have to look elsewhere." He had already told her the bad news. He was repeating his recommendations for my benefit, telling me to behave myself.

The conversation ended. If he was impatient, he didn't check his watch. But I guess we weren't going to chat about Italian wines. In her car, in the passenger seat, Millie scratched at her arm, rubbed it raw, so hard I thought she would damage it. "He only knew my husband," she said. I reached my hand across to stop her. "He never knew me. I have a mind of my own."

I told her not to worry. My voice was steady, and when she spoke again, hers was too.

"We will find someone else."

I agreed. There was always another lawyer willing to draw up papers for a fee. And when we located him, he was mostly the same vintage, although I can't say his services were as costly. His office wasn't in a converted house but a regular building, which felt more up-and-up, like he wasn't trying to be something he wasn't. No physical resemblance, but the same bookshelf of binders, the same wall display of diplomas. For all I knew, they probably owned the same coffee mug: "World's Greatest Golfer." He was legit. He wasn't some lawyer in a box. And even though he sat opposite from us, he was still on our side. Between us on the table was a vase of fake flowers, a calculator, and a plaque that read *The ABCs of Aging Gracefully*.

"In terms of P.O.A.," he explained, "it could be plain vanilla or it could be enhanced."

"I want it simple," Millie said.

"Sure thing." The rate, he said, would stay the same for either framework. "But while I have you both here, we should discuss health care proxy. It would be wise to tie that up, too."

You're probably thinking, Oh my God, he got power of attorney, he wiped her out, raided the bank account. Pointed himself to the Corvette Club. He signed a deed transferring the house. He left her with one spoon. No. None of that. I didn't move assets or change beneficiaries. I'm not saying I didn't pay myself a salary for time spent—and whenever I did, I felt like two people, the payee ("Don's Fix-It") and the rich guy beneath on the signature line ("Don Lank, P.O.A."), one version paying the other. Rarely, I—or the initialized me—would treat myself, just some minimal gift, but most of the gifts went to Millie, like a DVD player I thought we could use for watching old movies. But I didn't become some ogre, either.

Still, I thought about the money. A lot. About whose fund it was. The mindset was tricky: Is the money hers and I'm managing it, and I hope there's a little left over for me? Or the money, because I have access to it, is it in some way mine? These were the conversations I had with myself. Then I'd think about how I was acting like some greedy, entitled grandchild getting his inheritance now. Actually, I was thinking that I was acting *better* than that. And that's how you can get in trouble, when you think there's a gulf between you and wrong-doing—that because you hadn't parked the money elsewhere, you could still carve off some small amount and there'd be virtually all of the wealth left. But I stopped myself with a simple question: If I were someone else, and she *were* my grandmother, would I approve of this guy's behavior? And I would stay responsible.

Nothing changed. I kept working for her, visiting her. Or, what changed, what kept changing, was her.

Her words got worse. At times, they weren't close. "I'm gonna have one more episode," she said when she meant to say sip. The TV was off, but it had been on earlier. I don't know, maybe the word wasn't really wrong but just late. I thought about testing her, like the first lawyer had done. "Is it a good episode?" I might have asked, after she drank, but it seemed cruel, like added confusion. Another time, she said dog fuse instead of dog food. She kept saying it, "Dog fuse," even though she knew it sounded off, and was trying to make it right. We were in the grocery store. I had to remind her that she didn't need the food because she didn't have a dog. She laughed about the mental block to show she understood. But she knew she was slipping. "What the heck is it called?" she said, countless times. "I've lost track of myself totally."

"You're all right," I told her, unconvincingly.

Very quickly she was sad. "I am alone. I'm a one-person person."

"I'm here too, Millie."

I was there so long, and yet there were still more calls, some of them coming while I had minutes ago left, while I had barely driven distance. "Where are you?" she asked.

It felt like harassment, but not just. "On my way home."

"Are you on a microphone?"

"What?"

"There is an echo."

"No."

"Can you come back? I have misplaced—I don't know the name of it. I don't get it."

"What don't you get?"

"How can I understand life? When I can't understand anything that goes in it?"

It was harassment and heartbreak, equally. No, it wasn't harassment, at all. How could I use that word, much less call them equal? My blinker was on, I was already deviating from my destination, following the sadness and loss of her voice back to her house. "I'll see you soon."

"Soon is a terrible word."

"Millie, I'll be there in minutes." What was my apartment anyway? A rental barely furnished, a better place only because she wasn't there? Sure, a relief but nowhere. So why go?

"You're the only one who comes around. You are the key person." She told me she wanted to rewrite her will. So we went back to the lawyer, and replaced me for the charities. This should have been a moment where I told her to slow down, but instead I let her accelerate. "My husband was attached to these charities," she said. "I'm not." Millie and Jim had always been private people. The charities didn't know what was coming their way, and now they never would. I became the heir apparent.

And it wasn't long after when the niece called. Sometimes, I wondered if changing the will was what triggered it. Not in any direct sense of the lawyer calling (the first lawyer? the second?), and it's not that the niece was in the will to begin with, but just in the way that thoughts or actions travel. And then I thought maybe *my memories* had triggered it, that it was the remembering of another widow, another niece, the coveted car, that brought in Millie's niece. In any case, I was wrong about the reason for her calling, although after that, when she heard my voice, I guess I was right.

"Millie," the voice said, on the machine. I could already sense the worry, the tentativeness, even in the single mention of a name. I had stopped checking to see if Millie was listening, although she was always in the room with me, like she was now, and as soon as I heard her name, said in that nervous way, I turned to her. "It's Ann. Ann Lima. I thought I had the wrong number, but it says the Prall residence. But the voice ... Millie, please give me a call. It's your niece. I'm sorry I missed your birthday. That's why I was calling. You have my number, but I'm going to give it again." Which she did, first waiting for Millie to get an imaginary pen. And then she recited the information, slowly. After the numbers, there was a pause, and then, simply, a send-off, "Okay. Bye."

"Millie, did you hear all that?"

"Of course," she said, but she didn't say anything after or explain. I thought the television was competing with the voice, so I asked Millie if she could turn the TV down. Actually, I wanted her to turn it down for my benefit, because the swarm of noise overwhelmed. She lowered the volume, but I wanted it nearer to quiet. I tapped my hand in the air, until the person on the screen was just a mumble.

"Somebody called. Your niece. Ann."

"Good for her."

"You know about her?" Which was such a strange thing to say.

"What happened?"

"No, I mean—I've never heard you talk about her."

"She was like a child. A daughter."

"Oh, I've never heard you say that. Like that."

"I've never had a child."

"Okay. Where is she?" I remembered Millie saying something about California, so I repeated the state.

"I don't know where everyone landed."

"I think you said your brother's family was in California. Is she on your side?"

"Of course she is."

"No, not that—" Although maybe she'd understood me. Maybe she wasn't saying that her niece wasn't against her. I shook my head. I thought I'd ask for clarification. "Is she on Jim's side of the family?"

"Yes. That's where she came from."

I was about to ask where she lived, but I decided to find out myself. I entered the area code into my phone, and it came back Arizona. I tested her. "Where does she live? What state?"

It didn't take long for her to say it, to get it right. I was surprised by the clarity—maybe saying "state" helped her?—and I thought it was a good thing. For her. For me, for both of us.

"We should call her right now." I didn't like how my voice sounded, like I was telling her what to do, like I was worried, like I was acting the way the first lawyer warned me not to. All I had to do was to do what was right. Put Millie in touch with anyone that wanted to be in touch with her, especially family, even those members I hadn't known about.

"I don't need to talk to her."

"I think you do, Millie. She needs to hear from you. Calling back— it would be a problem if you didn't. Let me help you dial. I'm going to do that." I went to the phone. "Here I go." I pressed in the numbers from the pad, and I handed her the device and told her it was dialing. "Ringing," I said, louder, like I was waking her up, alerting her. I stepped away. I felt like I should step behind a wall, or excuse myself to sit in the bathroom, or even drive back to my own place.

"Where are you going?" Millie said.

"Just talk to her," I said, but I stopped retreating. "I'm right here. In the room with you."

I heard a voice inside the line, so I guess I'd stayed close. "Millie?"

"Hello," Millie said, and she looked at me, and I smiled back, like *we* were exchanging greetings. When she looked away, I raised my foot to step back, ready to freeze, like a game I'd played in the yard with Erin, I forget the name of it, and Erin would move in the opposite direction, starting from far away and then aiming to creep closer, undetected. Sometimes I'd catch her midmotion, her leg still tapping down, and I'd point at the offending body part and shout, "Aha," and she'd scream but also laugh. Other times, though, I didn't, I acted like I hadn't seen anything, because I knew she wanted to think she had magical powers, that she could anticipate exactly when to move when I turned away, and when to stop when I turned back. Actually, I think the reason I lied was less because of her and more because of me. What I mean is, for *both of us*, that we had a shared experience, an unspoken language, our body movements somehow in sync.

I didn't want to hear the voice on the other end of the line.

"Thank you," Millie said next, which probably meant the niece was repeating the birthday wish. Then Millie frowned. "He is a friend of mine . . . No, he's not a neighbor . . . He's right here . . . A while." Millie held the phone to me and said, "It's your turn. Good."

I grabbed the phone, and I was about to say hello, but first I listened. I didn't know what I was listening for. It was silent. I was on the phone, but the niece didn't know I was there. I knew only that she was family, Ann from Arizona, and that she was about to know about me—or the little she needed before she determined she'd heard everything. I said hello. It was silent again, but the silence felt different, a held breath.

"Who am I speaking with?"

"My name is Don."

"Your name is Don."

"Don Lank."

"Okay. Continue. Why are you in the house? Why are you on Millie's phone?"

"She asked me to do that. It wasn't my idea. She wanted a man's voice on the line. I knew it would be weird. Told her so. It was weird when I called it."

"When *you* called it?"

"A while back."

"Who are you?"

"Like Millie said, I'm a friend." But I felt like I needed to say more. I knew that what I said next would antagonize her, the same way the lawyer's verdict had rubbed wrong at Millie. But eventually we'd reach that point, and now was as good a time as any. "I'm a handyman."

"Oh God . . . my husband isn't home right now. When he gets home, you'll be hearing from him. We'll be in touch with people."

"I understand." I figured that meant the county, or something like that. "That's fine. I can talk to anyone."

"You . . . put *my aunt* back on the phone."

Which I did.

I walked away. I heard Millie yell, "Don't you dare call the government."

Whatever they said after that didn't matter.

By the end of the day, we received the other call. Not both of them—I never talked to the husband, although maybe he'd called the agency. Millie let it go to the answering machine, but I played it right after, a woman stating she was a social worker from protective services. There was no confusion in the woman's voice about whether she was contacting the right place. I told Millie we needed to call her, too. Millie shook her head, as if I'd told her we needed to make a hundred calls. Yes, I said. Very soon. Now. Again, I dialed, and again stepped away, but not too far so Millie would increase agitation. "Just tell them who you are," I said to her. "Tell them everything." Which felt right, but then a weird thing to say, because I didn't know how much she could tell, if *everything* was possible. I nodded, because I'd fill in the rest. Which wasn't the same.

"I don't want you to come over. I'm not letting you in."

"No," I said. "Millie, don't do that."

"What?" she said, and now I'd distracted her, and made the call a mess, I'm sure the woman on the phone was talking, too, I just needed to straighten out what was right.

"Tell them yes. Just . . . It's not good to say no. Tell them we're not doing anything. Tell them to come over. They can."

She shook her head. But she did. Still, when she hung up the phone, she was even more upset.

"They need to see how you're living." And I felt like I needed to see that, too.

But Millie was only crying and shaking her head, so certain about the plan. "She wants to take me out of the house."

The woman arrived the next morning. I answered the door. My preference had been for Millie to answer it, and I asked her to, but she said she wasn't moving, and I didn't want to stir up trouble, and have the doorbell ring again. Millie looked comfortable, which was important.

I opened the door, and we smiled at each other. She identified herself (her employee badge already said that), and I did, too, although I guess I just said my name. I'd save the rest for inside. We shook hands. She held a tablet in her other arm. I walked her in and stepped aside, but stayed close, for Millie's sake, but also for mine. I thought it would look weird if I stepped away like I was hiding. She gave Millie a friendly smile, maybe even friendlier than what she'd shown me, and while she smiled she studied the room, to see about clutter, which wasn't there. Nothing smelling either. I'd put her age at forty, and I say that only because I imagined she'd been in many rooms and houses, just like this, and was an expert at sight and sound and smell detection. She glanced back at Millie, probably to note if she was dressed appropriately, that her grooming was okay. But I'd been helping Millie, and I knew I hadn't let conditions get to that.

"You probably want to talk alone with her," I said, because she'd request that soon, and it was probably better if I offered it first. Although, I guess I *hadn't* been the first, since the lawyer had said it earlier, about private consultation.

"Thank you," she said.

Millie shook her head, so I said, "I'm just going in the kitchen."

"Millie," the woman said, "I just need some minutes with you. Would that be okay?"

I was in the kitchen before I heard the answer, or if Millie said anything back at all. Once I was there, though, I didn't know what to do with myself. The counter didn't need a cleanup. Nothing needed reorganizing. I was just waiting for my turn. I didn't even know if I was supposed to make noise, to signal I wasn't eavesdropping, or if making noise was a distraction, or if being too quiet meant I was up to something. Anyway, it was impossible not to hear the woman if I didn't keep busy, because the way she talked—just a bit slower and gently elevated, but not overboard to be offensive—was designed for Millie's hearing.

"How are you?"

"I'm fine. I have somebody great."

"I'm happy to hear that."

"He's my friend. He fixes things."

"Great. And how are your meals?"

"Delicious."

"Do you have plenty of them?"

"The same number."

"What do you have for dinner?"

"Rolls."

I thought to myself, who is good at remembering meals? Two days ago, I had what?

The conversation sent me to the fridge. Plus, I needed an activity. It felt like a moment from long before, when the deliveryman had arrived (it surprised me, to even have that memory, since I'd rendered him a nonentity), although this time I was studying me, and what I'd put there. And, honestly, I liked what I saw, and what I didn't. I didn't see a starving fridge. The shelves were stocked. The produce was there, and fresh. No slime stuck to the bottom. I heard the sound of the fruit tumbling (in my head, I mean), which was always a pleasurable sound.

I opened the freezer. A good assortment. Not just Eggo City. I stared at the cavernous space and heard the phrase, Cave City. Even when I shut the door, I was still back in that conversation, the surprises that popped from Millie's mouth, about twin Cadillacs, and husbands who were tyrannical, or maybe that's what you said to another one to make him think your life was sorry.

"We got a call. Your niece is a little worried about you. Do you remember her name?"

"I don't want to talk about that."

"That's fine. But can you tell me her name?"

"Her name is Ann."

I didn't know if I was surprised. Mostly, the name I'd heard from Millie was mine. Or Jim's. But, yes, hearing her say that correct word, that partial name, it felt like a full recitation.

"That's what she was to me."

"Your niece?"

"Ha. That was a long time ago. I don't consider her that anymore."

I wondered when she had confronted him. Jim. And where? Here, in the kitchen? Or maybe this is where she'd sat alone, at the table, for hours, after her friend had told her about seeing the two of them. Maybe Millie didn't want to talk about it at all, because she thought it would be gossip, because what Jim had done was hurtful but also embarrassing—maybe she carried that pain for days before any confrontation—and while she hated that lipsticked woman and her jerk husband, maybe she, or Millie's father, if she ever went to him, no, of course she wouldn't, she wouldn't discuss it with either parent, she'd keep that bad business to herself. And based on what she'd said long ago about him, he'd only tell her it was her fault, because she hadn't kept her husband happy, and maybe her mother would have believed that, too, and would have asked her, "What weren't you doing?" I sat down there, at the table, on Millie's side.

"Millie, you've been living here awhile. On your own. I'm sorry about your husband. Can I ask, how long ago did he die?"

"I don't talk about that."

"I understand. Maybe I can ask: do you know what season it is?"

"It's not the summer."

"No, it's not. I sure wish it was."

"That's what we're all waiting for."

"You and me both."

Maybe Millie, when she heard the story, she put on lipstick herself, changed out of her junk T-shirt, or the pullover top she was wearing to clean the kitchen and the garage, the whole house. I knew I was probably getting all of this confused, with a Millie I'd never known, only with the Millie I'd seen and was hearing now—and maybe I didn't like to think about cheating, anyone's, at all. Still, I wondered about Jim's side of it, if he apologized, or if he said something that men used to say or still do, "It wasn't my fault, she showed me her boobs." That's how my dad talked. Still does. Not me, I didn't think, even if I'd made the same mistakes. Maybe this was the part where Jim became different. Different in terms of pick of the litter. It wasn't just about what he'd done but how he accepted blame, asked for forgiveness. And Millie decided—or decided that she didn't have a choice—that she wasn't going to drag herself down by all this. And that's how they had a life after. Her gift to him, or just herself. Maybe gift was the wrong word.

"Would it be all right if we talked to him?"

"Why do you need to talk to him?"

"Well, so we can help you."

"He's doing that."

"I understand. We really need to, though."

Millie didn't respond, but whether she shrugged or nodded, the woman took it as acceptance. She entered the kitchen and smiled again. I wondered how many times she did that in a visit, in a day of interrogations, and a part of me thought she'd be really good at faking happiness, but I knew she was only doing her job, and that she wasn't acting wrong at all, and even her hard questions weren't meant to offend. Before she said a word, she walked to the fridge and opened it. I watched her study what I had just seen, even if she wasn't thinking what took place in my mind.

"Good."

I knew she wasn't seeing a bad one.

She opened the produce bins. Then the freezer. I was certain about what was there, but it was still strange when someone, someone like this, checked your freezer, like there was a nightmare story hidden inside—proof or revelation crackling out of the ice—something maybe even you didn't realize you'd put there. I was far enough away from the cold air, but I could still imagine it stinging.

"We like to see the nutrition," she said. She turned to me.

I nodded. "And I take her to restaurants. I get her out of the house." I glanced at the new stove, which looked out of place, shiny and suspicious. I wondered if she'd ask about it.

"Great," she said. "Where do you go?"

I named the names of the restaurants. Of course, she wasn't testing my recall but my truth.

"Can I have some information about you?" She cupped her tablet, to let me know she was ready to write, although she'd already started writing, so maybe she was noting down the fridge contents and condition, while I was about to talk about myself; still, the timing threw me off. I waited for her to finish the one thing, so I could discuss the other. A waiting game. I stared off at the fridge, and I had the funniest idea: that the woman could somehow open the door, peer inside, and know exactly what I'd been thinking. It was a scary thought, a mind reader inside the house, but also kind of comforting. That someone could know you like that. My mouth opened; I registered the sensation. Of course sharing that thought would be the absolute strangest thing to say. But I still could imagine saying it, some compliment that I paid and then it badly backfired. Thinking all of this only made me feel more secretive, which was exactly what I didn't want to feel, and I felt like I was badly using up my mental energy.

"Tell me about your job. How long have you known Millie?"

I told her, both.

"Do you have any other clients?"

"Not nearly the number I used to have, but I still get calls. It always slows down seasonally." I wondered if I spoke of seasons because of how Millie answered the question, but it still sounded like an abstract way of talking about my life. "I've asked her half a dozen times, is this what you want?"

"And you're helping her pay her bills?"

I nodded.

"And how are you paying *your* bills?"

"I'm doing a lot of work for her. Mostly, I work for her. I can explain that."

"Great," she said, smiling. "I want to give you a chance to explain."

"Aren't you done talking yet!"

Our conversation stopped. We both glanced in the direction of the yelling. Then we were back eye-to-eye. I was about to smile, when I thought I shouldn't, at all, and then I was about to grimace, which seemed off, too. I rubbed my face, wiped my tight lips. The woman signaled little. I read her expression as no-nonsense: I heard that. Now you.

"This is what she wants." My voice was quieter, to account for the yell, but not so quiet to sound secretive. "Every time I leave," I said, and I felt my voice strengthening, setting on the correct pitch, "she asks when am I coming back. I feel like I'm helping her. It's never been about me." I wondered about that last line.

"And how does she pay you?"

I explained the setup, the power of attorney, the progression of the past few months, and Millie asking every step of the way.

She nodded. "We'd like to get a release of information."

"Absolutely. Check everything." Which was true. I opened both of my hands in front of me. "Appointments. Prescriptions. Mail. I make sure she isn't missing anything."

"Good—"

"And I take her for drives." Because I felt like there was more to say. "Scenic stuff. High Falls, the lake. So she's not just seeing the television."

"We see that the food is in the fridge. Plenty of stuff. Nothing rotting." She glanced back at her tablet, and, for some reason, her words, about seeing all the food, sent me out to my van. To the Igloo sitting on the seat. I had my fridge at home—there was no need for my food, and Millie's, to be mingling in her fridge—and I still packed my lunch, an old habit, even if I often ate inside here. The cooler was out there now, like it usually was in the mornings, but I'd probably fetch it in a mere hour, so now it felt like some game of undetection. It was like she was hawkish, but based on the stove, and even the cooler, she also wasn't. But then I shook my head at myself, about the cooler. Because: how could she notice something that was unnoticeable?

"I'm going to give you my card," she said, "and we'll want to talk to her doctor and her lawyer."

Millie cried after she left, but I told her it was going to be okay, that the woman saw the stocked-up fridge, saw the rooms, saw her, and saw me. And in a few days it was. I wasn't sure what I had been expecting. Maybe fifty-fifty, in terms of the odds of the decision. I wasn't sure if that percentage sounded fair to myself. To us.

"We're closing the case," the woman said. I was on the other end of the phone, because Millie said she was finished with all that. "We don't think she's incompetent. We've talked with the doctors. We're pretty sure this is what she wants. What Millie wants. You're keeping her in her home. We're going to go along with that."

10

So that was settled but it wasn't, there was something else that unsettled me. A few things, actually. Millie's yell from the other room, its uncanny timing. Because when she said, "Aren't you done talking yet!" it was exactly what I was speaking from inside my head. Identical to how I'd lost patience with my younger self, and how I'd nixed him. I was thankful when Millie said it, doubly, because she'd shut that kid up for good, I hoped, but also because she was coming to my defenses. Even though, as I said, it didn't seem to have had any effect on the social worker. I didn't think. She kept steady with her questions, her listening, her tablet notations. But after she left, I heard Millie's line as if she were speaking directly from my mind, the same way I'd copied her when I said she had strong arms, even if she'd only heard it as compliment.

The second thing was also about timing, only not about Millie's line but the hour of the day. I wondered what might have happened if the social worker hadn't come in the morning, when Millie was clearer, but in the evening when she was less so. Not saying she was ever clear as a bell, but the woman could've seen her worse if the hour had been different. And certainly if she'd come a month later.

Because, as the days and weeks progressed, there were more signs of decline. Not just words out of place, but now paranoia. "The neighbors are taking my mail," Millie said, and I tried to assure her they weren't. She pointed out the window; she repeated the business about the dog pooping in her yard. "They never pick it up." Later, I checked but found nothing. When she asked me to feed some lettuce to a rabbit, was it a shadow or daydream or different time?

"The neighbors are taking my can opener." I showed her where it was in the drawer. Here it is, Millie. Can opener, corkscrew, measuring spoons.

Next: there were small children doing things. They were taking the bark off the trees. They were upstairs in the attic. There was a man who came in the middle of the night, to eat the cereal in her kitchen. She asked me to fix the locks. "He is taking things. I'm missing rings." I tried to convince her these people weren't real, that nothing was gone. She was worried about the garage; someone had broken in.

I tried to stick to the routine, to do what was the same, but I knew we had reached a crisis, that her mind was being robbed. I ready-mixed our cake. I baked it, set it down in the center. Fresh out of the oven, but she only stared.

"What should we talk about?" I asked.

"Blank."

"Blank?" I said back to her open eyes.

She looked straight at me, her face a mask. She nodded.

I pointed at her piece. When I first cut them, they were more or less the same, but now they were grossly uneven. "Don't you like it?"

She stared vaguely at the knife. "Of course I do. I've eaten it eleven sixty times. I don't think there's any of it that isn't any good." But her piece remained untouched. When I stared at my empty plate, it seemed I'd eaten an obscene helping, that there was something wrong with my appetite and I'd eaten seconds, thirds.

I had kept the card, the social worker's. A part of me thought of chucking it, instantly, which is why I didn't. But I didn't want to see it, either, so I'd put it in a drawer. I didn't bury it beneath papers—instead set it right on top, in front where it was findable, but also in a bottom drawer that I didn't use often or at all, so in essence it was hidden, dropped in a hole.

And when these conversations or episodes with Millie happened, soon after or even during, I thought about the card. And then I thought about the person. I saw her demeanor, her evenness, her unrattled face, after Millie had yelled, and I thought, *I can be that. I can be you.*

One night, after Millie called, she didn't call anymore. In the morning, there were still no messages. I tried her twice without answer.

I found her on the living room floor, propped against the chair. She was half leaning over, favoring a side. Her foot was rotated out. She had a bruise on her head. "Millie, what happened?" But of course I knew. I just didn't know how long she'd been there.

"My leg gave." She grimaced. "I went down." She sounded tired; her mouth was dry. "I'm going to stand soon."

"You shouldn't. You shouldn't be moved."

"I can walk. Period."

"You can?"

She thought about that. "Now, when you go out for a walk, what is your criteria?"

Her phone was nearby. Off the charger, but the battery wasn't dead. I called 911.

I was frightened—for the obvious reason, because I was dialing emergency, those three scary numbers, and in all my life I'd never dialed them—but I was also frightened because I looked at the drawer, with the card inside, and I wondered if Millie had fallen because I hadn't called her, the woman, called her before she called *us* with her decision. I should have said more during the protective-services visit. Millie fell because of my failings. But then again, I'd been thinking about her falling for months.

I told the dispatcher where I was, what was needed. The injury was likely a hip or pelvis. The woman asked if she was breathing, and whether she could move. I said yes, then no.

Millie stayed anchored to the chair. "Who are you on the phone with?" she asked. "I wouldn't overthink this."

"Someone to help," I said.

"I can see the need for it, but I don't want to get caught up in unnecessary beings. I know what you're talking about. But I'm just not sure it's necessary."

I sat with her. "Ow," she said when she shifted. I said they'd be here soon for the pain.

The ambulance and a police car arrived. The doorbell rang, and I called them in, and Millie asked if they just got here. Two EMTs, one cop. It had been a long time since any visitor, so this rescue felt like a team of home invaders. The male EMT crouched down and introduced himself. He asked Millie if she could tell him her name. Millie said who she was, first and last. The second question was the date, and Millie said, "Today. Or close to it." Next was the president, and Millie said she didn't care about any of that. "That's the simple answer."

"Can you tell me the place you're in?" and Millie said her house, of course. She said everyone was in her house.

"Can you tell us what happened?"

"I fell. Obviously."

"Did you pass out? Did you black out at all?"

"I was there"—her finger tremored back and forth in an either/or signal—"now I'm here."

They turned to me and asked who I was. I told them my relationship: a friend, and her health care proxy. "I'm a good friend." Had I witnessed the fall? No, I showed up after. They wanted my account of the story, and I told them about the unanswered calls, and what I discovered. They returned to her. Had she hurt her neck or back? She said no, a little.

The woman checked her vitals.

Millie stared at the sensor clipped to her finger. "This really has no bearing on what I do."

The numbers on the vitals were okay, they said.

The man said, "Millie, are you on any blood thinner?"

She looked at them, their uniforms, and then at me. "Why are they here?"

"They're here because you fell," I said. I didn't say I'd called them.

"That's what you're relaying to me."

They repeated the blood-thinner question, and when she didn't respond, I told them no. The woman asked if I knew about her medications. I brought her into the kitchen and showed her the basket of pills. While she copied down the information on the bottles, I heard the man say, "If I put this on right, it's gonna be uncomfortable." I walked back to see him fitting a collar around her neck.

"I'm . . . not whipped."

"This isn't just for whiplash," he assured her. Then he examined her body, touching her arms, her legs. It looked like a frisking. When he inched up to her hip and pushed on it, she cried out. "I'm sorry," he said.

"I think she was trying to say something else," I said. "When she said whipped." I said this all to myself, because I wasn't sure if I was wrong. And even when he hurt her hip, he was doing it only to make sure he wouldn't hurt her more.

The cop stood silent with his authority.

Millie thought the hospital was a very bad idea. "Why can't we just sit here and have fun. Let's have coffee. Let's leave it at that."

No one smiled, but the paramedic kept his voice gentle. "Well, you know, it's really best to check this out."

Millie said no one would be able to tell for sure. She said she might go yesterday, when she had the time. She said, "This is really the least of it."

The man spread his hands, flexed his fingers straight to frame a picture, to explain why it was necessary. Millie answered with more puzzlement and refusal. They indicated the problems with delaying. Millie said a hospital was nowhere. A detour. But she couldn't stop wincing. The EMTs conferred with the policeman. Millie said a hospital made no sense, that it had no meaning at all, that the only time she'd go there was on Thursday the third. Or two days before Easter. For now, the discussion was over. She wouldn't go, and get lost coming back. They had the wrong number, and they should call back and find the real person they were looking for. The person who fell off the train.

"You've hurt your hip."

"That's a separate problem."

"Well, that's really the main problem."

"No, it's not. It's not even half."

"Ma'am, the reason we know your hip is serious, we can see your leg is shorter." He said the last part mostly to me. "But the doctor will fix that."

"The doctors are violent." She would have been angry anyway, but because she couldn't twist or bend, her face looked choked into ferocity. "They will take me and slam me across two rooms. That is all that I can say about it. That is all anyone can say. They will attack you, and if they don't, they will come very close. The problem I have ... the problem ... this is smaller than a toothache. There's not even a name for it. The name is neither here nor there."

They were concerned about her hip injury, but also the bump on her head. They said they needed to rule out a brain bleed. And now they needed me to get her on their side. It was my turn to persuade. The policeman looked at me. I started talking. "Let them take care of you," I said. "Let them get your hip working." Everyone nodded at my coaching. Except for Millie, of course, and not just because of the neck restraint. "This is not the meeting of the minds," she said.

I tried more encouragement, but she still resisted. "I don't know where he's going with it."

"This will get you better," I said.

"It sounds like you've figured it all out."

"I'm just telling you the right thing." My words felt true but also rehearsed.

"You can't put your finger on it. There is no *because*. I don't understand the why of it. I'm not even sure I'm right. It's a lot to think about. I think we've all said enough."

"Will you go?" I said. What a strange thing to say to someone when you're in their house. But I needed to say it in order for her to come back.

She stared me in the face. "I will keep that in mind. You are a good person to have in mind. Because I know you care too much about people. When I intend to go, Jim will drive me."

I had to tell them Jim wasn't me.

"Is he here?" the policeman asked, and because Millie was still staring, I couldn't say no.

"How much is she like this?" the man asked, and I wasn't sure how to answer. I needed to assist them, but I knew she wanted me to minimize her condition. "A bit. I guess, more and more. But not this bad. Disoriented. Not always." I stared at her misdirected foot.

"Do we have your consent?" They were talking to Millie.

We waited. She looked at us, all above her head; we all looked down, zeroed in. And then she said, "I'll have to think about it some more. I think the future would be a good idea. Later is best."

"How about now?"

We waited again, longer this time for her decision. She kept contemplating. She looked, first at me, then at them, from face to face. Finally, she said, "Okay. Only because I'm bored." She glanced again at our many faces, as if there were more questions.

They carted in the gurney. A button was pushed and the legs collapsed. They logrolled her onto the board, put the board on the gurney, and slipped the board out from under. Like some expert tablecloth trick. She groaned with every shift. The hydraulics powered up. The equipment sounded just like my drill. I looked away as they fastened the seat belt harness. They rigged a belt around her middle. Secured her ankles, too. I wished they didn't have to be so careful. Straitjacketing her for safety. She was in a semi-upright position, just like the recliner I'd purchased.

"Wait!" she said, as if she'd been ambushed. "Wait! Wait! Don't you dare!" Her eyes blazed. She glared at me like I was an accomplice, like I was responsible for the horrible arrangement. When she'd asked them all to have coffee, I felt like she had invited them all to be me, or confused me with all of them.

But I hadn't done this. There was nothing to stop. It wasn't my mistake she was being taken. Wasn't anyone's. I hadn't deceived her. This was only helping hands, not a handover. And if she'd broken something, it was just protocol. She was trussed in a cage, but it was required for her protection. But I agreed with her: It was shocking that people could come into your house and help you by doing something so terrible.

"I am not in that category," she protested as they wheeled her to the open door.

I followed them out, and only when I saw the ambulance did I reregister the hospital. She would need important things. I reentered the house to find her purse, to fish out her wallet and locate her insurance card. Then I realized she might need her ID. I slid the card back in the wallet. I saw her glasses on the table, and I put the wallet back in the purse and added the glasses. I heard the ambulance doors shut. I had never been by myself in the house. Being alone here was as strange as when the first responders were just inside. I saw my lamp. Hers. It was, as usual, switched on. I remembered when I wrapped the original one up, the shades so fragile. Then I saw it, the antique, not just in my mind but here, too, an illusion. The police car backed out of the driveway, off to his next official business. What else was I forgetting? Health care proxy. There was a copy of the form in the cabinet. I searched for the documentation, collected it. What else was necessary? I didn't want to neglect a thing. I shook my head at the card in the drawer.

The ambulance left. I wanted to call someone else for help, the same way I called help for Millie. Millie was being transported, and it felt like she had disappeared. The room suddenly felt like an ending. The recliner was her bed, her resting place. Because it was vacant, I felt like the first customer at an estate sale. I walked over to the replica, switched it off. There were other lights on, but I felt like I had just switched off the entire house. I remembered when she first saw the replacement, and her confusion before she called it beautiful. It looked so small and shameful. I imagined the police officer, who had already reversed, somehow being here again, before, when I first removed the original. He stopped me in the driveway and asked what was in the box, and I told him I'd paid for it. "What are you doing here?" he persisted, and I blinked away the interrogation. "I know what it looks like," I said, "it looks like I'm trespassing," but when I glanced at him, he was already gone.

Outside, there were no cars, no wind, nothing in motion. I locked up the house and went to my van to catch up. I wouldn't take the other vehicle without Millie. The only reason I was thinking about the Cadillac was we always took it when she was leaving for anywhere. But of course it made no sense to think about that car, because the logistics of that meant I'd be abandoning my van, and I'd have to drive back later to get it, and I didn't know which direction I was heading after I went to the hospital. So, only the van made sense. I'd drive it there to keep her company.

But despite heading straight for the hospital, I felt like I was sneaking off.

In the parking garage, by the elevator, there were color-coded slips, so you wouldn't have to remember your level. I was on purple.

Millie had been transferred from stretcher to gurney. The emergency room team assessed her and whisked her off to X-ray. The fracture was significant. The CAT scan said no stroke, no bleed. Orthopedics scheduled surgery for the following morning. A dose of morphine was provided. She was curtained off from another patient. She remained flat on her back, hearing the thrum of voices, the parade of people coming in and out to examine her. "That is the weirdest people on Earth," she said. Technicians, nurses, doctors, even billing to collect copays. I glanced at the IV. Millie wanted to get out of bed. She demanded everyone leave her alone, stop controlling her. She swatted at clutching hands. "What sort of people," she tried to argue, to say more, which only made her more wild-eyed and enraged. It didn't matter how kindly the staff identified themselves and explained a procedure; she only heard deception and harm. Whatever friendly expression they wore, Millie saw only enemies with evil eyes.

"They're on your side," I said.

"No, they're not. The best they are is in the middle. They are being rough. They're trying to do the whole works. They're trying to do experiments."

"They just want to fix your hip."

"This doesn't have anything to do with my legs. It's intrusive. I want to prepare my case against it. I've been making laws for my room. I'm afraid of it. You try to stay away from it but you can't. It's a strong, powerfully led organization, and it will suck you in. We need to get out the other way."

The nurses tried to balance the pain control. They told me they didn't want her to be overstressed, but they couldn't risk suppressing her breathing.

Millie smacked the side rails. "Take these gates out of here." She lashed out—ragged tirades about meanness and attacks. "One by one, the group comes in here. And they do these horrible things. They toss me around. This is actual cruelty. I don't know why it is, and they think it's funny. You know what they are? A cult. They're pretty sure they're not a cult. They think *we* are. But it *is* a cult. And they make it seem like it's the greatest thing in the world. They all stick together, and it's very scary. I can't condone it. Never in all of my life would I have participated in a cult. They all think they're lovely." With more medicine delivered, and more nighttime arrived, she turned silent and gradually faded off to sleep. Some hours after waking, she was prepped and sedated for surgery.

The next time, I parked on orange. I went down to the lobby, got the room number from the reception desk, and followed the corridor signs to the green elevators. Inside, a pigtailed girl asked me, "Are you five? Are you six? Are you seven? It's gonna get to forever to get to how old you are."

Her dad was my age. He rolled his eyes, and I smiled.

"How old are *you?*" I asked.

"I'm six in two months."

"You're not a hundred?"

"N o !" she laughed. "I'm six in two months," she repeated. "That's how old I am for real life."

She looked different than Erin—the Erin, I mean, at six, going back in time—but the words from her mouth resembled her.

"Look under there," she said, pointing to the floor.

"Under where?" I asked.

She burst out laughing. "Ha. You said under where."

I didn't get it.

"Underwear. You said underwear."

"You got me," I said, and maybe I was just tired, or it had been a while since I'd been around those kinds of jokes, but once I'd heard the word I couldn't believe I hadn't heard it that way first, and now it was all I could hear, or see. The floor dinged.

We separated, and I followed the numbers to Millie's room. Masked nurses walked past. Gloved janitors wheeled carts. Everyone was on a round to elsewhere. They stopped only for hand hygiene or to type daily reports at hallway stations. In the doorway of one of the nearby rooms, a patient sat, his gown open, a shoulder exposed. He howled, "Doctor's Orders!" The next patient suffered mutely. Two more climbing numbers and I was there. I saw Millie's name on the door. Beside her name was a red sign, inside a plastic sleeve, identifying her as a High Fall Risk. I entered the room. Millie was asleep, the tube in her throat, her lips chapped and slack. I watched the rhythm of the monitor. The waves and spikes looked like bad handwriting.

I came back the next day. The gowned howler was still disheveled but tranquil now. The next room was empty, the bed stripped of sickness, just the shine of a wet floor and the waft of mops and disinfectants.

There were oxygen prongs in Millie's nostrils. There was always something going into her and attached, and so much less on her ashen face. She looked so tiny in the bed. But her eyes weren't shut. "Hi, Millie," I said.

She stared at me. "You look really different."

"Oh, yeah. Am I taller?"

"Something like that," she said, her voice calm and doctored.

"How are you?"

"Almost normal."

When she heard a noise in the hallway, she asked if it was the mailman. The next noise, she inquired, "Who's out on the porch?"

She stared past me. "What an awful painting." I turned around. There was only a clock. I pointed at it. "This?" I said.

"Yes. It's awful."

"What's wrong with it?"

"Oh, only a few minor things." She grinned as if there were nothing to interpret and we both knew what was obvious. "That man who made it should be shot. For what he's done."

"What's he done?"

"He was shooting people. He has an agenda. And there's a woman with him. Carmen. He knew what he was doing. And that was the end of the ladder."

Of course, I thought she was talking about no one, but I also thought she was talking about me. But minutes later, a nurse came in, and said hello to Millie and introduced herself. "I'm Carmen," she said.

"Are you from the church?" Millie asked.

"I might be."

I nodded at Carmen, but she was busy with her device.

"Can I borrow your arm?" she asked Millie. I was surprised to see Millie cooperate. I was sure she'd tell the nurse to cut it out. The cuff inflated with pumped air.

"Ow," Millie said at the tightness, but then the pressure released. "That one I know about," she said, about the thermometer, when Carmen asked to slide it beneath her arm. Again, Millie didn't fend her away. The thermometer wasn't a sharp weapon, just a harmless implement, and the nurse wasn't sinister but tender. Millie didn't seem bothered at all. "People forget to do this, and they lost ten points." Then she glanced back at the wall, at the clock face, the bad painting, but there was nothing adversarial. "Well, that is a pretty picture."

When Carmen left, Millie said, "She has a very strong accent. You can tell what she's talking. I hear her accent, but I don't hear her talking."

Later, the doctor came in. Maybe he was the bad man with Carmen, in Millie's dream. "Hi, Millie, how's it going?"

"What is *it?*" she asked. She looked at me and rolled her eyes, amused.

"Remember Blue," today's slip read, and it wasn't until my fourth time through the lobby that I discovered the music source: a player piano. I didn't even know those existed anymore. The piano was roped off, a *Not for Public Use* sign propped on its top. The bench was tucked under. The tune was light and bouncy, but it seemed the wrong kind of instrument for a hospital. The keys pressed down automatically as if by ghostly hands. If you'd never seen one, you'd think the piano, in the player's absence, had lost its mind.

In the elevator, because of what had happened before, I thought of Erin. Both of them. Both kids, meaning, Erin and Jack, not Erin and the pigtailed girl. All four of us, actually, the whole ex-family, a trip we took to Letchworth. No memory to speak of, just of going there, the gorge, the birds soaring. What were they called? Turkey vultures. Good memory, I said to myself.

Someone had combed Millie's hair. I saw her hairbrush, a tangle caught in the bristles.

"Have you been driving this whole time?" she asked. I wondered what she pictured when she said this. Me in the Cadillac? Me in the van? Me at all? "What are you doing up at this hour?"

"I thought I'd come visit you."

"Don was here this morning."

"I'm Don."

She smiled from the center of the bed. "Well, of course you are."

At some point, soon, she wouldn't be able to place me. I realized she would never call me again. Forever, when my phone rang, it would never be her. Too many numbers and buttons. Or maybe she'd come back a little, enough to accomplish that.

"What did you have to do to get in?"

"Oh, nothing. I just walked straight through."

She said she needed to go to the bathroom. I was about to alert a nurse when I saw the tube draining down, the drip of fluid collecting in a half-filled bag.

"I think you can go, Millie. To the bathroom."

"Sure I can go. I just need a sixteen-inch hammer."

The catheter was removed. She had a bedpan now. She had passed the swallow test, but she wasn't eating. The staff was concerned about nutrition. Finally, she found her appetite. I watched a shaky spoon rise to an open mouth.

"This did not come out right." I thought she would reject the rest, but then she spooned more of the same, and decided the liquid food was delicious. "They have good food there."

"Keep eating," I said.

"Why are you repeating yourself?" Millie said. "Did you make all this?"

I told her I hadn't, but maybe the next meal.

"There is radish in here," she said about the vanilla pudding. "It is very tasty," she said. "Doesn't that taste good, Don?"

I smiled from my chair.

"I'll just keep eating the raspberries," she said.

"Is it raspberries?" I said, but why did I correct her about pureed flavor?

"Unless you're telling me something I don't remember."

"Is it good?"

"Mmm," she said. "My God, is it good. The food is good here, no matter what."

But something on her tray agitated her. The plastic dome, the food lid. It reminded me of the climbing dome, the igloo. When I said the word "igloo" in my head, I went completely elsewhere, to the cooler in my van, and me in the kitchen with the social worker, and things I might have said, or said better. Millie tapped at the strange structure, prodded it with a finger. "What is this trying to be?"

She was a child. Her parents were alive again. And every pet. She asked if I saw them, along the wall, off to the side, in the corner. She smiled at their presence. Outside the window was a different season. She said, "I have spent all day trying to get from inside to outside."

She talked about a man on the bus. She thought she was in a restaurant that stayed open till twelve o'clock. She said she had to go to the airport. She asked if I would take the socks off her shoes. She said she'd seen the group again that was stealing everything from the high school. She said, "I am not going back to the night house."

I felt dumb for thinking she was my dead grandmother. She was never that person. She was only herself. And she wasn't even that anymore. I told her I had to go. I left her bedside, assured her I would come back.

"Will you come back *now?*"

And then, she recovered. Her head cleared a bit. One day, instead of finding her in bed, I saw her seated in a chair by the window. "Hey, look at you," I said. "Much better. You're yourself again."

She smiled. Her eyes looked brighter. "I guess I'll have to put on my duds. I could use a little hair spray, but big deal. I didn't do as bad as most people do when they fall. It is not usual to fall like that."

It may have been the drugs, what they stopped giving, what they switched to, some patch or injection or pill, some better balance or management. Whatever the case, I wanted to congratulate her. I wanted to say good job. "How are you?"

"Oh, three steps from hell. Get me out of this fiasco."

It was nice to hear jokes and memory recall. "Pretty bad, huh?"

"You don't even know a quarter of it from here. It was worse than jail." She talked in the past tense about the ordeal she'd been through. "They decided they were gonna tear me apart and spit me out," she said, and I said I understood. "My mother was opposed to this from the very beginning. And she knew that I needed none of this. She was very relieved after the tests said that. It was a learning experience, but it wasn't enough for me."

I still thought she sounded better, that she'd partly rebounded.

"Can I ask you a question?" she said.

"Sure."

"What does this room connect to?"

"Another room," I said. "Just like this one."

"Is that right? Imagine that."

"What did you think it was?"

"Well, gymnastic-type stuff."

"Could be, Millie. They might do that in there."

"I'm pretty sure that's what's on the other side of me."

And then she started talking about sand, how she wished there was some here, and why wasn't there any? I told her I didn't know.

At least her hip would heal—that disfigurement wasn't permanent.

"They have all odds of people floating around here. Camels, even." It didn't take her long to ask, "Is she eating at the restaurant or munching in the trees?"

I wondered what picture or sign she saw in the clock. On her face was no indication of her mind receding. I looked at the floor, and then up at the ceiling as if to measure the distance, to calculate how an actual camel could ever fit inside. Only a baby, or some no-necked mutant.

"Can you hand me that brick blanket?"

On the windowsill was a blanket, folded up. I guess it looked like that, a brick. What figment did Millie see in the sill? A diving board, a game table? Was the clock still forgotten, an imaginary planet with no time? I stared at the wall, wondered at the area beyond it.

"Are these the brick blankets that everyone is talking about?"

I stepped forward. Straight through the glass was a big, brick building. Down below were cars and people. If I were higher up, aloft, they might look altered—until I descended and saw the creatures for what they really were. "I think they are," I said. I unfolded it, covered her with the soft fabric.

"I can see why," she said.

11

I WANTED A LIFT. Or just to hear a normal voice, even to talk to
Renee, which kind of shocked me, to think of her and normalcy,
because when we were arguing at full tilt I'd call her a psychopath—
clearing my head was the *last* thing I thought about, when I thought
about talking to her. Calling or texting didn't feel right, so I decided
for less. Or more, depending on what happened, what I did, when I
got there. The house. Obviously, not my childhood one, I had already
gone there, and after I told Dad that I'd been to it, I didn't need that
reseeing. So, Renee's. It wasn't until I got behind a school bus, in the
afternoon, on my way, that I realized I was driving there at a problem-
atic time for voices—not just Renee's but Erin's, Jack's—but I'd lost
track of the hour. The lights blinked, then changed from orange to red
as the stop signs flapped out, which would normally drive me crazy,
getting caught like that, but I was in no hurry, and instead it reminded
me of mornings when we were. To get Erin out the door, five minutes
on the clock till pickup, some odd time like 8:17, and Renee would be
in one room, yelling to Erin about the bus coming and are you dressed?,
and Erin would say, "I'm kind of dressed, I just need to get dressed,"
something like that, that would make you scream, but after, you'd
laugh about it, when miraculously you got her onto the bus, even if
you had to hold up your frantic hand to the driver from your door
telling him wait, she'd be right there, while you yelled inside, "Let's go,

he's leaving," while Renee might yell, too, a yell inside a question, "Do you have everything?"

I didn't stop when I went by. I had already done that with the other house, and it hadn't gone well, and I knew I was picking the wrong time, with the kids maybe home and even outside, but I just wanted to feel what it would be like to be on that street—say what you want about Renee, but she lived in a pleasant neighborhood, wasn't trying to be anything else—and I glanced at the house, my neck kind of scrunching down as I rolled past, seeing nothing, of course, nothing different, because unless the house had collapsed, what are you going to notice if you're going at that speed? After I left (I guess I didn't need to speak to anyone), it wasn't long before I imagined being spotted, which I knew was paranoid thinking, but I even imagined Renee texting me saying, "Jack said he saw you?" In my mind, there was a question mark. And I was going to send a text back, lying, "He must be seeing things." But then I didn't want to do that to Jack. And to me. I felt like I was canceling myself out, to say where I wasn't when I was.

After having this imaginary conversation, I had another one, with myself. Or myself about how to talk to Renee. I think I wanted to tell her that I was in a situation. But I didn't like how that sounded. The meaning would be misinterpreted. If I'd told her that I'd met a woman, she'd've hung up instantly before she'd heard Millie's age—it was important to arrange the words carefully so that she knew who Millie wasn't, in terms of how she related to me. So I started to talk about her, Millie, to Renee, how there was this ninety-plus woman who'd been married for over sixty years, and she was permanently in love with her husband, Jim—I would say his name to establish his presence—and then at that point of the story it seemed safe to bring in my name and my connection, even if I didn't understand the point and where this was going, in telling it to my ex. The point, I argued with myself, was that Millie's fidelity and our close friendship would reflect something good or changed about me. I shook my head. Shaking my head was a way of hearing Renee's feelings, the silence on the line. And then the long silence would be followed by something like: "Do you know how late and wrong you are to tell me this?" I nodded at what she said. Because that was the only part of the story that made sense. Her imagined part. And I thought, is that how my life was winding up, with hypothetical fights, where Renee's side was right, and everything out of my mouth was foolishness?

The doctor diagnosed Millie with dementia. The social worker said they were planning to discharge her soon. "To where?" I asked, and they said they were recommending a rehabilitation center for the hip. Medicare would cover a twenty-one-day stint. As her health care proxy, I thought that sounded sensible. The social worker suggested I wait several hours after Millie arrived to settle in there, because she was going to be agitated by the foreign surroundings. I waited a full day.

On my first visit, I got stuck in the entrance, in the vestibule between the pair of electric doors. The outer door slid open automatically, but when I approached the interior one, nothing happened and I almost stumbled into the glass. I stood, clumsily, waiting. I searched the wall for a button to press, a microphone or a call box or an eye to wave at. I was about to knock on the glass or step backwards and retry the walk-through when the accordion doors folded open.

"Your second door's not working," I said to the receptionist. The desk was tucked around the corner from the entrance.

"You came through too fast," she said. "It's timed for our residents."

I had brought some items for Millie, and I set them on the counter while I signed in and asked what floor.

"It happens a lot with visitors." She located Millie's name on the admittance list, and told me four. "You must be the grandson."

"I'm a handyman," I answered. I didn't know why I said that. I remembered saying it to the niece, but it didn't seem as damning here, at least to this desk person. "We're very close."

"A handyman. We always need one of those."

I still had some cards in my wallet. I slipped one out and glanced at the face, and handed it, after an awkward pause, to her.

"Don's Fix-It," she said, eyeing both faces. "You do houses?"

"Sure."

"I'm in an apartment. But my brother's got one. I'll show him your card."

"I do apartments, too." Everything I said made total sense if I were speaking from an earlier time. "I got a new job I gotta keep close contact with. But, yeah, I'm still doing repair work." I turned away to locate the elevators; no more life talk.

Upstairs, the floor was split in two, with the nursing station and kitchen directly facing the elevators. To the left and right were wide dining areas, the back walls lined with windows. Hallways ran north and south from the rooms. I guess the floor plan was a big H, if I had to describe it in a letter.

I saw what I expected to see. The zonked bodies, the lifeless shapes, the whole floor deadened by sedatives, as if tranquilizers had been piped through the air. Even with four residents grouped around a table, each person was a marooned inhabitant. Most of the movement was the staff—and the fishes in the tank—although there was one woman who drifted aimlessly like a sleepwalker, never talking, just feeling surfaces and lids. Once, she neared the elevator, and a nurse called out her name, not unkindly, and approached without hurry and cupped her elbow and guided her away from the exit.

Millie was seated in a wheelchair, in the room off to the left. I carried over a blanket and her rosary, and one of the wedding pictures from the mantel. Instead of being thanked, I was reprimanded. "Put that away," she said. She glared as if I'd smuggled in contraband. "That isn't what's going on here." I looked around to see what was.

A man licked crumbs off the table, bending so slowly and lolling his tongue out. A woman chewed at her bib. I thought I was the only visitor, although I wasn't sure about the man in the corner armchair. He seemed sane and healthy, in his eighties and unimpaired. Unlike the other residents, he looked like he could rise and leave and go about his day. But then he lowered his head and spat on the carpet. Minutes later, he spat again. When he drank from a water glass, set on the window ledge, he spat it out like mouthwash.

The residents were either silent or shouting. Almost all were silent, but there was one woman, across the room, crying out like a sheep. Millie didn't seem to register the disturbance, but I could. It was a crazy sound. I kept waiting for someone to scream at her to stop, but the bleating didn't bother anyone but me, as if I were sealed off with her in a soundproof room.

"Will you look who came back?" Millie said, and she pointed, not at me, nor anyone, but at something in the air. She wore a childish grin. At her table, a woman attempted to suck ice cream through a spoon. Her name was Dorothy. I tried to tell her that was my grandmother's name, but her face jerked in a grin—a puppet pulled—before I completed the sentence. Her wide marionette smile was both kind and frightening.

Millie thought she was in a hotel. She said she spent the previous night in the hotel garage. She asked if I had registered. She said she was only staying today. "I'm in a one-night room," she said. "The stuff they make you do to go to the bathroom in a hotel." There was a phone book on the table. "How can people do that? Over a *pencil?*"

"What's the phone book for?" I asked.

"I was trying to call you."

"You were?"

"But none of the numbers are in the phone book."

"I'll give you my card."

"That's a good idea," she said. But then she said, "They take all the property that is personal. I don't know why. They treat it ... like a monastery. Yes, that would be the word for it."

At the next table, a woman played dress-up with a baby doll. She fiddled with the diaper, pulling it off and on.

"There's Ding Dong over there," Millie said, and I couldn't tell if she was pointing at an empty chair or the spitter in the corner. I watched him more. He twiddled his thumbs, counting. I saw his mouth move, "Forty-six, forty-seven," his eyes focused on his fingers. His shoes were caked with mud. "I don't know what he is. He's supposedly a painter. He thinks he's artistic. But he's not even close. He thinks a lot about himself, thinks he's a lot of things, but he doesn't come to any conclusions. He's just as good as Stan. You gotta count them the same."

In every visit, the man was either in that chair, or the chair was empty, as if the seat were only his. I never saw him elsewhere. Millie I found in different places, usually in the sitting rooms, on either side, but sometimes in bed, sleeping or just staring. She shared a room, but I hadn't encountered the roommate yet.

"I wish I would've found my room and my bed. Because this is not it. I got my own room and my own things."

"This is your bed, Millie."

"Yes, this is my bed."

She said she was having troubles with her neighbor. She meant the roommate. The front door listed both of them—(A) Millie Prall and, below her, (B) Arleen Springut. Shortly after Millie announced the conflict, the roommate appeared in the doorway as if she'd been summoned to defend herself. White-robed and ghostly, she shuffled behind the walker, dragging her body inside the metal legs. I thought she would pitch forward every time she maneuvered the frame. Her long, stringy hair was recently washed or greasy. She didn't resemble Millie. Her face was deep-lined and witchy, and her expression was angry with effort, with having to endure the strenuous journey down the hallway and now negotiating the turn and continuing forward, the corner room being extra spacious, which added to her hardship. It was easy to imagine how Millie had a difficult time with her. But when the woman reached the far side of the closer bed and lowered herself backwards, she grinned, a beaming smile animating her wrinkled face. "Hi, Grandma," she said. Her grimness was gone, and she became a different person. "She's my grandma," she said, staring at Millie. "I lost both my grandmas, so she's moved the place of my grandma. And I think the world of her. And my mother loves her, and my son loves her, and we all love her. Don't we, Mother?" She kept smiling at Millie. She seemed happier than anyone I'd ever seen here, but it may have been the relief of not falling. She hadn't tumbled on her walk, but now her words did. "She's a sweetheart. She is the sweetest little girl I ever could ask for in a sister. Because we all care too much about her, so we're not gonna let anything happen to her. She's the first one up in the morning, and it's so good to see someone that chipper. She is so precious. She's Grandma's mom. And she's *my* grandma, too. And we think the world of her." It was like watching a different part of her switch on, the one that could still go full speed but maybe couldn't stop, the burst of words both generous and frenzied.

Millie ignored the speech. It was as if no one had talked to her, or the words had been heard dimly across a too-great distance, or they were irrelevant to her current problem, which was her sock, namely the irritation beneath it. Her full attention was on her itching shin.

"We've known each other for a year. Worked together, and we made it fun. And we'll continue to make a good life together. We know together what we've been through. But I'm ready to start a new life, or get out of it. But I've got a husband I've gotta learn to live with. If he's around at all. He's hanging around with some friends, and he's with him."

"What's your name?" I asked, even though I'd already seen it printed. When she said hers, I said mine.

"Don, well that's . . ." And for a second I thought she was going to tell me it was her husband's name, or her son's name, someone related or recognizable—but she stopped, my name suddenly forgotten. "Is that right?" she said, and when I told her it was, she said, "If you say so, I believe it."

"Don Don," she echoed, which sounded like my assumed name, something anonymous, my last name gone. And it also made me feel like two things. An identical pair.

I sneezed, and she said bless you, and I mentioned allergies.

"I never saw a man yet who didn't identify what was wrong with him." She glanced at her pillow and was instantly tired. "Oh . . ." she sighed, her talk exhausted. "I need to take a nap."

"She's kind of a grandmother," I said to her. She had reclined on her bed, and the top half of her body was obscured behind the curtain pulled partway across the room. I looked at the doorway where she had first materialized. When would I need to reintroduce myself? Was I already a stranger?

"She sure is," I heard back, behind the divider.

Millie paid no attention to us, kept scratching at her skin, puzzled, as if she had come upon a part of her agitated body that she could not understand. She itched and searched, her fingers ever curious, her mind concentrating, until she found some source. Her eyes startled in astonishment. "Wow," she said.

Beth paid me the strangest compliment once. She said, "You have pretty skin." I was like, "Excuse me?" And she told me I did. "Okay," I said, "you mean *nice*?" And she said yeah, that's the word she meant. No one had ever said that to me before, pretty or nice.

"Is that your thing?" I asked.

"Yeah. Skin."

I didn't know how to feel about it. I mean, it's a compliment, so, good, put it in the plus column. And I could see by the way she smiled—which I told her about, right there—that it made her happy. So, great, she saw something she liked in me. I guess she could have said something more pointless (*gosh, you have great ankles*). But as far as compliments go, it felt kind of thin. Like if she had complimented my entire body, which I guess she had—it's skin—and not like I cared much about my body anyway, but I knew most people did, especially when you first started dating, but it just felt like she was talking about these two tiny areas on my cheeks, real small. But then again, I was also like, this is my skin, and it's good that she likes it, and it's not going anywhere, other than changing when I get old, older.

But I think it would have been better if we had talked longer about what we liked, if after we each made our one compliment (me with the smile), we'd kept going, I like your hair, I like your et cetera, and that way established more positives, and I would have been on solid ground with her, or, I would've known if she stopped with one, that there was a problem, a shortcoming, and I wouldn't've been so blind-sided by what she said when she said she wasn't feeling it. When she ended it, I wished she had said something different, because skin—it's one of the things you *can't not see* in the mirror.

She was the last woman I'd seen naked. I remembered when we had sex, that night, after we'd said nice things, I was on top of her, and I leaned in close, pressed my forehead against hers, so our eyes were almost touching, and I said, "Do you like my skin?" And she laughed and pushed me away and said, "You're crazy." And I was like, "What, you said it first." And she kept laughing, and I said sorry, but in a mocking way, and then I leaned into her smile and said, "I guess your words just made me aggressive."

Money was a problem. Or it was about to be. Not for Millie. And not just because of Medicare coverage but also because of her bank balance, the cushion. But *I* didn't have that. I looked at my own account, and because I wasn't working, only visiting (the hospital and now here—two nonbillable places, for me), the number was low, getting lower. I hated when I talked like this. *Thought* like this. If I kept going in this direction, soon my life would be pointing backwards, downwards, again toward that hole. I thought, If only I could find another Tiffany lamp. I meant it as a joke, to myself, although I remembered Millie saying, "We'd be rich," so I guess she was there, too.

I went out on a job. Had to, given my measly dollar figure. I stood inside a living room while a couple pointed out their damaged wall. It was all pretty standard, the water getting behind the chimney, and now the internal evidence, the line of bubbling paint traveling down. The couple was especially distressed about the condition of the built-in bookcase. I was about to assure them it was all easily fixable when I heard myself go in another direction. I started talking about plaster dust. "You're"—I spread my arms wide, to gesture at the rectangular section of the wall that I'd need to cut out, but I think what I was really doing was encompassing the whole room—"you're really going down a dangerous road here." By the time I'd finished talking, I'd made them think their old house existed somewhere in a hazardous mine shaft, with toxins released if they opened up this wall. It was a good story. If I knew less, I'd have believed it. I told them I could try to cordon off the area while I worked, to make sure the stuff, the dangerous dust, didn't get everywhere—they had a young child, another on the way—and that I was busy now, I'd check my schedule, and it might take me some time to acquire the necessary equipment. I was already out of the house, hearing myself on the phone when and if they called again, days later, adding to my runaround. I shrugged at them now, at the wall. "Can of worms," I said.

When I left their house, I didn't feel like myself. And I knew exactly who I felt like. Decades ago, there'd been a handyman. Lubo. I didn't know where he was originally from, to get a name like that. Faint trace of an accent, but I couldn't pin the region. I had assisted him on a few jobs, and eventually he referred customers to me when there was a job he didn't want. Which got to be often. This was how he phased into retirement. By phasing himself out. He was just over sixty, I think. His wife still worked. They had enough money between them. So, I'd go to these jobs in place of him.

One time I went on a job, and it wasn't one of his referrals, but it turned out Lubo had been there, not only because the homeowner said his name but also by the way he talked about him. "He told us that this was really something we could do on our own." It was a casement-window job, the old, rusted originals. "He said it was easy, we could just get a . . . tool and grind the rust on the . . ."

"Cranks," I said.

"Yeah, he used a different word. *Arms.* That's what he called them."

I nodded.

"Just file down the rust. He said we could do it ourselves. He was really nice about it. Explained it step by step. I think I was supposed to take notes." And the guy smiled at me and waved his hand at some nonsensical paper. "But I was like, 'Uh, that's why we called *you.*'"

And by you, he now meant me. I smiled back and said, "Yeah, that's Lubo for you." I rolled my eyes at his crazy talk.

If I say that when I pictured Lubo at the end, I saw a guy that didn't even want to climb a stepladder, I don't mean it as a sad story. At all. His life was a happy ending. Workwise, at least, since I can't say how it all ended. I lost touch with him after the referrals. But long before that, back when I was assisting, I'd been out to his house, and I'd seen the deck he'd constructed. Triple-tiered. They had a good house, with a pretty piece of property behind it. Backed up to woods. He was really into birds, it turned out. Birds, and soccer, for some reason, so maybe he was from a soccer country. Maybe his wife had as much to do with how they could live like that, out there. She had some job at the hospital. Administrative, I think. So good for him that he'd stopped, that he was able to, even if it was partly because she hadn't yet, but might soon. Good for them.

But when I left that house, not Lubo's but the mine shaft, I realized that I was becoming him, *had become* him, prematurely. I didn't know it would happen at such an early date, and honestly, because I always thought of it as Lubo's story, and Lubo's story only, I didn't know it would ever happen at all.

The aim was to use a walker, but Millie wasn't responding well to the rehab. The last time she walked, she fell, so she was scared to walk again.

"You come at the darndest times," she said. She turned her attention to her shirt, which had come untied. "I get so angry at this. At the size and the fact that they're too small. There is no way that I am going to be wearing that in a year."

One day, a man arrived. He wore a suit and carried a clipboard, and he walked from chair to chair, smiling, saying names. When he got to the spitter, he said, "Hello, Detective."

A cloth lay on the ground, and most of the meal was heaped there, which explained the traces of food on his shoes. Briefly, the suited man glanced at the waste, as if it were some minor table-manners quirk, but then he paid it no mind and kept mingling, his friendly hand extending to another shoulder.

I don't know why I was amazed. Why not a detective?

"All these people," Millie said, "are relatives of people that were here before. I know all the people over there. They all know each other very, very well. My gosh, they all look like they're twins."

It was as if her pointing activated a conversation; two lady residents began communicating back and forth, old friends. "Are you all packed?" one of them said.

"I'm not either."

"We gotta get all packed ourselves."

Millie saying twins—it reminded me of her roommate saying my name twice, doubling me. I looked back to the detective against the wall. Did he know what he'd been? When he walked the hallways here, did he think he was patrolling his old beat? I watched him blink and squint. I imagined that he was still that same person, that I was only seeing a disguise. He was here for his final assignment, incognito with his fake imbecilic spitting, his messy etiquette, his strategic silence. He was The Spitter, pretend-crazy with his food spatter— when he fiddled his fingers he was actually doing a head count—the crime stopper in the corner, the perfect vantage point to prevent future escapes.

"I've gotta get home. Maybe I can get a taxi from your house to get home. I'm talking to my girlfriend across the street. Yes."

"What did you ask me?"

"I don't know if I asked you anything. I was just trying to ask you how many were going."

"You said your answer was yes. To what? Are you talking to yourself?"

"I was—"

"I'm only taking two people. So stop asking me."

"Oh, bunk!"

"For somebody as nosy as you, you deserve it."

"I'm not nosy at all." She was outraged, but then she wasn't.

Millie laughed. "This one is a real close pal of mine. She's on like a . . . the word is like a kaleidoscope, only it's not."

In the corner, the drop cloth was gathered up with all the muck inside it.

I couldn't keep going like this. I scheduled some little jobs. Painting. Yard care. Shelving. I even called the couple, and told them I could do the wall.

"Oh," she said.

I told her it wouldn't be too difficult. She brought up the bad words I'd said, but I acted like I hadn't really said them, or said them in a way that didn't quite mirror their meaning, or that *she* was seeing them in the wrong context. We both fell silent. I said I was just trying to be extra careful, with an old house, something near historic. The job didn't seem to exist anymore, and I could tell she was resentful that I'd used words I hadn't really meant, scary ones, worrying. "The way you talked about it . . ." I sensed she was thinking about her child and pregnancy and exposure and sickness.

Soon, though, we were able to concentrate on the mere dimensions of a cutout rectangle. We could forget what I said before, and not be anxious about particulates in the air. The project shrunk back down to the designated area. By the end of the conversation, they were excited to get their wall repaired, maybe she was even feeling that it was no longer a mistake to live somewhere ancient with who knows what in the walls, and to have their bookcase returned to what it was, the books lined up on the shelves.

"It'll be okay," I said. *Dust, dangerous, can of worms*: after all of Millie's unremembering, her incomprehensibility, I felt a kind of amazement that a set of words and phrases I'd used, on another day, could be recalled. "I'll have the tarps," I said. "I'll set up tight barriers, contain all the work. *Insulate*," I said. I stressed that word. "I'll make sure you're safe."

They said Millie kept rejecting the therapy, that her walking wasn't improving. The nursing home recommended she stay. Just paperwork, my hand. She could remain on the same floor, which was a memory care unit, that's what this floor was, the same room, even. Medicare had ended, so now Millie had been converted to private pay, a sky-high cost, fifteen thousand a month. I'd see the reduced number reflected on Millie's next statement.

Viva Las Vegas played on the flat-screen. When the janitor passed by, Millie told me he was good looking. She eyed me, conspiratorially. "I said, 'Listen, buddy, if I had two more fingers, I would've killed you.'"

"You like this movie?"

"It's movie time. This is when the men gather. They somehow know what's coming up. And then you see that they get free dinners. It's a good life. I bet there are twenty men that do that. Their idea of fun is pretty raucous. They take stuff away from like a child. I stay away from them is what it boils down to ... This is not a favorable atmosphere and it talks. A lot. Lots of amenities. But it's an odd place. I was trying to get somebody to keep my ice skates in the closet."

"You like to ice-skate?"

"I would never classify myself as an ice skater."

"Me neither," I said.

"We have a lot in common. You're a loyal friend, but I haven't seen you in a while."

"I was just here yesterday."

"I didn't pay attention then. You probably don't remember that."

The staff wheeled a man in. Not a wheelchair, or a gurney, but somewhere in between. He wore large protective boots on his feet. He cursed the staff as they tried to navigate him toward the window. And then he started growling. Like a beast. I expected him to spread his arms and beat his chest.

I looked at Millie. She watched the man. I think she glanced at his padded extremities. But I didn't know what she could see, or what impression it made.

"There couldn't possibly be a human being growling over there."

Which was strange, because that was exactly my perspective.

She smiled. "Geez, people are so weird." She started chuckling away. I realized that her quilt was on wrong. I didn't mean that it was falling off. What I meant was that it was upside down, and when I saw it that way, when I thought of it—when I *processed* that word, or words—I thought of the upside-down pineapple cake, like cake and quilt were the same thing. Anyway, the quilt, there was a worn corner, and when I used to see the quilt covering her, at home, sitting in her chair, she would worry that corner with her hands. But now this favorite corner was at her feet. So I lifted it off her, rotated it, draped it back down, and I placed this corner in her hands. Her fingers groped the familiar material. A calmness spread across her face. I would show the staff which direction the blanket was supposed to be. And then, I thought, decades from now, who might do this for me?

"I don't know why it closed up so quickly," Millie said. "How do you figure out where I am? Which one of these multitudes of places I inhabit?"

"Where do you think you are?"

"I guess I'm . . . right where I'm at, too."

"Me, too." I wasn't unemployed. But—I wanted to cut ties to that business.

I still spent a chunk of daytime here. I rarely saw visitors during working hours, although there was one today. A son. Leather-jacketed, with a motorcycle helmet beside him on a spare chair, and he sat with his mother, holding both of her hands, his forehead touching hers. They didn't speak. Occasionally he pulled away, leaned back in his chair, and then he tapped skulls again. Sometimes he kissed her forehead, her cheeks, even her lips.

"What's wrong?" I asked Millie, although she didn't look any more unhappy. I think it was just the contrast of this picture in my mind.

"I don't see anything wrong with myself. It's just the outside world, and I don't know why. I'm tired of staying in a motel. It doesn't make any sense. I want to go live in a different . . . back to the station I was living."

Here wasn't a bad place. The patients got three squares a day. Today's dinner menu was cabbage roll, ham sandwich, and carrot coins. An hour ago, there was a kind of volleyball. The staff arranged the tables in a long rectangle, with patients placed lengthwise to face each other. "Who wants it?" the therapist said. She bounced a blue beach ball on the table and sent it in an arc. The resident missed, but the ball was retrieved and tapped back into the air, a hand twitched from a stagnant body, and with a second spasm from the other side there was a small rally. Then more bright colors—red ball, yellow ball—floated in, and more patients were wheeled over to play the game, fingers flicked, limbs activated and circuits functioned, faces came to life, eyes shining with delight. *You missed it, Roberta. It's yours, Sabita.*

But yesterday, there were guinea pigs like some sick joke. Two rodents quivering in an enclosure. And the woman cradling the baby doll— why all this kiddy stuff? They weren't children. Maybe the men wanted to play poker. Maybe everyone wanted cocktail hour? I know. But that guy I saw with his tongue put out for crumbs; maybe he was a former hell-raiser who, if they weren't gonna pour him hard stuff, maybe he didn't want another round of goddamn Jell-O.

"What do you think of this place?" I asked her. The corner chair was empty. It was like it was a good time to talk, because the spitting detective had left his position, and no one could be monitored, all actions unsolved and unwitnessed, all clues missed.

"I just don't have a feeling for what anyone is doing. It just doesn't make any sense at all. What do you do when you've got really, sensibly, no place to go?"

"Millie." It's possible I spoke too softly to be audible. But when she didn't make eye contact, instead casting her glance away, it felt as if she'd changed her name or I'd misremembered it, that the name was meant for someone else. The man with massive feet growled louder, like he would devour the room. I didn't want to visit here anymore. To hell with second childhood. And I didn't want to have to apologize for neglect. I had to take her out, back. Because of what she'd said in her kitchen. And maybe even because of what she *did*, what I'd seen. What I meant was, I could do the thing that Millie had tried to do— I was talking about the up/down alphabets—or that I *thought* she had tried to do. Do two things at once. I could care for Millie, and care for myself. (The second part of that thought stung a bit.) And just like with Millie, it didn't have to be a mistake, even though that's what it looked like, and odds were, that's probably what it was. I owed her that promise. I could bring her back to where she wanted to go, and where I needed to bring her. (Again, me.) Even in her familiar surroundings, she would be miserable. But she was miserable here. Her house couldn't possibly be this grim, this lonely. Every floor of this building was filled with anguish and defeat. Every space, no matter how well-lit, was dark. The bib-gnawing, the dulled and scrambled minds and broken forms: at least at home the craziness and bad wiring could be all hers.

She was crying. But no one noticed or cared, not even the staff. It was like Millie wasn't crying, or she was, but the audience was oblivious. The sadness meant nothing. A phantom noise.

Even if the detective was in his same spot, that person disappeared a decade ago. His name was Walt Furtsch, and his room was near Millie's, two doors away on the same passage. There were several pictures of him on the door, but the images weren't old enough—in his prime or newly retired—to see the earlier person he'd stopped being. They went back a little, a faint difference, but I felt like I'd already seen them. I wished the pictures were like the ones on Millie's mantel, a series of successive shots, the lifespan of a marriage. One photo showed him sitting in the passenger seat; the picture was taken from the driver's seat, so it only captured a side angle of his face. Another was a close-up, like a passport photo. His eyes, his surveillant squint, confused me, because he seemed to see something and nothing, both tracking and absent. His door was always closed. The roommate's name was Stan. One of the nurses had caught me once, studying the photos, peering at his face and trying to go back ten, twenty years—no, further, thirty, forty, to see him half his age, around me, similar, or even younger, in his twenties and nimble—and she'd asked if I was lost. Furtsch: sounded German. I wondered where he had lived. She directed me to the correct room farther down at the end.

The last time I wheeled Millie back to her room, a patient, gray and nameless, pointed at Millie and said, "This is Pastor Cindy. She's going to be living with me now on."

"Let's get you home," I said. I was scared when I said it—in my mind, alarms sounded—but enough of me thought I was right. I repeated it, "Let's get you out of here," so it felt like a shared opinion, my own company.

"When?" she said.

"As soon as we can." She didn't like the word soon, never did. "Early. Quick. Right away."

"Let's not wait for the yes answers."

This place was exorbitant, but around-the-clock home care would cost even more. I felt ashamed for thinking about money, for always thinking about it. "Let's get you out of this fiasco," I said. I remembered her saying that, even though she wouldn't. And then I wondered how many of her sentences I'd committed to memory.

She smiled at my right words. "That's the idea."

Someone else began crying, at another table, as if Millie, done with sadness, had handed it off, as if the room couldn't permit such quiet, or always had to carry some amount of that sound. The room felt so simultaneously crowded and deserted—all the spaces at the tables were filled, but no one was left.

"Why are you crying?" a nurse asked quickly and walked over to console. "What's wrong?"

Millie was now happy, calm, as if she'd been that way for hours. Her body was slumped but comfortable in her wheelchair. She lifted her head, her eyes wandering across the low white sky of the ceiling. "I mean, this is a nice place, really."

12

When Renee cheated, she confessed it. Not right away, but close. She said, "I'm just as bad as you. We're both terrible." And I was like, wait a second, slow down here, let's not talk about me, I'm not interested in assessing my value at this particular moment. My voice raised as I spoke like that. I wanted to know who was the guy and did I know him, and what had she done—I didn't want to say the two of them *together*, so I was asking for specifics and pushing him out of the picture simultaneously—and how often. She told me everything, one after the other, that he was a stranger, a guy from the restaurant, and she'd waited on him, and it was a couple of times, the sex, and, no, not here in this house, and I didn't ask where. Knowing it didn't happen here, and not knowing where, meant it existed in some nonexistent place, although I was never gonna step foot again in that restaurant. She said she'd ended it. I asked if it was payback for what I'd done, and she said no, she didn't think so, maybe. Then again no. I didn't think I was as mad at her as she'd been for me. Actually I'm sure I was exactly as mad, madder, I just remembered feeling like I was copying her hurt behavior for a few days.

When she caught me cheating again, it wasn't text messages this time that tipped her, it was something in my actions or mannerisms, she didn't even tell me what it was, just accused me so fast that my face and voice couldn't prepare a credible denial. When she had finished yelling, or she didn't even yell this time, she just said, "You must really want to be alone." I remembered her expression. Baffled. It wasn't shock, like the first time, when I seemed to hit her out of the blue. Looking back on this, her face mirrored the open face that Erin gave us soon after, when we sat her down. Although, I think Renee was more baffled at *herself*—I didn't mean that as deflection. She exhaled, like everything was too late, then shook her head at me like I wasn't there, like what was coming next for me was nothing.

"You remember what you promised?" she said. She meant, of course, when I cheated before.

"Of course," I said, but I also knew my memory at that point would do me no good.

"You're really great at going back on your words."

"We don't have to do this," I remembered saying, and she said sure, let's just go on serial cheating, and by us she meant me, even if it had been her once, too, but less, plus the confession, or minus. I asked, kind of desperate, at least that's how my voice sounded to me, if it would have been better if I'd confessed, too, and she said she was done with my stupidity. Then she said something really trite, "What's done is done." Something people have been saying for ages. Then she said or clarified, besides, we weren't. Doing this. *She* was.

I informed the nurse manager Millie would be leaving. I was taking her home. The manager's mood changed. She asked me to wait a moment, and suddenly I was talking to two more people: a social worker and some coordinator, admin something. The three wanted to know my course of treatment, and whether there was a safe plan. "Are you going to move in with her?"

"Yes," I said. I hadn't planned to say that, but I knew that I would. I was terrified, but another side of me thought it was the wisest option. I wasn't sure if I was sacrificing my life or investing in it.

"What if you need to leave? Is there a backup?"

"Who's gonna keep her safe twenty-four seven?"

"Do you have the proper supplies at home?"

It didn't matter who said what, because all sides—A, B and C—were alike. No one approved, but I didn't need their approval, not legally. They couldn't say a word. Although, maybe I was wrong. Maybe there was some stipulation or policy, that if they didn't see this as a safe discharge, they could set up roadblocks. I saw three: a lawyer in his office, a police officer in Millie's living room, even a card in a drawer. "You don't want to deal with this," they said. And they were right. But I'd already made up my mind.

"Are you prepared to change her diapers?"

"Are you prepared to turn and position her in bed, every two hours, so that there isn't any skin breakdown?"

"Are you capable of overseeing the medicine regimen?"

The next round of questions. I told them I would ensure the house was handicap-accessible. "She doesn't want to be in a facility," I said.

"Well," the manager said, "we don't really think of ourselves as a facility. We're a community."

It sounded part caring, part sales talk, but I nodded.

"She's been participating in activities. She'll be losing a lot. The socialization. It's not just staring out a window."

I thought about that. Millie's window. Her point of view. "This is a good place." I remembered her line to the ceiling, her eyes on the whiteness.

My point of view: Sorry, but this place is a horror show. People are rotting in cages. It had to be affecting her, the hopelessness. It was affecting me. They cared about her, but they cared about their formula, too. She was still a bed. A number. And they were minus one. They didn't want to lose her, this gold-plated customer. A thought moved through me, but there was no time to examine it with all this attention.

"You've been here a lot," the manager said. I heard both compliment and criticism. I could tell she wasn't just talking about devotion. Her eyes measured me, but I stared back, at all of them. I didn't think I was seeing the Sisters of Charity. While we're discussing judgments and clear conscience: I know you have a soft spot for your private-pay people. Don't tell me you have *my* number.

And what had they seen me do? Had I eaten off her tray? Had I ever snapped at her? No. No. What peculiar? I guess there was the moment where I was caught gawking at the photographs, where I looked like some prowler at the door. I wondered if, after the nurse directed me down the hallway, she reported my suspicious behavior to her superiors, these people here. So what? I'd been bored. Eyeing a picture doesn't make you a rip-off artist. Nonsense. Why is it a bad thing if I'm here more than anyone else? Maybe that means Millie has more.

"You're a family friend," the manager said, and I detected the stress at the end, the final word louder, overpronounced, rounding into insult.

"She has no family here," I said. "I'm it," I said, my own emphasis.

"But you're not."

"Yes, I am." I didn't feel like a liar, even an honest one, when I said it. If I claimed I was a distant cousin—a good catchall term—I'd be lying, but somehow saying family rang true. Not to them. All around me, in a half circle, eyebrows arched, lips pinched, mouths opened in disbelief, like some single doubting body. My words were worse than hollow talk.

"On paper. When we did the intake—"

"Not on paper," I said to their combined skepticism. "Not real family."

"Okay. Just to be clear." She flashed a plastic smile. They nodded at my statements to show I was making enough sense, that I was who I said I was, not some fake nephew.

A friend, I heard her say, the extra decibel in my head, and it was strange that it would sound like its opposite. "She doesn't speak to her family." I remembered the document. I was the first contact. The second contact I'd left blank. "I'm stepping up here."

"Can I be candid?" The manager threaded her fingers. "Sometimes the elderly dig their own holes." She made a nest of her hands, then lowered it until it touched the edge of her desk, touching bottom. I had the strangest impulse to open the drawer, on her side, and rifle through it until I found some incriminating item, so I'd pull it out and wave it with my fingers—some compromised pictures of the residents, a flask of alcohol, unethical monitoring of staff activity, evidence of weird tendencies, my mind went everywhere—and I could say to the others, "See, you didn't know she was doing this," and the dynamics in the room would reconfigure to a new three against one.

I shook my head. "I'm solid." Worth it.

"Good." She searched the papers on her desk. She opened her hands, flung them in opposite directions. Then she nodded, as if she'd decided there was no choice, and exchanged glances with the other two. "We'll hope for the best. We're all on the same side. What matters is her happiness and her comfort." They all smiled at me like they were pleased.

The conversation had closed, but for me something was still the matter. "Where do you think she's at?"

"Things can change rapidly. Could change in two days. Right now, she's nearly bedbound."

"That's not what I'm asking. I want . . ." I suddenly wanted her to know it all, the thing I'd most resented during the entire conversation, but I wanted her to tell me everything. I needed that from her. "I want to know . . . what she is."

She didn't answer for a while—a long enough silence that I felt as if I'd asked her a question about a person she knew nothing about, or that she was done thinking—but when she finally spoke, it was swift and perfectly simple. "She's still in there."

I cleaned out her room, collected her few possessions. (The sterile room somehow became even more so.) At the medical-supply store, I picked out a hospital bed and a mattress with alternate pressures, plus a three-in-one commode and an over-the-bed table. I got her the Cadillac of everything. I didn't purchase a Hoyer lift, because I didn't like the way her body folded up when it suspended her, and she didn't like it, either, the manhandling. I had seen her scared when they used the machine at the nursing home. If need be, I could carry her.

When the bed was delivered, I positioned it in the living room so Millie would still be in the central part of the house. It was a big room, and I just needed to shift the recliner toward the couch to allow each piece of equipment to fit beside the other.

I set up a care area. I went through it in my mind, so everything—diapers, sheets, clothes, towels, cleaning supplies—would be ready at my fingertips.

I got out of my apartment lease and had my mailing address switched to Millie's.

My phone rang. It was Dad. I was back at her place, in the chair I bought her with her money, when the call came in. I figured I should take it, because I didn't know what would happen with my future, alone with her. I imagined her right here, before, calling me for the nth time, and I tapped Answer, suddenly craving a back-and-forth.

"I can't believe it," I heard him say. "Am I really talking to my son? Is it really him?"

I apologized.

"What's that? There must be static on the line. I'm sure I'm hearing things."

I said sorry again.

"You don't return my calls. How many? This must be the third time—I finally get the person."

"I know, you've called."

"Called plural. Figured the voice mail again. At least I know you exist."

I laughed. "How're the nuptials coming?"

"Huh? Oh, Stacy. Well, no, we've kind of put the brakes on the engagement."

"You're over?"

"No, no. Off and on."

"What happened?"

"She did the math. Ten plus ten plus ten. She didn't like the age difference. It gave her the thirty-year itch. Seventy/forty. Eighty/fifty. The wrong split. Suddenly, she's sixty . . . uh oh, where'd he go?"

"That's a long way off." The aging and the years and disappearance brought me to the series of pictures, Millie's marriage.

"Not in her mind. I might as well be a hundred. She said as much: 'I'm seventy, you're a hundred.' I said, 'Geez, you're really keeping score.' I said, 'Hey, ninety-three isn't what it used to be. It's the new ninety-two.' She thought it was funny, sort of. Still, once she'd skipped ahead, it was hard to bring her back to the actual me. I think it gave her the creeps."

"Happy ninety-ninth. How old is she exactly?"

"She's forty-three, and she wanted me to be fortyish too. Then fifty/ fifty, then sixties, you get the picture. I said, 'Those ain't our numbers.'"

I stared at the bed. My dad talking about his nineties—if I took away the house, it almost made sense that the bed was here for him, one day. "Didn't she know this would be a thing, when you started?"

"That point was mentioned."

"Didn't *you?*"

"I'm not stupid. I may have underestimated it. But: I'm younger. Healthier. My stamina is terrific. That gimp I was, before the hip replacement, and the knee operation—*he's* the slow mover. Three years since the stent. The man with the geriatric hip, the plugged-up heart. I'm glad we said goodbye to that geezer. Thank God I'm not what I used to be."

I remembered the surgery for the blood vessel, but I had forgotten about the degenerative hip. But the surgery was years in the making, not caused by a sudden fall.

"Really, I feel like I've been revived. I eat better now. More will-power. Sure, bad eyesight, and the other knee that won't cooperate."

I heard a honk—the first sound that said he was driving—then my dad telling a car to pass already. "Maybe you find someone closer to you, in years. Better match."

"We're not over yet. No one's pulling the pin. But: point taken. Or, I just never fess up to my real age. You know, who's counting? 'How old are you?' 'Old enough. Okay, fine, fine, I'm forty-five.'"

"Can't be forty-five. That's me."

"Well, then, I guess I'm you. We're twins. Or maybe I should do something with my face. There's a lot of that down here. You see these prunish hands but the no-wrinkles face. Anyway, seventy is where I'm at. And I'm working."

"I know you are."

"No, I mean—I'm *working* working. A job. I don't mean my body. Intact. Helps with the living expenses. *Pocket* money. Actually, it makes up the difference of the pension cuts."

I asked him what he was doing, and he said same as the old. Driving. Instructing, mostly.

"It's sort of like *no* money," he said, "because it's just replacing the deficit that shouldn't have been there in the first place. How's that for a second income?"

I looked outside, at the street, the sparse traffic. I thought about how this would be my primary view. In a direct diagonal, past the bogus lamp, a lamp you could hardly see by, I could imagine myself at the beginning, when I passed and saw the different lily, with the multitude of lights, the dozen gleaming shades. When it happened, did she notice me stop and come back? Did she think I was some wrong-way driver, mindlessly overshooting the mark? I pictured her, long ago, seeing everything. "Huh," I said. "Unretired."

"How about you?"

I laughed. Maybe at the combination of my dad working again, or that when he said he was, I thought he was bragging about body parts. "I've sort of been phasing things out."

"Oh yeah? What you been phasing in?"

So I told him, how I met Millie and what had transpired—the lamp and the dealer, the initial tasks and repairs and general upkeep, her struggles leading to her reliance on me to sort through the mishmash of mail and the transacting of all the bills, and then her entrusting, followed by the accident, and the health crisis, right up to where she was. I hadn't told anyone the full story. The closest I'd come was the imagined conversation with Renee, and even now, I suppose I hadn't, because I'd left out the part with the patterned towels. Still, it didn't feel like an outline, but more like a very long and unreal speech, like Millie's roommate's stream of words—and when my dad was silent, it almost reminded me of that gap when I first got on the line with Millie's niece.

"You're living there? With her?"

"Hey, you told me to bag the rental."

"I told you what?"

"You said not to get stuck in that spot."

"Wait, are you putting me on? This is really happening? You're like a . . . nursemaid? Is that what you call it?"

"Caretaker. Caregiver."

"Who . . . What's she got to do with you? Why is this your problem?"

"I've stopped with roofing."

"I understand that. You ain't some spunky kid anymore . . . Where are *her* kids?"

I guess I hadn't told him that part, only about her husband, and how she had drawn away from everyone else, into her own bubble.

"Donny . . . I realize I haven't seen you in a while, but I'd like to think I know you after forty-plus years. You've known her *months*?"

I looked up at the mantel clock, which read the time as past five. I imagined it was a calendar, showing dates, a numbers grid. "Almost a year."

"That's months. You've been doing one line of work for twenty years. Half your life."

"It's been on my mind." I thought, My father has known me my lifetime, but he doesn't know me this year, so he's missing a lot.

"Wait. Let me slow . . . I'm gonna pull over somewhere. Hold a sec." I heard more horns, a louder volume. *Careful*, I almost said. "Yeah, yeah, no blinker."

I studied the room. I said to myself, *This is where I live now.* Outside were no cars, no lettered vans. I could see clear again to my old self, arriving here for the first time. An unexpected car in the driveway, the driver stepping out. Of course it was *me*—except, sitting in the chair now, it felt like the double wasn't me on the other side of the door but *her* walking toward it. Perhaps she climbed from the chair before the doorbell even rang, her age the only hesitation to answering. "Just a second," she might have whispered, maybe even repeating it, her words keeping her company until she reached me, enough time in her slow hurry that, if it happened later, when her mind had worsened, she might have forgotten midstride the reason for the walk.

"Just turning here," I heard my father say.

A youngish man asking gently about a lamp? What could that possibly mean? Where was the talk going? How peculiar. Who was he, some scavenger? She let him in. Let *me* in. He pointed at the wall, the corner, the window, the lamp. And now both sets of eyes were on the burning object in the corner. Suddenly I wanted it back. All that vivid color for her. Could it still be at the store, unsold? No, it must be gone, passed from my hand to the dealer's and then on to someone else's.

"Okay, I'm parked. No more loud. Where was I?"

Beats me, I thought. "My change," I said. "My whole life." I didn't like how the conversation was narrowing down, and I didn't like looking at this bed and seeing my dad, and I didn't like sitting here idly while my retired dad told me he was driving, still. I wanted to have this conversation at least outside. I grabbed the Cadillac keys from the mantel. It would be good to do that anyway, to make sure the battery didn't die again.

"I'm trying—"

"Hold on, I gotta do something." I walked out to the garage and got in the car. Dad was driving, so I was too. I put the phone on speaker, set it down on Millie's seat. The mirrors were all set up for me, but after I opened the garage door and backed out, I couldn't go anywhere because the van blocked me in the driveway. I guess I could move that out to the street, but I felt like some parking-lot attendant, shuffling cars, and I didn't really want to take a drive with my dad anyway, especially not in Millie's vehicle.

"Are we talking yet?" I heard from the phone, the seat.

I set the car in park, looked at my van in the rearview mirror. "Yeah, where were we?"

"*Where were we?* You tell me. I'm trying to make a mental picture. If this were some volunteer work. I don't mean free, but you know . . . you pay a visit to a widow, help out. *She* pays. A pair of hands. But to quit your job."

The windows were rolled up. "I didn't quit. I just . . . stopped doing it."

"Same difference. You're saying this all in a normal voice, but it's not you. Obviously, she's—how old is she?"

"Ninety-five."

"Ninety-five—*that's* a number. Hey, I'm young again. Anyway, she's fifty years older, so there's nothing between you, so I gotta ask. I'm not gonna tiptoe. Is there something . . ."

"Dad." Maybe I did want to go driving, needed to. There was no one behind me, but the van looked like there was, and if I moved it—or even if I edged the Cadillac around it, which I couldn't do without driving on the lawn—it would be good for this car to take it out for a stretch, and I could feel my body anticipating the fast twists and turns.

"Well, I don't know what this is. You hear stories. I'm not saying you are. No one is. But people—they do things underneath."

"Who are you talking to?"

"*Exactly!* You're living with her, can I speak plain? You're . . . are you wiping her ass? Okay. Sorry. You do some rough stuff with the houses, but you do all right, and who's got the perfect job? You just gotta out-smart the heavier things. There's hard work everywhere, so why throw your career in the ground like this? And why the mess?"

"Shit and sugar."

"What?"

"That's what you used to call it." And honestly I didn't even know that I'd remembered the phrase until I said it.

"When?"

"I don't know. When I was a kid."

"Okay—"

"You were explaining two sides of life, the good and the bad, and how everybody had to live in both."

"Fine. I don't think I was being literal."

"I'm not either. It just popped into my head."

"Can we just talk about *right now* for a second. Your future. This *thing*. This is not some plum gig. If you're looking to switch, there are lots of trades you could do between what you used to do and now this. A thousand second careers."

Truth was, I had been preparing myself for the nasty tasks, the difficulties. I'd watched internet videos about changing and bathing, about anger management and refusal, which were just demonstrations, but they still gave me pointers about proper steps. I went out shopping for more necessities. A baby monitor with a screen. A bed alarm. Disposable underpads for the bed. I put jingle bells on the front door, even though she was probably past the point of wandering. I remembered the brochures and pamphlets at the law office—no, that was the first attorney, and I probably wouldn't want to go back there for any advice.

"Who's helping you?" he asked, and I explained that it was just me.

"You're crazy," he said. "All you? Have you flipped? Kid, you're in over your head."

I wasn't. He was wrong. I had everything set up. I had my care station. Even from out here, I could see it. I was ready for Millie to come home. "I've worked long hours before. I can handle it."

"Why are you in her corner? What am I missing? And what do the neighbors think? Here's this old lady, she doesn't know what's what. Here comes this guy. Is he a nice person? Some pirate?"

"I'm me. Why do you keep bringing up rotten people?"

"I'm talking about how this looks."

"No one's looking," I wanted to say, but then I didn't. I thought, *The neighborhood rallies around her*—a quaint old story. It must still exist in places, but not here on this block. If I drove on the lawn right now, no one would even see me. "You sound like other people, the people at the nursing home. Worse than them—"

"Well, why'd they—"

"Because it's *you*." I wanted to turn the radio on and blast him.

I heard him pause, a moment of silence, to separate himself from the crosstalk. "Hey. Maybe they—me—the *world* gets a bad vibe because it looks ... questionable. The handyman and the old lady. I mean, come on, anyone, what's on his agenda?"

"You think I'm holding her hostage in the basement? Bringing her out to get cash?"

"Hey, bud—"

"What kind of creep—"

"Now you're talking to yourself. Is this because of your mother? We split, she gets sick, and maybe you should have done more? Some issue?"

I didn't have a response to that. I said, No, to myself.

"Because she had her new man taking care of her. And he had a daughter. She had enough help, enough family there. But you felt left out?"

"No, I didn't. I saw her enough."

"Okay. Good, because if anyone turned their back, it was me, the divorce. I'm just ... Is this about Renee? You're on bad terms?"

I lied and said I had amnesia about her. "She doesn't exist."

"Well, if it's not family history, make me understand. Can we just be honest for a second? Cause I'm having trouble. My mind's an entire blank. Or, fine, it's your path. But: I got a son, he's nearing middle age, and suddenly he wants his grandma who's not his grandma back in his life? Is that the why?"

"She's no one's grandmother. She was married sixty years. They never called it quits." But I didn't want to discuss that past, not with my dad. "I'm being very nice. To her. Nicer than I've ever been. Nicer than when I was married. I'm just trying to be someone else." Being honest, I mentioned the money.

"Aha."

"Wait, no."

"We get to the kernel. The loaded widow."

"No, you don't, you're not."

"There's the sugar, I guess."

I yelled at him to stop, even though he wasn't saying anything sharply. I couldn't have any more of this conversation stuck in the driveway. He was parked, and I was parked, and I wanted to put some distance—some difference—between us, and now I wanted to stare at him from inside, to see him on that bed. "Hold on again," I said, and I stepped out of the car, kept it running, and reentered through the front door, which was shut but unlocked from my earlier entrance. Out the back door, and back in through the front—I felt like I was circling through the house. "Why can't I be a nice person and be in it for the money, too? Why can't I be *both*?" But then I thought, how can I be a nice person if I'm picturing him debilitated?

He was silent. "You put it that way. I guess if we're speaking the whole truth . . . But—how much money?"

I didn't want to share with him the total. It felt like childhood again, where you'd done something wrong at home, or made trouble at school, and you didn't want to admit it to the adult who looked you in the eye and didn't think your mischief was funny. And I didn't know why I had to feel that way, a grown-up child, when I'd done so much right. And important. I felt like I should be thanked—but then say sorry for the umpteenth time. No, that was disproportionate. Too much sorry. I meant apologize once but then get thanked repeatedly. Because the right far outweighed the wrong.

"I'm making myself better," I said.

I didn't mean richer—even if that, too. But, for all I knew, Millie would live till there would be nothing left. And now that I'd mentioned the money part, he wouldn't hear both sides, the pros and cons, not the kindness. Only the greed, not the redeemable parts of me.

I surveyed my surroundings. The shut drawer that once contained the cash. The other drawer. "It's a lot of money." And because I wanted a clear conscience, I told him the complete amount. "Over half a million," I said, and when he yelled I pulled the phone away, but I could still hear the noise, a voice dislodged into the room—and I'd already pictured his body inhabiting the bed. I heard him echo my phrase, "Over half a million," as I pulled the phone back to my ear, and it sounded like too much, inflated, an upper-end figure, but maybe that was also because we'd together said it twice. "Six fifty," I said. I had tried to switch to some thin number, but I just ended up saying more. "Give or take," I said, and I shook my head because I kept wanting to speak simpler. "She's got a nest egg, but she's gonna spend it down."

"That'll take a while."

"Not really," I said, and I was about to talk about at-home health care costs, when I realized I'd be talking about me. I had already decided to charge myself twenty-five dollars an hour—I had gotten this number from a couple of places. In other words, my caregiver rate would be far less than my handyman rate—almost slashed in half—but since I'd be working here around the clock, night and day, I'd clear more. But maybe I wasn't going to charge her for sleep, when we both did. Although, why not? Weren't those hours part of the work, if I still had to stay here, inside? Yes, each hour she should pay out, even rest. That's how any agency would charge her. I shook my head, as if the generation of income were some complicated equation. "It might be a house, too. I don't mean I'm angling. I'm not doing anything wrong." I heard my voice, the effort to sound certain.

"A *house*? Where's she live?" he asked, and I told him, the street, the cross street. He paused, and then he said, "That's a nice area." I didn't know what to add. And I couldn't tell the quality of his voice, if there was a hint of admiration, not for me but for the address and her life, for living there, here. Or if it was disapproval, or confusion. "What if she gets hurt?"

It was easier to understand his anxiousness. I eyed the floor. I thought about the last time she was here, her contorted leg. Now I wasn't wordless. "She won't. Not with me."

"Not with *you*. Who are you? You have no training. No experience. You're not qualified. You're walking into this cold."

"I'm her one person."

"Her one what?"

"I upset her the least."

"The least . . . Donny, be straightforward, please."

But I was only explaining her happiness. I wasn't trying to be clever. "I'm being truthful. I am. I'm saying what exists." I couldn't convey it, her ease, and our connection, what we had and why we were close. I remembered that guy with the motorcycle helmet, the tender gestures with his mother. I had thought about him and her often, the silence and the sorrow, their two heads together like conjoined twins.

When would the meals become silent feedings? How long before no talk remained? I had seen so many patients at the nursing home, seated at tables with their voices gone to sleep, as if the act of speech had been taken away on a tray. That would be Millie. A murmur, a disturbed voice disappearing. She was already so thin. So little left. Why was I bringing Millie home, this stick figure? *Six figures*—those were the words it slipped into. Right then, I despised how my mind worked, unspeakable, turning weakness into wealth.

"What happens when you're done with her? I mean, when *she's* done, what's next for you? You gonna do this again, with someone else? Is this you now—or some temporary you?"

I was answerless. I was in her chair, like a squatter, or, if I was being her, an impostor. "You should mind your own beeswax," she might have said, even though I knew she hadn't. I sat here as a bystander, or like some hallucinator, watching the two of them, one of which was me. I saw myself at the door, with the envelope of cash, the second visit—no, the third one. Wait, the second time I brought eight hundred, the third time it was ten grand, so much more. I watched the succession. There I was, twice, side by side, like an optical illusion, bringing money time and time again, both of them the same person and neither of them completely me. But of course they both were, even with the changes. And here was an even stranger thought: Because I imagined this from Millie's side, I imagined that I was lined up with her, keeping her from being outnumbered by the two me's. I heard my dad call my name, and wait again for my response, about what was temporary and what was permanent.

"Alright, I give up. Your life. I'm not gonna say I understand it. Or maybe I do, but not in the way you want. And I tell you, I don't know why you're so eager to be around old age. I don't. Don't and won't. You don't gotta worry about me. I'm one tough onion. When I get too old and decrepit, you ain't gonna have to lift a finger."

"Dad—" I saw him, flat on the bed, looking so much worse than I'd ever seen him.

"I'm serious. I'm not living forever. Or dying forever. No infinity for me. When I start losing my faculties, I'm shutting it down. Terminate. Forget it, goodbye."

"Dad!"

"Dad, Dad. Never mind. When am I gonna see you? We can't just stay voices."

I told him I didn't even know where he was right now, which state.

"I'm back here. Florida. I was up in Lake George, but I never made my way over. Sorry. I went the other direction. Up through Maine. Bounced around Canada. Sightseeing the Maritimes. I was all over."

His actions made no sense, crisscrossing territory and heading south before summer's end. "August—that must be the worst month to go back."

"You ever heard of air conditioning? Don't matter tropical. Sides, it was hot up there, too. So what's the difference, hot and hotter. I tell you, it's not the summers I remembered. Everywhere down here is AC. Maybe we have the cooler summer."

"That's cracked logic."

"Well, Stacy says I need to get my brain waves checked. She's got her own crazy talk—the gobbledygook from the shows. I gotta watch her with my food. 'Hey, stop adulterating my drink.' So how 'bout, since I know you're not gonna get down here—next year, when I head north, we plan that we're actually gonna see each other. We need to do person-to-person. I mean, come on, no more stretches of not seeing. Forget this year. Next year, we're not gonna become invisible to each other. I'm proposing I come to you. Heck, I feel like the prodigal son. How's that for a parent?"

"Sounds good." I wondered what he meant. Would he visit me here? I had a crazy notion of not giving him the address, so he couldn't locate me, the mental image of my dad driving up and down the street, which I'd given him, but not the number. There he'd go, crawling past the house, half seeing.

"Maybe I'll meet your . . . lady friend."

The future meeting frightened me—not the awkward introduction but the thought of a passing year, which seemed forever, some interminable, everlasting torment—so I switched people. "Maybe I'll meet Stacy."

"Right, you never met. Maybe to that. Hope for both, I guess. Hey, what's her name?"

I told him.

"Millie. Okay. Probably short for Millicent. Birth name. That's probably who she was."

I studied the single stem, the one blossom, the lone bulb in its solitary socket, like some broken-off piece of the twelve-light lamp. I imagined the first lilies as actual flowers, taken apart, a separated bouquet, a flower given to so many other people, *Here's one for you, here's one for you,* until all that remained was the one central, delicate stalk. The lamplight needed more brightness. It could use a three-way bulb, but I'd have to check the socket. If need be, I could change it so it had an extra contact. If not, the bulb would only function on its middle setting.

The street looked deserted. I suddenly realized that I'd answered the phone not to have a conversation but to admit to him I was scared. Because I was bringing Millie home to help her die with dignity, but what happened if she didn't, only lived, a dozen years? Her survival felt like a nightmare—which was the meanest thought I could have. But how could it be mean if it was only a borrowed thought, Millie's nightly prayer? Would she stop aching for her end of days? Can a thought like that ever become unremembered? I hoped so. If so much else had gone, shouldn't the pain go, too? What happened if she forgot everything except her own anguish? And how could she communicate it if she only stared into space like nobody? I saw my time ahead as fighting through fog. I wanted to be younger, a kid again, so my dad could help with my dreams and fears, even the times I got in trouble.

"Hope you'll recognize me after all the plastic surgery."

"What?"

"Geez," he said, "you zone out on my jokes. Come on, keep up with me. What I was saying before, about the face."

"Oh, sorry. I must be half-deaf."

"'Doc, time for the makeover.'"

I pictured my dad with some guy in a lab coat, holding a chart and a clipboard, going over the changes. "Don't do it, Doctor," I said, playing along.

"Who was that?" my dad continued. "A mirage? Oh, right. That's my son. See the family resemblance. Make me look like him. Forty-five. Make me in Donny's image. Ha. Junior over there—he's the one I'll be impersonating."

The call ended and I looked at the clock. Mere minutes. And since we had been talking about months and years, it felt like no time, or a backwards increment. What if I called my dad back, and said it was all a joke? *I told you what? When I said I lived there, I was being euphemistic. It's like my home. You misunderstood me.* I'd keep talking till I directed him to his initial disbelief. "So I'm not wearing an eye patch," I would say.

"Huh?"

"You called me a pirate."

"Oh, right, right, forgot I did."

"'Are you some pirate?'" I said, imitating him. "That was cuckoo," I said, cracking myself up, and was it the clock, albeit a different one, or the picture of Millie that formed these words in my head? The pictures of Millie, her life and possessions, were all around me. Which was okay. My apartment wasn't home.

Dale Tiffany. Robert Louis Tiffany. Meyda Tiffany. So many fakers—a bogus family tree—all with the same last name so you'd think they were someone else, a different kind. So easy to mix up with the original brand. Louis Comfort: that's the person you're looking for.

Another glance at the electrical device. No more devising, I thought. I'll never take. And no hiding, I thought, and I didn't need to turn to the dresser to remind me of my conduct. When you're gone, I can take what's given, but only if it's there. You won't fall again, I said to the imagined Millie, on the floor, on her side. I won't fail, I said to myself. I promise. I'm capable. Dependable. It was time to go shopping for food. I'd spend her money on good food, none of the nursing home mush. She wasn't here yet, but my new occupation had started. Nurse. Caregiver. Helper. I'd become all of them. Triple-duty. I felt like a three-way bulb switching on, then brighter, then brighter again. I looked at the door, where before I had envisioned the imaginary me's, and where soon Millie would be conveyed inside. The supply store sold portable ramps, and I'd need to return there to purchase that forgotten item. No more forgetting.

I scanned the interior, her favorite room, my care area, my mind rehearsing. I wanted this. I was scared but also exhilarated. The job felt bigger and more substantial than the large-scale construction jobs I'd never gotten the opportunity, on my own, to do. Building a house from earth to a finished product—sure, an accomplishment. But now I'd found something else to do from beginning to end. And how could anyone say this service wasn't more valuable? Except, working day in and day out, how would I sleep? But I had seen so much sleep at the nursing home. Some residents, I'd barely seen awake. There was the commotion, all the warped talk, but more than anything else was rest. Dead time. I was sure I would get plenty.

Her phone sat on its cradle. I had found it, earlier, wedged between the cushion and the recliner's arm, and I'd set it back to recharge. Maybe I should watch more of the videos, over and over. No, I didn't need to. My memory was fine.

Has it been a thousand years?

Who said that? At first, I thought it was the girl from the elevator, in the hospital, who said I was forever years old. But then I realized it was Erin.

"Has it been a thousand years what?" I'd said back, then.

"Has it been a thousand years since I've been alive?"

This is how she asked when she was six or seven, the age when I first knew her. And I laughed, both at the memory and in it, when I told her, No, it hadn't been that long.

"Were you living in 1764?" she asked me once, another time but still young again. She was looking at a magazine. No, a doll catalog.

"No," I said. "Do you really think I was alive then?"

"You were saying something about it once."

The window screens: It was getting time to think about the storms again. Get to work, I said. I shook my head, at my old job, which I guess I was still doing.

Her name was Mildred. Not Millicent. That's what Millie was shortened from. I knew because she told me once. And I don't know why I didn't correct Dad. You were wrong, Dad. Wrong about Millie. I was talking to my dad again, now.

The battery was sufficiently warmed up. I could go outside and return the car to the garage, and shut the engine off. Close the garage doors. And then I'd come back inside. Return the keys to the mantel so I wouldn't forget where they were.

When I had found Millie's hat in my van, I was surprised it wasn't in one of the places I'd thought of, sunk down on either side of the passenger seat. Instead it was on her all along, tucked behind, in her jacket's neck. But I guess I was right to think it was missing, to see that it wasn't where it was supposed to be.

13

SOMETHING I MISSED ABOUT BEING A STEPFATHER was
making chocolate-chip pancakes. My specialty. Every Saturday morning, or at least it seemed that way for a very long while. Even now, I
still remembered the ingredients, the measurements, which I always
doubled. A happy memory, even if the kids always fought about who
got the first batch, or the best one of the first, and they'd scream in my
ears, which was so irritating, and sometimes I'd call them ingrates, and
threaten that I wasn't gonna make pancakes if they were just gonna
fight like that. (I didn't really think about it at the time, and it's probably wrong to say it now, but in a way they were fighting about me.)
I'd have to act like an arbiter: you get the first one, and the fourth one.
And the other one gets the second and the third. That way, neither of
them felt shortchanged.

One birthday, they bought me a spatula. I joked, "You bought this
for yourself." I mean, obviously Renee bought it, but same difference.
The spatula was gigantic, industrial-size, like a giant flyswatter, and it
didn't work well for pancakes, even though that's actually what it was
called, a pancake spatula. It was so huge, it took up so much space,
and the way the metal bar was angled up, you could barely fit it in the
drawer. Whenever the kids were in another room, I'd use the smaller
spatula, because it was easier. And sometimes they'd catch me using
it, and I'd feel bad, or I'd lie and say I was just using it for this one

pancake in the corner. It'd be weird if it was still there, and maybe Renee chucked it, although I don't think she would have done that to the kids. Anyway, it was nice, for a while, to be The Pancake Man.

The opposite of making pancakes was doing math with Erin. In terms of what I missed or didn't. Not at first. At first, she learned simple stuff, adding or the size of numbers, I can't remember the order of it now, but it was fun. She'd ask me something like, "Is it a million or a billion?" And I'd tell her a million had six zeroes, and it would have to have nine of them to be a billion. And she'd say, "Oh, I guess this is a hundred million." I checked the zeroes. "That's right." And Renee was happy, too, because I was helping. And then, or maybe this was earlier, Erin went on to basic multiplication, and I could catch her mistakes. No, seven times four is twenty-eight, not twenty-four. "How do you know all the answers?" A happy question. *I just do.* Next problem: eight times what is seventy-two?

"Seven."

"No, nine," I corrected.

"Wait, that's what I said."

"You did?"

"Yes!"

"I thought you said seven."

"I did. But then I said nine. I said both."

"Sorry, I was distracted."

One day the problems leapt ahead:

"What is an improper fraction?"

I remembered her saying that because it was so unfamiliar. It sounded like the beginning of a dirty joke. "Uh . . ."

"What does thirty-three-eighths equal?"

"Thirty-three eights?" I had to see it on the page, one number on top of the other, to understand what she meant. I thought I could still help. The word denominator was known to me, but numerator took longer to remember, and divisor was completely foreign.

A story problem: two kids shared a batch of twelve pancakes. No, that didn't happen, I'm combining memories here, but the point was that Erin *would* ask me to help her with these tricky puzzles, but they'd grown so complicated or elongated, like, instead of two children and five pancakes, it was five children and two pancakes, and one of the boys gets a fifth of the pancakes, so how many pancakes do the others have? How many cookies—no, pancakes—will they each get? And the teacher wanted to see the order you went in, she wanted to see you write down the steps, like you were following the recipe.

"You're not even listening!"

"I think I need a break."

"Help me!"

"I'm sorry. My brain can't make sense of it. That's what your teacher is for."

"But you're not paying attention," she'd say, and I'd ask where her brother was, and Renee, any chance you want to step in?, and Erin was screaming and crying and saying even if Jack knew this stuff, he'd never explain it because he was the worst brother ever, and this math problem was the stupidest, and she was the stupidest, and none of these made any sense and she'd done it *completely* wrong, and no one here knew how to help.

"Hi, Millie," I said.

She reacted like I'd been gone not since breakfast but from long, long ago, some older historical time farther back than me. "I'm kind of shocked," she said.

I was here to meet up with MediMotors, to transport her home, but the driver hadn't arrived yet. The nurse was the youngest person present, in her midtwenties, not yet thirty, and everyone else, including me, was far beyond her. Three people dozed in a row like a sleeping section. Music played from the stereo system, a happy tune. "What's the song?" the nurse asked. "One two three go!" a resident yelled so fast I didn't know its origin, much less if she was right, or if she was shouting a different thing or rhythm. "Tequila!" the singer shouted, and, of course, I remembered the mambo tune. Rumba? Whatever it's called. The music felt like a celebration of Millie's going.

"Okay, let's get in the car!" the resident across from Millie shouted, a louder sound than the song's volume. "Let's get in the car! Let's get in the car!"

"Oh, shut up!" Millie said. It had been a while since I'd seen her so mad. But I wasn't sure if she was really upset at the ranting, or if she only wanted to copy the woman and shout at the top of her lungs.

"The car's out there. Right in front. Got your hat and coat? Your umbrella? Cars are going. See 'em down there. We gotta go out the door. It's ten after eleven. We gotta go. That clock over there says eleven. It's after eleven."

A physical therapist approached another resident. "I'm just gonna move your arms. I ain't gonna be a moment." Her voice sounded so low and controlled after the other resident's spew of words. "Great," she said, testing his flexibility. "Terricky." When she walked past, Millie rolled her eyes and said, "I want to watch them leave."

Next it was "Great Balls of Fire," and I sang along, knowing most of the words, the chorus, the signature line, and tapped my feet to the raucous energy, all that fast running piano power, and then came an olden song about sugar in the morning.

"Do you know this song?" Erin asked, many times, when one of her favorites came on the radio.

"No." It sounded like all the other poppy ones she liked.

"Of course you don't—because it's new."

I thought music might be something we could listen to at home, but Millie said now, "Turn it off. Totally."

The decals on the windows were different, the changing season. The birds and flowers had been replaced by leaves and a couple of pumpkins. "Isn't it pretty outside?" I asked. Probably in a month or so, they'd pull down the scarecrow and stick a turkey or two up there. Then the winter picture, snowflakes and a snowman and a chimney with a puff of smoke. Hearts for Valentine's, then birds again, never chirping.

"You know what, I could care less."

And I didn't blame her irritation, the life outdoors signaled by synthetic decorations fastened on glass, as if the windows were the *view* from the windows.

"That one over there, particularly. It makes no sense. And if it doesn't make any sense, where does it?"

"Millie," the nurse said, "where's your smile?"

"In the water."

"In the water? Well, what's it doing in the water?"

I imagined a thrown smile hitting the surface, the water ringing out.

An administrator wheeled binders of papers on a wheelchair. The stacked binders were the tiniest body here. Like some maimed figure, only lap.

"Get all of that equipment," Millie said. "Anything you can get your hands on. Get it to my house."

"That's right," I said. I glanced at the administrator behind the chair, pushing paper. "That's what I'm doing." But then, a jolt, a distress signal: I realized I hadn't. Her wheelchair. Millie's. It wasn't hers and I hadn't bought one. I had seen her for so long in one, I had forgotten what she didn't own. It had her name on it, but of course that label meant something else. They were coming, and it was too late to leave now, and I couldn't ask anyone here for help because it would confirm their worst suspicions. I was the wrong person. I wasn't just inadequate but dangerous. Up to no good. How could my mind mess up so badly? I'd been distracted by pancakes and monster spatulas and picture alphabets on a classroom wall, when all I should've concentrated on was Millie's chair, and ownership. How, after all this time, did I not know what was hers, and what wasn't?

I looked around at the residents' expressions—no answers on their faces. The deep sleepers with their bodies knocked sideways. Wheelchairs, more than the people sunk inside them, filled the room. I wanted to smack my head. I couldn't trust it. What a ding-a-ling, a chickenshit. I heard the string of words from my brain. I hated me more than anyone ever did, even through a messy divorce.

Everyone was in a chair, so it felt like the stupidest thing I could do was forget what every person needed. Dumbbell. The sound of the elevator doors opening was like the room spinning. Of course he would arrive now. *Wrong time*, I wanted to shout. Which was confusing, since earlier I had asked myself, Where was he? The uniformed man stepped out, and he walked to the right, Unit A, the other side of the doubled room. He would consult with the nurse's station, and they would send him over to Unit B. But for now, he wasn't here. He was around the corner, hidden from view, so in my mind I made him farther.

I was paralyzed, but then, my phone—I jerked for it, yanked it from my pocket, and thumbed through the product line at Wilson Wheelchair. There were too many things, the options and designs went on and on, but I located the right one, a match to what Millie sat in. I called and while the phone rang, the many, many wheelchairs all around me were thirty reminders of what I'd impossibly forgotten. My idiocy. Dodo. I heard a lady's voice in my ear, and I said to it, "The standard manual," careful not to raise my voice above the song and whatever outburst. The room wasn't listening, no one looked at me, but I couldn't help but be cryptic. "Excuse me?" said the phone, and I had to explain more information to be understood. I asked if the model was in, and I waited, petrified. Thank God, I almost shouted, when she responded yes. Did I want that model or the next generation? she asked, and I said, "The one I said." She told me the price, which seemed high enough to be good, if not premium, quality, and I gave her my name and said I'd be there soon. The call ended. Because I'd kept quiet throughout, I felt I'd been lying. I breathed heavily. Calm down, I told myself. This wasn't serious, not a do-or-die crisis, just a minor blunder simply solvable. No more mad internal words.

When I saw the woman munching hungrily on her blanket, I still felt fine, not frightened, even though her bared teeth looked like the worst toothache. Her hurt turned the blanket into a soft and soggy sponge. Or like a tongue fed back into her mouth. But I wouldn't shudder. Because it wasn't Millie. It could be one day, just like it could be me, or anyone, late in life, which was why it was terrifying, seeing someone returned to childhood, teething on a wet length of blanket. But it felt, for Millie's well-being, essential to keep looking, like I was watching another video, Exhibit A of dementia. The woman's eyes stayed shut—her mouth, with its gritting teeth, was her only body part awake. I wouldn't miss again, like I'd done with the chair. No more negligence. I got you a chair, I said to Millie, not out loud. "Terricky," I said, my mouth like a hiccup, mimicking the odd encouragement, flattering myself. I gave myself a confident nod. "I got you a chair," I said again.

Millie shook her head. "I don't want anything that keeps this place open."

"What else can I put in here?" A voice spoke from the near corner of the room, where a group of women sat tidily around the square table. The speaker's hair was groomed and poofed, fixed in place like a wig, but I didn't think it was one. I studied Millie's hair, nearly falling into her eyes, and she'd probably need a haircut, or just her bangs to be clipped. Maybe I should have combed her hair for going home. "I don't want it to taste even better than it does," the woman said. Her hairdo looked so different than the words coming out of her mouth.

The woman beside her said, "I don't know what you mean by that, but that's not my kind of language."

The uniformed man rounded the corner. "About time," I would have said, if it hadn't been for the mental lapse with the wheelchair. He passed the elevator as if he were here again, a second visit. When he approached, I motioned to identify us. I stood up alone. Millie didn't move. My legs didn't wobble, no dizzy spell. The man and I were about the same age, but when he reached me he was years younger and inches taller. I shook his hand. He still wore a wedding ring. He looked like a sports ref, but maybe that was because in this room I'd seen a sort-of volleyball game. "You're the person I'm looking for," he said to me. He asked if I was accompanying her, and I told him I couldn't, because I'd driven here, and he shrugged and said we'd do caravan. Then he said hi to Millie but she ignored him. It reminded me of the time the EMTs arrived, and she wanted nothing to do with them. I didn't want to remember that strap-down. He tried once more. "How are you, Millie?" he said, starting over.

"I am so mad at the world."

"Well, I'm very sorry to hear that." He crouched down to console. Like some compassion expert. "I'm Monty. From MediMotors."

She made a face. "Who's that?"

Monty, I thought. Who has that name?

"I'm the people mover," he said. "I'm here to get you home."

"That's right," she said, and her irritation ended. Her mind changed with the news. She smiled and smiled, her face lighting up like she was riding the Ferris wheel in the summer. "I can't wait to see . . . I can't wait to see . . ." She didn't finish what sight it was.

"Okay," Monty said, "here goes my driving skills." He unclamped the wheels and we moved off together to the elevator, passing the not-quite quarrelers, Monty pushing Millie, and me behind at a near distance, my hands not connected to anything. "I'm the best driver in the building," he said.

I don't like that speed at all, I imagined her saying.

"That was very nice of you," she said.

He pressed the down arrow. I turned around, gave one last look to the left and right, to take in the parallel rooms, the identical shapes. The letter *H*, I remembered thinking. Straight ahead, in the kitchen, an aproned man plated out pink slabs of ham, an uncountable monotony. He used an ice cream scooper for something that wasn't ice cream. Maybe pudding, some paste or filling. Whatever mud it was, it didn't seem like a color. I shook my head at the glum meal, the ham and the bad helping, the strange combo, the firm food and the gloppy fixing. Enough with the diet kitchen. *I don't trust my stove.* When did she say that?

"They serve lunch here," Millie said, "every week."

The elevator dinged. We entered and he pressed the button for the first floor. The door closed, always, slower. On both handrails were mechanisms that sent signals to alert the staff when residents crossed the threshold and wandered into the moving box. Millie said something about her mother, but my mind was elsewhere. "My words are telling me to go home." This was Erin, again when she was six. I remembered it because the four of us were at a Red Wings game, and she wanted to go home, and even though the late-inning game was close, it was Triple-A and meaningless, and I wanted to go home, too. This was during the early years of the marriage. When we were both still people the other one wanted us to be. Jack was there, but he wasn't acting up. He had a lot of quirks. The initials, the diagnosis the schools and doctors gave him. The glitter jar to calm him down for stress. For timeouts and fits. But that night, he was fine. He liked baseball.

Blue numbers flashed the countdown on a digital display, 3, 2, 1, while a buzzer sounded out the descent. Now Millie was saying more about her mother. I couldn't make it out. But little by little, I grasped its meaning: she thought she was going back to her childhood home. I wondered if I needed to clarify the situation. I started half thinking ahead to her confusion, "No, Millie, not *that* family home, the one *after*." I didn't know what to say to Monty. "Any questions for me?" I asked him. I didn't know why I bothered.

"Sure," he said. "What's tonight's lotto numbers?"

The punch line was funny until he belly-laughed over me. No need for both of us to find his loud voice humorous. I busied myself with my phone. It told me the day and month. I registered the time. 11:43 a.m. The minute changed.

"It's not too cold out," he said, "but it's gonna get cold."

"Again?" Millie asked.

I followed them to leave, until, the muscle memory, I realized I should sign out. I angled to the front desk. It didn't really matter—no crime in not signing—but there was something about my name saying that I was only *in* that bothered me. I didn't want my name signed in where I wasn't gonna be anymore.

"Coming and going," said the lady behind the desk.

I nodded. Except I couldn't find my name. I scanned the page, but I was nowhere, I felt like I'd been erased, or renamed, until I found me, listed above twenty others, names long and short, some with first initials, others written full, in hands neat and indecipherable, who'd arrived in the interval between then and now. Next to my name was hers, Millie's. Today might be the final time I'd see us like that. I stared at our names linked there, side by side, almost merged. My handwriting was mostly legible.

"Yeah, people have trouble finding where they are sometimes," said the lady. She wasn't the same person who told me how to walk through the entrance doors. Or maybe she was. There were a number of different people with her job. I tried to remember the incident before. "A lot of people here," I said, talking like some bad icebreaker.

I read the clock on the wall—11:45 sharp—and wrote the time out in the empty space. Because this was the last time signing, it didn't feel like just time out but time ending. The door opened for another arrival. I set the pen down beside the ledger. Then I was out in the open air. A brisk wind. I thought of the stickers on the windowpanes, the colored leaves like bits of stained glass. The wind picked up. I walked into it. *This* was where the weather outside was.

The company van was parked in the fire lane of the circular drive. The platform raised Millie from the ground; her hand flinched. I had a vision of the vertical ride at Seabreeze, where you climbed straight up and plunged partway down, then rose high, high again and dropped— you went up and down like some towering yo-yo—and you laughed with relief when you were back on solid ground. I did that once or twice with the kids. With four or five seats across, we could all ride together. Erin screamed and screamed with each dive, but when it was finished she yelled, "Again!"

Monty rode the lift with Millie, then rolled her backwards inside. Then he stepped out and down from the platform. He held a control box in his hand, which he pressed, and the platform tilted like a hand coming up to a face. Or like a gangplank, or drawbridge, some dream you had about castles and armor and storming the tower. Whatever it was, it was now a metal gate. And then the double doors closed over the gate like another pair of hands. Watching it was like watching a lot of things.

Still, Millie had been outside for such a short time.

Monty walked from the back to the front and into the cab, so they were both gone. I imagined the van driving off while I stood here, a spectator, immobilized. *My favorite moment in life is when you're not there.* This was Renee, acting like a child. "What are you, five years old?" I said—or maybe not—during the fight. I said it now, maybe again, to my infantile ex.

I followed him in. "Why are you under me?" Millie said as he braced the chair with tie-downs. He looked like a dog about to bite her ankles.

"Well, we wanna make sure you don't go flying. That feel okay?" he asked, and I heard her reply, "Average."

I felt like she was being taken to another operation.

"You leave it to me, Millie. I've been doing this eighteen years."

"I remember that," Millie said.

I could just say the wheelchair was in a closet; he would transfer her to the bed, and then I'd somehow bring Millie back with me to the supply store. Somehow. I'd have to do better than that word.

I didn't want to start with a mistake. The wheelchair should be there before she got home. This was the time to do that. "You know what?" I said to him, as if the thought were first crossing my mind, and I told him I was just gonna make a quick detour, this little thing. "Grocery run," I heard myself explain, like some flake. I thought he'd have a problem with that, but he didn't see it as complication. I guess it was all the same to him: me as a passenger or a caravanner, or just forget about me till he reached the next point.

Caravan was how I'd pictured it on the way over, which was why I hadn't taken the van but the Cadillac. I didn't want the guy asking about the lettering, about my line of work. The car seemed a more logical and direct connection to Millie. But now I'd have to buy a wheelchair and place it in the trunk, which was spacious and would be fine, just a moment to collapse and fit in, but I didn't have extra time.

"Looks like we'll rendezvous at your house," he said to Millie. "That sound okay?"

We both faced her and waited for a statement.

"This room is made of noise."

I said nothing.

"Yeah?" he said. He glanced at the interior and listened. Then he nodded definitively, as if the compartment were high-ceilinged and echoing. "It *is* kind of loud in here."

"You certainly are."

Her language made me smile. Although, I had to admit, Monty seemed like an understanding guy, considerate of her feelings and what she thought inside. Compared to the upstairs racket, this space was silent.

"It's not too loud," she said, "it's just the noisy."

I asked if he had the address, and he said he was all set, knew the way. "See you soon," he said. "See you," I said, shorter and not quite copying.

I stepped out of the van and ran away, feeling foolish but I didn't care how it looked, I had to gain time. I got to the car and drove out of the lot, and accelerated at breakneck for the needed chair. I pictured myself as a superhero on a mission to save Millie from someone's— my—incompetence. When I'd driven to Renee's, I'd almost wished I had taken the Cadillac, for camouflaging, and now I wished I was in my van, because speeding in the Cadillac felt like I was being even less of me, only some crazy version of Jim, tearing away at some uncontrollable speed like he'd lost his mind. A traffic signal stopped me. "Go, go," I said. The light stayed red so long I thought it was broken. I wanted to run it, but getting caught would only delay me more. I dashed off again, flew through a string of green lights, but a red light—again—made me hit the brakes. The stop felt like days. "Forget it!" I said, and this time I really did almost drive through, who cared what menace I was, cutting cars off. But it switched and I drove on and finally I turned into the shopping center and parked close and hurried for doors.

Inside were chairs and chair and chairs. Items to assist with this and that. Nothing dismal, I told myself, not even the disposable pads. Along the wall were racks of clean clothes, but it was hard to see them as fresh. The new clothes looked out of place because everything else seemed like what came *after*. I matched the wheelchair model to the product on the floor. "I called someone about a wheelchair," I said at the counter, and mentioned which version, and when the salesperson nodded and reached behind her for the orange Medicare form, I told her to forget that. "I just need one," I said. "A chair. Gotta go." And I sounded freakish, like the fuzzball from the nursing home. But there was no time to check boxes, fill out documents. I used my own credit card, because I didn't know if I was doing something wrong by not filling out the form. Waiving coverage wasn't wrong, but it *felt* wrong. Which made no sense. No, it *did* make sense, if I was giving away her money—so here I was, the next dilemma. I wanted to switch cards, but she was already taking payment. They had Millie's card on file, I'm sure, because of my earlier visits. On the wall behind the salesperson's head was a display case of rows of stethoscopes, like thirty bad hearts.

I probably had a five-minute head start, but I'd lost the ground I'd gained. I wasn't getting back fast enough; I should've already left. Monty wouldn't speed, but I wished he would drive the way he walked, when he meandered from one side of the room to the other. The clock said past noontime, which felt late. The minute hand on the one was like an extra hour. The second hand was flying. The next leg of the drive felt like distance personified. I pressed a finger against my temple; my head was splitting. Finally, I was out the door. I found the car. Again, I wished for the van, to throw the chair right in the back (I felt like I'd used the wrong car, the wrong credit card), but the wheelchair weighed practically nothing and it was easy to collapse, a piece of cake. I dashed home. The store was only partly out of the way, and I arrived in the driveway before them. Faster than a caravan. I brought the wheelchair inside. Then I went to the garage for the ramp and, as I carried it out to the front steps, I heard the tires. Beat them by a whole minute. Perfect timing.

Monty parked and hopped out and walked to the back. I met him there. I hid my heavy breathing, turned my head, and set my hand at the corner of my mouth and exhaled a few hisses. I didn't say anything about being early and first. But I remembered his laughing, "Ha ha," in the elevator. The doors parted. The gangplank lowered. It was like a sci-fi movie, where the UFO landed and I was the human being saying, What in the world? and, afterward, no one would believe what I saw from outer space. Except this encounter was happening in someone's driveway, not in some field. Still, I looked around and nobody watched. No one saw me. Nobody would watch the house. Which was scary, the days and days ahead, the mornings and nights, so unnoticed. *Millie* wouldn't notice. "Forget about me," I said.

Millie was expelled, and I came out of my thoughts.

"What's keeping you?" she said.

"What?" I asked.

"She was asking where you were," Monty said.

"I took a shortcut," I said, which I guess was a joke. "I was waiting for you. Just in time."

"That's right," she said. "You've been traveling."

I walked in first, with Millie in the middle. "We're here, Millie." I flipped on the overhead light. "You're home." I waited to see her register the destination. "It's all the same," she might have said. But she didn't. And it wasn't—not with the care area, the new furniture cramping the room's dimensions. Or, wait a minute, maybe it *was*—too much like the nursing home. "I don't like the looks of that," she said. And I remembered her wanting to be in her childhood home. I thought she was about to berate me for bringing her somewhere wrong, not her birthplace, and I'd have to say, "But that's not where you really are." But then she saw the personal effects, the photos on the mantel, her mind lighting on the familiar faces. "My word," she said. She wasn't clapping her hands, but I felt like she was. The homecoming was, I don't know, amazing. Very, very. Never, ever been a person happier. I spread my arms wide like here was the whole world.

"That's right," I told her. "You're the queen of the castle."

"There's my Jim," she said.

"He sure is," I said. "Both of you," I added. I looked at the series, at the man she outlived. She smiled, she kept seeing her and him, the two of them, one by one by one. The most recent shot didn't show what had become of her. Which, in a way, was like saying she still looked young there. On the mantel, she was younger and younger—and I stared at the oldest one, the first faces, and I felt somewhere, maybe here, that I was only a boy.

"This part's you," Monty said. "I can't do that." I thought he was having an identity crisis, but then he said, "Liability," and he meant company rules, and the wheelchair transfer.

Fine, I thought. The transfer was me. My hands alone. My new skill set. Easy, I breathed, and I stepped forward, feeling something rise in me, something I wouldn't let linger or even identify. I wouldn't listen to what my body was telling me. I shook my head at it. Blinked to make myself go blank. But the nervousness was still there. I lowered my legs, like I was squatting, and placed one arm under her legs, the other grazing then guiding her in the back, feeling her brittle bones. "Looks like that arm lifts up." This was Monty, behind me. I thought he was talking about Millie, but he meant the chair. Both of them. The two chairs side by side reminded me of being back in the store, when there were chairs everywhere. The chairs were closely alike, these exact two, and I was glad for that. It meant my eyes were working, that I was in the right frame of mind.

"Right," I said. "I was forgetting that."

"Getting what?" Millie said.

"Huh?"

"I think she misheard you," Monty said.

"Oh. *Forgetting*," I corrected. I flipped the armrest—the right one—out of the way, and did the same thing with the left one of the other chair. This meant I could go lower, straight across. A second turn touching her; I went back to holding, anchoring my hands to Millie. "I'm gonna sit you in a chair," I said, but when I went to lift, her hand gripped the other armrest. I was surprised by the strength. "Millie, can you give yourself a hug?" I asked, and I told her it was just gonna be two secs. She listened, crossing her arms. I tried again, closer, and she cuddled in, and I scooched her from one chair to the next. I exhaled, but tried to hide it with a smile.

Now it was just the right wheelchair that only looked like a shell, although Millie in the left one didn't look like much more.

Monty didn't evaluate. He put the appendage down like he knew everything, then wheeled off what had always been theirs. To his back, and the empty object, I said, "Looks like you're wheeling a ghost."

"What's that?" he said, and I said forget it. I turned the other way, too, readjusted the raised arm. I don't know, I just wanted to say something to him after his loud lotto laugh. Three, two, one down the elevator, all the way down till he's numberless. I smiled to myself, and I heard him say goodbye, but, I don't mean this in a forgetful way, he wasn't really there anymore. Whether I was pretending or not, he was just an imaginary so-and-so who didn't exist. The door opened and closed on the third person.

I realized, after moving Millie, that I had been not just afraid but terrified to make the transfer, and I only knew this from my accelerated breathing now. I listened to my breaths, thought of what I'd suppressed before. I blinked several times, which felt strange, because I couldn't be *more* awake. Partly, it felt like a good thing, that I'd buried my fear, necessary to hide a piece of you so another part can accomplish the task at hand, but it also seemed deceptive, that I'd hidden something from myself, which I wasn't supposed to do. For some reason, I looked over at the mantel series. None of them was a picture of maniac driving.

I wondered if she had felt the terror in my body, and that was why she had clutched at the armrest pad. I'd have to be better with my fears. Or more honest with them. To control my nervous hands when carrying. "Okay, Millie," I said, and I felt like I was in a different time, here at a beginning, just us. "We're home." I stepped to the wall and turned up the thermostat, a couple of degrees, because the house had to be warmer now. It was comfortable, but probably for her it was frigid. The care area was in good shape. No shortages. At least, not yet. I was hungry and, given the time we left, skipping out on lunch, she had to be, too. "I'll make lunch," I said. "You must be famished." And later, I'd bring dinner.

Millie stared at me, perplexed, then beyond, as if pondering what was there. Her hunger, maybe, up on the wall. I turned to the kitchen and heard her say, "That's a whole different word I don't know."

14

SHE CALLED ME AN ANGEL, she called me a liar. She called me sweetie, she called me her protector, she called me funny, she said I was fat, she said I was short, she said my smile was crooked, she said my checkered shirt was stupid, she called me savior, she called me manipulative, she said I was trying to get her out of her house, she told me to get out of the room, she told me to shove it, she said, "I don't know what I would have done without you. That's the truth." She said, "I believe Don the least." She said, "I don't know how you know all this stuff." She said I was the bad guy, she said thank you, she said, "You're nice on the surface," she said, "I can still do this." She said, "You're worthless, I don't need your help, I'll do it myself." She said, "You're lying like a liar." She said, "When am I going to see you again?"

In two days, I was so many things. I was a punching bag, sure, but also it felt like family.

Of course I had to change her. Many times. She was my first diaper. My stepkids were always older. I'm not gonna pretend it was a cute little baby butt. It was a saggy, skinny bone butt. I put on gloves and bent her legs and rolled her on her side—no, first I told her, "I'm going to roll you to your left side." I told her everything I'd do, so I'd never startle her, but also, I think, to convince myself that I was doing it. I removed the Depends. I had the wipes, the cream, the trash bag. Everything organized, within reach. I winced at the sight and the odor, but that was it. The stench I could stomach. I didn't need to chew gum or sniff Vicks. But the videos provided only so much guidance. They helped, but they couldn't prevent mistakes, because Millie wasn't a mannequin or paid actor, and of course I wasn't the efficient instructor who knew every step automatically. I turned her over and she shat again, and I didn't see the incontinence so I rolled her into a bigger mess. I ran around the bed four different times, like some quack doctor at the operating table performing some mad experiment. Millie wasn't any of the problem; every one was me. I thought she'd fight me on the changing, but I guess she'd gotten used to it at the nursing home. She didn't mind—or she did, but only a little. She said she was embarrassed. Or she'd inquire, "Why are you touching me?" Or, not so much critically, "Aren't you done yet?" She'd tell me not to miss a spot. She said, "You're careful with me because you know I won't tolerate it." Or she was off somewhere, talking to a squirrel out the window, or about the cow in the bathtub. Or she was—I didn't know—maybe back in the bedlam of the nursing home, saying she was afraid to keep going but afraid to quit, but she had to stay there because there was a contract involved.

Once she said, "Oh, Jim, I'm sorry you have to do this." Which was okay. I didn't mind being somebody else. Even him, or especially. It meant she felt safe. I guess I had to take what I could get. "It's okay," I said, "I don't mind doing it." "You'd like to think you're a nurse," she replied, which could have sounded mean, but coming from her, it was just a believable statement about me. "You must just like to do this," she said.

There were pills throughout the day. Some of the pain pills were long-acting, others were as needed for spikes. Sometimes, she took them without complaint; other times she wouldn't. "The only thing that's gonna make me feel better is to say no." She'd shake her head and say she didn't know what that was. "Come on, Millie, you gotta take it." Which increased her resistance. "Not today," she said. "Not taking this, that, or the other thing." And I told her no, she had to, but she didn't understand the term no. "You need to take it now," I said, and we went back and forth with no. Then she answered, "The way that it is unfolding is quickly. And pressure." If I tried to impose my will, it only worsened her suspicion. "You're trying to poison me, you're trying to kill me." I quickly learned that instead of struggling with reason, I could just walk away and try again in minutes. Later, I realized there was room to play with the timing, that it didn't have to be on the dot, just within the hour. And still later, I learned I could hide the pill in the applesauce or yogurt, to help it go down, because I had to get it into her however I could. Except one time, when I didn't tell her, she started chewing it; I watched her face frown, some mystery in her mouth, which I knew would mess with how the medicine worked, and then she found it in her throat and spat it out. And accused me of tricking her. "You don't miss a trick," she said. So I stopped hiding it. Still, I could make a game of it, tell her it was candy, which wasn't the same as hiding.

Eventually, with the pain spikes, I learned how to read her face, her gestures, when she clenched her fists, furrowed her brow, even when she worked the bedsheet, picking at the material. I watched her jaw muscles, her temples. I learned these were all signs of pain. I'd ask her, "Are you in pain? From one to ten, how bad is it?" But then I got rid of the pain scale, because maybe her ten was different from my ten. Are you hurting? Show me where it hurts? I learned to be aggressive with pain management.

But the first day, the second dispensing, she dropped the pill and my god, where'd it go? It wasn't on the floor, and it wasn't underneath her, on either side of the chair, and it wasn't inside the neck of her nightgown—I thought I'd have to go searching there, because what happened if she found it and ate it and I didn't know and I dosed her again? I found the pill. A spot on the floor I'd somehow missed. I shook my head, because I'd eyed every square inch, as if the pill were coated in invisible ink. The pill was like a tiny grain or a baby tooth. Once my stepdaughter, Erin, had lost her tooth—I mean, not from her mouth but after, she dropped it and it was *gone*—and she cried about the tooth fairy not coming, and we searched the carpet and found it, and later my hand slid under her pillow to leave the night-time money. "Did she wake up?" Renee asked when I came back to bed, and I said, "Sound asleep." The best part was the morning: you'd wake up, and your kid was so happy about the midnight visitor, and you had to act surprised. *He did?* That was, like, one of my favorite parts, being the tooth fairy. Me and the tooth fairy, all in one. I was good at it, I never forgot, I even reminded Renee a few times, Hey, we gotta do the dollar. One time, neither of us had a dollar in our wallets, and we debated about whether we could use change, four quarters. It was a fun argument, we laughed about it, and we both said how it was a quarter back in the day, if our parents even remembered, but also we really wanted to find the dollar, and finally we did, me or Renee, somewhere, the little money in a drawer or pocket. There's no way I would have gotten divorced if the kids lost a tooth every day. I know that sounds strange.

But bathing was something else. The private thing I dreaded more than the diaper change. I explained that she needed one, but Millie thought otherwise. "I didn't do anything to get dirty," she said. I explained, gently, that her clothes were a bit smelly. And I said she'd feel better after. "Let me just wash your face, and see how it feels." She said no to all of that, and I wished she was right. I tried the reward system. "You can have all the ice cream you want," I said, which got her on board, which was good—necessary—for her hygiene, but now I had to complete the scary task and touch her everywhere. I closed the curtains. I swished soapy water in the basin. The water was the right temperature, warm but not hot. I started with her face. Actually, first I told her what I needed to do for her body, what I was washing. The videos even demonstrated how to clean her eyes. I wiped in the right direction, from inside to outside. I worked section by section. The chin, the neck, et cetera. Wash, rinse, dry. Before each one, I said, "I have to clean you here." When I washed her front, I kept her covered for modesty's sake. The videos said I should lift her breasts to clean under them, so I did that. Her arms were dry, so I applied lotion. First, I warmed it in my hands. I cleaned her hands, her fingers. She still wore her wedding ring. I saved the middle parts for last, skipping to her legs, which also needed lotion, then down to the toes. I soaked her feet. I turned her toward me and cleaned her shoulders and back. I felt her soften. All that was left were the parts of her I didn't want to do but couldn't neglect for infection. "Gonna clean you down below," I said. I felt like I was especially violating her privacy when I touched her there. But I decided it wasn't a private area. I mean, of course it was, but I decided it wasn't because it was also a job. My job to provide quality of life.

I'd never bathed my ex. Sure, we had fun in the showers at first. With Beth, we never got to that point, although I think showering with someone, at least in my experience, was something you did early, for kicks, and then stopped doing, but I guess I never reached that early point with Beth. I couldn't get over her body, Millie's, its thinness. I could feel so much of her, her skeleton, where a muscle began and attached to bone. She complained about being cold so I tried to dry quicker. I had to get everything out from under her and put everything clean around in place of it. Which was so difficult, pulling up the dirty sheets and tucking the new ones under, but I did it, and I was so happy, admiring myself, because I thought I'd done a pretty good impression of the video experts, even if they weren't sweating by the end. But then Millie knocked over the pan with the dirty solution, and she was damp and scared and terrified, not knowing where she was. I had to calm her and reclean her and remake the bed, changing the sheets another time with her in it. Now I was dripping. Next time, I didn't put the water so close.

The meals were always together, unless she was asleep, and I'd take mine in the kitchen during the nap break. "Is that yours or mine?" she asked when I cut up the meat on her plate. "Yours," I said, and I explained what I was doing. She said she wanted cake, so I made it, the upside-down kind, and brought a piece to her, but then she said, "Get it out of here. I didn't want it." And I tried telling her what she'd said earlier—I didn't want an argument, but I'd baked a cake, I had the recipe nearly memorized, and I'd accomplished this between checking her diaper and turning her position in bed, and so I told her, "Yes, you did," and she said, "I don't want some special cake in the morning."

The pancake spatula. The thing that Renee probably threw out, she did or she didn't, I almost wanted to call her up to ask which one, to tell her I understood either. I imagined her saying, what the hell, to my question, to me. I wondered if the kids ever thought about what was gone, like the way I'd come into Millie's house the first time the lamp wasn't there, and seen the missing spot. Did they say anything? Did they cry? Would they take their distress to Renee? Did I wish that, too, that sad scene? How selfish. Would Renee get angry, lose it, or probably just roll her eyes, that what was gone was about as significant as a table lamp, an artificial one? If I went there again, and went slower, stopped, parked, got out, would I be able to detect the emptiness, like I'd been able to do with Millie's, when from outside I'd seen the dimness in the window? I didn't think I was being unreasonable with Millie, to want her to eat the thing she'd wanted to eat, the thing she'd asked me to make. I wasn't bitter or anything, and it wasn't wasteful, I could save all the pieces for later feedings, and it's not like I expected elation, like her face when she saw the photos, and I didn't need or even expect a thank you, but I just wanted her to understand what I'd done for her: that between the diaper check and eyeing her skin for any bedsores and making sure to reposition her, I'd baked her requested cake and now I was serving it. I'd never brought a cake to anyone, much less in bed. Her saying she didn't want the cake felt like a wrong answer, like she didn't really want to say no, but the illness in her head was making her say it to drive me crazy. "It's cake," I said. I just wanted to remind her that we were talking about a sweet category of food. A fresh bite in the stale air of a sick room. I wasn't forcing her. If you feel full, you gotta stop, but she wasn't full because she hadn't eaten in hours, so she was wrong about herself. I tried to make a joke of it. "Come on, free sample."

"I know what it is, but I don't have it."

"You asked for it," I said.

"Maybe I did, but I forgot to name it all."

"Please," I said.

"You want to be in charge of some kind of wild dream of yours."

I held the plate closer to her so she'd smell what she was missing, and change her mind, change her mind *back*, and then her arm came out and the plate went flying and when it crashed suddenly she was my mother throwing things and next Dad was cursing, "You fucking lunatic," and Mom, face rigid with fury, "You're the lunatic, you fucking shithead!" I was swooped right back to childhood, the two of them gigantic and lighting into each other. I thought I'd taken care of this stuff, decided it hadn't mattered, what my parents did to each other, to me, the home they made, or mostly didn't. Fine, I buried the fights again, now. Two people saying blankety-blank. They never attacked each other, it only looked extreme when I was young. Wasn't ever fists, just thrown objects and noise, threats and tears.

"That's enough," Millie said. "I told you I didn't want to do this. Get out of here."

Okay, I said. I said I was sorry. I felt like I wasn't apologizing to her, but I didn't know what that meant: I wasn't apologizing to her because she wasn't herself anymore, or was I apologizing to other people? Then I felt like I was apologizing *for* her, because she was at her worst now. I told her sorry. "We can eat this later."

"Thank you," she said. "Thank you so much." It sounded like the way she used to talk and acknowledge me.

"Let's watch a movie," I said. I thought we'd watch an old one together. "That is Cary Grant," I said when he first appeared. "That is Cary Grant," I said, again. But she didn't like it. The bright lights, the stimulation, overwhelmed. "I didn't do any of this," she said. I hadn't counted on movies not working anymore as a babysitter. I tried regular TV. A cooking show, which seemed slower and calmer, a better diversion, where maybe the lagging of her mind wasn't such a problem. I couldn't tell if it was a new program, or if it aired originally in the '70s or something. "How about this?" I asked, making my voice as soft as the host, but she said, "Never."

"Oh, you used to like it," I tried. I wanted to watch the show, to listen to the lull of the stirrings and the steps, so mind-numbing, even if it reminded me of the rejection of the cake.

"That was ages ago. That's nonexistent anymore."

So I shut it off and sat down, remained there. "It's windy out," I said, and I imagined the noise it made, welcomed it, because the silence inside here wasn't at all peaceful.

"We discovered that this morning. It was awful."

I watched the bare branches shake.

"They still threaten it. We all remember that. Everyone was surprised when we got up this morning and saw that."

A mail truck drove by and I felt strangely sad that it didn't brake but kept going.

"What's *your* weather been like?" she asked.

"Same as yours," I said.

"It must be the way it is out there."

I nodded.

"Is it still morning?" she asked. Erin used to ask that, sometimes in the afternoon. *Is it night or day?* Although, when she would ask me this, I wasn't as confused, the setting sun now not meaning evening or anything, the phases of the day blurring for me, too. "Not anymore," I said. "It's Tuesday," I said to myself, which felt irritating, like it would be much better if it was Sunday, which then bothered me because it made no sense, the days being identical, the time all the same, although the nights were getting longer now.

"The day after . . . what is the name of that holiday?" Millie asked, so I guess I was talking out loud.

It was late, which didn't mean downtime if she was winding up for the hours ahead. It could be the hardest shift. And I knew I couldn't keep working all three. I needed to clock out. I needed my nights. I needed time during the day to run out and get things. I could only do two shifts, max; other people had to take turns. Too much of the job was beyond my scope of expertise, so a shift took more out of me. I was prepared for X, Y and Z, except it was A to Z all at once.

There were sleeping pills to help with normalcy, but the drugs would probably snow her, and I was worried about side effects, like constipation, so I thought I'd just take my chances without them. She gave a big yawn; the night itself seemed to be still working. "Night-night,"

I said when she fell asleep, and I felt like her roommate with her double talk, and then I went upstairs to her old bedroom. There were other rooms, but they only contained couches, no pullouts, so the master was the best place to sleep, even if every room felt overheated. Lengthwise was a body pillow. Millie had probably purchased it as a replacement, to feel Jim against her, to hug her from behind after he was no longer there. I moved it off the bed, onto the window bench. It felt odd carrying it, because of what it was supposed to be, a substitute body. It was so much lighter than that, even a child's that you carried off to sleep. Sometimes, Erin slept with us, at the beginning, if she was having trouble sleeping, and I'd wind up switching to her bed because she'd kick in her sleep, and I'd tell Renee in the morning, "Now I know what it was like for you to be pregnant with her." Renee told me I snored. Badly. And how could I argue against it, when you weren't awake to tell them otherwise. It was the perfect lie. Maybe I'll record you once, she said, to prove it. I wanted them both in the bed now to keep me company, in the bed that I wasn't yet in. I wasn't sure what side to sleep on. Both hers and his felt wrong. My eyes seesawed left and right, then settled on the center. Maybe that space wasn't anyone's? No, the middle seemed like the intersection of the two of them. I decided to flip the mattress over. For some reason, the underside didn't feel like married life. But I still didn't know which place to pick. I'd flipped it from the bottom, so the sides were still the same. I went with hers, not wanting to be the dead man, which felt harsh to think of him that way. The deceased, I corrected in my mind. The husband, Jim. I looked back to the window bench, as if he was there.

I had already unpacked. The two bottom drawers of the chest were empty, his belongings probably donated to the church or Goodwill, so I filled them with my folded clothes. I had tried to be neat and respectful with this room. I didn't want to be as messy as I'd been formerly living. On the nightstand, I set a baby monitor with a video. I was sleeping in her old spot, and she was in the monitor, like I was her and she'd been shifted over. I stayed up hours watching it, her. She rustled and I was up. I couldn't take my eyes off the image. I'd be almost asleep and she'd groan, and I was wide awake again. And if she wasn't making noise, if I wasn't watching the little screen, I was seeing the episodes behind my eyelids—the dumped water, the thrown plate, the invisible pill. I even thought of my angry parents, angrier in marriage. I could move the TV up here, if she wasn't going to watch it anymore, but I didn't want the noise to distract me from the transmission of the downstairs noise I needed to listen to, which is why I'd put my phone away, on the nightstand, too. Car lights swept across the room. I knew I would have more nightmares here. Or maybe the nightmares were the whole day, Millie's life, that I already existed in. I remembered the high wind and imagined the electricity short-circuiting, a power outage, a house without a generator. I thought of racing to the medical supply store, no, to Lowe's for a generator, of running red lights, of cars hitting cars. My head whirled with what had happened and what could have or might still. And I had to be up every two to three hours, anyway, to rotate her position, because the websites said I had to be vigilant about skin integrity. I imagined sores on her body, skin tears, bruises. I fell asleep and dreamed I was talking to her, mostly mumbling, I wanted to say more but my mouth was shut, and then I realized the noise was her, but also not, that it came from out of nowhere but was also increasing, and I woke to the monitor, she sounded like she was in excruciating pain, and I had forgotten to give her her 2 a.m. meds. How long had I been sleeping? Minutes, hours? I thought I'd set the alarm on the phone. When had I given the previous dosage? Why hadn't I written the time down? I stumbled downstairs and took care of the medicine and repositioning, and I went back upstairs, where Millie was again only the small gray image inside the monitor square, and the husband was the pillow way over on the bench, and I was the body between them on their bed, and of course there were more pictures of them up here, too, so I felt like they were on every side of me, and I shut my eyes tight, and when I slept I dreamed I had driven back to the house, and I was waiting for Monty and Millie, and they hadn't arrived, and suddenly I suspected that Monty had taken her elsewhere and he wasn't coming here, and it would just be me, and finally he arrived, but not until night, and he had earbuds in his ears so he wasn't listening, and I screamed at him, like Millie did when I stepped away, "Where in the world were you?!" and Millie was up on the platform, and I yelled at him to get her down but he couldn't hear me, and he kept not pressing the button to lower her, so Millie looked like some statue, and Monty's hair had started turning gray, which I could see in the dark because of the bright lights shining in her window, and I kept telling him to push the button, to flip the switch, and I was pointing at his ears, to take the headphones out, because that was a really stupid way to do your job.

Within two days, I was gone. Four intermittent hours of sleep total. I had circles under my eyes. My personal self was in the back seat. I felt like *I* was the one dying and losing my mind. I was so thirsty. In the kitchen, when I filled her a glass of water, I chugged it for myself first. Then I refilled and drank again. The water gushed from the faucet, and I splashed my face awake. On day three, she woke up mad at me. Every command was unfollowable, and when she yelled at me my exhaustion made it seem like she was yelling more. I yelled back at her, which I knew was a no-no, but I couldn't help it. She said, "You're not in charge. You don't have the power of the place." My voice raised again. I'd lost control in the night. She said, "You're a show-off," which made me so mad, the nonsense. I needed sleep. She lifted the plate behind her and the eggs went all over the wall. "Fine!" I said, and I couldn't tighten my lips. "You don't want these things." I saw the mug of coffee and the saucer, and I imagined them flying, too, everything I'd prepared and cooked up. I stopped myself, but I felt it flare in my body, my turn as the thrower. I sat in her chair, angled myself away from her. The lamp looked so stupid and phony, the whole corner looked fake.

"I don't have it," she said.

I cupped my face, as if I were shielding her from me, and I clenched my teeth and cringed into the cage of twitching fingers. I imagined the lamp shattering against the wall. I groaned, and the noise turned me into the growler, and I shook my head, because I didn't want to become that strange immensity.

"You've got everybody around here just paralyzed with fear!"
I heard her anger climb.

The phone rang. Which didn't matter to me, except I was sitting in the chair, the same as when my dad called, and even though it was a different phone, and it wasn't him, I still grabbed it, Millie's phone, just to see what person, even though it was always junk or spam. Caller ID said the niece. Or not. Byron Lima, said the name—so maybe that was the husband, had to be, of course, but maybe she was still the one on the phone now. Or maybe it was both. Or him first, he was waiting to see what I would do, and if I picked up, another part of their house would pick up, too, and I would deal with both of them. I let it ring.

The phone call was the opposite of protective services coming too late in the day, to notice Millie at her worst. The Limas had timed it just right, as if they'd waited for some horribly confused moment, like when Millie said cake/no cake, although there were so many of these worst moments, so I couldn't really call it timing. Still, I felt as if they had a camera on me, just like I had a monitor on Millie, which sounded like a math problem, where Millie had to have a camera on *them*—something like A to B to C—to complete the terrible triangle. "You've been waiting for just the right moment," I said.

"I never do," Millie said. "Everybody is. It just went downward."

And I'm sure she thought I was talking to her, accusing her, but what did it matter? I almost wanted her to hear me that way. "I'm not touching that!" I said. I meant the phone. The ringing stopped. I'd check the message later.

"Me neither!" she yelled back, and when was the last time we'd agreed on anything? "You've gotten yourself into a wad of trouble!"

When I looked at her, her eyes were enormous.

"I'm sorry," I said. "I'm very sorry."

The message was blank. I checked it right away, and it was just a hang-up. That's right, I thought, you hung up because you couldn't begin to know what is happening here. I wanted to call them right back and scream, "YOU WANT TO SEE WHAT I'M DOING?!" And I'd hold up the phone as a camera.

I told Millie I was sorry again. And I was, I wanted her to know she was safe, not vulnerable at all. I wanted it to be ten minutes later, when the anger inside me was not just out but forgotten. "What do you want me to do?"

"Sit there and stare into the sky!"

I wanted her—everyone, including me—to stop yelling. The yelling felt like hell. I remembered what she'd said, in the van, about the room of noise, and I looked up at the ceiling like we were in some vaulted space. I waited for the phone to ring again. She, the niece, probably wasn't ready to leave a message the first time, or she had second thoughts about it, but now she was prepared to say her piece. The phone kept not ringing. I kept hearing it, but it wasn't. You can call back right now, I said to it, to myself. We're still in that worst moment. I pressed every finger against my face and it felt like a cave-in.

I wanted to hear someone else. Some*thing* else. What was it that my stepdaughter said? Erin. It was great. I mean, the words. I remember, I can't remember what she said. *The word hello has a swear in it.* Yes, that was it. She was sounding out syllables. I laughed now. The hell in hello. I was so happy it came back to me. It was like a healing memory. What was another Erin moment? Ha, the hat. We were coming out of a store, I can't remember where, and I reached into my pocket and pulled out my hat. Except it wasn't mine. It was hers. I must've grabbed the wrong one when we left the house together. So I said, "Look what I've got," and Erin looked at the hat, kind of amazed, and said, "How are you a magician?"

But it didn't change anything now, because there were so many ways to hurt Millie. I was so afraid that I'd make a fatal mistake. I was afraid of twisting her arm too much when I dressed her. I was petrified that I'd make her die. Her skin: it wasn't a toddler's. Her *mind* was a toddler's, but her skin was like a premature baby's. Like tissue paper. The bone-on-bone of heels touching; I had to prevent heel sores; I put the heels between pillows. She complained about the weight of the blankets on her toes, so I made a tent of the blankets over the pillows. But it wasn't enough. The washcloth could be too rough. She was so fragile even a wrinkle in her sheet made her uncomfortable, so I needed to smooth out every crease.

Millie stayed mad all morning and past lunch, and it was like something had escalated without knowing what I'd done to get us there. I wanted to back the day up to a beginning we'd skipped. "I'll do anything you need, Millie, but you need to say hello first." I felt like some '50s housewife whose husband came home from work and all he said was "Where's my supper?" That wasn't my dad and mom; I'd have to go back one more generation, to my grandfather and grandmother. I was the grandmother. Dot. And Millie was the SOB. You can hate me and tell me how terrible I am. This was me talking to Millie in my head. Just say hello first. Then you can hate me after.

But she just looked numbly at my face like it wasn't a face. So I said hello. "Hello, Millie." It didn't matter that it was midday. I wanted hello. She said nothing back. So I tried again, like I was teaching her to talk, till I got a greeting out of her. And then I said, "Hello, Don," and she said it back, our words in agreement. Which brought me back to the phone ringing, when Millie and I both wouldn't touch that call. Me and the niece, we'd probably be in agreement, too. We'd probably both say the same things to each other: *Why are you between Millie and me? Why is that even you?*

"You sound like me," she said. Millie.

I smiled. It didn't matter who said what first. "You sound like me," I said back to her, which made her laugh.

"We sound like us," I said, and I knew I was being monotonous, even adding to the repetition by laughing.

The day had finally settled down. I went into the kitchen. When I saw the faucet, it reminded me how tired I was. I carried out the cake. "Surprise!" I said. "I have a gift for you."

"Is this mine for life?" she asked. She sounded so much like Erin when I gave her one of the first presents, or maybe it was what my six-year-old self might have said when Grandma Dot gave me that sailboat.

"Absolutely!" I said, but I wasn't sure if I was excited for her, or for the memory of me getting that gift. I wished I could give her something bigger, a six-figure equivalent. I'd never be able to give her that much. I'd always reciprocate with less.

"This is kind of good," she said, but by the way she was eating it, I could tell it was better. "I never loved it."

"There's more in the kitchen," I said.

"I'll eat it twice," she said. "You can have the fourth part."

15

I THOUGHT OF THE NIECE. Truth was, when protective services had called to say they were closing the case, I hadn't expected the niece to stop calling. I'm not counting the hang-up, either. Mostly, it still felt like a ghosting. If anything, I thought the calls would increase, that I'd get more from her, her anger plus the added threats from the husband. *We haven't forgotten about you.* That was her. *We know where you live.* That was him. I almost wanted to say, Where'd the two of you go? Glad to hear from you. I wanted to turn accusatory: *What kind of family are you, to disappear like that?*

I thought about the call they must have received from the agency, how the social worker must have assured them of my treatment, that the problem signs weren't there. I was tempted to call the niece and say, "I just want you to know, everything is alright." I thought that sounded better than my imagined screaming. More measured. But then I would have to tell her, them, about Millie's fall, and about the hospitalization, and the rehab, and how I'd brought her home, and all the physical stuff, the touching, and all I heard was the niece saying, "You you you!" And I didn't like how that sounded.

After she called, that night, when Millie was sleeping and I couldn't, I searched her name on Facebook. The niece's. But I couldn't find her. I mean, I found a bunch of hers, the same name, but I couldn't be sure which one, and I knew where my mind was going, back to Beth, and

I didn't want to see pictures of DJs. I wondered if the niece, or the husband, ever did the same. With me. And I'm sure there were a bunch of me, too, but in terms of my profile, there was nothing. No pictures, not even the one, the main one, that clarified it was you. I just stayed with that blank silhouette that Facebook gave you when you started. I remembered joking with Renee about it, "Hey, they got the good side of me."

Next, I searched for my dad. I went on my profile to click on him. He was like me, didn't say much, or anything, except he posted pictures. So that it looked like he still had a life. He looked the same. And there he was with her, Stacy, on the beach, and in front of the RV, and they looked entirely happy—and I knew she was gonna break up with him. It wasn't anything in the body language. Wasn't even anything on their faces. Maybe it was the RV picture, seated like a pair of retirees, except *she* wasn't. Or maybe I was seeing the last conversation superimposed over the photo. But I just thought they weren't about to get married, but were headed in the opposite direction, and that they were almost over.

I called for help. I didn't mean any card in a drawer. I was in a different situation now. When Millie napped, I went on Lifespan's website and scrolled through a list of home health care agencies, all the peaceful-sounding names, like a carousel of greeting cards. I picked a company close by, with good ratings. While the phone rang, I walked into the next room for some semblance of privacy. A woman answered and I told her my story, Millie's—that she'd been basically limping along at home and then she fell, and now here we were. The woman asked about the level of care, about Millie's physical and mental status. I told her those, too. I said I needed some time every day. "She needs someone here more than me." I figured the first thing I could let go of was the bathing. "Maybe you could freshen her up in the morning."

"We can do personal care. Of course."

"Good. I'm not really . . . versed in that area."

Her voice sort of laughed. "I understand." It felt good to hear another woman sound that way.

"I'm kind of skittish about that," I said, and maybe I'd stayed on the subject too long. "Maybe do the same thing at night. Get her ready for bed."

"We can do those shifts." She told me the standard rate, which of course I knew because I'd been charging it for myself.

"Fine," I said, maybe too quickly, because she said "okay" with a light hitch—I guess she thought I was supposed to drop the phone.

She asked if Millie had long-term care insurance, and if she or her husband had been a veteran. Just like the nursing home questionnaire, and I said no to both, and again I remembered Millie talking way back when about her Navy brother.

"We can have someone come out for an assessment on Friday, and then start the day after."

"No," I said, "I need someone now."

"It takes time. I'm sorry. It's based on availability of nurses."

"Sooner than that. Please. I'll take any time."

"We try to move fast. The nurse must go in first and do an evaluation. She'll come up with the care plan for the aide to follow."

I told her Millie could do private pay. I figured it couldn't hurt to say she wasn't poor, to stress Millie's resources. I didn't know how much easier that would make it for the agency, but I figured it sounded easier, if not in terms of getting paid, then maybe in terms of scheduling, adding hours. "I'll pay on time," I said. Then I told her I was going crazy.

"Lemme take another peek at the scheduling." She sounded like a roofer, who first said they couldn't do your roof until next spring, and then suddenly got free that week. *I can get you in on Thursday*, I might have said, long ago. I knew she was honestly trying, checking spreadsheets, but part of me thought she was just squiggling a pen, making doodles. "Okay, let's do the paperwork backwards. We'll start service tomorrow. We can go right away with companion care. That should give you some relief. And we can make-shift assessment the next morning. You can fill out the forms then."

"Thank you so much."

She asked if I would pay cash, check, electronic transfer, or credit card, and I said the last one. She asked for a two-week deposit. Fine, I thought, let the money go out the door. The first-visit schedule was repeated and confirmed. "How'd you find us?" she asked, and I didn't know what to say, so I just said, "Word of mouth."

She was really good. The aide, I had to admit, she had a real knack for it. She held Millie's hand, she hummed and sang. Her name was Terri and I was amazed how quickly she created a relationship. She massaged Millie's hands with lotion, she gave her a foot rub. She fluffed pillows endlessly. "What else do you need me to do?" she asked if she had a break, but mostly she didn't need any prompting. She'd go right to dirty dishes. She'd wipe something clean. The water glass was always full, the Kleenex box never empty. Even if she had to say something a hundred times, Terri never got tired of it. She was so attentive, so maternal.

The nurse showed up with a batch of papers. She did a physical assessment, a home safety check. She noted the grab bars. "That was me," I said, although I didn't say I was a handyman doing it. My mind went back to telling, or selling, Millie about a stair rail. And then my mind returned to the bank statement, or maybe it went forward, what I would see the next time, and it made me feel less guilty, some of the money going to other people. It wouldn't just be money seesawing from Millie's account into mine, but then I realized I was on both sides of the seesaw.

"Good for you," she said. "For her." Which felt nice, but I knew I hadn't admitted everything.

With the free time, I was able to run errands, to catch up on sleep. Whatever noise there was downstairs, my ears stayed closed to it. And my mind could move to other things. The calendar came back to me. Dates. My stepson, Jack, he had a birthday soon. When I lived there, he loved video games. Probably still did. Like I said, he had some problems. He'd scream, "I want a better life!" And I'd say, "You and me both."

"I have a terrible life! I don't want it worse!"

I went to the store and found something age appropriate. It hadn't been so long, so I figured he was still the same kid. Maybe on a different device. I bought it with my money. Of the gifts I considered, I picked the most expensive. I drove by the old house, when I thought they might be home—I guess I could have texted Renee and double-checked whereabouts—and I parked and got out with the gift, feeling like two-thirds of a deliveryman, one-third of an ex-stepdad, and walked to the door. I rang the bell, waited. No one answered. I stared at the front steps, which could be pressure-washed, and I recognized the cracks I'd patched. I never worked enough on my own house. The exterior could use maintenance. Still no one. I rang it again. I had a sudden thought that Renee had moved with the kids elsewhere, which she wouldn't do, she was never fast with decisions, the only time she'd acted fast (rashly, in my opinion) was with the divorce, although if she did take them and go, she wouldn't have told me, and I peeked inside the front door, my hands cupping, and it was them. Meaning, the same couch, table, rug. So, same people. Of course it was. What did I expect, a family of squirrels? Still, I was relieved no departure had happened. I grabbed one of my business cards and wrote on the back, "From Don," and tucked it under the gift-wrapping ribbon. I was about to leave the present inside the door when I had another thought, that I could just walk with the present back to the van and drive away and try the presentation later. I looked around. No one had noticed me. I decided to do it. I returned to my van, but I hadn't really figured out what *later* meant, so I just ended up driving aimlessly for ten minutes, and by the time I pulled up in the driveway again, I was angry at myself for my ridiculousness. I brought the present back to the door, rang the doorbell, knowing they still weren't home—it felt like they were even *more* away—and I left the present just like I'd done before, I certainly wasn't going to repeat the routine a third time, and I looked around to make sure I hadn't been spotted again. I shook my head, at myself, but also, looking at my watch, at them, because it always seemed like we were in the house when we lived there.

Then I drove home to Millie's. I stayed in the driveway, idling. Maybe I should have stayed like that at Renee's, just waiting it out for a long time, instead of aimless driving loops. Something I felt when I looked at Renee's house, which was something I *didn't* feel when I looked at my childhood home, was homesickness. Terri was visible in the window, dressed all in green. I sat there wondering which house was stranger, Terri here or no one there. I thought of arranging 24/7 care with the agency, of packing up and moving out, going back to my recent life of being a handyman, and a tenant. For an instant, I wanted to own an RV like my dad. But it made no sense for my life now.

I slipped inside (I heard Terri in the kitchen, she had another hour) and climbed upstairs. I lay on the bed. I heard footsteps on the floor below. Terri sounded more alive than me. There was Millie, and then me, and then Terri, in ascending order of who was most alive, despite my being the youngest by a good ten years. I texted Renee: "I dropped off a gift for J's bday next week. I know I'm early."

The closet doors were closed, but not completely, one slightly ajar, and at some point I felt like I'd get up and shut them properly. In the bathroom was only my toothbrush, which was just like the bathroom in my apartment, but when I would enter here, I would see the empty slots and I would think of Millie and Jim, but more often I would think of the ceramic holder in my former house, which held Renee's toothbrush and mine and the kids', and the different tubes of paste on the counter. The bathroom fixtures here, the sky-blue sink and toilet, were outdated. Another house I worked on, this one thrifty lady, she'd put a Band-Aid on her padded toilet seat. A bunch of minutes went by before my phone chimed: "Thanks for remembering."

I was tempted to ask, "Where were you guys?" but I knew it wasn't my place. "I hope he doesn't own it already," I texted back. I couldn't help myself, so I told her what I'd gotten, but I figured that didn't matter, because I'm sure Renee wouldn't spoil the surprise.

"No."

I closed my eyes, pictured Jack's eagerness opening it. "How's he doing?"

"Better. Not always."

"How's Erin?"

"Everyone's good."

I wished Erin had her own phone—maybe she did now?—so I could communicate with her directly. I'd send her a bunch of emojis. "How's her math?" I already knew the conversation was getting long, but I liked the sound of the phone chiming again and again, and it had been so long since I'd heard it repeat like that, like talking, even if it wasn't face-to-face.

"Her teacher is really tough."

I stared at the words, and I was surprised she'd kept responding to me. "You dating?" Which—my fingers just went ahead and asked that. I didn't know why I typed that question, spoiling the messaging, when I didn't even care. I stared at the ceiling, baffled, some idiotic propositioner. Some weirdo, some insane guy showing up at the door in only underwear. She texted me back a question mark. It was hard not to hear her voice saying Drop Dead. The air in the room felt suddenly cold, even though, because of Millie, it was exactly the opposite.

I looked over at the monitor and almost responded, "I'm seeing someone." When I shifted, the bed made a noise. Maybe Terri thought I was a ghost. No, if she didn't hear me come in, or the weight of my steps on the stairs, she would have seen the car, my van, which I'd driven, in the driveway. I knew I wasn't hidden. I could have called down to confirm my presence, but I didn't want to interfere. I wanted her to continue doing all that she could do with her remaining time.

"Not me," I texted back, "no time for that. Too busy with water aerobics." I didn't wait for the next question mark. I silenced the phone. And threw it on the bed, my hand twinging. The room felt frigid. Nonwinterized. I glanced at the old windows. Their room, Renee's, when I peeked through the front window at the furnishings, it hadn't looked bare. I suppose I expected things to look half-gone, with me not there, but of course there were four of us, so maybe it should have just looked a quarter. Maybe I hadn't been searching for things I recognized, but I wanted to find some stark spot, some emptiness where I would go. I wondered if Millie's missing lamp had got me thinking like that.

Instead of thinking about Millie, or Renee, I thought about him. I remembered when Jack—we called him Jackster, sometimes—got into fights with one of his classmates. I mean, he was always doing that, but that was something I remembered being a problem when I first came in the picture. He was having difficulty with one of his classmates, and the school counselor made the two of them sign a friendship contract. It was hard not to laugh when I heard the term. Me and Renee both laughed about excessive feelings. We give up, we said. We kept shaking our heads about the way kids were being brought up nowadays. The next argument we had, me and Renee, we joked after about writing up one of those. Even Jack thought the school was stupid, because he was already acting nice to the other kid, despite fighting sometimes. It was probably one of the times that I most agreed with him, the school making him be friends on paper. Brice. Wow, that was the kid Jack had a problem with. Who knew it was still there. Brice. In my brain. Crazy, what you find. *Remember Brice?* Wait, I don't think that's right. I think that was just one of his *real* friends. Jack's real friends. Never mind.

"Leaving now," Terri called up. Her voice came from two places, from downstairs and amplified beside me, where Millie was visible, as if she had spoken.

My hand almost lifted to wave goodbye. I could have talked through the two-way monitor, but I didn't. "You mean it's already nighttime?" I thought to myself. I glanced at the window. On the window bench was the dead pillow. The front door closed and the sound bounced up to here. Terri would return tomorrow, but right now it felt like she never would.

I wanted more, hours and services every day, but the agency said I'd have to add a second aide. I tried to like her, the next one, but I couldn't.

It was the way she tried to take over. *This is how you set up your supplies. Why are you using this brand? You should empty the bag before that. She should only be eating finger foods. Elbow macaroni is way better than spaghetti.* I'm not saying I disagreed with these ideas. I even appreciated the input, and if I was making errors about Millie's digestive system and her ease of eating, I wanted them corrected. But I didn't like when this lady started talking about who I was, and wasn't. The agency must have told her I wasn't family, because when I said that Millie didn't have kids, or grandchildren, that being a grandson wasn't me, she said, "Oh, I know who you are."

"Excuse me?"

"You're the name on the checklist. The main contact. The man of the house." She said this with a grin on her face, like she knew what I was after. Like I was some squatter. Like I was waiting for Millie to kick off. She thought it was really funny. And beyond the innuendos, her voice was loud. Her loudness was a problem. I started to feel like there weren't any good ideas anywhere in the world except for what exited her big mouth. I didn't want to hear it four or eight hours of the day, and I couldn't imagine it was good for Millie, either. It had to be upsetting. I hadn't seen them click, not like with Terri. I told the agency things weren't jelling with the second one, that Millie needed a softer voice, that her loudness was really setting Millie off.

"Sure," the manager said, "we can try someone else."

"She was getting on her nerves. She was really forward."

"Sometimes people just don't match well. We want compatibility."

"And another thing," I said, because I was still angered by the loud-mouth. "Why are your caregivers wearing uniforms?"

"Excuse me? You mean the scrubs?"

"Millie thinks something is wrong with her. Like she's in the hospital. Or the nursing home. This is *her* home. It's not a hospital, so why do you wanna make her feel like it is? It's confusing when they show up looking that way." I knew I sounded too angry, but I wanted to let them have it. "I mean, who came up with that idea? If you're giving care at *home*, why would you dress these people up like a hospital?"

"I understand. It's pretty standard. But if Millie would prefer they wear regular clothes, we can certainly accommodate that."

"It just seems like you'd want them to wear *exactly the opposite clothes*, you know. Than a hospital. Think about how it *looks*, to someone who's been in the hospital, in a nursing home, who's not really sure where they are anymore."

"I'm making a note of it right now."

"I mean, you got this Hallmark name, but you're—they're dressed for surgery!"

She was silent, which I knew was her way of noting my state of mind. *Who is this dope?* "Okay," she finally said. "I've figured it out. A replacement. A better fit."

The third aide was even worse. Almost like a punishment for my insulting the agency. To put me in my place. She talked on the phone all the time. Her interaction with Millie was almost nil. She'd finish a task and stare at her pink gizmo, not making a sound, her thumbs texting at hyper speed. That device had her undivided attention. God forbid if her phone rang when she was transferring Millie to the chair or back to bed; I imagined she'd pivot Millie back to not lose the call. She was young. Too young. Too quiet. And her hands, she had long nails, with bright nail polish, and I thought they would hurt Millie. I called the agency and said they needed to swap out the third for a fourth. Get rid of scratching fingers, of eyes glued to a phone.

The fourth one, I thought, was the worst. A thief. I came home once to find Millie asleep and the aide not there, and when I went upstairs, I caught her rushing out of a guest room. "What the hell are you doing?" I said from the landing, pointing behind her at the incriminating space.

"It's not what you think," she said, but the panic on her face said it was. "I just . . . I found something." And for a second I thought she meant the money I used to hide, but only downstairs, so it had to be something else.

"What is it?" I said.

She turned around and I followed her back into the room. She walked past the couch, with a crazy quilt draped across the back, to the far wall with a dresser against it. She opened the middle drawer and pulled out a thick book.

"We were talking about the pictures downstairs," and now I could see it was a photo album, "and I thought more pictures would give us more to talk about." She scanned the facing pages up and down as if she was trying to find some convincing example. Then she looked straight at me. "I would never take anything," she said. "That's not me." She looked off. "I didn't go—where there might be . . . confidential stuff. I didn't go into your room." She looked at me again, then away. "I just thought this might be the place to find something more. The spare room."

"And you were right," I said, and she didn't say anything back.

I wasn't sure what to say or do, if I was supposed to order her to return the album, and then to leave. It seemed like both a violation of privacy and an act of kindness. She'd broken some protocol, she must have, and I still wasn't convinced she was telling the whole truth and this wasn't just a cover for other snooping, and I was already thinking about the call to the manager, to report her and maybe she'd get fired from the agency?—but it also felt like we were a pair of siblings discovering an old photo album of Mom and Dad, like she was my sister, which I didn't have, saying, "Can you believe our parents once looked like this?" "What's in it?" I asked, which seemed like a stupid question, and I was hoping she didn't just say photos. *Pictures, duh* would be the thing you'd say back to a brother. And because I was still confused about what she'd done, and whether this room and the whole top floor were off-limits, and because I was seeing her as a sibling, I felt like yelling, "You're not allowed to do this!"

"Not much," she said. "They don't go back that far. Maybe they're somewhere else in the house. Or she could have chucked them."

I thought about that. "She's not really a hoarder."

"No."

"She liked to knit," I said, and I decided she didn't need permission to be here.

"Yeah?" She looked back at the album, and I didn't know if it was what I said or what she saw on the page, or both, but she made this giddy laugh.

"That's what she told me. Before we met. I mean, when we first met, she told me she did that. Before."

"You should give her some yarn. Probably some lying around. Her hands. Let her remember the feel." She rubbed her fingers. It looked like the moneymaking gesture, but I knew what she meant.

Her nails were red but clipped short. I stared at her fingers, her wrists, the hem of her shirtsleeves touching them. I asked if her clothes were a problem. "I told your boss to nix the scrubs."

"Yeah, I heard about that," and she probably meant not just the request, but my attitude.

"It was all me. I didn't really ask Millie if it was bothering her."

"It might have been," she shrugged. "I probably wouldn't like it, if I was her."

"I thought maybe she hated them."

She nodded, looked down at the page, squinting as if to read some inscription.

"Is it a pain? A hassle?"

"What, wearing these clothes? No, not really. Either way. You're not the first one."

"Oh, really?"

"Yeah. Others have requested it. Here and there. Not many."

She was young. I had a decade or more. Put her at thirty, thirty-two, somewhere in there. I felt like my dad liking her, so I tried not to. Also, I felt differently. The sibling thing. Or like an older cousin. Or, no, like half children, with one of our parents being the same. This fourth aide, her name was Carla. I knew that both of us felt uncomfortable being there, so I nodded and left the room and went into mine with the giant bed, and I heard her go downstairs. I remembered when Erin used to say, "You're one year older than her, you should know better." She was talking about Renee, and I always thought it was funny, getting scolded by Erin, who was acting like an adult.

When Carla left, I imagined someone else walking in on me, from another room, the same way I'd walked in on Carla. The person I imagined was Millie's husband, Jim, seeing me holding the bank statement. *Get your hands off my money.* It's amazing that I could hear him, so clearly, when I'd never heard him in life. His didn't sound like a voice that angered easily, although he was certainly angry with me. I knew that if I had met him, he probably never would have let me through the door. Even Millie, six months earlier, might have done the same. Then again, maybe the person they *would* have let in would be me now. *This* me. No, I was probably thinking too much of myself. If I heard myself say sorry to Jim, or to Millie, I also heard myself say thank you and, maybe defensively, you're welcome. I didn't really need the memory of him, or some fabricated conversation, to hear the phrases, because I could hear all three of them when I self-interrogated. *Sorry. Thank you. You're welcome.* A rotation of apology and multiple responses pressing against my head. Sometimes, one of them seemed louder than the other two, and sometimes I heard all three together in some nonsense blur, which I didn't mean to say that they canceled each other out, just that the noise was more bothersome, because I felt each was important to clearly hear. So I would separate them. I preferred to hear them one by one, even if one of them was painful.

Millie was still asleep, and I found some yarn in the closet. I brought it to her when she woke. It kept her hands busy. "Can you put this in a ball, Millie?" I asked, and she rolled it back up. We went through several skeins of color like that. Carla was right. The family album was nearby, beside the tissue box, the spine over the edge of the table, which wasn't a careless position because the album wasn't close to falling and the table was out of reach. Millie and I went through the pages front to back.

There were street photos of the house after a big snowfall, and others inside of a decorated Christmas tree; of the front door; of Millie out in the backyard (I could tell that from the V-tree, in the background, that was no longer there); of Jim, with a shovel, in the driveway; of just the shovel, stuck in the snowbank. There was a photo of a young girl, a kid kneeling under a drop-leaf table, smiling like she was playing hide-and-go-seek, or maybe she was imitating a pet who had walked under there before. I didn't recognize her, and she couldn't have been Millie, based on the age of the picture, but I recognized the room, not because of the table but because, at the edge of the frame, I could see several drooping shades of the Tiffany lamp. So it must have been taken from here. A few pages later, I saw the same girl, a few years older, third grade or thereabouts, sitting on a bench, grinning, a yellow balloon in her lap. I had my suspicion. But I didn't say the name in my mind, in case it might be upsetting. I'd let Millie say whatever she thought to say. But I thought about the lamp peeking out, and I wanted to say something about it. I wanted to say The Lamp Man, to see if she remembered. But I didn't say that, either.

I didn't check for any signs that Carla had been anywhere else. I trusted her, even if I wasn't certain if I was supposed to for Millie's sake. I suppose a part of me didn't want to discover Carla had been lying. I wondered if I was also thinking there was a rationale for my being around when Carla was here, at least at first, to keep watch, to verify things. I imagined myself installing closed-circuit cameras and sitting upstairs with a bank of monitors—not just the baby one—like some woman at the front desk of the nursing home. I'd already cycled through a bunch of aides, and I'm sure the next one wouldn't speak English. And the next one after that. In my mind, those were the options. Perhaps to be on the safe side, I should move any valuables up to the attic, away from Carla—or even Terri, because you never knew. But if I did move them, I'd be moving them from Millie, which meant I'd be moving them to me. So I just left everything as is. And I suppose the big thing had already been boxed up and taken out. I'm speaking about the lamp.

"Who is the person in black and white?" Millie asked.

"That's you. And this must be Jim."

"I went by that whole period in life without him."

Which was interesting, since the photos weren't of that earlier time. Unless she meant now.

"I have no idea what the status of my mother is. I hope she's alive, but I don't know. You can check on that."

I told her I would do that.

"Find out again for yourself. It shouldn't be too hard to find."

I glanced at the big pictures on the mantel, which now looked magnified. That night, I remembered when my stepkids bickered and tattled on each other, to get on the good side of me. When I left, the back deck needed staining.

For days, I opened drawers, searched the entire house, to learn about Millie, to uncover what every part could tell me. Like a scavenger hunt, for conversation pieces. In the attic, I found her wedding dress, some vintage period. (I found the drop-leaf table, too.) When I touched the sheer material, these tiny dots came off, so I set it back in the box, sorry for the damage. But I kept looking. I wanted to spur memories, to connect her to the person she'd always been. Stored away in a Sibley's gift box were more photos, the kinds Carla said she'd wanted, if that was really what she was only looking for. There was one of Millie with three other young women. She wore this big smile— she looked happier than I'd ever seen her. The photo wasn't from the marriage but from her previous life.

"A family farm," she said when I showed the image to her. "That was a man with money."

"Oh yeah?" I said, curious.

"Should I tell you the story of the family farm?"

"Sure."

"I've never seen it. Except her."

I pointed at the photo, at the girl with the hat, and said the hat was pretty. "High occasion," Millie said. I asked where she liked to go in high school, or when she was twenty. That seemed to be about the age on the girls' faces.

"We didn't go anywhere," she said.

It was fine, the stories weren't mine, but I wished they were still hers.

"Where are you staying?" she asked.

"Upstairs."

"Are there places to live up there?"

I nodded that there were.

"You're upstairs in a cubbyhole."

I brought her a cookbook and turned to the pages that were full of splatter. I read out the spaghetti-sauce recipe with the red stains. "That's a good one," Millie said. "You ever make meatballs?" I asked, and when she didn't answer, I told her my grandma had. In the spare room, I found a Poconos guidebook. Back in the attic, I uncovered needlepoints, and an unfinished mosaic, with the pattern penciled on the base. The foundation, whatever it was called. The leftover glass tiles were in a baggie. I asked Millie if she wanted to finish it together, but she said she'd never been able to tolerate that kind of group. So I glued the remaining pieces. The pattern was off, but it didn't matter. It filled X amount of time. I grouted the gaps when she napped.

The three of us—or I should say four, counting Millie—fell into a rotation. Millie got along well with Terri; she'd often scream at Carla. If Terri trimmed her fingernails, she'd say, "Wow you're fast," but when Carla attempted a diaper change, Millie yelled, "How dare you!"

Carla tried to calm her, to tell her she was almost done.

"Can't you please leave it alone! What are you doing in here?"

The excitement could be just as bad with the dispensing of medicine.

"Open up," Carla said.

"You're not in the hospital business," Millie said, and I blamed myself for that. Not only because I'd asked Carla to help with meds, but maybe it would be clearer if the clothes were identifiable. Maybe medication wouldn't be such a battle.

I went downstairs to explain the outfit and help with the clamor.

"I would like my problems taken care of for a few minutes, if you don't mind!"

"That's what I'm trying to do, Millie," Carla said.

Millie looked at me. She twirled a finger and rolled her eyes to let me know who she thought was crazy. "Why don't you stop this person before it gets hairy."

"It's for your hip," Carla said, trying to stay pleasant.

"Then I'll talk to the doctor about it. It's getting to the point where the pain is easing. And then I'll go in one of the other rooms so you can talk."

"That's good," Carla said, and she held out the spoon. "Let's get your throat ready." I expected Millie to smack it—the way you'd bat at some colored ball coming at you.

"This stops if I stop!" Millie said. "My mouth doesn't have anything to do with you!"

"Absolutely," Carla said, and she nudged Millie's lips, "open big big big," like she was talking to a three-year-old, which I wasn't saying was wrong. Down the medicine went.

Millie swallowed. "In the future, if you come to visit, which I know you will, leave this one home." She wasn't looking at either of us when she spoke.

I watched Carla's face sink. She exhaled. She crossed herself. Then she repeated the word "calm" and said to me, "That's how I stay centered," to let me know she wasn't bothered. "I'm quieting my body."

When she touched Millie's shoulder to say goodbye, Millie said, "You can leave now!" And after Carla left, and before Millie forgot about her, Millie stayed mad. "He has all of us on alert." I thought she was talking about Carla, but seeing me confused the sex. Unless she couldn't tell us apart.

"I won't be sad to see it go," Millie said.

"Oh, I think she's alright."

"They're not nice people," she said.

"Oh, sure she is," I said. I wondered if after Carla stepped outside, she started crying. I imagined her face breaking apart right on the other side of the door. "She's got heart."

"She's too happy. She's after Don," she said, and I told her I didn't think so. "Did she come for a reason?"

"To help you."

"Never mind. I'll talk to my lawyer. I can take every person here and wring their necks." Her fist shook. "This is true what happened here. There are reasons for what went on this afternoon. Two days ago, she said, 'Oh I love you,' and it went on like that. And now it's 'Awful, and imagine doing that.' So that's what I was talking about. How quickly people change."

"I think she just has a lot of energy."

"She did a job on me and she was ready to go again. I've had it drained out of me from every single person in this place. I still don't know what they do. This is why I was trying so hard to protect my head and whatever I had. Because I was gonna be splattered outside. She threw me all over the place. Everybody's got me programmed for death here. It was all about the kill. It was gonna turn into something fierce, if you let it."

"I think she's just going through something," I said, and I didn't know what I was talking about.

"None of us have been perfectly lovely," Millie said, and she nodded, and Carla was no longer an opponent. "She wants to be included. She's got a car that her daughter stole from her. Literally."

"Yeah?"

"She's named after my grandmother. I know exactly what happened. Because it happened to me."

"I understand."

"Here's the other side agreeing with me. Everybody I know is like her." She looked at me and said, "How did I ever get to be a part of this family?"

I told her I didn't know, but I was glad she was.

"What do you call this thing you're in?"

"Me?" I asked.

"It's a very detailed kind of game." But the way she said it, it wasn't antagonistic.

"No game," I said. We looked at each other, whatever that meant now. "I'm just wondering what we should have for dinner."

"I thought you were gonna ask me that."

"You did?"

"Dinner. Foreign concept."

I laughed at that.

"I've never seen you smile," she said.

I glanced at my watch. "I guess we have a few hours before dinner."

Millie nodded. "Holidays are coming up. I'm just glad Christmas will be over soon."

"We'll be having something good for dinner tonight."

"Don't do me any favors." And then she said, "Am I supposed to just sit in the midst of this?"

"No, I can move you if you want." And I prepared her for a transfer.

"You don't even know how to check a chair," she said. "Pull up a chair, or two or three. He thinks he's a big shot."

No, I said, no.

"It's not a slightly little thing. I'm talking about people dropping bombs. It's not unseriously. Now I know how to attack her."

"Millie. It's okay," and in my head I searched for some kind of baby-ish talk, like Carla's.

"Is this the demise of the place, or people thinking they can take everything they want, or what causes this?"

She was moving back toward her agitation, where she was mad at someone, everyone. No one else would be here for hours. It was only me.

"Pretty soon the day will be over," she said. "Is there a vote tomorrow or something?"

16

SHE NEEDED A HAIRCUT. Her bangs were shaggy and hanging over her eyes. I combed her head, patting down the static in the back, things I had never done with any woman, not even close. I couldn't remember the name of the salon, but I got the plaza. My phone did the rest. I tapped the number, gave them Millie's name, and they located her in the system. I asked if the hairdresser was working now, and if we could speak, and when the person got on the phone, I told her what had happened to Millie.

"I've been wondering where she was," the voice said.

"Speaking of wondering . . ." I asked if she ever made house calls.

She said she would do that for Millie. "Millie was one of my first-ever clients," she said.

I felt like responding, "She was my *last* one."

When she arrived in the driveway, her car sounded like a putt-putt boat—some exhaust-system stutter. She carried in a duffel bag. "Hi, Millie," she said. I remembered her face. It was kind of doughy, but who isn't heavier at this age? "I haven't seen you in forever and a day."

"Well, I'll be . . ."

"Who's been cutting your hair?" she said, and while she unpacked the bag—the dryer, scissors, rollers, a portable bowl—I told her they cut it once at the nursing home. She touched Millie's shoulder before she touched her hair, so as not to scare her. I noticed that kindness.

I excused myself and went to the kitchen. I heard footsteps go in the other direction, then water running, then footsteps back. I heard her say something about removing Millie's hearing aids, so they didn't get wet. "I promise to return your hardware." Then she apologized for the temperature. "That was cold, sorry about that. It'll wake you up a little bit." I thought to myself: I am listening to a haircut. I ran the sink, so my life was more than that. But whenever I turned off the water, I couldn't help but pick up pieces.

"Millie, I forget, does it part on the left or the right?"

No response.

"Whichever way it wants to go? Whatever it wants to do. We're taking liberties. Oh, wait a minute, I'm seeing those pictures. We'll go with that." The photo album was still nearby, but I knew she was talking about the mantelpiece.

For some reason, listening to her doing a job I couldn't do made me think about Terri and Carla, how they often did my job better. I should just let them run the show. There were no new messages on my phone, but someone had called days ago about a repair, a leak. I'd already deleted it, but the phone still had the number. I pressed it and when a voice answered, I said, "This is Don Lank."

"Who?"

I said my company name. It was like saying a married name I'd dropped.

"Oh, right, yeah. Sorry, I got someone else."

"Not a problem. You're all set?"

"We are."

"Sorry. Just buried in work. Crazy time of year."

"I understand," he said.

"Alright. Just keep my name for future projects," I said, and he said he'd certainly do that. I sorted out the pills in the pillbox. I checked the fridge for expired food. There were dishes in the sink so I started them, but then I thought about the number of aides—I wondered if I needed a bigger pool—and I looked over the aide schedule for the week. Sometimes Carla called in sick. In which case, I needed backup.

Sometimes she had car trouble—she drove more of a clunker than Terri did—and once she missed the bus. The woman's voice, not Millie's, called me from the other room. The sink was still running, so I shut it off.

"That was fast," I told her when I walked back in.

"I got speedy fingers," she said. "Okay, hot stuff," she said to Millie, but Millie was asleep. "Geez, she's out. What you been giving her—martinis?"

I laughed. I thought it was a good line, and I tried to think of some exotic drink, but I blanked. "Shots, too," I said.

She woke her with several hellos and gentle taps, and then she said, "Miss Millie, you look gorgeous." I watched her hold the hand mirror up to Millie's face. Millie stared at the riddle, expressionless. "Oh, I forgot to put her ears in." I watched her insert them on each side. She was quick, fitting them in the correct position. "You got the easy ones." She sprayed her hair. "You are ready for the Easter Bunny," she said.

"She looks like what she used to," I said, by which I meant months ago, before she fell.

"You hear that, Millie? You're back to your old self. You have the best hair." She turned to me and said, "I've always told her that."

"You can come wherever I am," Millie said to her.

"I appreciate that," she responded.

"This is what the others are preaching," Millie said.

"Who cuts *yours*?" I asked, for some reason.

"Me," she said, and she laughed. "And my daughter. She's been working on a mannequin." She wasn't wearing a ring. So, maybe, available, if I was looking. "We comb it. We work on parting. Just the simple basics. She's ten. She's OCD. So I tell her don't worry about your perfection. Just worry about getting your technique down. She plays chess, too. Kind of opposite ends of the spectrum."

"What does she owe?" I asked.

"Honestly, I have no idea. Normally, it's thirty. That's what I charged in the shop."

"Say double?" I asked. "For your time and energy."

"That'd work."

I reached for my wallet. I didn't want to write it out on Millie's checkbook. "I didn't get your name," I said.

"Melis."

I had her spell it out. "What's that?" I asked.

"Greek. Turkish, too. I've heard it sounds like all sorts of things. I tell people, it's Melissa, but a little less."

Both of us, I thought, weren't bad looking, as far as appearance go. Besides, I didn't really trust anyone my age who was the picture of health. She seemed like a real person. I handed her the sixty, and then I realized I should probably tip, so I went to give her more, but she stopped me.

"That's plenty," she said. She held a hand up to the side of her mouth, screened it from Millie. "Millie wasn't a big tipper," she whispered.

"Would you come back next month?" I asked.

She said she would. She left immediately, like she was having a really busy day, although, with her car, it sounded like she couldn't go very fast.

"She comes back in the middle of the night," Millie said.

I nodded.

"The last time I saw her was before you saw her."

We were doing everything, even physical therapy, a band that Millie could use from a seated position, which maintained some motion, but mostly there was always less. I'd never seen someone ingest so much medicine and only wither. Her brain stopped sending messages to her legs. If I was getting her dressed, I had to tell her what to do with her arms. I had to guide every limb. "Let's take this leg," I said. And when she sat up, she would tilt, so even in bed, she needed help balancing.

But every morning, her eyes would open. She was dying, but she also wasn't, and I didn't know where she was—at the end, obviously, but maybe not the *very*, and when she said, one night, "We're the invincible group," I thought maybe this stage would lengthen indefinitely. What if she had not months but a year? A second year? Which scared me, that this was the rest of my life, that she'd outlast me, that I'd never get past her, that this was every subsequent day, month, year. I imagined waking up one morning to find Millie standing over my bed, doing jumping jacks, while I struggled to move my body slightly. Her voice grew stronger too. "Don, get up, your slow body needs calisthenics!" Her hands attempted to straighten my slumped posture. My crooked spine. Then she danced down the stairs, promising to visit later. "I'll quilt you an extra bedspread if you're cold." Her voice continued to call back to me, "I'll get started. As soon as I finish this braided rug!" What a nightmare, Millie frighteningly lively—like some monster who'd stolen my energy, who'd lured me with her money— and what a terrible thought, to hope that someone never regained youthfulness, to think that she'd planned this reversal, where if anyone was guilty of planning, it was me. No, I wanted to say, not me neither. *Stop*, I wanted to say, and I was confused by the word, whether its meaning applied to Millie or to the thoughts I was having. When I'd worked a lot on roofs, I used to dream about them, and now I thought I would only have dreams about Millie. Soon, she'd reach ninety-six. Then ninety-seven, ninety-eight, ninety-nine—a final sequence. Why not a century? I sounded like my kids talking about a video game, about getting to Level 100. "I'm sitting here for three more years," she'd said, as if we shared one mind about her endurance. But another time, it was, "I'm already close to death today." And still another, she was someone voicing a midlife crisis: *What am I going to do with the rest of my life?* Which I guess was another way of her being me. So it was hard to tell, about her condition. Besides her hip, which, the staff told me, didn't knit very well, and her dementia, there was nothing compromised with her heart or lungs. She was relatively healthy, whatever that meant.

One day, there were hundreds of ants crawling along the base of the front wall of the living room. They looked like the type of thing you were hallucinating, but it wasn't my faulty impression. They were really there. I set bait stations, and within days the problem was gone.

I thought Millie's hair was getting long again, coming over the collar. I called the salon and asked for—I suddenly forgot who. The woman with the name from all over. I told them Millie's name instead. And I wished I'd written it down when she spelled it out, and I couldn't see the letters on the imaginary page, but then I remembered her saying Melissa, and I tried to work backwards from there, but I couldn't. "It's Melissa," I said, "but it's not." I was about to clarify when the woman said she already knew who I meant.

When she arrived, I realized I had wished she was here more than once a month. "Hi," I said, sounding too welcoming, but I couldn't help the happiness. She smiled back and I stepped aside, with an uncoordinated lurch, and when she got to Millie, again I saw the conscientious gesture, the shoulder touch. It seemed to come naturally. I told her how I'd mixed up her name, and she told me she thought she had, too. I asked what she meant by that.

"Is your name John or Don?"

"Don," I said.

"First time on the phone, I thought that's what you said, but I heard it different after that. John or Don," she said again, with a little sing-song, sounding funnier this time.

"I'm Ron," I said.

"Nice to meet you, Tom," she said, playing along. It had been so long, I wondered if this might be flirting.

"I met her already," Millie said. "The next occasion, she should've been there."

I asked if she wanted water or coffee—I asked both of them this—and she declined. Millie just stared. Out came the contents of the bag, which seemed like a signal to get lost.

"Do you know what you're doing?" Millie asked behind me.

"Well, I've been doing it twenty-four years, so I hope so."

I went to the kitchen. No spoilage in the fridge. I sat alone in the corner nook. Outside was a nice dogwood in the yard, and it would bloom in a few weeks. I was so cooped up. I missed the rest of the world. New people, new layouts, different furniture. *Hey, that's a nice credenza.* A new job every day. Sure, paycheck to paycheck, one injury away from disaster, but I missed walking into people's houses. I missed swinging a hammer. Sometimes, I'd go back to a house I'd already done, and I'd realize I'd done a good job. "Hey, I did a good job on that tile. It came out nice."

"Yeah, we're enjoying it," they'd say.

"Looks like a million bucks," I'd say.

"Yeah, it does."

"Good. You owe me 997,000." And they'd chuckle. If they knew how to laugh.

A small thing, but the world needs a decent handyman.

After a while, I heard her summon me: "We're all done."

"She went out quick this time," she said. Melis.

"I used to work with a guy named Lubo," I said. And I thought, What the hell?

"Oh, okay."

"I was just thinking about foreign names."

Something I noticed about her now were her cheeks. They were red. They were red last time, too, but I think I just figured it was the weather (although I wasn't sure if it was cold that day), or nerves, since she hadn't seen Millie in a while, but she certainly didn't act like she was embarrassed. If anyone was embarrassed it was me. So I wondered if it was some circulation issue, or maybe, for both times, she'd needed water. I asked now if she was thirsty. (And then I realized I'd already offered that, but maybe she'd declined out of politeness.)

"No, I'm good."

"Okay."

It must have been the way I looked at her, because I saw something quickly register. "Oh, my cheeks," she said. "They're just like that. Rosacea."

I didn't recognize the word. "Row . . . ?"

She repeated it, and the second part sounded like a continent.

"Asia," I said.

"Spelled differently. But you get the gist."

"I thought you were embarrassed."

"Yeah, I get that a lot. Some people are like, 'Hey, relax. You need to sit.' When I was a kid, it embarrassed me. Which was awful. You were embarrassed about looking embarrassed. Like living in a circle. I don't think about it anymore, unless people bring it up, but when I was a kid, it made me miserable. Like having bad acne."

I shook my head. "No. I don't think it's like that at all." I thought if I told her it looked like the opposite, I'd be pushing it. But now I realized she hadn't meant rows, but rose, which explained the redness, in terms of words. I thought it was interesting, someone seeming perpetually embarrassed or overly sensitive, when they weren't. Like a disguise, or a feature you had to ask about to understand. *You look flushed?* No, not. I felt like she'd taught me something.

I liked the way her face had been so responsive to what I'd said. It had been a while since that had happened. I wanted to be attentive back. I looked at her face again. The distinguishing trait of her cheeks. I glanced lower. The top two buttons of her shirt were unbuttoned, the fabric pulled tight at her breasts. I snuck a peek, then looked away before she caught me.

I pulled the money from my pocket. I had already taken the bills from my wallet earlier, so I'd be ready to pay her.

"I thought you were the caregiver," she said. "But then, this . . ." And she gestured at the money I was handing over. "So then I thought you were family. But Millie never talked about family. Except for her husband. She talked about him all the time. And her pets. So I'm a little confused."

I nodded and paid her, an extra five hidden inside the larger bills. "She talked about her husband with me, too. Jim." I felt I was saying it for familiarity.

She tilted her head, to suggest maybe a window, the outside, a neighbor. For an instant, her gesture reminded me of Millie's lopsided body. "So who are you? I mean, I'm guessing nephew?" Her look— I didn't think she was eyeing me like the first lawyer, whose face said, Who is he masquerading as? But she sort of *was* that person, too.

"No . . . it's a funny thing. I'm not family. Exactly. I'm just—" I tried to verbalize it. To explain me, or not just me, but the story *around* me. "I met her a year ago. Little more than that. And I did work on her house. This."

"Oh, like a handyman."

I nodded at the word. "And then I—she asked me to do other stuff. Driving. Groceries. We'd eat dinner together. Here and there. With the divorce, the kids were hers. I mean, with my divorce. Not Millie's. She was married longer than I've been alive. And the work I did, this and that, it got all the way to . . . *this*."

"Oh. That's really nice of you." Her smile seemed genuine.

I liked that she was seeing the honest side of me, but it also made me mad. It just felt like other smiles I'd seen that stopped. "I'm not family." Which I'd already said, I'd *just* said, so I had to say more. "I'm like the underground."

"Underground?"

I didn't know why I said that—it felt like a big lie, some conflict of interest that didn't exist—but I kept saying it. "The handyman, the gardener. All these people that might be looking in on a person like her, if I wasn't family. If the family wasn't doing it. The underground," I said, and I knew I was repeating myself.

She stepped over to Millie, moved her hand through her hair, fluffing it, but Millie was still asleep.

"Those kinds of people can be sketchy. Right? Sometimes. I mean, that's what the majority of your average person would say." But I didn't know why I was representing me as some cruel mastermind, some lowlife. I didn't think I was being fair to myself. I felt like I was someone else calling me out.

She nodded, No question.

"I live upstairs," I said, which sounded like more connivance. I only meant to sound closer, more caring, but the arrangement came across scarier. I could tell that from her eyes. "Thought I could help more that way." The handle of the portable hair dryer was folded up. The problem with this conversation was we were having it in a large house. And that I was a non-nephew.

"Well, that's different." Her eyes lowered, as if I'd been talking pure deceit.

"A life changer, that's for sure." Her red cheeks felt like my embarrassment. My eyes followed hers to the floor, but even if our gazes were fixed on the same place, I knew we weren't focused on the same thing. "Don't know what it is. I'm like you. Not married anymore."

"Yeah. You said that."

"And I've got kids. She did. So I wouldn't say that I'm still their father."

Her brow furrowed. "Is this, like, opening up?"

"Huh?"

"You just go around telling people you're the underground stepfather? Or, they come here and this is what you tell them? Or is it just because of me?"

"You?"

"You know, the hairdresser. People like to confess. I'm second only to the bartender."

"No. I'm just talking generally. The thing about me is ..." I didn't know what to say after that. "I guess what I was describing, it was someone else. Like a sort-of thing. Other people, but also somewhat me, if I wanted to look at it being critical. But mostly different." I waved my hand to brush aside the mentioning.

She pointed the scissors like a long fingernail, like self-defense, but the way she talked wasn't apprehensive at all. "I see. Like I'm sort of *not* the mayor. I sort of didn't marry into the Wegmans fortune. I sort of don't own Paychex." I couldn't tell if she was angry or having fun at my expense. "Like I sort of don't live at the George Eastman House."

The scissors resembled the nails of the worse caregiver, but her words sounded more like the second-to-worst, who knew everything about elbow pasta. But I liked her a lot more than those two other people. "I cheated on my wife."

"Ha—you're just full of virtues." She looked at me cross-eyed like, *Why should I care?* "Is that, like, your pickup line? Because it's the worst one ever." She took a step back, but it could have been to see me better, or more likely to stand closer to Millie. I was staring at her too long.

"I'm trying to be up-front."

"Up-front?" she said, and she blinked like some blinkering light. "With who? Bet you didn't tell *her* that."

These were old arguments, or somewhat recent—I'd had them with Renee, with my dad, with Millie's husband, and even with me—but Melis's voice, though it wasn't raised, felt louder. Maybe because I thought she was talking for all of them. I didn't hear my ex-kids in the chorus, but I was sure that's how Jack felt, and probably eventually Erin. I wanted to change that before it happened, and I felt my face flush in a panic—Erin's opinion was too late for salvaging. "No, I didn't." I touched my face. Every response sounded like some impairment. I looked at her and then at Millie.

"Probably told her at the opposite time," she said.

"Opposite time?"

"After."

"When I got caught."

"You should meet my ex-husband. The two of you are two-timers. If you met him, there'd be four of you. You could have a foursome. You could all be friendly together. That is, when you weren't cheating on each other." She shook her head, like she'd talked herself dizzy. "He said it wasn't his fault. Said he liked a challenge. Can you believe that?"

"Pretty stupid," I said.

The scissors sort of flip-flopped in her hand. Then they moved through the air, like swordplay, and I couldn't tell if it was meant as a threat or if it was kind of funny, like if she had caught him right then, this is what she would have done to him, snip-snip.

"Hello, you got three kids. Geez, I guess you're not the perfect person you thought you were. So much for my instincts." She placed her hands on her hips. She looked at me like it was obvious I should apologize. "Some people are really lacking. Some people—they just take up space."

I wanted this conversation to be about someone else, so I looked at Millie. "She would've been a good mother."

"Yeah. I used to tell her about my life. My problems. She'd give advice and then say, 'That's the dog lover in me.'" Her voice softened, speaking as Millie, and I knew I'd used Millie for the subject change, but I also wanted to talk about her with someone who shared the connection, who knew her before me. "Gosh, just saying that, I really hear her. We used to talk. She knew everything about me. She's really lost some pounds. Not me," she said, and she patted her stomach.

"Not me neither," I said. Then I said, "She should have had more family."

Melis shook her head. "No. She did. She had her husband." She nodded decisively. "Jim," she said, squinting, and nodding again, and I couldn't tell if she was signaling that she'd already known the name, before I said it, or if she was thanking me for reminding her, or if she just knew we had both said the name, together.

"Three kids," I said. "I guess you told me about one of them. The haircutter. The chess-playing mannequin." Which, I didn't mean it as offensive. Only as a joke. "I didn't mean it like that."

She laughed at my mistake. "She's the middle one. She's got an older sister. And a younger brother."

"What're their names?" I asked, but I knew I'd been too personal. I told her I had two kids, too, but they were stepkids. I wasn't discounting them, I said, I was just talking about fathering, just calling them for what they were. I named them. I told her my ex's name was Renee. I said we were on good terms, but then I said we weren't. Five kids— my eyes widened. I imagined the chatter of five kids, a handful, talking, a whole population, but I realized that couldn't happen, that combination, not unless Renee and Melis blended families. Still, I asked if she wanted to go out one time.

Her face showed only lukewarm feelings. "Why do you think I'm not dating anyone?"

I was about to answer, but then I wasn't sure how I'd heard it. I couldn't tell if it was a question, or an aggressive statement about why she wouldn't date. "Do you mean, why do I think it, or why aren't you?"

"Huh?"

"Do you mean, why didn't I think you were dating someone? Or, why did I think ... why did I assume that, because you were already married and it didn't work, so you don't want to do that again, you're staying away from men?"

Her eyes popped at my speech defect. She looked over her glasses at me, like I was half-crazy. "The more you say ..." And before I could try to clarify, she said, "I *mean*, I'm not wearing a ring but that doesn't mean I'm single."

"I know. I know. I thought that's what you were saying. I just, the way I heard it, I wasn't sure if it was ... one of those questions without an answer. You know, where the answer is already obvious. So you don't have to say it."

Again, my talking was on the blink. She packed her bag. She told me she'd been broken up for two years. I told her it had been almost that for me.

"Less kids, less time," she said. She hesitated. Then she shrugged at the comparison. "Sounds like we're in the same boat."

Which meant, I thought, that we could like each other. "So, are you dating anyone?"

"Honestly," she said, and she looked at me square, and then angled her head upward, as if someone were listening above. But I knew what she meant, she meant that territory, that second story, which was me, where I lived, a problem area. Not some higher place, but the opposite. Some subbasement. Like if I were younger, and I didn't own a car. Like if I still lived at home. Like some adult adolescent. She still hadn't completed the sentence, it felt like an eternal pause, but I knew her opinion even before she'd stated it: "I think you've said enough for the both of us."

17

SOMETIMES I DIDN'T KNOW what to do with truth. When Millie asked where Jim was, I wasn't sure if I was supposed to bring her back to reality or if I should bend the facts for her own good. Sometimes I'd tell her he was at work, or I might ask, "Where do you think he is?"

"He is all around the world."

It made her happier if I said he'd just stepped out, but I got tired of repeating that line, so I might just say he was upstairs, and count on her not asking for me to call him down. She never did. Instead, she'd nod and say something like, "He's sitting in the back row."

It was interesting to think that lying might be the right approach, as long as you didn't *start* it, and I felt like I was learning about older fibs (no, fibs was too polite a word), damaging ones, when I did. But you had to be careful with distortion, even if I felt encouraged to play along. With Millie, I mean. I learned my lesson when one time I went overboard and said, "He came in and kissed you while you were sleeping."

"Why didn't he wake me up?!"

Suddenly damage control: I apologized for saying the wrong thing. With trial and error, I learned the right way of talking. The residents from the nursing home—like the woman who pointed out the window and asked, "Is that the bridge to Lima?" before asking me if I thought her car would be out of the shop today . . . Remembering this, I suddenly realized the niece's name echoed the name of the nearby town, and then of course there was the food, the bean, but connecting this trio didn't really lead me anywhere. Anyway, the point I was making was, it was nice that I didn't have to mislead Millie about getting home. The problem, though, was in convincing her she was really here and nowhere else. "Where have you put me?" she asked often. I'd tell her, and I tried using the photos as a reference point. "It's hard not to relate them to my own life," she said. "It's very important to me." Eventually they meant nothing. I brought them closer because I was unsure if it was a problem with her mind or her eyes. Still, there was no recognition. I fetched a hand mirror from the bathroom, and when I returned, I pointed the reflection at her and asked what she saw. "I see a very young woman," she said.

"You," I said.

"If there was something in it, it would be beautiful."

She talked about Jim and herself, and mysterious others. "Why isn't Tony here?" she asked.

"Who's Tony?" I never learned if he was anyone.

One afternoon the doorbell rang. A Bible thumper, maybe. And when I answered it, I thought he was a local politician canvassing, but instead he was a lawn-care guy. He stood not on the steps but down on the driveway to demonstrate how friendly and hands-off he was. He introduced himself, and I told him, "Not interested." I knew he'd heard that stock answer a million times.

"Absolutely," he said. "Could I just ask what you did to the lawn last year?"

"I cut it."

"Okay, and how many applications did—"

"Buddy," I said, trying to kill the rapport-building, "I'm really busy." I gestured back inside, at the chaos behind me, even though Millie was just asleep. He couldn't detect that from his position. She was twenty feet away, as far from him as he was from the edge of the lawn.

"I hear you. Home is busy. It's just . . . you got a lot of stuff going on out there." He gave me a wink about weeds. In my mind, I saw a cardboard cutout of the second aide, her mouth, her extra commentary about the household.

"It's green," I said. "We're good. Listen, just give me the door hanger."

He looked down at his hand, finally untalkative. "Oh, okay," and he stepped onto the stoop, careful with his footing, and reached out and passed me the paper. When I grabbed it, it switched from a company advertisement to a Do Not Disturb sign. I think he was aware of that. He was stumpier than I thought.

Of course I was glad he was leaving, but I also felt bad that he was still traipsing door-to-door. He probably had five years on me. "I saw some yards up the street," I said, "grass was looking patchy." Which was true, but I didn't realize I'd recorded that info. "Don't know which way you're going." The hanger was still in my hand, but I'd already folded it in half for garbage. One of the yards was across the street, and the other was a corner lot on this side, and I was reminded of my yard-work life. I pointed over his shoulder. In my other hand, I unpinched the hanger so it became triangular, a paper hut. "That direction."

He was almost encouraged. "That's where I'm going."

My next break, I cut the grass so he, or anyone like him, wouldn't come back. Later, I treated it, just to be sure.

The first sunny seventy-degree day, my phone rang off the hook. This happened every year. I called this the Motorcycle Weekend, when everyone wanted to take their motorcycle out. I think it was like a chemical thing. Serotonin levels going up. First sunny day, people think, "Hey, let's remodel the basement," and I was always like, "Where the F were you in January?" Of course, I wasn't thinking that this past winter. With the schedule solidified, I went out on small jobs. I fixed a kitchen plug. Patched a wall. I installed vinyl replacement windows; they inset right into the existing frame, pop in easy. One job, I was mounting a spigot on the outside of a house, so the man could water his front garden, when his neighbor came over and asked about fencing. I checked and it was just putting up three sections—Terri had a couple of hours left on her shift. Sure, I thought, I jumped right on it.

Being outside, I realized how much Millie needed to feel the outside, too. So when I got back there and cut the grass, I brought her some blades. I placed them in her hand. She stared at the thin stalks. She closed her eyes and felt them. One time, she put them in her mouth, which was sort of like the opposite of when she looked at a grape and mistook it for a toy. "No, no," I said, but it was all okay, everything was okay. Like when she asked me to put socks on her feet when they were already there. "Can you put these back onto me?" Or when she put the Styrofoam coffee cup on her foot, so it looked like a snout or bad skin.

"That was my coffee," she said, pointing to my cup, the other one, on the table, not on her.

"Oh, really."

"Don't worry. It was, but it's yours now. I'm leaving."

Her meal wasn't finished. I fed her. She moved toward me and opened her mouth like a baby bird. After she swallowed, I asked about her food.

"You had a so-called salad. It worked out, but it wasn't terrific. And she ate it."

One night, I woke to her screaming. "I'm so scared. I don't know what's happening to me!" I ran down and told her it was okay. I stroked her arm, but I couldn't do anything about the fright on her face. She called for Jim. I told her Jim was here. I told her he was right here. She said, "I don't know how to die!" I climbed into bed. I held her. We spooned. I wiped the tears from her eyes. She fell asleep so fast, it was as if the incident had never happened. I stayed there for a stretch of time, just to convince myself that it had. Earlier that day, she had said, "And then at night, she goes asleep and stays asleep."

Melis visited again, even though Millie's hair didn't need it. Her car didn't make the stop-and-start sound; I didn't ask if she got it fixed. "You know, she can't get her hair cut this much," she said.

"I know that," I said. "It's my money." And it was. I was paying for this too-soon visit. I guess the term "my money" was relative. "She likes it. She likes you. Just do some . . . cosmetic thing. I'm not doing anything wrong by bringing you here." Which I thought was also true.

"Not wrong but weird. You know, like, *underground*."

I was insulted—like a culprit, again, the subhuman in the subbasement—and embarrassed, but also kind of flattered, that she was keeping track of what I'd said. I asked her again if she was dating anyone.

"You're really stuck on that word."

"Dating?"

"That one."

"Are you?"

Instead she said, "What would *Millie* say about you?"

"I don't know. Ask her." Because I was curious. The last time she mentioned me, she said, "Don's been very good, sort of."

Millie hadn't said anything, but she hadn't fallen asleep yet.

"Millie, what do you think of Don?"

"We've kind of gotten involved in a friendship."

"He feeding you alright?"

"The meals here are very good. The lunch usually includes soup."

"Sounds like he's running a good program," Melis said.

"A bonfire," Millie replied.

"But it sounds like you're okay here."

"It's a long story," Millie said. "You know what? I will never do this again."

"It's good that you're home," I said. I wanted to be a part of this.

"I went home first, middle and last. I don't know what to do with this *mmmm* place."

We were both quiet after that sound.

"Every time I turn around, she's gone. I'm hoping to get her back," Millie said, but Melis hadn't left, she hadn't even started whatever she would do with Millie's hair.

"I'm right here," Melis said.

Millie asked her, "Do you have any candy in your hand at all?"

And before Melis could open her empty hands, Millie asked her, and not me, "How long are you in this vicinity till you move out?"

It was summertime, and I took on more deck work. I hired another aide. She couldn't think for herself, couldn't anticipate, which was fine because I'd just write out a checklist: Millie needs breakfast at such-and-such a time, et cetera. She did the job.

Carla, I knew she cared, but she was like two people. There was one part of her that, I swear, was gonna tattoo Millie's name on her arm. The other part, though, her car kept breaking down and she couldn't seem to remember the bus schedule. But then again, Carla was the one who found the radio, still working, and plugged it into the living-room outlet. She turned the dial to the old-timey station, and the music made Millie so happy. "I can't believe I'm not of that era," I heard Millie say. I couldn't believe I'd stopped trying with TV, that I hadn't gone backwards with entertainment to radio. I'd forgotten about our car rides together. Erin said this thing about me; I guess I'm thinking about it, because of the phrase she used. I liked to listen to classic rock, always have, and Erin had this phrase, "Classic *you*," when I did something that she thought was familiar. Characteristic of me. Most of the times she said it, it wasn't a compliment, it might have been when I was stuck in my annoying ways, or when I was saying no. I didn't think much about it then—I probably just responded, "yeah yeah," if I said anything at all—but it meant a lot to me now, that Erin knew enough about me to recognize a pattern in my behavior. But this is all a long way of saying about *Carla*—that I appreciated her thoughtfulness, and if she was worse than Terri, she was also at times better, and her better part was her true nature, her *inside* part, because once she was here, she always knew what to do with the rooms.

I opened windows for the fresh air. I brought in Millie's lilacs. She felt the greenery, the moisture. Then I realized that bringing the outdoors inside to her wasn't as good as bringing her out to it. I wheeled her to the garden, and I placed a flowerpot of soil in her lap. I watched her pat and tap the dirt.

There was the inevitable switch to a pureed diet, which made it difficult when Millie's favorites came back to her. The upside-down cake, for instance. She asked for it, which created a tension between safety and comfort. I worried about choking. Instead, I blended it together. "What the hell is this?" she asked, and I explained that it was her cake. "No it isn't," she said, and she was right, just baby food. But I had to account for her trouble swallowing. I gave her protein shakes, pudding, ice cream. Lucid moments, if there were any, were mostly in the morning. But then again, it might be any time when her brain fired recognition: *Don.*

"Hey, you got my name," I said.

"That's what your mother called you."

"Yes, she called me Donny."

"That too." Then she looked at the floor, talked to it. "He's attracting attention." I couldn't tell if she was speaking to me about some imaginary being, or vice versa. At least she wasn't agitated. When that occurred, she looked like she wanted to tear the curtains off. "What is it?" I asked.

"The drawers. They're just useless. The way they are. I want them all open."

I did what she said.

Even the one with the card, although I'd thrown that out some time ago.

One time, when I was dividing up the pills, I discovered that the week's supply of pain meds was far short. I thought I'd been careless with the medication, that I'd somehow double-dosed her several times, but then I realized: No. I knew it was Carla. I didn't know why. It just wasn't anyone else. Her next shift, I ordered her to follow me and I walked her into the kitchen, and her reddened cheeks told me right off. I knew that redness wasn't Melis's, and it wasn't the complexion Carla wore when she held the photo album and looked up at me and said she never took things. "You wanna tell me why I'm needing a refill so early?"

Her eyes dodged mine. "My boyfriend made me do it." I didn't know if I believed her. I did and I didn't, but I didn't want to be double-minded. She didn't look like a user. What was I supposed to look for, anyway: pinpoint pupils? Maybe she was a better liar than I thought. At least this wasn't full denial. I didn't care to know about some boyfriend, if he was selling or using it to tide him over.

"The pharmacy is gonna question this," I said. "What am I supposed to tell them? I dropped the pills in the sink? I tipped them over? They fell in the toilet?" These were red-flag excuses, even if they were all plausible. "It won't be a big deal now. Happens once, maybe it was my error." I was rehearsing what I would tell them, because I had already convinced myself. "But I can't make this mistake again."

She nodded.

I pointed at the initialed slots of the pill organizer. "It can't! Never again." I didn't want to report her. Because she was so good with Millie. And that's why it didn't matter, not yet. And it was partly my fault, since I'd let her administer medicine. "I've been through two others before you. You're doing a good job. You're good at this," I said, repeating the compliment, but her downward glance and shrinking body suggested she took it another way.

She *was* good, but no longer better than Terri, who I needed more for this phase. Millie developed a urinary tract infection—Terri detected the odor, the increased confusion—and we treated the fever with Tylenol and cold compresses, and the infection with antibiotics. The infection cleared, but she was weaker, and in two weeks it happened again, so I wasn't even sure if the course of antibiotics had taken effect. Everything was cycling down.

"She's pale," Terri said. "I can barely get her awake to eat. She's breathing a lot faster. She's working hard to breathe. Air hungry," she said in a way that I knew was a coined term. Terri spoke all this without alarm, but hearing all of this talk about troubled breathing and starving air made me hyperventilate. Her hands rose between us, and she floated them gently, bobbed them up and down, some signaling of calm. "I know," she whispered, "talking about breathing can make you breathy." She breathed in through her nose, exhaled slowly. I followed, rubbed my ribs. I felt my lungs restore, the air returning. I nodded, thanks. "This is what we see," she said. She was back to talking about Millie, I think. She knew everything that was happening because it had happened before, so many times. Although, there were things about Terri that I was seeing now, her spiritual side. She told me she always opened the windows because the windows needed to be open for the soul to leave, which was like the opposite of me doing the same thing, for bringing the outside in. She said I needed to call a priest, to give the sacrament of the sick.

"What's that?" I asked.

"Last rites."

"That's what it's called now?"

"It's part of it. The terminology has changed."

I was grateful for her knowledge and experience, but I wasn't sure if she was imposing her belief. "This wasn't really discussed," I said. In the time that I knew Millie, she was mostly angry at God, but I knew her anger had stemmed from devotion. The rosary had to mean something. I wanted to cover all the bases, including faith. I asked Terri to make the call, to arrange the appointment around her next shift, and I slipped out for the blessing and whatever holiness and anointing.

Before I did, though, I called the niece in Arizona. It seemed the right thing to do. Only, I picked the time when, if she didn't answer, I might not be there when she returned it. The phone rang and rang, and I kept hoping to reach the voice mail. When the dialing stopped, it was strange for me to be relieved to hear the niece's voice, just because it was recorded. The niece's message was short, to the point; I thought I'd be that way, too. I told her where Millie was at, and that if she wanted to see her before she passed away, she would need to come visit soon.

When I hung up, it seemed my life had gone in circles. What I mean is, I remembered not only how the niece had first called Millie but also how she'd then reported me to protective services, and how I had almost recently reported Carla. I guess those weren't all the same thing. Another thing that *wasn't* the same was that the last time the niece (or her husband) had called, she'd hung up—but at least I'd said something. In that regard, I felt like I'd done more.

Anyway, I never heard back. So I don't know if the niece ever gave it much thought.

Terri made a cloud of pillows around Millie's body—she looked like she was floating. When Terri turned her, she made sure to flatten Millie's ear so it wasn't folded and hitting the pillow. Millie's mouth stopped working. Every question became unanswerable. Once when I said something, she flinched, as if I'd spoken from an unthinkable distance. She wasn't here, and I wasn't either. Everything we talked about, everything I told her, everything I built and repaired was forgotten, the stories, the work I'd done, my face, my voice. But it didn't matter if she'd forgotten everything, because I was remembering it, and I would long after she was gone. Terri told me hearing was the last sense to go, that I should keep talking. Millie wouldn't respond but she could still hear me. "She can't open her eyes," Terri said, "but she knows you're there." I told Millie thank you, and that I wished I'd known her longer. I reminisced about our drives, our sightseeing, the lakeshore and the downtown landmarks.

Terri switched her focus; she rotated the care to me. "You're looking tired," she said. And now I saw the concerned look. "Are you taking a break? I'm seeing a lot of pizza boxes. I'm noticing the beer, too." She sort of toggled her finger from the counter to the fridge. It was maybe a little bit more advice than I'd like, but I didn't mind the attention, being told to eat a balanced diet, to watch my beverage intake. It felt like she'd caught me the way I'd caught Carla. And going back further, it felt like the protective-services visit, but now Terri, as that woman, was seeing something off, and not what it should be.

Pizza, I wanted to say, who even thinks about it? I sure didn't, and I felt like I'd hidden the behavior from myself, if it even *was* behavior, because pizza is like nonthinking food, your brain on autopilot. Although, I certainly hadn't hidden it, because I'd left the box, this one, out on the counter, and why hadn't I taken it out to recycling? Had I just been tired, or had I wanted someone, someone like Terri, to notice? Not like stuffing towels down a toilet, but still, if I looked at myself, some kind of attention-getting gesture. I stared at the box as if to understand my past intention.

As for the beer, did I really need to justify it? In all the time I'd been here, two had only been my max, and that was just the once. So, no effect. Still, I saw what Terri was saying, seeing.

"I'm here," she said, "why don't you go?" She meant Wegmans, and I did. I didn't mind the direction, the dos and don'ts. She was saying Millie needed me to be healthy.

Millie's lower legs turned mottled. Her hands and feet got cold. Her brain wouldn't fire signals to her heart and lungs. Her body couldn't manage; resources went in sixteen different directions. The delirium worsened. We gave her a cocktail of Haldol, Ativan and morphine, in a concentrated dose squirted in with a syringe, but the drugs only made her more sleepy. She forgot how to swallow; she pocketed the liquid in her cheek, and then it would dribble out. To remedy her dry mouth, we inserted sponges on a stick, and Terri showed me how to slide them in on either side, so Millie wouldn't bite down on them. Terri applied Vaseline to Millie's lips. "Would you like to put lotion on her hands?" Terri asked me, and I did, I wanted to do something, more.

We weren't going to put in a feeding tube. We'd already filled out the DNR form; the MOLST form was posted on the fridge, with most of the boxes checked off. Those choices were made when Millie went to the hospital for her hip. So we were counting down the days, of living without nutrition. Terri put in a catheter; she inserted nasal prongs. Millie reached her hands out with her eyes closed. I held her hand. I told her what she meant to me. Terri told me to encourage her to go. "Tell her she doesn't need to hang around." I sat at her bedside. I told her she was going to see Jim. I made cooing noises. Except, then

I remembered that the last person she'd called out for wasn't Jim but her mother. That's what she'd said, yesterday morning. I had thought she was calling out in agony, saying "ow," but when she said it again, I realized it was "Mom." She'd said the word loud and clear. So I said she would see her, too. I said that now. I placed a good-night kiss on her forehead. She breathed in a heavy and irregular pattern, but I couldn't be terrified. I told myself this was dignified. I told myself this was life. A peaceful death. She took a couple of big breaths and then she was done. Seconds before, she was a person, and suddenly, just a body, unanimated. I was so used to seeing her chest rise and fall. I turned away to not remember this. But then I ordered myself to look. To feel. It seemed like it was Terri calmly advising me to do both things. I almost wished her expertise had been there for other women. In my life. I mean, their deaths. My mother's, foremost. Grief, relief, guilt. And of that trio, I think I felt grief and relief the most, and maybe even relief more so, because I was feeling it both for Millie and myself, but as soon as I thought that, my grief intensified, and of course my guilt. So maybe an even trio.

I called 911. The medical examiner arrived and checked her pulse and pronounced her time of death. The sheriff's office asked for my name and date of birth, so he could run my criminal record, which was understandable. He asked who I was, and I showed him the paperwork and said, "I'm as close to family as she has." I switched the tense to had. The undertaker's manner was very gentle, like he was a friend or family member of Terri's. "We're going to remove her now," he said before ever touching her, and I nodded, and then he went out again and wheeled in the gurney. When he finished with the body bag and the terrible zipping, he placed a blanket over her. I accompanied Millie out of the house to the hearse. I called the funeral home and told them about Millie, and about me, that I was the executor of the will. They asked who wrote it, and I gave them the attorney's name, so they'd know I had the legal right to be in this position, that I wasn't just some person in off the street. I supposed they would then ask the attorney if there were assets to cover the burial. Millie and I had barely talked about final arrangements, other than her telling me a plot had been purchased, and a gravestone inscribed, but she had talked about Jim's funeral, and they used the husband's death as a template and went backwards to mirror the merchandise. They'd done an open casket, but Millie had told me once she didn't want anyone looking at her, so I requested closed.

I called the niece again. As it rang, I realized how much I hoped she'd answer, because I didn't know how to say this into the phone. When I heard her answer, I realized I didn't know how to say it in person, either.

"Hello?" she said.

"Hi," I said back. I was surprised she picked up, but then I remembered I was calling from Millie's phone, so maybe, with caller ID, she thought I was miraculously her. No, she wouldn't. I suppose I could have cleared up any confusion, if there was any, but I hadn't wanted to use my phone. I exhaled. And then I told her about Millie.

There was a pause, and then she said, "I figured. Why else." She seemed half-angry, maybe less. "Based on your previous message."

When I gave her the funeral info, she said, "I can't come." A blunt response, but then she said, "Thank you," and it seemed like she should've said those two things in reverse. "I can't travel out there right now. It's a bad time. I'm busy with my husband."

"I hope he's okay."

"I don't talk about my husband with you."

I nodded. I said his name in my head, but not out loud. She wouldn't want to hear that.

I didn't call anyone else. I figured the announcement in the D & C would be sufficient invitation to family and friends. The funeral home helped me write the obituary. They had an outline, and I answered their list of questions, first Millie's information, followed by the predeceased.

"Survived by—"

Part of me felt it was me—that it was only me, in her family circle—and part of me felt it was everyone *but* me, and I wondered how many members were printed on their page: parents, sons, daughters, grandchildren, great-grandchildren, sisters, brothers, nieces and nephews.

"No. Don't put anyone." If I mentioned in-laws, it would only be to explain Millie's estrangement from extended family.

"Any societies or clubs?"

I repeated the things Millie had told me about herself. I tried to speak her words. She loved knitting.

"Very good. We can say she was an avid knitter."

"That's nice. A good way to put it."

"Anything else?"

"Can you go back to the husband? Add something to him. Say 'loving.' Say 'devoted.'"

"Of course. Beloved husband."

"Beloved and devoted husband." I wanted to keep adding, but it would sound like embellishment.

"And do you want a picture?"

I looked at the photos on the mantel, the last of them together. Or should I go with an earlier one, all the way back to the beginning, or maybe the middle pictures, when they had years behind them and ahead?

"It does cost extra," she said, misreading my silence for finances.

"Can I send one to you?"

"Of course. Or you can bring it in."

"It's of the two of them."

"We can crop him out, if that's what you'd like?"

"Is that what you'd normally do?"

"Yes. Not always."

"I guess I could just do that here, though. I'd be taking a picture of a picture, with my phone, so I could just take it of her."

"Whatever's easiest."

So that's what I did. I framed the shot to capture her half.

"Any contributions?"

"From me?" I asked.

"No. For the announcement. In lieu of flowers. If there's an organization or charity she particularly cared about."

"Oh. I guess not. I guess just leave that blank."

"And how would you like her buried?"

"Excuse me?"

"In what clothes?"

"Oh . . ."

"Maybe she had a favorite outfit? Sometimes people make prior wishes."

"We didn't talk about that."

"We can provide garments."

"No," I said. I thought, Carla would help me with this. I would call the agency and ask if Carla would come back one last time. I would bring her into Millie's bedroom, to look through Millie's closet and find the correct attire. I knew the wedding dress would be too much, but I thought pajamas or sweatpants were the wrong choices, too, and I thought Carla would identify something special in between. "She has a wedding ring," I said to the woman on the phone. "She wanted to be buried with it. Those were her wishes." Millie had never told me that—had we discussed so little?—but I still knew I was right.

She was a private person. I arranged the service accordingly. No pomp and circumstance, no clergy. A spray of sympathy flowers by the casket, but just a morning visitation, and then we needed to be at the cemetery by 2 p.m. Terri showed up at calling hours to kneel and pray, and then promptly left. Carla was a no-show. Transportation problems, maybe, but I took it as deep mourning, that if she'd been here she would have been overcome by grief and weeping. I'd prefer to remember her that way, even if it never happened, rather than the ducked head and blushed face she wore in the kitchen when it did. Or I could just remember her from the day before, when she opened the closet doors and helped me settle on a dress. "That one," she said, as if she'd seen it in an old picture, but no, she told me, you could see Millie had hardly worn it, that she'd kept it for rare occasions.

During the visitation, I sat midway. But since the first few rows, reserved for immediate family, were empty, and since it hurt to see them unoccupied, I moved closer to up front.

I imagined what this ceremony might have been if it had been years before, if Jim had been alive, if Millie had been the one to predecease him. We'd be in a different room, in the church, and he'd be up at the pulpit, sharing stories, about Millie's goodness, and he'd keep a part of himself hidden—I stopped where this was going. I felt terrible for bringing that episode into this room right now. I shook my head at the casket to tell Millie I'd never heard that story, or only the good part of it, which was her. I heard Jim talk about other things, trips and knitting, and maybe some inside joke, and I imagined the smiles and nods of recognition of the audience, and I thought of the room filled with other people, with everyone who should've been here, church attendees and neighbors, which also meant minus me, I wouldn't have been there at all.

Melis arrived. I waved at her, and she walked up the aisle. She looked at the empty spot beside me, but then thought better of it, to leave some room between us. She sat and stared straight ahead. But then she turned and smiled, and I returned it because I appreciated her proximity.

18

DAD SAID THINGS HAD ENDED WITH STACY. "It was her birthday that did it," he said. "She got a year older. She said, 'I'm forty-four now. You're fill-in-the-blank.' Then she started singing *me* the happy birthday song. 'Happy Birthday to you. You're a hundred and two.' Then she made a joke about tying a balloon to my chair. My *wheelchair*. Ha ha. I thought it was pretty childish. Or, abusive, maybe. Somebody says something like that, you wonder if they ever felt anything."

I felt sad for him. But I also wanted to scream at him to act his age. This Stacy, this forty-four-year-old, would have been a real proper spouse for him—if he was *me*. "Dad. Why'd Mom marry you?"

"Ha. To get out of the house."

"Really?"

"I never told you that?"

"Maybe."

"I thought I did. She wasn't the only one."

When I heard a dog barking in the background, I stopped being mad, or maybe it's that I tried to hear if the *dog* was upset, which lessened it for me. "Is that you?" I asked. "Yours?"

"What, the dog? Yeah. Trusty companion. He's great. I love this guy." His spirits sounded revitalized. "You should see the way he's taken to me. I'm like his adoptive father."

"Where'd you get him?"

"A friend. He got too old. Actually, he died. I mean, I took the dog when he went into the hospital, and then he died. He's got kids, but they don't want it. He'd asked me about the dog, before he got sick, when he wasn't doing too well, and I said no thanks, but then with the breakup, I thought, why not? It's good for my activity."

I was going to tell him about Millie, but then I decided not to. We'd already talked enough about those circumstances. Another time.

"Did I tell you what kind of dog he is? Spoiled kind. Papillon. He's French. His name is Sergeant Tuffy. Little dog with a big name. Wasn't me that gave him that."

I looked in the corner. I wondered if a standing lamp would be better there.

"So ... what was I starting to say? You remember when you lost that jacket?"

"Yeah, yeah, it's like the thing you always remember. I'm the kid that lost his jacket. I left my jacket on the bus, and you're still talking about it."

"Alright, I'll drop it. I just, I love that story. I see a school bus sometime ... Anyway, I feel like I was gonna say something else. Senior moment. Donny, why are you listening to all this? I'm just going on and on."

"I'm in no hurry," I said. I told him I didn't need to be elsewhere.

"Whatcha gonna do next?" he asked. "When you're through with this."

I didn't tell him I was. And I felt like I sort of *wasn't*.

The windows: another month or so of colder weather, and I'd put up the storms. The house across the street had a nice tile roof. The value of the lamp in the corner would never increase in my lifetime. "I thought I'd go into the thatched-roof business."

"Ha. Yeah. That's what everybody wants now. A thatched roof. That, and geez, I don't know, something from another century." The dog barked again. "He's gotta take a leak. So do I. We got the same bladder. I can take the phone with us, if you want, while we go wee-wee. Put you on speaker."

I heard the dog scamper, my dad fumbling with the leash, the door opening, more barking mixed with my dad's baby talk. While this was all happening, I stepped outside, too, so I wouldn't feel motionless, but also to feel closer to him in the outer world.

"So . . ." my dad said, his voice muffled then clear again, "you climbing walls?"

"Climbing what?" I said, and then I understood the figure of speech; I'd thought he meant actual scaling. But I still wanted to keep silent, so now I had to lie and tell him I was doing fine. "I've brought some other people in, so I've been getting out to other houses. I should probably get back to it." I didn't clarify what clientele. "Duplex," I said, for no reason.

"Sounds good," he said, satisfied about my nonconfinement. "And don't you worry, you ain't gonna have to do this again for me. Ain't leaving a mess for you to sort out." Then he told me he wanted to be cremated.

It scared me, hearing him use a word like that, talking about incineration. "Dad, slow down. It's kind of early to be talking about all this."

"*Early?* Is there something you wanna tell me about mortality? You still think I'm in my middle years?"

I didn't say that, I said. Only that he had a long time before he cashed in, which I guess I was partly saying for myself. I glanced at the big houses in my neighborhood. I told him that when the time came, I'd build him a mausoleum. I'd never thought of that, but I was seeing it now.

"No thanks," he said.

"What, you don't want a fancy house?"

"Sure," he said. "Like I wanna be buried in a drawer."

Erin asked once, when we passed a cemetery, "Is those graves heaven?"

"I guess it could it be," I said. "But also there," and I pointed up. I missed that kind of talk. Like when we were in the car and she said from the back seat, "I don't like Scare City."

"What's that?" I asked.

"When you don't get a choice that you want. So you have to get something else."

It took me a moment to realize she'd meant scarcity—and maybe she'd said it like that the first time, and I was only mishearing. I was backing up in the driveway, so I might have been distracted. "Where'd you learn that word?" I asked.

"In school."

"I thought you were talking about a video game."

"No," she said, "I don't really play video games that much."

By the time I left the house, we didn't have these kinds of conversations.

"Why are shatters so tall?"

Shadows, she meant, when we were walking together.

One day, the phone rang. Millie's phone. It was the first time it had rung since her death, and a part of me almost felt like it was her, even though I knew that was irrational—but I think I picked it up because of that connection.

"I want the lamp," the niece said.

I had said hello first, but she hadn't said it back. Didn't even say who she was, although I didn't need help identifying, and not just because of ID but because I'd heard her voice in so many different ways and places, on the phone, on Millie's machine, and on hers.

"I'm not contesting the will. I don't care what you're getting. We're fine out here. I was never calling about that anyway. But the lamp. There was a lamp in the corner of the front room. I used to sit beside it and play with the switch. I remember that."

I remembered the photograph of her, or, at least, what I thought was her, under the table. The balloon one, too. I looked over at the reproduction—which morphed, terribly, into the original, the dozen shades like some twelve-headed being. I blinked, shook my head straight. "I sold it."

"You what?"

"I mean, I bought it."

"What the hell are you talking about?"

So, I explained it. I started from the beginning.

I heard her huff into the phone. "I don't understand a thing about you. My aunt and the grifter. That's the title of your story."

Fine. I thought I had earned the insult, or she'd earned the right to say it. "Listen. I could try to track it down. It might be online somewhere. If I don't find it, I'll send you the money."

"That lamp belonged to us!"

"I . . ." I didn't want to say that I knew that. "You could buy another one."

"It's not about the money. It's about the lamp. It's my family. I'm talking about my childhood!"

I wanted to say I was sorry, but if I talked about her childhood, I wouldn't know where I was at.

"You know what. Fine. Send me the money. I'll use it for—I don't need to tell you what."

"Okay. I'll need your address."

She paused. "You know where the whole family lives, don't you?"

"I . . . could wire it."

"Ha!"

I decided to let her talk to herself for a while. In the silence, I thought about three figures: five thousand (the share I kept), ten thousand (the number I brought back to Millie), and fifteen (the full value of the lamp, at least until the dealer sold it again). Fifteen would be the amount I would send to the niece, but I wouldn't tell her anything about the odd combination I'd been working through in my head, the simple multiplication.

"If I give you my address, you better never show up here. I don't want to hear from you again."

I agreed. I didn't bother clarifying who called who.

I thought we had finished talking, but then she said, louder, "I don't want you stuck in my head."

So, I'd mail her the check. And maybe, sometime later, I'd mail the photo album, too, but I wasn't sure if, from her perspective, that would mean hearing from me or from Millie.

When it was all said and done (the will, I mean), six figures remained, well into it, which I realize is a big cushion. And the house. I thought I'd renovate. But I didn't want to spruce things up. Sure, I took out the grab bars. And I donated the bed and the wheelchair to the fire department. New sheets and pillows and cases, so they'd smell of no one, and new towels for the bathrooms. But the rest of the house I left as is. Even the window inefficiencies. I know I'm living with ghosts. But I can't change anything yet. Maybe later. Next year's spring cleaning. Right now, renovating it would only make me lonelier. But I think it's past time to drop the landline.

Still, I wanted to keep my hands busy. I worked on another house— meaning, I worked on other homes, as a handyman, but what I mean is the house of my ex. How that started was, I texted her and told her I had free time, and I was hoping to do any necessary repairs. Just make a punch list, I said. No charge. I would only work on the house during the off hours, when no one was home, because I didn't want to confuse the kids, or even her. No one would even know it was me.

"What are you talking about?" she texted.

"The shutters. The front steps. The paint."

"That's not what I'm asking."

"Well, that's what it is. Just that."

My phone rang. "Hi," I answered, but she didn't reply back with a greeting. Instead, she said, "*Now* you wanna work on the house?" Her voice sounded so much older than Millie's. I mean, in the chronology of my life. But of course it sounded like hers. Renee's. No reason for it to change in that short span.

"If you don't believe me, you could put a camera on me while I'm working." But I knew that wasn't the right way to provide assurance. I waited for a response, but I didn't get one. "Look, if you're antsy about it—"

"Antsy?" she said.

"Yeah, I mean, I don't want to argue about a word."

"What's your angle? What you trying to get at?"

252

"Nothing. I'm just ... I've gone through something." I wondered when or if I would ever tell her about Millie's death, and her bequest. "It won't cost a cent. No strings attached. It's just about a debt."

"Your father?"

"What?"

"He died."

"What? No ...'"

"Who died?"

"What are you talking about?"

"You said death."

"No, I ... *Debt*." But now *I* was confused, having a flashback to Dad talking about one foot in the grave, and maybe I *had* said the wrong word, since I was thinking about Millie's dying right before. The words were so close, hard to tell if it was her mishearing, or my misspeaking, or somewhere in between.

"Oh. You said you were going through something. So when I heard the word—"

"The house needs *work. Your* house."

"No duh."

"So I'd like to do that."

"You want to make *amends*." And then she huffed, which made the word sound like a curse word. Her exhalation reminded me of a recent awkward talk, but I didn't speak of that memory.

I just said yes. "The work I didn't do before. I wouldn't start till nine. I'd be out by three. By two, if you don't want me to cut it close." I sounded like I was giving myself some afternoon curfew. I'd keep talking till we reached a compromise.

"If the kids get sick, if one of them—"

"Just text me in the morning, and I won't show."

Finally, she said, "The gutter came down from the wind."

"I'm on it."

"Not the gutters. The downspout. It disconnected. I hate ladders."

"That's me," I said.

"Jack liked the present."

For a second, I had to remind myself, but I was so happy to hear it. I pictured him opening it, the grin on his face. Then I backed up to replay the celebration, Erin and Renee and Jack seated on three sides in a semicircle. Obviously I was missing, the absence at the far end of the rectangle, opposite Jack, the birthday boy, growing up, but I guess the gift was sort of me, the centerpiece, so I was closer. But if I thought harder, Renee wouldn't have waited for the actual birthday. She'd just hand the package to Jack on the day of my delivery, say, with a shrug, "This is for you," and Jack would carry it up to his room without comment. So no table with all of them plus me. I wished I had included a birthday card. Now that I was thinking about it, I should have driven to the store when I saw that no one was home at first—it would have been a way to kill time while I was driving around—and I could have picked something more personalized. Although, if anything the card would have been more *de*-personalized, since it wouldn't have been my words. Except, I could have at least written "For Jack." I remembered I'd written "From Don" on my business card, and of course it was from me, dumb repeating. I realized I could have done the card part better.

Renee would've probably done her own gift separately, on the proper day, with the cake, the candles flickering. I understood why. Their moment. Couldn't blame her for that. And now that I kept thinking, I couldn't see Renee handling my gift, once it was inside. The gift might have been buried under the day's mail, and she would have gestured at it with her eyes, some neck twist or uptilt of the chin. Which was fine, too. No resentment, from my end. I nodded at her, in my mind, but when she finally looked right at me, all I saw was disappointment.

I reattached it, the downspout. When I climbed up to repair the flapping shutters, a bonus was I could look in and see the bedroom. Nothing had changed, which was strange, since so much had, but it was like I was seeing the same hour as when I left, like my leaving meant no time at all. And I guess I had anticipated that sameness, because of what I'd seen through their front door, earlier, but upstairs on the second story, I thought more would have happened. It was almost dizzying, and not because I was high up on the ladder, but to be right there (here, at the window), it was like I *wasn't*. There. I was about to tap the window to prove to myself that I *was*, that I wasn't just some nonoccupant in the air. I imagined the sound, the tapping, which wasn't hollow, it was more like a knock, and it brought me back, restored me. And then it felt like it wasn't me that was the imaginary part. Maybe it was what I was *seeing* that was unreal, like I was looking at some effect, some replica room. I gripped the side rails to steady myself; dug my feet into the rung below. Maybe my perception was off. Maybe the situation wasn't so bad. Maybe it didn't only mean that my absence was insignificant but that the kids hadn't changed so much. Or at all. If I looked closer, I bet I could see the same dust on the shelves. I wanted to climb inside, trace the substance with my fingers. How strange that would look, some thief, some second-story man, breaking in to capture dust. What a sight for the neighbors. But of course they wouldn't know that from the outside.

I haven't really met them yet. The neighbors. Over here, at Millie's house. They wave, that's it. Once, a couple from down the street introduced themselves when I was in the yard. They had two toddlers in a double stroller, and the young dad said hi from the sidewalk. They looked like the complete picture. They were off to a flying start. I'm sure they were curious about the property changing hands, because the house was never listed, and also confused, because there had never been a moving truck. The wife glanced at the front door, like she expected a family to appear. They probably would have preferred that I was younger and had kids cartwheeling across the lawn. But both of them were too polite to say the wrong thing. "We live at fifty-three," the husband said, and he pointed in the direction the house numbers were going.

I tended to talk more to myself at nighttime. One night, a word I wrestled with was *intent*. "In tent," I said innocently, stupidly, dumb wordplay, like something misheard over the phone, but I knew I shouldn't play with such a word. I'd ask myself, posing the numbers problem: Say there was a man, a stranger, who met an elderly woman at the final stages of her life, he worked for her, cared for her, and when she died he inherited her big house plus the remainder of her bank account. *Geez, he really got ahold of her,* was my quick response. Well, that's your answer with the short version. The skeleton story. To really understand it properly and fairly, you'd have to hear me out. You'd need the full accounting, and not just listen but experience every long day, the lack of contact, the constant drudgery and torment, the frantic concern, along with the company and the closeness and the sharing and the discoveries, about yourself and about her, but all the days and nights—up at all hours—in a scary state, the months that felt like hundreds of them, the year of unreason, the fear that where you were was forever and endless, that the continual decline of her life was an entire existence (just recounting this, I needed help again with breathlessness), until it was over, she'd perished, at which point you felt all sorts of emotions, not exhilaration, which would be shameful, although once you thought of that, you were ashamed, deeply—and maybe your answer would surprise you.

I think I was telling the story to some imaginary guy who worked at an agency that monitored these situations. Sometimes the man behind the desk was my dad, sometimes it was Jim, but mostly he was me. I'd start explaining it, preparing for a lengthy presentation, but then I'd skip ahead to the ending, because I knew everything, and I just wanted to hear his final judgment. He was back to being an authority figure, not me, which was good, because he could be impartial, and I asked if what he'd heard was different, and his brow furrowed, a finger played with his bottom lip, which meant he was considering. "It all boils down to that one word." A short sentence, but his voice was very loud. Then he made a cage of his fingers, to enforce the principle, like he was in charge of that important word, and I thought he should be a nursing home executive, with that kind of gesture. Amazing how some people thought they knew you more than you did. I stayed quiet. I wanted to say that maybe intent should be two words, because it felt too simple as one, and I thought it could be a lot of things, broken into pieces. But I held my breath. This didn't feel like a tactic or concealment. I'd said everything, and now it was his turn to render his verdict on that word.

I heard him shift in his seat. Was he about to say he'd misjudged me? But he only looked to the wall, which was crowded with pictures of people who had done bad things, a nasty clientele, in their capacity as caregivers, and I squinted, I tracked his eyes to identify if I was up there, which meant there were two of us in this room, me posted on the wall and me seated before him. I wanted him, if he located my picture, if it was even there—a part of me rebutted, defensively, insistently, why *would* it be?—to pull it down, to find a different place, slip it in some album he kept of better people. He nodded and then he tilted his head one way, then the other, like he was figuring a complicated equation, a set of plusses and minuses, positives and negatives, and as he calculated—calculated me—I thought of him not as some expert at the geriatric center but as some professor of advanced mathematics. And when I thought of him as a mathematician, I wondered: What if the intent, mine, was point zero zero zero zero something? *Dot* zero zero zero zero? He squinted his eyes as if he'd heard me thinking aloud, and he was waiting for the key number that came after the zeroes, the only one that counted. No, I imagined all that. I was back to him, only him, working through the formula. I waited for his answer, but the fact that his answer was so delayed, that he was still processing and there was a real chance, the odds maybe in my favor, that his conclusion might defy his (my) initial response—I thought I could live with that uncertainty.

Except, then I imagined him as a different mathematician. The bank teller. Someone who knew me, my value, then and now. "Here's the thing," she said, and I guess she was the person behind the counter that day I first walked in with Millie—except I was the only customer this time, and this bank was only me. "Here's the thing," she said, again, "before this all started, you were worth X, but now look at you." She eyed me as if she saw my old decimal wealth, what I was before the lamp.

And I nodded, because she was right. I repeated the statement back, "Yes, now look at me. I'm worth a lot more than X."

The last time Melis had visited, I'd told her about these specialty shower caps. They had shampoo in them, so you didn't have to rinse the hair. They didn't require water, I said. Melis squinted back at me. She said she'd heard of them. "You know, you look familiar," she said, and she gave me a funny face.

"Well, I should be, right? You've met me a bunch of times now."

"No, I don't mean that."

"Well, I've got generic face number twelve. People tell me I look like other people, all the time. I've always said I could rob a bank because my face would match everyone's."

She laughed. I complimented her cheeks again. I wasn't sure if I'd actually done that the first time, with the coloring of her skin, which gave me an unpleasant memory, but I pushed it away.

"Thanks," she said, "I'm blushing."

And I laughed at a statement that was both true and false. "I knew I could get to you." I asked her the dating question again, and she didn't accuse me of being fixated. The way she answered was to say there was no one else. Then I asked her her last name. I thought she was just gonna leave it blank, but she said, "Gary." I repeated them together, first and last, and it sounded like I was saying them in reverse. "My maiden name was Arena," she said. "I haven't changed it back."

"Melis Arena," I said, and I nodded, because it sounded more like one thing. "I like it better than Gary."

"Me, too," she said. "But now, with my kids, it would confuse them if I switched."

I told her my full name, middle included. It felt like a background check. Which gave me butterflies. No, it felt like we were grade-school kids at attendance. It's funny, it felt like some next step, trading full names, family names. She told me she was leaving something out—that her first kid, her oldest, was from a different father. Never married.

"I'm just telling you. Anyway, she's out of the house. My daughter. Other two are home with me."

"The other two were with your ex." I was only saying that to make conversation. It didn't change my mind about her.

"Of course," she said. "Who do you think I am?"

But I wasn't judging her. I liked that she was telling me more about herself.

"My oldest, Lauren, she has my name, my surname." Then she shrugged her shoulders and said, "It's not all that complicated." She gave a look—I couldn't tell if she was estimating something about herself or me. "I saw your name outside."

"Huh?"

"On the van."

"Oh, right."

"Handyman man. Not too original."

No, I said, it wasn't.

"Don's Fix-It," she said, lower, whispery, like she was trying to add some intrigue to it, a code name. Like she was trying to make me sound better. I nodded at her, as if the phrase had been on the tips of our tongues, but I was probably overthinking that, some shared fantasy.

I was about to tell her The Lamp Man, how the name came to be, but then I'd have to explain the purchase, and I didn't want to talk about money, or even visualize some aggressive gesture—the cord yank. But I wanted to talk about Millie, and to tell Melis this old story. I thought, on balance, it was a good story. I mean, a good story about me. Only, parts of it just didn't feel answerable. At least not now, not yet.

"Who cuts your hair?" she asked.

I said no one, I just go to the cheapest place.

"I can tell," she said. But I didn't feel insulted at all. It felt almost the opposite, in fact, that she was taking the time to look. She was seeing some potential for improvement.

I went to our restaurant. Me and Millie's. I didn't mean that I went there with Melis, but maybe the two of us in the future. (On the way over, I decided to listen to the golden oldies station—even though some of the songs didn't seem that old to me. Maybe the station changed formats.) The place was so packed, you'd think it was Mother's Day. It was weird being there alone. "You ready?" the waiter asked, and I told her I wasn't, which was odd—wrong—because I knew what I was having. "Take your time," she said, and walked off, and I almost called her back. I looked around at the other tables. I wanted to ask one of the customers, "How am I doing?" I thought I was doing okay, but I wanted confirmation. A few tables away was a family of four, the two kids smack-dab in the awkward age with their braces and gangliness and soccer uniforms, their parents ignored. Beyond them an elderly man worked on a brainteaser. A man and a woman sat across from each other, with their waters, and maybe that could be a picture of me and Melis, drinking coffee at the kitchen table, like I used to do, at my new home. I'd say my chances of having a relationship with her are better than fifty-fifty. When I finished my meal, I walked up to the counter to pay. I handed a twenty to the cashier, who doubled as the greeter. She pulled singles out of the register. "There you are, there you are," she said, counting out the change.

I'm still a handyman. But there are things I won't do, that I don't need to do for years, probably, until maybe I get to the age where my body couldn't do them anyway—if that makes sense. I'm done digging postholes. For decks, forget it, you hit a rock and it's two hours. And roofing. Somebody called me about a garage roof, and I said, "Sorry, my schedule is a bit skewed right now." I think I can take a long vacation on heavy labor. The tedious jobs—painting, drywall—I can pick and choose.

I texted Renee about paint colors, about whether she wanted to go with the same ones. I remembered when she looked at the colors years ago, and she wanted numbers, oh, I don't know, one and six, and I thought two and three were better. One of her choices was awful. I thought it looked like baby-poop brown. And we got acrimonious about that.

"Okay, I just wanna be clear on all this," she said, now.

I assured her I knew I was out of the picture. I wasn't hoping for a change of heart. Ours was a botched marriage. But postmarriage, maybe we'd have a reconciliation, if that's not too big a word. I might put some blobs on the wall, so that way she could see what they really looked like. But I'm not gonna argue about color scheme. The customer is always right. I pictured myself climbing the ladder again, only this time to paint the exterior, and I hoped I wouldn't feel as bodiless as I did before.

I remembered her furnace, how old it was, over twenty years when I was still there, just a matter of time, and I didn't want her going into debt on that. I felt like I was already offering to pay for a replacement.

Maybe if I did fix up this house, I wouldn't work solo. I don't mean adding a crew, but maybe Jack could help me with projects. I didn't teach him anything. He didn't know what a hammer or a screwdriver was, because I didn't take the time. So maybe we could work on that together.

I looked at the room. Mine. The inferior lamp. An hour ago, I took it out to the curb but the moment I turned my back, the disposal felt like a disinheritance. I changed my mind and brought the reproduction back inside like some collectible. But then I threw out the radio and the old TV and some other devices, because things have to go, and I'm not gonna embalm the place. Em *bomb?* you might ask, if you were a kid. Like Erin, when she was wondering about shots for school, and she asked if she had to get an attendance shot. She was talking about tetanus. It's too bad, now that Erin was years older, that she probably no longer used a child's vocabulary. I wondered if she couldn't stand math anymore. And back to Renee's furnace, which I thought I'd dropped, as a topic—she wouldn't even know about the dangers, a potential crack in the heat exchanger, the carbon monoxide leaking out (I should probably make sure her detector was working).

I don't want to be the person I was before Millie. I thought of returning to the original will and bequeathing the money—some of it—to the charities. But, no, I'm not gonna do that. The money means too much. It'll keep me going for a long time. I'm not saying I won't part with some portion, throw conscience money at a cause. And Renee's kids, when they get to college, because everyone goes now, harder to be someone like me, like I was back in my twenties, just following what my dad did, or *didn't* do, back when I hadn't felt the need to be different—and all the colleges cost something, community colleges, state branches. I know I'm getting ahead of myself, but it would be nice to provide for that. For now, I'll just look after that furnace. I could bring another monitor over if the batteries were dead (might ask if she's heard a noise, a chirp), because things can get serious. Might tell her to crack a window just in case.

Maybe one day I'll branch out to a different trade. But I'm in no hurry to make these donations and decisions. I have a house now. It's a dream house, but I'd like to have some people go inside. Some company. A family, a close one, like Millie and Jim's. I'd like to really get to know someone, ask about their life, their kids, their parents. Still alive? Both of them? Maybe this person would return my questions. *Me? No, not my mom. My dad, the last time we talked, he acted like he was on borrowed time, but he's got years left. Right now he's born-again with a dog.* And I'm glad he's not neglecting the pet like the Martinengos did. Moonie—the name of their dog was Moonie. Wow, my head! Such memory. Didn't know the spelling, but still. I imagined a room of lights thrown on, like I was the prizewinner of a game show. Game of concentration. It still feels wrong that my dad and my ex-wife, so many people, don't know about Millie, about what happened to her, and to me, like some conspiracy of silence. Better to talk more.

I thought again of having coffee with Melis. It was the shoulder season now, and then the work would keep slowing, more and more, so I had ample time to spend with her. I would sit where Millie used to sit, or maybe I'd switch places. Either way. The chairs would be interchangeable, so both sides would be not just mine or hers, but ours. And maybe we'd move on to romantic dinners, not just the old familiars but new spots, *Hey, I heard this one just opened*, so the experience would be ours together, begin with us.

And with Melis's kids, we'd have a use for all the rooms. Even her oldest might come over and spend the night if she needed a place to crash. She could sleep downstairs, if she wanted a separate floor, or even below that, the basement, which I could renovate into a guest room. It would be nice to turn the house into that, a spill of kids, because without them, it's too much space for just me.

This morning, in the mirror, I thought my hair was getting crazy. I should probably make an appointment with the person to fix it.

Acknowledgments

Many thanks to: Ann G.; Marjorie A. Smith, LCSW; Sally Norton; Bob Weston; Art Mason; Christine Peck; Amy Belliveau; Craig R. Sellers, PhD, NP; Karen Kuebler; Joe Lima; Mike Kramer; Carolyn Reardon; Miles P. Zatkowsky, Esq.; Lorie Myers; Martha Mock; Dr. Elizabeth J. Santos; Dr. Carol Podgorski; Tziporah Rosenberg; Mary Judge; Jim Memmott; Jesse Lee Kercheval; Ted Avgerinos; Jim Howard; Charles Zlotkus; April Hill; Carmen Santora; Frank Liberti; Lisa Kibler, RN; Rosemary Kegl; and Katherine Mannheimer.

To generous and invaluable readers: Jake Morrill, Joanna Scott, Debra Spark, and Reader B.

To Dennis Lloyd, Jackie Krass, Michelle Wing, and the entire staff at the University of Wisconsin Press.

To my English department colleagues at the University of Rochester.

To Marilyn Uselmann.

To my dad, and in memory of my mom.

To Susan and Henry and Ella.

About the Author

Stephen Schottenfeld's first novel is *Bluff City Pawn*. His stories have appeared in the *Gettysburg Review, TriQuarterly, StoryQuarterly,* the *Virginia Quarterly Review, New England Review,* the *Iowa Review,* and other journals. He teaches English at the University of Rochester.